Praise for the novels of
Jasmine Haynes

"Deliciously erotic and completely captivating."

—Susan Johnson, *New York Times* bestselling author

"An erotic, emotional adventure of discovery you don't want to miss."

—Lora Leigh, #1 *New York Times* bestselling author

"So incredibly hot that I'm trying to find the right words to describe it without having to be edited for content . . . extremely stimulating from the first page to the last! Of course, that means that I loved it! . . . One of the hottest, sexiest erotic books I have read so far."

—*Romance Reader at Heart*

"Sexy."   —*Sensual Romance Reviews*

"Delightfully torrid."   —*Midwest Book Review*

"More than a fast-paced erotic romance, this is a story of family, filled with memorable characters who will keep you engaged in the plot and the great sex. A good read to warm a winter's night."

—*Romantic Times*

"Bursting with sensuality and eroticism."   —*In the Library Reviews*

"The passion is intense, hot, and purely erotic . . . recommended for any reader who likes their stories realistic, hot, captivating, and very, very well written."   —*Road to Romance*

"Not your typical romance. This one's going to remain one of my favorites."   —*The Romance Studio*

"Jasmine Haynes keeps the plot moving and the love scenes very hot."   —*Just Erotic Romance Reviews*

"A wonderful novel . . . Try this one—you won't be sorry."

—*The Best Reviews*

PAST MIDNIGHT

Jasmine Haynes

HEAT
New York

THE BERKLEY PUBLISHING GROUP
Published by the Penguin Group
Penguin Group (USA) Inc.
375 Hudson Street, New York, New York 10014, USA

Penguin Group (Canada), 90 Eglinton Avenue East, Suite 700, Toronto, Ontario M4P 2Y3, Canada
(a division of Pearson Penguin Canada Inc.)
Penguin Books Ltd., 80 Strand, London WC2R 0RL, England
Penguin Group Ireland, 25 St. Stephen's Green, Dublin 2, Ireland (a division of Penguin Books Ltd.)
Penguin Group (Australia), 250 Camberwell Road, Camberwell, Victoria 3124, Australia
(a division of Pearson Australia Group Pty. Ltd.)
Penguin Books India Pvt. Ltd., 11 Community Centre, Panchsheel Park, New Delhi—110 017, India
Penguin Group (NZ), 67 Apollo Drive, Rosedale, Auckland 0632, New Zealand
(a division of Pearson New Zealand Ltd.)
Penguin Books (South Africa) (Pty.) Ltd., 24 Sturdee Avenue, Rosebank, Johannesburg 2196,
South Africa

Penguin Books Ltd., Registered Offices: 80 Strand, London WC2R 0RL, England

This book is an original publication of The Berkley Publishing Group.

This is a work of fiction. Names, characters, places, and incidents either are the product of the author's imagination or are used fictitiously, and any resemblance to actual persons, living or dead, business establishments, events, or locales is entirely coincidental. The publisher does not have any control over and does not assume any responsibility for author or third-party websites or their content.

PRINTING HISTORY
Heat trade paperback edition / May 2011

Library of Congress Cataloging-in-Publication Data

Haynes, Jasmine.
    Past midnight / Jasmine Haynes.—Heat trade pbk. ed.
        p. cm.
    ISBN 978-0-425-24094-6 (trade pbk.)
I. Title.
PS3608.A936P37   2011
813'.6—dc22

                                    2010036500

PRINTED IN THE UNITED STATES OF AMERICA

10   9   8   7   6   5   4   3   2   1

To my husband, Ole,
for all the years of believing in me

ACKNOWLEDGMENTS

Thank you to my wonderful network of friends who support me, brainstorm with me, and encourage me: Laurel Jacobson, Bella Andre, Shelley Bates, Jenny Andersen, Jackie Yau, Ellen Higuchi, Kathy Coatney, Pamela Fryer, Rita Hogan, Terri Schaefer, and Jenn Mason. What would I do without you? Thanks also to my friends Teresa and Marty and my brother Michael for their technical help, and to Lynn for her insights. And, of course, to my agent, Lucienne Diver, and my editor, Wendy McCurdy.

PROLOGUE

JUST PAST MIDNIGHT, SHE REACHED FOR HIM IN THE DARK. A SLIVER of moonlight illuminated the bare wood bureau and blue carpet, its fingers creeping up the bedspread, ending at their feet, leaving the rest in darkness.

It was always past midnight when she turned to him, as if touching him in the daylight or at bedtime, when he wasn't sleep-drowsed, was sacrilege. He lived for the nights she reached out, as if his flesh were touch-starved. After a year and a month, he *was* starving, body, mind, and soul. He slept naked, terrified of missing a single moment. They never spoke. She wouldn't cry out even when she came, her silence as essential to her as the dark. He used to beg for a word, a sound. *Talk to me.* He would have accepted anything—her anger, her pain, her guilt, her tears. But he'd always lost her as soon as his voice broke the quiet. He'd stopped asking and took what she allowed him; this, her hands on him, her mouth, her body. Without words, sex was anti-intimacy, yet this was all he had left of their marriage, these dark moments after midnight, and he would not let them go. He would not let *her* go.

Her hand skimmed over his nipple, pinching, turning the nub pebble hard. She'd always known the things that drove him crazy.

Then she followed the arrow of hair down his abdomen to wrap her fingers around him. She stroked him softly, gently, to hardness. It didn't take much, he was so on edge for her. He held his breath, afraid to disturb the silence, afraid he might cry out with the heat of her touch. Pushing the covers back, she laid her lips on his crown as the November night air rolled like a cold wave over his hot skin, the silk of her long red hair a curtain over his lap.

She engulfed him to the root. Her mouth on him was heaven and hell. God have mercy. He fisted his hands in the sheets, his body wanting to rock, thrust, drive deep into the recesses of her mouth. Yet he held still, so still but for the throbbing of his blood and the pounding of his heart. The sounds of her mouth, her tongue, her lips taking him was like a gentle melody on the wind, caressing him, stealing through his mind. She reached between his legs and squeezed the heart of his manhood, bringing him to an aching, crushing need, his body arching involuntarily. But still not a sound, not even a groan.

God, how he'd loved her, wanted her, still loved her even after all the pain, the guilt, the blame. Once upon a time he would have told her so, hauled her up along his chest to take her mouth, to taste his essence on her tongue. But those days were long gone; a year, four weeks, and a lifetime gone. Now all he could do was grit his teeth and try not to spend himself now, in her mouth. Because there was more. She would give him more, at least physically, but only in darkness and silence, only past midnight.

She shifted, then slid back with a suctioned pop as her mouth left him. A moment later, her firm thighs gripped his hips, the heat of her core close, so close he could feel her all the way up to his throat.

He didn't enter her; she simply took him. As if he were nothing more than a solid piece of flesh to fill her emptiness and assuage her guilt and pain for this short space of time. She didn't kiss him, didn't brace herself on his chest to smile down at him. Their lovemaking used to be rich with talk and laughter, dirty talk, nasty talk, sexy talk, spinning ever kinkier fantasies for each other. It had been hot, exciting, priming him with the hope that someday they would act on those fantasies. Now she merely leaned back and rode him silently, hands splayed against her ass for support. For her, it was pure physicality, a way to stop the whirling thoughts and memories, the rawness of the act exhausting her into sleep.

For him, it was touch, connection, life. For a little while, he could pretend that she had forgiven him. His body rose to meet her, overcome by a blinding, aching need he dulled with physical pleasure and the remembered taste of her, the sweetness of her juice, the softness of her skin, the flowery scent of her body lotion, pungent now with her arousal.

She began to tremble with impending orgasm, her inner muscles working him. The barely there grunt of exertion remained her only sound, yet it was so erotic and beguiling in the deep after-midnight quiet.

She spasmed around him, her body curling over his, but not touching, never touching beyond the fusion of their hips. He shoved his head back into the pillow, thrusting hard and deep as her climax rippled over him, around him, inside him. He filled her, forcing her to feel him, bucking hard against her, limbs trembling, sweat beading his forehead with the effort it took not to scream out his orgasm. Explosive and mind-altering in the dark, the silence, her body, her heat. They ended with quivering bodies and harsh breathing, until finally she slipped away, tipping to her side of the bed.

Even as aftershocks jolted through him, she fell into the regular cadence of sleep, what she'd been striving toward when she reached for him. Sleep. Oblivion. The place where she could dream the dead alive again. She couldn't talk about Jay, but she could dream of him.

He was glad for her, yet he envied the ability. He'd never dreamed his son alive. For him, there were only dreams of Jay's face the last time he saw him, in the hospital.

Long past midnight, he lay in the dark, wide awake, his body sated, his heart bleeding and in shreds.

1

MONDAY. THANK GOD. SHE'D MADE IT THROUGH THANKSGIVING. One more holiday to go.

She didn't know how to tell Dominic that he was the only reason she got through the nights. Maybe it wasn't fair to use him that way, but when she touched him, she didn't have to remember anything. When they were done, she could finally sleep. The sex was how she managed to forget that she'd lost Jay a year ago last month, how she forgot that most people were starting their Christmas shopping, how she ignored that she didn't need to shop anymore.

Her parents had wanted them to come home to Michigan this year. She couldn't handle it, the memories, the one little boy no one would talk about, driving it home that he wasn't there. She'd told her folks no. Dominic hadn't complained, even though his parents had been hoping for a visit, too. Last year she'd been too numb to even notice Christmas or the holiday season. This year . . . she wanted to pretend it didn't exist.

Erin DeKnight stared at the reorder point list. Dominic saved her nights. Work saved her days. There was a ton of stuff to do before the December year-end. The contract with Wrainger Electronics was up for renegotiation, ripe for eking out a few extra pennies for the bottom line. Costs had to be revised for raw materials and outsourced parts so they could roll standards for work-in-progress and finished goods, and revalue their inventory for the upcoming year. Two years ago, they'd purchased an on-line enterprise system, which saved them having to house their own server to run an integrated accounting and manufacturing software package, not to mention the data backups. In order for the system to operate properly, you had to feed it good raw data, which was a hell of lot of work before year-end. Work to keep her occupied. Dominic said she was a workaholic. She was. It kept her from thinking too much.

Puffing out a breath, Erin flipped the report page, hitting the transducer part numbers. Which made her think of Leon. Leon had been fabricating transducers for DeKnight Gauges the entire ten years since she and Dominic had first started DKG. He was seventy-five and fabbed the parts out of his garage. No else did it cheaper. But Leon had decided to retire.

Erin should have been finding another source, but instead she was searching for the perfect argument to change his mind. Leon was young at heart. He'd hate being retired, having nothing to do. She couldn't let him do that to himself. He was more than a vendor. Truth was, Erin didn't want to let him go. He was part of the DKG family. A talented whittler, he'd crafted a different animal for her birthday every year. He'd whittled for Dominic's birthday, too.

And for Jay's.

An image of Leon burrowed into her mind. Jay's memorial. Leon's grizzled face, eyes sunken. The words of grief she hadn't let him express. He'd said them to Dominic instead. When Erin thought about Leon retiring, she felt queasy.

Erin glanced up at the light rap on her doorjamb. Rachel, a paper in her hand, her smile too exuberant. "Morning."

Ah, saved from her own thoughts. Erin smiled a greeting. A newly divorced mother of two, Rachel Delaney had started as receptionist a couple of months ago, also handling filing, mailing, and a myriad of everyday jobs. She was blond, pretty, and curvy in a way that drew male attention. That wasn't always good. Erin had felt sorry for her, a woman suddenly thrust into a man's work world for which she had few marketable skills. She could easily have been taken advantage of by an unscrupulous boss.

"What do you need?" Erin said pleasantly. She'd practiced the art of smiling. She might not always feel like it, but people needed normalcy, and that's what she gave her employees at DKG. They were like a family, and for family, you presented the illusion that everything was all right. Even when it had stopped being all right over a year ago. But Rachel didn't know; she hadn't been at DKG then.

"I printed out your itinerary." Rachel laid it on Erin's desk. "I sent it in an e-mail, too," she added with the hint of a question, as if unsure whether she'd covered all the bases.

The printing far too small for her to read, Erin reached out an index finger to slide the sheet of paper across the desk. "What itinerary?"

"For the PRI Trade Show."

DKG manufactured ultrasonic thickness gauges. While the gauges had testing applications in a variety of industries, high-performance racing was one of their biggest markets, and the Performance Racing Industry Trade Show, held every year in Orlando during the second weekend of December, was *the* show. But Dominic, not Erin, represented DKG.

Erin didn't sigh. She smiled. Rachel did her best, and honestly, she rarely made mistakes. "You know, this was supposed to be for Dominic, not me."

Rachel smiled with equal courtesy. "I booked his, too."

Erin kept her patience. She didn't have as much of it as she used to. She hated to think of herself as a bitch, but sometimes, if she didn't think before she spoke, she came off sounding pretty damn snippy.

"Dominic handles our exhibit booth," she said. Though he'd missed last year for the first time since they'd started DKG. He'd sent Cam Phan, their software engineer, in his stead. Far be it for them to actually miss the show altogether. This year, things were supposed to get back to normal.

Not that things could ever be the same again.

"He told me to book yours as well." Rachel paused, her lips pursed as if she were slightly irritated now. "He's going early on Wednesday, and he had me book a late-afternoon flight out for you on Thursday so you'd only miss one day of work. You'll fly back Sunday with him."

She'd been tamping it down, but suddenly Erin couldn't rein in her anger. "He did *what?*" She hated the trade shows, she hated schmoozing, especially *now*, with the holidays, and hell no, she wasn't going. What was he *thinking?*

Rachel gave her a look that clearly said, *Don't you even know what your own husband's doing?*

Well, no, she *didn't* know what Dominic was doing. They didn't talk much unless it was about business. Even in the dark, when she couldn't sleep, weakened by the need to blot out everything for a little while, even then, they didn't talk. What was there to say?

With careful movements and a deep breath, Erin stood. "Don't worry. I'll talk to Dominic about it myself." And she would be calm, swear it.

Rachel nodded and scurried out as if afraid she'd get caught in the cross fire.

God, had she looked *that* scary to Rachel? Erin followed her out of the office, the itinerary in hand.

Like cogs in a wheel, the DKG offices ringed a large common area housing their office equipment, copier, fax, high-volume wireless printer, mail machine, and a conference table. Everything out in the open, shared by all. They called it the roundhouse, though Erin couldn't remember who'd started that. On the far side, she'd had a break nook installed, with a sink, plumbed coffee machine, microwave, and refrigerator stocked with water, juice, and other goodies. Her motto: Happy employees didn't waste time gossiping around the watercooler. On the left lay their manufacturing area with assembly, warehousing, shipping, and receiving. To the right was the engineering wing and the no-man's-land of Dominic's testing lab.

She stomped down the engineering hallway. He wasn't in his office. She found him in the lab with its walls the sterile white of a hospital room. Shoving a scrap of paper beneath the mouse pad next to his computer when she walked in, he was seated on one of the three metal stools amid parts, disassembled gauges, and test equipment that beeped too loudly. Another stool sat forlorn in a corner, its seat ratcheted higher than the others to accommodate a shorter, smaller body. It hadn't moved from that spot in over a year. A cold cup of coffee sat on the speckled white Formica counter beside him, "World's Best Dad" emblazoned on the mug in big red letters. She wondered how he could still use it. Her "World's Best Mom" mug was gone; she didn't know where and hadn't looked.

Mother's Day had been the worst. Jay's birthday, or the anniversary of the day she'd lost him, she'd thought those days would be the most unbearable. But if no one reminded you, you could lie to yourself about what day it was. Mother's Day, though, it was everywhere you looked, on TV, store flyers, even shouting at you from spam e-mails the filters didn't catch; *everywhere*, reminding her that she wasn't a mother anymore.

Erin swallowed past the lump in her throat. Aware of the sudden silence out in the roundhouse, she closed the lab door gently. That was the problem with working together; all your employees knew about your marital squabbles. Not that she and Dominic fought much anymore. They didn't talk enough to do that.

She slapped down the flight schedule on the counter next to Dominic. "What the *hell* is this?"

A gauge in his hand, he glanced at it, then up to her. "It's your itinerary for the PRI show," he said mildly, his charcoal-colored eyes so dark they could appear black in certain lighting. Now they smoked, like coals on the edge of blazing.

"I *never* go to that show," she said, her teeth gritted.

He wore his thick hair short. Despite being forty-three, he didn't have even a hint of gray, and the overhead fluorescents gleamed in the black strands. He was more handsome than the day she'd first seen him in a university night class back in Michigan. Over the last year, she'd forgotten how good-looking he was. She'd looked at him, but she hadn't really seen him. Just as she couldn't really see him in the dark when it was long past midnight.

"We need some time away from here," Dominic said, flicking a button on the gauge. "Together." He watched something on the piece of test equipment he was working, and she hated the way he didn't even look at her as he added, "Don't tell me you've got too much to do for year-end because I'm only talking about one work day."

Damn him for circumventing her argument. "You should have asked me."

"You would have told me no."

She could feel her heart's vicious pounding against the wall of her chest. "I hate it when you make decisions for me."

He turned his head, smiled. It didn't reach his eyes. "Like when you decided we wouldn't go to Michigan?"

"All right, so I didn't consult you about that. I didn't want . . ."

She hadn't wanted to argue. Because he made her *think* when they argued. He made her feel. In a terrifying way, feeling something, anything, even anger, was dangerous. It opened her up to emotions she couldn't deal with, things she couldn't think about. It wasn't like in the middle of the night when she reached for him. That was physical, akin to taking a sleeping pill, a matter of survival.

He was making her feel now, and she didn't like it.

He flipped a switch on the meter, and it pinged at him. "It's nonrefundable, and I'm not cancelling it," he said, anticipating her objections again.

That just pissed her off more. "Screw the money." Why was he being such an asshole about this?

All right, *she* was being more of an asshole than he was. First with Rachel, now with Dominic. But she couldn't go to that goddamn show, couldn't wear the game face, or pretend with all those strangers. It was bad enough pretending she was fine with people she knew.

"WHOA, I DIDN'T MEAN TO START WORLD WAR THREE," RACHEL whispered to Yvonne after Erin disappeared into Dominic's lab.

"It's not your fault, honey." Yvonne tried to assure her.

In the break nook, they poured themselves fresh coffees. Rachel loaded hers with creamer. The coffee was made from expensive, freshly ground beans, and the creamer came in a variety of flavors. The DeKnights treated their employees well. Rachel didn't have to make a copayment on the medical or dental insurance, and the benefits were so good that she and her ex had taken the boys off his plan and added them to hers. Then there was the profit sharing, which was based not on salary level, but divided equally among the thirteen employees. Everyone had equal incentive and was equally rewarded. Rachel had her own office, too. Where else did a receptionist get an office, even if it did open right into the front entrance? She needed this job, and she wished she hadn't gotten testy with Erin even if she'd only been following Dominic's instructions.

Beside her, Yvonne eyed the hallway leading to Dominic's lab. "They're on edge with the holidays, and it being a year and all. You know how it is."

No, Rachel didn't know. But she'd felt the tension around DKG growing over the last month. She was the newbie. Almost everyone else had worked for the DeKnights at least five years. Yvonne herself had been with them the full ten years DKG had been in business. She was inside sales, handling all the existing customers with repeat business. Yvonne Colbert was a big woman, not fat, but husky and tall, over six feet. In her midfifties, she was soft-spoken, with caramel skin and gentle brown eyes. If Rachel made a mistake, Yvonne was the first to say, "It's okay, honey, don't worry about it."

Rachel sipped her coffee. God, it was good. She couldn't afford stuff like this. She was strictly freeze-dried. "Okay, here's the thing. I feel like I need to walk on eggshells, but nobody tells me why." She didn't want to screw up this job by putting her foot in her mouth when she didn't even know what she wasn't supposed to say. Or do.

"Aw, honey, I'm sorry. We just don't talk about it, that's all, and we all figure that someone else has told you."

"Like who? Bree?" Rachel glanced over her shoulder at Bree's office, the fourth that circled the roundhouse along with Erin's, Yvonne's, and Rachel's.

Bree Mason was DKG's bookkeeper. She sat at her desk, her long black hair pulled back in a severe ponytail that looked downright painful it was so tight. She was *always* at her desk working hard. While she was helpful, smiled, and talked like a normal person when you were face-to-face with her, alone in her office, when she didn't think anyone was looking, she was almost a shadow of herself. So no, Bree wouldn't have said a thing about Erin. Rachel had yet to figure out if Bree was always so quiet or if this was something new, like Erin's increasing tension. All Rachel knew was that Bree didn't gossip. In fact, no one gossiped about the DeKnights. They were a tight family, and Rachel felt like the interloper.

Yvonne patted her hand. "I'll say it once, then we don't talk about it again, all right?"

"I won't say anything." Rachel zipped her lips, but she had to admit, her curiosity was killing her.

"Their little boy died last year, the end of October."

Rachel took the words like a body blow. "Oh my God. Was he in a car accident?" She couldn't imagine what it would be like to lose one of her sons. Even if lately they'd been acting like they hated her guts, as if the divorce were her fault. Maybe that was the typical reaction of all teenage boys who adored their fathers.

Yvonne sighed deeply. "He picked up some parasite while he was on a day trip with his school class. Little itty-bitty amoeba thingies the doctors couldn't figure out were there. He died two weeks later." Yvonne's eyes misted. She blinked away a tear. "Wouldn't have mattered if they had known, though. There wasn't anything the doctors could do after the parasites got into his brain."

"I'm so sorry." Rachel's heart was racing, the horror of the loss washing over her, leaving her hands clammy. Yet she'd wondered about Dominic's "World's Best Dad" mug and assumed in the end he'd taken whatever was available in the cupboard.

"It was awful," Yvonne murmured. "I knew Jay all his life.

And Erin had an awful time of it when she was pregnant with him, too. Fibroids in her uterus. She spent the last couple of months in bed so the baby wouldn't come too soon, then she had him caesarean. They ended up giving her a hysterectomy afterward." She shook her head sadly. "So no more babies." Yvonne had three grown kids she doted on, two sons and a daughter, and Rachel knew she was thinking that Erin had lost more than her son; she'd lost the chance at more children.

Though who would even think that having another child could replace the one you'd lost?

Rachel's stomach crimped. How could Erin DeKnight even get up in the morning? Every morning, knowing her little boy wouldn't be in his bedroom. Never again. One day he was laughing and playing, then he was gone. Just like that. Rachel didn't think she'd have survived. "How old was he?"

"Eight. I tell you those two adored him." Yvonne glanced at the closed door down the engineering hall. "Nothing's been the same around here since. Nothing ever will be. It's like we all lost Jay that day."

Rachel's boys were thirteen and fifteen. Even now she sometimes got a sick feeling letting them out of her sight, though that was probably an aftereffect of the divorce.

"Dominic was supposed to go on the school trip." Yvonne wore a faraway look, her gaze fixed on the closed door. "But there was some problem with one of the new product releases, and he didn't." Quickly, she touched Rachel's hand, her fingers cold. "Not that I blame him. It would have happened anyway."

Dominic must be racked with guilt.

"Poor Erin, she was always taking care of everyone else, including all of us, and now, when she needs it, she doesn't know how to ask."

From down the engineering hallway, despite the closed door,

they could hear voices, not yelling, just tense. Rachel realized that for a woman who didn't gossip, Yvonne was revealing things far beyond anything Rachel needed to know. It was like reading someone's private diary.

And yet, Rachel didn't know how she was going to resist the urge to tell Erin how very, very sorry she felt for her.

2

DOMINIC SET DOWN THE GAUGE, BUT HE DIDN'T LET GO OF IT NOR did he look at her. He could feel the steady *shoosh* of his blood through his veins. "Don't make me go alone, Erin," he said softly.

"You always go alone."

"Not this time." He hadn't gone last year. He didn't believe she'd considered that this time of year held as many reminders for him as it did for her, that his guts ached with loss, with guilt for not being there that day, that at times he was as close to despair as she was. She wasn't unfeeling, but she didn't . . . notice him. Yet no matter how much you didn't want it to, life kept right on going, rolling over you if you didn't get out of its way. The trade show was important for them, a venue to show off their new products. He had to go.

Around him, equipment hummed, beeped. Something scrabbled on the roof, maybe a bird, or a squirrel snatching up acorns that had fallen off the oaks surrounding the industrial park. He could smell Erin, the sweet shampoo he sometimes borrowed when his ran out. He liked having her scent on him.

"I'm not sure I can." Her voice lacked the tension she'd entered the lab with.

"Do it for me," Dominic said, his fingers tight on the gauge. "I need you."

It was dirty pool and he knew it, but he was tired of fighting fair with her. In past years, he'd spent the entire week in Orlando because a hell of a lot went on even before the actual trade show got underway. This year, though, he'd opted for the earliest flight out Wednesday morning to have time to set up the booth before the show started on Thursday. He'd had Rachel book a late Thursday afternoon flight for Erin. Last Christmas was a blur for both of them. They'd moved in a haze of grief. But this year, the holiday season was proving to be far more brutal on her, and he would not leave her alone for that many days, especially not over the weekend. But he'd already cancelled on several trade shows and conferences over the past year, places he should have been, networking he should have done. He couldn't miss the PRI show. So instead, he'd decided to take her with him. No matter what kind of fight she put up.

He held his breath, waiting, the animals scrabbling on the roof the only sound in the lab. *Say yes,* he willed her. *Don't fight me.* He needed this. He needed her, but he was so damn terrified she was too far gone to ever find her way back to him. He should have forced her into counseling. He'd needed it, too. But she'd refused, and any pressure he'd put on her had only driven her further away.

"All right," she said.

His heart started beating again, and he resisted the urge to punch his fist in the air. Unsportsmanlike conduct. He'd like to say it was all for her own good, but he was the one that had to have it. For the last eighteen years, even before they were married, every decision he'd made had been with her in mind. If she left him, he had no idea what would replace her. Without her, he could not bear Jay's loss. He was willing to do anything to get her back. "Thank you."

"You owe me," she said, trying to make light of it, but he recognized the huskiness of emotion in her voice.

"I got us a room at the Crown Royal."

She raised a brow. "That's a little swank, isn't it?"

"It's nice enough." On his own, he wouldn't have spent the extra money, but he'd wanted to give her the best. At forty, she was still gorgeous to him, with a body women ten years younger would envy and long red hair that made him tremble when he buried his fingers in it. Yet her eyes, a pretty robin's-egg blue, were blemished by dark circles, and her brow furrowed with a frown she probably didn't even realize was there most of the time. It didn't used to be that way. She used to laugh a lot. "Pack a bathing suit. The weather's supposed to be nice." Unseasonably warm, in fact.

Her lips thinned. "It's a working trip."

"I'll be working. You can lay by the pool if you want."

"If I'm going, I won't waste time at the pool. I'll sit in the booth with you and talk to people."

She'd hate it, but he didn't argue. He saw many of the same customers and suppliers year after year, and he liked the idea of introducing his wife around. "You'll need a couple of cocktail dresses. There are evening parties we'll have to attend."

She raised a brow. "Oh yeah, I remember. All the business gets done at the parties."

Among other things. He grinned, feeling a little lighter now that she'd agreed. Of course, he'd told her about the parties. All the dirty details. And some of them did get pretty damn dirty. "I have to make a showing."

"Sure, right." She smirked at him as she left. In that moment, there had been some remnant in her unguarded expression, the

Erin of old, the girl he'd fallen head over heels for, the woman he missed as much as he missed Jay.

They'd been together almost half their lives, meeting in night school at the local university in Kalamazoo. They'd both been working full time as well, and they had the same goals, the same dreams. Neither of them wanted to spend their lives worrying about where the next paycheck was coming from. They wanted control over their destiny, wanted a better life for their children. They'd married fifteen years ago, after he graduated with his mechanical engineering degree, but they put off having kids until Erin finished business school, until they owned their home out in sunny California, away from the Michigan winters. Building the life they wanted had been a struggle, but they'd done it together. He designed the products, courted the new customers. She did everything from purchasing to operations, handled the entire office. They were a team, DKG a second family to them. Everything had been perfect.

Until last October. Now they lived in a darkness that seemed to have taken over their souls. They could never go back to that perfect life.

He withdrew the photo from beneath the mouse pad, where he'd stashed it when Erin walked in. Jay had his dark hair and Erin's pale skin, the wiry body of Dominic's youth, but Erin's smile. Jay had loved hanging out here in the lab after school, sometimes on weekends. He'd been smart as a whip, helped out with the testing, knew how to run the instruments.

The photograph was all Dominic had left. She wouldn't let him talk about Jay. There wasn't a grave to visit. Erin wouldn't have it. She'd wanted Jay cremated. That was the only real fight they'd had afterward. Dominic closed his eyes, his heart pumping hard, his chest tight, his temples suddenly throbbing. He could still hear her screaming at him.

I won't let those things keep eating him. I won't. I won't.

He'd given in because he couldn't stand the anguish in her, or thinking about it, imagining that she was right.

Dominic tucked the picture at the bottom of the drawer. He usually kept it there, beneath a pile of outdated transducers and cables.

They couldn't go on like this much longer. Unless they wanted to lose each other forever. Sometimes he wondered if that's what she intended. Despite all the pain, all the sorrow, he couldn't allow that. She was his other half and though they'd lost everything else, he could not lose her. Without her, he would . . . the thought wouldn't complete itself.

Instead, he swore he would find a way to bring her with him into the light, even if he had to drag her kicking and screaming.

A WEEK AND A HALF LATER, THURSDAY, FIRST DAY OF THE PRI SHOW: The Orange County Convention Center was a madhouse. Dominic loved it. He enjoyed people, loved the schmoozing and the talking until his voice got hoarse. Even if the noise level made his ears ring after a while, the atmosphere energized him; meeting new contacts, reconnecting with old. He felt like a different man here. He was into the whole design phase of a new gauge or even upgrading existing products, but sometimes he craved recharging his batteries by hanging out with a bunch of guys shooting the breeze. That's why it had worked so well that he'd done the trade shows and Erin had stayed back in the office.

Even though she'd been out of sight back then, she hadn't been out of mind. Thank God for the three-hour time difference. He'd enjoyed calling her late at night, regaling her with stories about the after-hours parties. They weren't sanctioned by the show's organizers, but no one could stop the private get-togethers. Some of them could get pretty damn wild. Erin had soaked up every naughty detail. He'd get her really worked up, too, telling her how he'd love to watch her with another man at one of these shindigs, just sit back and enjoy her pleasure. Oh, she'd gotten into that one all right, and they'd had some of the best phone sex after that particular fantasy.

But all that was before. Life was different now. Over the last ten days, since he'd finagled Erin into attending the trade show, they'd hardly spoken beyond the necessities of working in the same facility and living in the same house. With emotion slicing through his gut, he admitted she hadn't even reached for him in the night. The only hope he still harbored was that she hadn't backed out of the trip.

By five o'clock in the evening, the trade show crowds had thinned, with attendees heading to dinner or the bar or the cocktail mixer. Dominic began locking away his sample gauges.

"Dude, it's great to see ya here." Stomping into the DKG booth, Jamison grabbed Dominic's hand, pumped his arm in a merciless handshake, then slapped him on the back.

"Good to see you, too, man." Dominic put his tongue to his teeth to make sure they hadn't been rattled out of his head.

Jamison was a big man with an expanded midsection, a bald pate, and a huge pinkie ring with a ginormous diamond. He was in carburetors. The racing industry had strict guidelines on the thickness of everything from car panels to holes bored through a carburetor for increasing performance. And they used DKG gauges. Jamison was a good customer, and despite his bluster, Dominic had always liked him. He and his wife had flown from Palm Beach to attend Jay's memorial service.

Jamison boomed a laugh that still managed to turn heads despite the noise level in the hall. "I tell ya, Cam was a peach last year, but I had to watch all my p's and q's with that little gal."

Dominic had a hard time believing Jamison could actually accomplish that. With the fees already paid, Dominic had sent Cam Phan in his place last year. She'd been new at DKG, replacing his previous software engineer when Reggie up and quit because Dominic refused to give him a higher percentage of the profit sharing. From day one, he and Erin had agreed everyone would profit equally. Even their share was the same. As good an engineer as he was, Reggie had always been a pain in the ass. Cam might not have his genius, but she was a quiet little thing and she worked hard.

"She didn't speak for a month straight after she got back." Not true, but Dominic couldn't help ribbing Jamison.

Jamison smacked his forehead. "I'm such a jerk." But he smiled, not minding the dig at all. "Ryan's got the penthouse at the Milton. Nine o'clock, party hearty. You comin'?"

Dominic glanced at his watch. The Budweiser mixer would get under way in a few minutes, and he could sure as hell use a beer. After that? He had to fetch Erin from the airport. Her flight came in just past midnight. He hoped she'd sleep on the plane. "Not tonight," he said. "Anything going on tomorrow?"

"I heard Miterberg is putting on something. And man"— Jamison shook his fingers as if he'd touched a hot stove—"he's rented a freaking palace."

"Miterberg usually puts on a good party," Dominic said mildly. A *good* party was understating it. Miterberg was a so-called silent partner of a high-profile racing team, and everything he did, he did big. He'd have rented a mansion with acres of grounds and fifty million bedrooms (slight exaggeration). Lobster, crab legs, jumbo prawns, caviar, anything you could think of to drink, and the entertainment would be risqué. Erin would finally get to see what he'd told her about. That had been his plan since the moment he'd decided to bring her. "Erin'll love it."

Jamison's bushy eyebrows, in dire contrast to his bare scalp, shot up. "Dude. You can't take your *wife* there."

Dominic laughed. "I won't let her venture too far from me." He'd let Erin go anywhere she wanted. He would encourage her. His pulse quickened with the possibilities. He had no clue why he was wired this way, why jealousy wasn't a factor for him. Maybe it was plain old desperation now, anything to get her to see him again, interact with him, play with him the way she used to. Perhaps he'd be jealous if fantasy actually became reality, but whenever he thought about it, whenever he'd told Erin the stories about what he'd seen and how he'd love to watch a guy doing her, he'd become so hard he couldn't think straight. Miterberg's party could be the big test. Would he let someone touch her? Would she?

Jamison shook his fingers again, his pinkie ring glittering in the overhead lights. "Man, you're taking a chance," he said, punctuating with another boom of laughter. "My wife would castrate me if she knew what went on at some of the parties."

It wasn't only PRI. It happened at a lot of trade shows. Okay, maybe not the National Association of Accountants annual conference, but he'd worked in an industrial environment long enough to know there was a fair amount of kink going on out there. Not every party, of course; sometimes, he'd had to make things up for Erin, but he was hoping he could find something hot for her to see. A Miterberg party was a damn good bet. Dominic winked at Jamison. "Get me an invitation, would ya?"

"Will do. Catch up with you later." Jamison followed the crowd into another of the exhibit halls, where the beer would already be flowing and the Budweiser girls mingling. That was part of the charm of this particular show, the scantily clad ladies hawking their sponsors' wares. Dominic did his share of looking, but he'd never cheated. He didn't want other women. He wanted to watch Erin with another man.

Their one kinky experience had been unintentional. A hiking trip, they'd gone off trail. Thinking they were out of sight, Dominic had turned her around, pushed her up against a sturdy redwood, tugged down her hiking shorts, and done her standing up as she braced herself against the tree. *Hot* didn't cover it. The ultimate was when they realized the trail they'd been on wound around, and they were on display for a couple coming from the opposite direction. It hadn't stopped him. It hadn't stopped Erin. In fact, her moans got louder. There in the forest, they'd had some of the hottest sex of their marriage, all while that couple watched. Hell, they'd relived that one event for a lot of fantastic sex later.

Dominic thought of the silent nights in their bed, her hands, her mouth. He needed more, wanted her to touch him, kiss him, talk to him. The only way they connected these days was sexually, in the dark and the silence. But he needed her to connect with him outside of their bed. Even if she got pissed about the party, at least there'd be some sort of connection. She'd actually have to talk to him. Just as she'd had to acknowledge him when he had Rachel make the reservation.

A little kink could be exactly what he needed to crack the shell she'd grown around herself, and an elaborate party at a mansion would be the perfect place to find it.

3

"THANKS, RACHEL, I APPRECIATE THE RIDE TO THE AIRPORT." ERIN hadn't been comfortable accepting, but when Rachel offered, turning her down had seemed churlish.

"I don't mind." Though Rachel had bargained for not having to return to work. At least she'd gotten something out of it.

The San Jose airport was only twenty minutes from DKG, especially at freeway speed. Erin remembered the days when Highway 880 was gridlocked at almost any time of day, not just commute hours, but you could see the recession's hit in lighter traffic on the roads and rental signs in building after building lining the freeway.

"You seem to be settling in well at the job," she said, making polite conversation. She'd lost some of her interpersonal skills in the last year. While never an extrovert like Dominic, she used to at least be able to keep up her end of meaningless chitchat without excruciating minute-long silences. A minute could be a very long time.

"Oh, it's going great," Rachel said brightly, as if she had to force it. She'd been stilted since the episode over the itinerary. "It'll be nice to get home a little early and cook dinner," she added. "Sometimes I'm rushing so much that I end up making something out of a box or picking up fast food. I hate giving the boys fast food all the time."

Erin closed her eyes two seconds longer than necessary. "Yes," she agreed, "kids eat too much fast food these days." She admired that Rachel had been a stay-at-home mom until her divorce. Erin herself could never have given over her independence to a man, not even Dominic, but she remembered the effort it took to provide nutritious meals. Now . . . well, now she didn't plan anything until she got home and saw what hadn't gone bad in the fridge. Or they got takeout. Usually takeout, come to think of it.

She never thought to ask how Dominic felt about that. Another weed of guilt sprouted in the backyard of her mind.

"The boys are good about helping to get stuff ready." Rachel flipped her visor down against the sun's sudden glare on the windshield.

The rain had stopped for the first time in a week. Since Dominic had gotten Erin to agree to the trip, every day had been cloudy and rainy, some days a drizzle, others a downpour. She'd hardly noticed; it shocked her more when the sun came out, as if the gloom suited her better. She should have used the weather as an excuse not to travel. She hadn't. She'd made no excuses whatsoever. If she got it over with, showed Dominic how miserable she was, he wouldn't ask again. Yet there was the niggling guilt that she'd forced him to beg for attention.

Don't make me go alone, Erin.

Standing in his lab, her fingers had tingled as if they'd fallen asleep, and her anger vanished. They didn't talk about it, but she knew Dominic had just as many hard memories. She was so me-me-me, she ignored him. In her defense, Dominic seemed so much more . . . even-keeled. She'd always been the moody one, even before. He'd wanted to do grief counseling. She didn't know why. He hadn't needed it. He'd come to terms with everything after the first few months.

The silence in the car was suddenly expectant. God, she'd totally missed what Rachel had said. "I'm sorry, what was that?"

"Nothing important."

Damn. It probably was. But there she'd gone being me-me-me again. "I really like that sweater you're wearing." Totally inane, but on the fly, she couldn't come up with anything else. God, her social skills sucked. She should have driven herself to the airport and left the car in the long-term lot.

Rachel plucked at the fake fur collar of her cardigan. Black, short, the sweater was made of a wool that looked both soft and warm. "This?" She laughed. "I bought it at the thrift store for a dollar. It was a deal."

Erin stopped the gape before her mouth actually dropped open. "It's nice." It was, honestly, but she wouldn't be caught buying at secondhand places. As a kid, secondhand was all she wore, either from her sisters or cousins, or they were Salvation Army issue. After she and Dominic moved to California and made a bit of money, she'd never stepped foot in another thrift store. Not that she begrudged other people who did. Rachel was a single mother on a tight budget. The difference was that Erin would never have admitted where she got the sweater.

"Thanks." Rachel accepted the compliment without a blink, attesting to the fact that she couldn't have grown up poor.

They fell into silence, cars winging by Rachel's minivan on either side as she stuck to the speed limit. Erin once again searched for something to say.

Rachel pursed her lips, gaze straight ahead on the road. "Yvonne told me not to say anything, but I need to." Erin's stomach rolled as Rachel quickly glanced at her before going on. "I'm feeling uncomfortable with this hanging between us."

What? Erin couldn't manage the word. She didn't want to hear. Yet she knew.

"I'm so sorry about your little boy." Rachel shook her head slowly, back and forth, her eyes on the road.

Erin's insides hollowed out, nothing but a vast empty space left inside her. "That's okay." She felt as if someone else said the words.

"I had to say it, mother to mother, not employee to boss."

Erin's throat hurt. "Thank you." She wasn't thankful at all. For a moment, part of her hated the other woman. Rachel had two boys to rush home to. Erin would have sold her soul to be rushing home to make her son's dinner.

But her emotions weren't fair to Rachel. Face on, the woman was pretty in an ordinary way, but from the side, she suddenly seemed so much stronger. She probably only saw the ordinary, straight-forward view of herself, not the strength in her profile. You never saw yourself the way other people did. Erin didn't want to know how others saw her. Yvonne had warned Rachel not to say anything. Because she didn't think Erin was strong enough?

"I won't say anything else about it," Rachel added as if more was necessary. "I just wanted you to know how I felt."

No one ever talked about Jay at DKG. She and Dominic didn't talk about him. If she said anything, all her feelings might come spilling out, her guilt, her fear, her insanity.

A man from the Centers for Disease Control and Prevention had come. A month after. To interview them about what happened. The CDC documented all these kinds of "events." He'd said it was extremely rare, and she'd wanted to scream at him. If it was so rare, then why *her* child? Why, God, *why?* She'd said nothing, though. Dominic had answered the questions: where Jay had been, the school trip. How Dominic should have been there that day, but they'd had a difficult product release, and he'd opted to let Jay go on the day trip with the teachers and other parent chaperones. He'd taken his blame. Dominic had always taken his blame. They went on to how the doctors figured Jay had gotten the amoeba. Horse playing in the hot springs. A cannonball. Water up his nose carrying the tiny microscopic things that . . . She couldn't even think about what those *things* had done to him. Almost the first words out of the CDC man's mouth were that it wasn't their fault, nothing they could have done. Nothing. But he didn't know what she'd said to Jay, what she'd done. No one knew. Especially not Dominic.

Erin bit the inside of her cheek until she tasted blood. Otherwise, she might have screamed. "Thank you. You're very caring. I appreciate your concern."

Rachel reached over to pat her knee. It felt . . . odd, like an out of body of experience, not her knee at all. Erin knew the only way she could go on was to keep pretending that everything was okay, nothing had gone wrong, her life hadn't fallen apart a year ago.

God, she needed something, anything to stop the freight train of memories and guilt bearing down on her. She needed Dominic. Needed a shot of hot sex that would make everything go away. It was easier to push aside the black thoughts in the dark, where there was nothing but the physical. Sometimes the need felt almost like an addiction, have another shot of Jack Daniels to make you forget, pop another of those pills. Or have hot, quick, mind-numbing sex. In the dark, she didn't think about Jay; she simply acted, reaching for Dominic, driving out every other thought. She needed that fix now. How was she supposed to make it through the whole plane trip by herself? Last night alone in their bed had been bad enough, but Rachel's words had pushed her to the wall.

Rachel pulled into the roundabout at the airport. Erin hadn't even been aware of exiting the freeway.

She blew out a breath. "Thanks a lot," she said, forcing a semblance of normalcy into her voice as she gathered her purse and laptop case. She'd brought her MP3 player as well, equipped with a couple of mysteries she'd downloaded from the library. She could plug in and tune out. That would work. She could do this. She'd be fine. Nothing was different than it had been half an hour ago.

ERIN HAD UTTERED NOTHING MORE THAN MONOSYLLABIC AN-swers during the thirty minutes since Dominic had grabbed her bag off the luggage carousel. Despite the late hour, the baggage claim had swarmed with people, sound, laughter, the shrieks of families finding one another, so he hadn't noticed how quiet she was. Her relative silence wasn't uncharacteristic either; she'd been like this for months. Except that tonight, there was an odd tenseness about her. He could actually hear her breath coming in short puffs of air like an uneasy animal. Once they were in the rental car and away from the crowd, her stress had become obvious.

Goddammit. He'd thought getting her out of the Bay Area might help. It hadn't. After the long flight, she was probably pissed he'd goaded her into the trip. He tried engaging her anyway. "How was the flight?" He was pretty sure he'd already asked. He couldn't remember if she'd answered.

"Fine." Monosyllabic.

Fuck. Dominic breathed deeply. The Florida air was sultry, the December weather unseasonably warm even for Orlando. He'd worn short sleeves. Erin arrived in jeans and a jacket she'd re-moved to reveal a tight, long-sleeved white T-shirt that scooped low on her cleavage and seemed to make her red gold hair a richer shade. Back in the airport, he'd intercepted many a male glance Erin hadn't noticed.

Fine. He'd try again. "Were you able to sleep on the plane?"

"No."

The street was noisy with cars and people, vacationers in sum-mer wear still strolling the sidewalks despite the late hour. Garish neon lights reflected on the water to one side, high-rise hotels like behemoths against the night sky on the other, the ubiquitous palm trees lining the road.

"I downloaded a mystery from the library," she said.

He glanced over. She wasn't looking at him, but gazing out at the darkened shoreline instead. All he could think was that at least it was more than one syllable. A whole sentence. "Great."

"It helped pass the hours."

He couldn't remember the last time she'd gotten out her MP3. Never one to sit down and read, she'd listen to a book while do-ing chores, making dinner. Always multitasking, that was Erin. But she hadn't taken out the player in ages.

He capitalized on her sudden talkativeness. "You can hang out on the beach tomorrow and listen to a book if you want."

"I'll come with you to the show. See you in action."

She was talking, but she still wasn't looking at him. He watched her a few seconds too long and almost ran a red light. A young guy in the crosswalk, neon light playing colors across his shaved scalp, shook his fist.

"That sounds great," he said once the light had changed and they were moving again. It would be better if he knew what she meant by *in action*. Good or bad? He wanted action, but not in the exhibit hall. Might as well lay out his plans now and get the fight over with. "I got us a party invitation for tomorrow night. It's out in Windermere." Windermere was a posh burb on the Butler Chain of Lakes about twenty minutes outside Orlando.

"Isn't that where Tiger Woods lives?"

"I don't remember." But it wasn't unlikely. The area was home to a lot of celebrities. "There's the Crown Royal." He pointed, the hotel a block ahead, lights blazing across a semicircular drive, fountain, rock garden, and palm trees.

She turned in her seat, hooking a leg beneath her, and braced a hand on the dashboard to look up at the facade through the windshield. "Nice." A pulse fluttered at her throat, and he noticed again her odd intensity, foot bobbing on the floorboard as if nervous tension vibrated through her.

He passed the entrance and took the next drive heading into the underground parking garage. Circling once and finding nothing, he took the ramp down another level. Erin stretched, shoved her hands through her hair and fluffed it. Her nipples beaded beneath the thin T-shirt material.

Dominic suddenly felt parched. The tires squealed on the concrete despite the fact that he wasn't going more than five miles an hour. Spying a spot just past the end of the last row and flush up against the wall, he wheeled in.

She was on him the moment he shut off the engine, fingers at his belt.

"Do me," she whispered, her breath minty from a freshening strip she'd popped in her mouth.

His cock was hard before she even got to the button on his jeans. "Here?" Late, the lighting unexceptional, the back window of the rental car darkened with some film against the heat, they may or may not be seen. But he'd sure as hell hear the squeal of tires announcing another car's arrival.

"Here," she insisted, tugging on his zipper. Her lips were close but not touching, her skin flushed with heat, her eyes bright with something close to fever.

"We could get thrown out of the hotel or arrested." He didn't stop her as she shoved her hand in his jeans, found his cock, molded her palm to it.

"Do you care?" She squeezed.

"Christ." He felt his eyes roll back. "No, I don't care."

"Then fuck me, Dominic." She hadn't said his name in a year's worth of post-midnight sex.

In that moment, he was hers completely.

4

DOMINIC FELT GOOD BENEATH HER HANDS, HIS FLESH SLICK AND hard within her grip. Smelled good, too, his subtle aftershave muskier and more sensual on his skin than when sniffed from the bottle. Touching him drove Rachel's words in the car right out of Erin's mind. Sleeping on the plane had been impossible, and the audio book didn't help. Erin hadn't stopped thinking. Not until this moment, when there was only the impulse to take him. Here, now, not waiting for the room.

Hand on her nape, he pulled her close, his touch hot, his eyes dark. "Kiss me."

"Taste you," she said, pulling back and bending down to his lap, feeling only the slightest bite of guilt for not giving him what he wanted. A bead of pre-come on the tip of his cock seemed to glitter in the garage light falling through the side window. She closed her eyes as she took him, reveling in the physical, where there was nothing but his salty-sweet taste, the harsh sound of his breath, his fingers fisting in her hair, and his body surging deeper into her mouth. The console and handbrake between them dug into her abdomen, and even that was good, physical. She slid her hand deeper into his jeans and squeezed his balls as she sucked.

"Aw, Christ," he whispered.

Tires squealed on the concrete. The risk fueled her. Like that time in the woods, someone coming. *Do it anyway,* she'd told him. She hadn't cared, her excitement drowning out all common sense, all thought. Just as his musky sexual scent did now.

She sucked harder, deeper, then slid all the way up to circle the ridge of his cock, darting her tongue in his slit. He groaned; the sound was her reward. She used him, took from him, but he got something in return, even if it was only physical.

She was still thinking too much. With one last suck, she let him pop from her lips. A vein pulsed along his cock, his skin glistening with her saliva, the crown purple with need. She swiped away another drop of pre-come with her tongue, swallowed, and raised her eyes to meet his hooded gaze.

"Tell me what you want," he said.

She tore at the snap of her jeans. She should have worn a skirt. It was warm enough, the Florida night sultry compared to the Bay Area.

He grabbed her chin, held her still. "Tell me."

"Make me come." She didn't know what he wanted to hear, but what she said seemed to be good enough.

He helped her tug on the zipper, then she rolled in her seat, toed off one tennis shoe, and shoved her jeans and panties down. One free leg was all she required.

"Come here." Dominic helped pull her over. She slid her bare leg down by the side of the door, her jeans trailing her on the other side in kinky disarray.

He held her a couple of inches off him, his cock between her legs. "Someone might see," he said, his gaze dark in the shadowed interior of the car.

Her hair brushing the roof, she hunched slightly, braced herself on his shoulders, and glanced through the back window. Fluorescent lighting gleamed on the concrete, but their spot was to the right of the aisle, not clearly in the line of anyone's sight unless they were actually getting in or out of a car. "Yeah," she answered. "It's hot. Getting caught in the act again. It's what you always used to talk about." In long-ago phone calls and fantasies.

"Fuck, yeah," he agreed, his fingers flexing at her waist.

He'd always been that way, liking things a little left of center, kinky, making her like them, too. When he'd called to check on her last night, he'd tried one of those sexy phone sessions. She'd shut him down; it just hadn't felt right. She had little to offer these days, had fought going on this weekend trip even as she knew he needed more from her. The connection between them would never be the same. This—kinky, mind-numbing sex—was all she had left to give. Like an addict used drugs, she used him to make the pain go away, but at least when she did it, she made him feel good. Somehow, this place, away from home and the real world, made letting go seem all right. Here, it didn't have to be in the dark. It didn't have to be silent.

She wrapped her hand around his cock, grazed her pussy with the tip, leaving a trail of moisture along both of them. "Oh my God," she whispered, keeping her gaze trained over his shoulder. Then she lied. "There's a couple walking to their car."

Dominic played the game as he raised his hips to breach her with half an inch of cock. "What do they look like?"

She made it up. "Our age." She gasped at the feel of him filling her, sensitizing her skin but numbing her brain cells. "No, wait, he's about fifty, she's more like thirty." She bit her lower lip. "Blond, blue-eyed, and buxom, the way you like."

"I like red hair better." He curled his arms around her waist, pulled her flush against his chest until his breath caressed her ear. "Tell me when they see us."

He was hot, hard, and high inside her now, pumping out a slow, mesmerizing rhythm.

"Now," she told him. "The woman's caressing his arm and indicating our car with a jut of her chin at us."

Dominic thrust deep at her use of the word *us*, and she closed her eyes a moment to relish the sensation.

Holding her hip, he shoved a hand between them to find the button of her clit. "Tell me more."

"They've stopped completely . . . watching . . . like they're in a trance." Just the way Dominic entranced her with his touch on her clit, swirling, circling, and driving his cock deep in smooth motions. She let him do the work despite the fact that she was on top. He could pat his head and rub his stomach the same time, too. That used to be their joke about how good he was at bedroom-multitasking.

They hadn't joked or fantasized like this in so long. These days sex was relegated to silence and darkness. Erin felt a dangerous wave of emotion rising.

"Tell me when he starts to touch her."

She let Dominic's voice drag her back, concentrated on it. "He's running his hand up her skirt." Of course a fantasy woman would be wearing a skirt to make it all easier. "He's pulling her back against him, his hand moving between her legs."

Dominic's breath ratcheted up a notch, and her body swelled to the rhythm of his touch inside and out. On the phone, he used to drive her crazy with the after-show parties, describing the naughty doings, telling her how he wanted to watch her. Dominic had always loved talking sex. There were so many things she hadn't given him in such a long time.

"Oh, Nickie, he's shoving her skirt over her hips now," she teased him. "And *he's* huge. So thick and long." Then she chuckled. "Not as big as you, though."

He harrumphed and punctuated with a plunge of his hips she felt clear to her chest. She had pretending down to an art form now, yet it had been so long since she'd done this kind of pretending with him. For this short space of time in the cramped confines of the rental car, nothing else existed but his cock, her beating heart, and the imaginary couple.

Her ears hummed with the rush of blood through her body. She closed her eyes, chanting her little story. "He's shoving her against the car. Taking her hard. Pounding into her." And Dominic took her equally as hard, pinning her to him as he plunged deep. "Oh God, he's fucking her, and she's screaming out how good it is."

The orgasm came without warning, a burst of heat shooting out. She clamped down on his neck with her teeth like an animal taking her mate instead of the other way around. Dominic's come filled her, warmed her insides. For long moments, there was only exhaustion and mindlessness, exactly what she'd been searching for, the fix to drive out everything else. Maybe in Orlando, away from home, work, memories, and bad thoughts, she could let go of the lassitude. Maybe, for this one weekend, she could give Dominic the closeness he'd been silently begging for, and find a respite from her guilt for longer than one night.

NICKIE. SHE HADN'T CALLED HIM THE PET NAME, THE BEDROOM name, in more than a year. She hadn't played voyeuristic sex games that tied in with their long-ago hike. She hadn't talked to him while she fucked him.

Yet now she lay peacefully beside him in the hotel bed, no bad dreams disturbing her sleep.

She'd left him sated yet strangely nervous. Dominic couldn't gauge her mood, so different from the desperate forays in the dark of their own bedroom. Edgier, for sure, and he'd loved the added risk factor. Loved that she'd played into his desire for sexual banter and fantasy. He didn't know what had changed, but his heart raced with the memory. The transformation might not last through the weekend or even past the first rays of morning light, but she was here, she'd brought the cocktail dresses he'd requested, and she wanted to man the DKG booth with him instead of spending the day alone on the beach.

He'd take what he could get.

IT WAS BARELY TWO THIRTY IN THE AFTERNOON, AND ERIN FELT AS if her head might explode.

"Honey, come and meet Ryan." In the cacophony of the exhibit hall, she read his lips as Dominic waggled his fingers at her.

The man called Ryan folded her hand in both of his. He was short and slight like a jockey, blond and good-looking in an ethereal way, his skin pale, blue veins close to the surface. She preferred a hardier type, like Dominic.

"It's so nice to meet you, Mrs. DeKnight."

"You can call her Erin," Dominic said, adding the name of the team Ryan either owned or worked for. His words, though, were washed away in a burst of laughter from the next booth.

Her head ached beneath the overhead lights beating down, accompanied by the noise magnified in the high-ceilinged hall and an overabundance of cologne that didn't quite mask the odor of too many sweaty male bodies.

Dominic loved it all—the people, the loud voices, the activity, the endless schmoozing. He actually seemed proud showing her off to the cast of characters he'd met over the years. Now let's see, Ryan was the one who liked . . . She couldn't remember.

"Yes, please call me Erin." She echoed Dominic.

Ryan—was that his first or last name—dropped her hand as if sensing he'd held on too long. "You're as beautiful as your husband claimed."

Dominic stamped her with a hand on her nape, drawing her closer. He leaned over to whisper in her hair—"More so"—then raised his voice to include Ryan. "I'm glad Erin could finally make it here with me this year."

Most men would shrivel having to introduce their wives at this traditionally male-dominated trade show. If the parties afterward were anything to go by, trade shows and conferences were where guys went for a week away from the wife. But not Dominic. He was different.

She owed it to him to put on a good face for his friends. They were her customers, too. She searched for a topic . . . and Ryan's preferences hit her. He liked twins, as in a threesome with female twins. She hid a smile. Okay, not the topic she'd bring up now, but maybe she'd tease Dominic with it later.

But while she was thinking of what to say, Ryan moved on to the reason he'd stopped by the booth. "I hear you've got a through-coat gauge now."

Erin could feel each breath in and out of her chest. Dominic had been working on the gauge last year when . . . She swallowed past the lump in her throat.

"Sure we've got one." Dominic's voice had gone oddly flat, his eyes darkening. He bent to pull the sample locker from beneath the table.

The gauge had become one of their top sellers this year, yet this was the first time during the trade show that Dominic had brought out the sample, let alone set it out among the others he'd put in the display cases.

Rising, Dominic laid the instrument across Ryan's palm. "Check it out." He held up a painted metal pipe. With an ultrasonic gauge, you didn't have to cut the pipe to measure the center thickness. Only one available side was necessary, an important characteristic when you were trying to measure corrosion on the inside. With the through-coat gauge, you could obtain accurate measurements even on a piece of metal with a coating such as rubber or paint, which made it essential in high-performance racing.

Dominic was knowledgeable, personable, and he loved talking with people. He knew something about everything, could offer an insight on almost any subject. He was a charmer, not in a male-female way—though he was certainly capable of that—but he knew how to put people at ease, how to talk to them, how to bring them around to his way of thinking. If there was something wrong with a hotel room, he sweet-talked the front desk clerk into fixing it and ended up with accommodations twice as nice.

The trade show was more about showing off your wares, making an indelible impression, getting people to call you on Monday morning with the order. Yet with this gauge, Dominic was monotone, almost an automaton, reciting the features as if he were a disinterested telemarketer reading lines from a brochure. He didn't look at Ryan. He didn't look at her. A tick fluttered momentarily beneath his eye.

Still, Ryan walked away after ordering five of the gauges. Dominic laid the instrument back in the sample locker and shoved it out of sight under the table again.

In her worst moments, she'd hated Dominic for how easily he put aside his guilt, how easily he forgave himself, as if all he'd done that day last year was miss a meeting. She'd even envied his ability to forget. Yet watching him now, her whole body trembled. Maybe the only difference between them was that Dominic was better at hiding his grief and guilt. Suddenly, she couldn't stand his silence, his brooding. And that gave her the tiniest inkling of how he must feel when she was in one of her moods.

"Twins," she said, grabbing his hand. "Ryan was the one who was always looking for twins." The smile she pasted on was so big and so phony it made her cheeks hurt.

He looked at her then, and each facet of his face seemed to shift; the tense line of his jaw eased, the frown slipped from his brow, his eyes lost the deep obsidian cast, and finally, his lips curved slightly. "You always said you were falling asleep when I told you that stuff on the phone."

She'd *never* fallen asleep on those nights, had loved them. She wished she had the words to tell him that now. Something held her back. Something always did these days.

"It's the little lady." The voice boomed across the hall as if he were on the other end instead of standing outside their booth. Jamison. Erin couldn't remember his first name. For all intents and purposes, these guys didn't have first names. And she'd never been so happy to see anyone, as if he'd saved them from something terrible.

Before she could open her mouth, he gathered her up in a bear hug, his belt buckle pressing into her belly. She almost squeaked, staring helplessly at Dominic over the man's shoulder.

She'd met him once. Jay's memorial. He and his wife had been kind. *Please don't say anything about that now.*

"Pretty as a picture." Jamison beamed with his big Yogi Bear smile as he set her back on her feet.

"Schmoozer," Dominic said without inflection. Then he squeezed her hand. He held on for a few minutes of conversation that didn't require her input. Slowly, his grip relaxed, the tense moments over the through-coat gauge drifting away. Maybe she'd imagined them in the first place.

"HERE'S THE INVITE." JAMISON HANDED DOMINIC AN EMBOSSED card. "You know how to get there?"

"Looked it up on the Web. You weren't kidding about posh."

Dominic had even looked up the prices of houses out in Windermere. *Definitely* posh.

Jamison shook his fingers in the air, then blew on them as if he were trying to put out a fire. "That husband of yours says he's bringing you to Miterberg's party tonight." He socked Dominic in the arm, then leaned in close to Erin. "Do not *ever* tell my wife what goes on." He zipped his lips. "I'm trusting you."

"Not a word," she promised.

He guffawed. "Right. I know you ladies stick together." Soon after, with another hardy hand clasp, Jamison moved on.

"Why don't you take the car and go back to the room?" Dominic said. They'd been at it since nine that morning, without even a break for lunch. He'd sent her off for a salad and a burger, but she'd brought the food back to the booth to eat with him. Now, she was sagging, shoulders drooping, eyes glassy from too much frenetic activity going on around her. She wasn't used to men bear-hugging her, but she'd handled it well.

At work, when she had her fill of people, she could close her office door. Here, you couldn't get away from the noise. It never bothered Dominic. Erin was different.

She hadn't said a word while Ryan was here, not a thing when he retrieved the through-coat gauge. Dominic's gut had clenched, partly from the things it made him remember, partly from fear of how she'd react if he showed the slightest enthusiasm about it. For a couple of months after Jay died, he'd considered scrapping the project altogether, probably would have if Cam Phan hadn't stepped in until he could get his bearings.

Yet, despite his fears, Erin had bounced back after Ryan's visit. She'd even joked about the twins as if *she* had to bring *him* out of a funk. It gave Dominic hope for the weekend, hope in general. Wrapping his arms across her back, he pulled her flush against his chest. She didn't fight it. He nuzzled her ear, drinking in her scent, his heart thumping in his chest. It had been so long since she'd allowed him small intimacies like this. "Take a bath, get all gussied up for tonight."

She opened her mouth. He knew what was coming. She didn't want to go to the party. She'd tell him to go alone.

Instead, she dropped her eyelids to half-mast. "Your friends at the next booth are staring."

"Because you're beautiful," he whispered.

"It's because your hand is on my ass."

She wore tight jeans again and a thin sweater that molded to her breasts. He hadn't felt his hand drifting lower. "Does it make you hot?"

"That you have your hand on my ass?"

"No." He shook his head slowly. "That they're watching."

The blue of her eyes deepened, and she moistened her lips, catching his gaze on the sight. "It does," she admitted. "As if I'm on display."

His skin felt suddenly stretched tightly over his bones. Giving her butt a one-handed squeeze, he pressed her hard to his cock. "A bath, a glass of wine. Get ready for anything, baby."

Tonight, he was going to see how far he could push a few limits.

5

WINDERMERE WAS AN UPSCALE TOWN OUT ON THE ISTHMUS IN the Butler Chain of Lakes. Quaint, it was like something Erin pictured up in the northeast, with a pretty town square and a landmark town hall. Though it was close to nine o'clock, the ice-cream shop was still doing a brisk business and couples walked hand in hand on the sidewalk, navigating around families with strollers. Everyone was taking advantage of the unusually warm December air.

Fifteen or so miles southwest of Orlando, Windermere was idyllic. On the way in, they'd passed a sign for a nearby prep school. No ordinary public school for Windermere. This was where the rich came to live and play. It was the kind of place where you'd have to get a permit to have a garage sale and pay a deposit for the signage to make sure you took it down afterward. Then again, Windermere residents wouldn't have garage sales; they'd do auctions at Sotheby's.

Driving out toward the lake waters—which of the Butler Chain, Erin wasn't sure—they left behind the houses and hit mansion central, the lakefront properties.

"Don't be nervous," Dominic said, anticipating her mood.

It was one of the habits she'd driven him to, anticipate and circumvent. It made her more determined to keep any black mood at bay for the evening. "I'm not nervous," she gave the obligatory white lie. Her mother had cleaned houses like this for a living.

Dominic turned down a lane framed by trees, something tall, thin, and evergreen. Cypress maybe. Or juniper. He drove with his hand draped over the wheel. "You look sexy in that dress."

It felt like a throwaway compliment, something said to make conversation. She didn't call him on it. "Thank you." Ever so polite. Yeah, she was more than a little nervous. The black velvet number hadn't been out of its plastic hanging bag in a very long time.

Ground lights flanked the drive he pulled into. There was no gate, but a uniformed man stood by a pillar topped with a lion's head. Dominic lowered the window and handed over the embossed card Jamison had given him.

Beyond the entry pillars, the front yard was a vast expanse of grass dotted with flowering bushes and a huge box hedge on either side, separating the property from the next estate. Lights gleamed along the front of the two-story house, illuminating the three-car garage and the walkway to the front portico and open double doors.

Invitation inspected and accepted, Dominic rolled away, stashing the card on the dash. He smiled at her, his teeth gleaming. "What do you think?"

He'd described the opulence of some of these parties, but she hadn't quite believed him. "I hope the food is just as good because I'm starving." He'd brought her a salad when he returned from the show, telling her to save her appetite.

"I guarantee you'll be totally satisfied."

With another flash of his teeth, she was pretty sure he wasn't referring to food. Since the time that couple had stumbled upon them in the woods, they'd gotten a kick out of fantasizing about watching and being watched. But though Dominic had ventured to the Internet to scope out sex clubs, they'd never acted on it. Just the phone sex after some trade show or conference he'd attended. She'd suspected he made up half of it merely to excite her. And it had worked.

They pulled their nondescript rental car in among Mercedes, Jags, BMWs, and a fire-engine-red Mustang. A young parking valet with short blond hair opened her door and held out his hand to help Erin from the car.

Dominic loved people and parties, but he was also looking for something from her. Connection. She owed him at least this, a little pretending, a little forgetting. Why the hell not?

SHE WAS GORGEOUS IN BLACK VELVET, A DRESS HE HADN'T SEEN IN longer than he cared to admit. Even before they lost Jay, she'd worked too hard. He'd allowed her to. She'd paired black suede high heels with sheer black stockings. Wanting to save the surprise and heighten his anticipation, he hadn't watched her dress and wasn't sure if they were thigh highs. His skin heated in hope.

He knew her well, her signals, the nuances by which he gauged her mood. He also knew she hated it when he read her correctly. Now she was playing the dutiful wife. *This is what he wants, so this is what I'll do and then maybe he'll get off my case.* That wasn't good enough for him.

Dominic laced his fingers through hers and led her across the marble foyer. "Food first," he told her. Maslow's hierarchy of needs; air, food, drink, then sex, though that wasn't exactly how Maslow would have expressed it.

Like something out of an antebellum mansion, a wide carpeted staircase rose before them, then parted at a small landing to climb in opposite directions to the second floor. On the left of the stairs, wide doors led to a large sitting room that extruded voices and laughter like a well-oiled machine, but, like carnivores on the hunt, most of the throng followed the sweet and tangy scents wafting through the archway to the right. The attire was anything from jeans and polo shirts to fancy cocktail dresses, the colors as vivid as a peacock's feathers. There were more men than women, and the women, for the most part, were under the age of thirty. Stereotypical playthings for rich, old men. Dominic preferred his own woman to any twentysomething.

He jumped in line behind one of the few middle-aged couples, snagged a flute of champagne from a huge tray set by the door, and handed it to Erin.

"Oh my God." Her voice was breathy against his ear, awe-struck. "Would you look at that spread."

She gazed in wonder at the magnificent buffet. Trust food to bring her to life. Thank God he hadn't fed her well. It was as if they'd entered another time, another place, a foreign setting, where their past didn't have to exist and Erin could forget for a while, be the woman he'd married rather than the mother who'd lost everything. He squeezed her hand. "Hungry?"

"You know I'm famished. A salad," she scoffed. "What were you thinking?"

"I was thinking about this." He swept his hand before them, but it wasn't the platters stacked high with fresh shrimp, lobster, and crab that made his mouth water. It was the sudden animation on her face, the sparkle in her eyes. So what if it didn't last? He was living for the moment.

The meat had already been pulled from the cracked shells. He held her champagne and a plate to share while she mounded it with shellfish. "So this guy is rich?"

He hadn't seen Miterberg yet, but the man was known for

ostentation and risky business. By midnight, his guests would be swimming naked in the heated pool. And a whole lot more.

If everything went according to plan, Erin would be crazy with desire in a couple of hours. He wasn't hoping for a public display at the party. That was asking way too much. He was thinking about after that. She might not even be able to wait for the hotel. He imagined doing her in a secluded glade off the highway. He'd been on the lookout as he drove.

"Do you want some Brie?" She held up a small knife.

He wanted something smooth, hot, and creamy, and it wasn't Brie. She laid a few crackers alongside the cheese on the plate. Then she raised her eyes and batted her lashes. "Maybe you need your own plate. This one's getting full."

He felt himself coming to life right along with her. The trip could work. It could be a new beginning for them.

While she concentrated on a tray of fruit cut in intricate designs, he let his gaze wander the room and found himself captured by a man leaving the head of the line. His eyes on Erin's ass as she leaned slightly over the table, the guy almost bumped into a woman passing by him.

Though his hair was silver, the lines on his face didn't make him out to be more than in his midforties. Where Dominic had chosen slacks and a button-down shirt, this guy had gone the tuxedo route. Erin liked a sharp dresser, James Bond style as played by Sean Connery. Elegant without being prissy.

As he watched his wife being assessed, something hot blossomed in his gut. He wasn't ashamed to admit that. It was partly pride of ownership, and he enjoyed that this man couldn't tear his gaze from the sexy sway of his wife's ass as, oblivious, she picked through the buffet.

Before he could point the guy out, though, he'd disappeared through the open doors at the far end.

Erin walked away with a full plate. "God, this is seductive," she said as he caught up. She dipped a morsel of lobster in a little tub of drawn butter she'd poured.

Seductive? An odd word. "The food?"

She shrugged. "The opulence. Like hanging around sports pros or rock stars. You can see why people become groupies." She held up a shrimp dredged in cocktail sauce.

He ate from her fingers, licking away the remaining sauce, his blood starting to rush. "Yeah, sex, drugs, and rock 'n' roll." He steered her to the same open doorway through which her admirer had vanished. Beyond lay a large sunroom cascading with hanging plants and potted ferns, rattan chairs, chaises, and rag rugs. A citrus scent from indoor fruit trees perfumed the air. Couples lounged and laughed, exchanging seductive glances and touches, but nothing untoward. Yet.

He didn't see the man among them.

"Have a cracker." She fed him one slathered in a delicious cheese, watching his mouth as he ate. Beneath the velvet of her dress, he detected the pearl of a nipple.

She was seduced, stepping out of herself. She hated party schmoozing. Especially when he talked business and wasn't paying as much attention as he should. Thus was the difference. Here, she was the center of his attention. He noticed everything, her tongue slipping along her finger to catch a drop of butter, the rich shade of her lipstick, the fall of her red hair across her shoulders and back. The way men looked at her.

He wanted to toss aside the plate, lay her down on a chaise lounge, and fuck her right here in front of everyone. The way they'd fantasized in their previous life. The way he'd done her up against that tree with a pair of hikers watching. He wanted that other life.

All he had was this weekend.

"Drink your champagne." He traded her for the plate, taking her hand as they wended their way through the crowd.

She sipped. "Wow, this is the expensive stuff."

She noticed things like that, her childhood having been poor. His had been hard, too, but money had always seemed more important to her than to him. Not that he didn't like or appreciate having it, and he'd worked hard to get it.

They feasted, sipped champagne, and wandered the room for a bit, then headed out to the patio. He laid the plate on a table by the French door as the scent of chlorine overlaid the citrus. Tiny lights illuminated the edge of the kidney-shaped pool, and water bubbled over a rock formation at the far end, simulating a waterfall. In the shadow of the rocks, a Jacuzzi frothed, vapor rising into the cooler air. From its depths, three couples and a man saluted with champagne glasses, a heap of clothing on several chaises next to the pool. It wasn't midnight, and they were already getting naked.

Erin skirted the hot tub and headed out to the boat dock. Lights twinkled along the opposite shore. The night having grown cooler, goose bumps pebbled her bare arms, but he didn't move to touch her beyond their clasped hands.

Sometimes he was incapable of taking the slam when she turned him down. He couldn't bear it now.

She drew in a deep breath, staring across the water. "Thank you." She sipped the good champagne.

"You're welcome." For what?

"I was really hungry. And that was good."

He had a feeling she was speaking of something else entirely, sustenance, maybe, but not food. Maybe something a little bit higher on Maslow's hierarchy.

She didn't specify. He didn't ask. *Thank you* was enough. A moment later he led her away from the boat dock. Something creaked in the virtual darkness at the edge of the patio, on the backside of the Jacuzzi and waterfall. Erin stopped, tugging his hand.

The darkness coalesced into shapes. A couple of lounge chairs. One of them was . . . moving, then, his eyes adjusting, he made out the twin moons of a man's ass surrounded by a pair of alabaster legs gleaming in the moonlight.

Erin put her lips to his ear. "You weren't joking all those times."

"I told you there was a lot of sex going on."

"I thought you made a lot of it up."

He grinned. "Some. But certainly not all."

"They're fucking." She sidled close, hugging his arm. "God, that's hot."

"Yes." The first time you actually saw live spontaneous sex, it was hot and exciting simply for the novelty. Though he couldn't say this was exactly a seductive sight, the ass in question a bit too large and flabby.

For a moment he wondered if it was Jamison. But Jamison, despite his talk about not telling his wife, had never actually done anything at any of the parties Dominic had seen him at.

"What wasn't real in all the stories you told me?" Her breath was a warm puff fanning his neck. She still hadn't taken her gaze off the oblivious couple.

"There was no orgy."

He imagined he could actually feel her body heating against him. "But everything else?" she prodded.

He tried to remember what he'd thought would excite her, the things he'd exaggerated or downright made up. "Give me a reminder."

"Two guys taking that woman between them."

"DP?"

She rolled her eyes, still watching the tableau by the patio corner. "Glad you know all the lingo. Yes, double penetration."

"I made it up. They did her separately."

She looked at him then, arching a brow.

"All three played together, sucking and kissing, but one of them did her first, then the other."

"You were a lot sexier at this over the phone."

He grinned. "Sorry. I'm out of practice."

A loud groan punctuated the laughter coming from the Jacuzzi. Moon-Ass was closing in on his climactic moment, and he followed the groan with a series of long grunts.

Erin laughed. He couldn't remember the last time he'd heard that particular husky unselfconscious tone.

"He sounds like those turtles we saw at the zoo," she whispered, laughter in her words.

The mating turtles. They'd gone at it for damn near half an hour. Jay had asked what they were doing. After the first few weeks, she didn't bring up anything they'd done with Jay, as if all the memories had been expunged. She hadn't even spoken Jay's name and pulled up short if even the slightest reference reminded her. But here, she'd recalled that scene with the turtles. And she'd smiled at the memory. He didn't comment, didn't want to break the moment, saying instead, "Not as sexy as you hoped, huh."

"The night's young." Then she touched his arm, and her voice dipped to a seductive note. "Show me more."

6

HER WORDS WERE MORE THAN DOMINIC COULD HAVE HOPED FOR, more than he'd dreamed. Back in the house, he led her to a vacant rattan sofa in the sunroom. The lighting here was more ambient, unlike the brightly lit, open-beamed living room on the other side of a set of open French doors.

"Would you get me another, honey?" Erin waggled her empty champagne glass.

When he returned, the silver-haired man had found her. Standing by a potted lemon tree, the guy hung back, watching her as Dominic passed.

"Your wife is very beautiful." His voice was a deep baritone Erin would love.

"Yes, she is."

He was an inch or so shorter than Dominic, his eyes blue. "You're a lucky man."

"I know." Then he left the man and joined his beautiful wife on the sofa. She'd curled herself into the corner, kicked off her shoes and tucked her feet beneath her.

"What did he want?" she asked.

"You."

She glanced at the man. He'd remained by the lemon tree. "Aren't you jealous?"

Dominic tried to gauge what she wanted. "Yes and no." He tipped his head to take in the man. "Feeling a little possessive over you makes me hot. Makes me want to test my reactions."

She sighed, propped her elbow on the back of the couch and leaned her chin on her fist. Finally, her lips curved. Not quite a smile, but not a sneer either. He'd said the right thing.

Another man, in his midfifties maybe, joined Silver Hair; they talked, then a young blonde dressed in blue laid her head on the older guy's shoulder. Curling his arms around her waist, he squeezed her breast without even a break in his conversation. He strummed her nipple, pinching it until she was clinging to him just as Erin had hugged Dominic's arm out on the patio. Silver Hair let his gaze pass between the blonde and Erin, as if suggesting he'd like to give Erin the same treatment.

Erin laid her arm along the sofa back. "He's touching her boob in front of everyone." Her voice rose slightly on an incredulous high note. "It's one thing out back on the patio in the dark, where it's hard to make everything out. But here?"

"Told ya you'd get an eyeful."

"Is that how it all starts?" She passed her tongue over her upper lip, leaving her lipstick glistening.

"Sometimes it's slow and subtle, others it's damn near a free-for-all." But Dominic liked Silver Hair's style. Appreciative rather than slimy.

"Oh my God." This time her words were nothing more than a breath against him. He cocked his head, following her gaze.

The man and woman she'd spotted weren't hidden well. They probably didn't mean to hide at all and merely found the ficus by the door a convenient place for her to drop to her knees out of the flow of foot traffic. Dominic couldn't see her face, just a rear view of a trim body, dark hair tumbling down her bare back, and the soles of her high-heeled shoes as she unzipped her partner's slacks. Closer to forty than thirty but in regular workout shape, his canary yellow polo shirt sported a team logo on the pocket. Dominic couldn't read which one.

Erin's fingers bit into his arm as the kneeling woman drew out an exceptionally imposing cock, enough to make you turn in the men's room with envy in your heart and *whoa* on your lips before you stopped yourself.

"Whoa," she whispered, echoing his thought.

Dominic absorbed the voyeuristic gleam in her dilated eyes. Her breasts rose and fell, noticeably faster than before. He should have brought her here years ago. Then again, if he had, he would have nothing new or intriguing or mind-blowing to tempt her out of the shell she'd built around herself.

He leaned in close, scenting the fragrant bath waters still lingering on her skin, and something more, something sensual; arousal. His balls tightened, his cock flexed, hardened. "Would you like to suck something as big as that?"

She slid only her eyes to him, then back to the couple. "Size doesn't matter."

He laughed. "Hell, yes, it does."

She shook her head, still watching. "It's about how much he likes it, how much he wants what *you* do, not some other woman, but *you* and you alone."

Dominic had never thought about it that way. Maybe that was the difference between the sexes. He held her chin, the flutter of a rapid pulse at her throat, then captured her gaze. "You're the best cocksucker I've ever had."

Emotions swept across her face. He couldn't read them, but he sensed some good, some bad. The place was so perfect for seduction; decadent, hedonistic, the kind of atmosphere they'd talked about over the phone. He knew she'd been turned on by it back then. But that was before, another life. Tonight could backfire on him, push her further away.

Yet the emotional distance between them couldn't get any wider than it was in their own bed. What the fuck did he have to lose? He'd dreamed big as a kid, and bigger when he grew up. He had to dream big now.

Feeling the scrutiny of the silver-haired man, Dominic trailed a finger down to the pulse beating at Erin's throat, then followed the line of her bodice to the swell of her breast, rising, falling with each quickened breath. "I'd love to watch you suck cock."

"No way."

No way, he wouldn't love it? Or no way, she'd never do it? He caught motion in his periphery. Then Silver Hair made his move, taking the chair next to Erin's side of the rattan sofa.

Dominic decided to put his fantasy to the test.

"YOUR WIFE HAS GORGEOUS BREASTS."

"They're absolutely perfect." Dominic agreed with the man he'd pointed out to her earlier. "They're very sensitive. She loves to have them pinched."

"Hard?" the man asked.

"Mildly hard, not too much pain."

The man nodded, smiling slightly, looking at her nipples already beaded beneath the soft velvet.

They talked about her like she was a sex object and didn't have a thought to add to the conversation. Their gazes traced her curves as if she were nothing more than a piece of flesh. It was horrifyingly sexist.

Erin was so wet she could feel the cream on the inside of her thighs.

Mid- to late forties, the man was clean-shaven and dark-skinned. The color was natural, not from the sun or a tanning salon, but speaking to a Mediterranean ancestry. His eyes were a searing blue even in the relatively dim light of the sunroom.

"Call me Winter," he said. Somehow, the name seemed perfectly appropriate. "I heard what you said to her."

Dominic raised one dark brow.

"That she was the best cocksucker you've ever had."

He must have been adept at reading lips because Dominic had not said that loudly enough to carry over the party noise.

"The very best," Dominic reiterated. He kept his hand moving on her as they spoke, her throat, shoulder, arm, thigh, his touch warm and so very *there*.

Winter focused on her lips. "How many cocks has she sucked?"

"We've been married a long time." Dominic knew she'd had three lovers before they were married, but he revealed nothing.

"I can tell."

She wondered how. It was more than the matching wedding rings.

"I can smell her juice." Winter dropped his voice. "I believe she will be so very sweet."

Under his penetrating gaze, her skin flushed, heat blossoming deep inside. But it was Dominic's voice that made her feel wild. "Her pussy is beautiful. Pink and lush and plump when she's aroused."

She sure as hell must be pink, lush, and plump right now.

"A woman's pussy is a beautiful thing." Winter didn't talk to her, he talked over her. Like a horse trader getting ready to put in a bid.

A normal woman would have walked out on the two of them. She wasn't normal. She couldn't move. She didn't want to. Sex had become her crutch, a high to make her forget, and this was the biggest high of all. Her physical cravings had crossed some sort of line, and her needs were no longer about blotting out memories or emotions or guilt; they were about the sex itself, the heat of it, the desire.

"What does she taste like?" Winter murmured, his voice low, sexy, setting her on fire.

She held her breath waiting for Dominic's answer.

"Sweet yet tangy and succulent like fruit."

"Christ." Winter unbuttoned his tux jacket as if he couldn't breathe with it fastened. Beneath the pants, his cock filled the material, but he didn't touch the bulge.

"Do you want to know the thing I love best?" Dominic's dark gaze fell to Erin's lap.

Yes, God, yes, she wanted to know. He'd seduced her like he'd done with his phone calls, making her breasts heavy and her clitoris throb. All the more so because he was telling another man the intimate secrets of their marriage.

"Tell me," Winter begged as if the dialogue were part of some male ritual.

"I love it when she spreads her legs and masturbates for me."

Her ears hummed as if she were about to faint, and her arms tingled with pins and needles as her skin seemed to come alive, an entity all its own. The fast hard sex in the dark when she couldn't sleep was nothing compared to this. This drowned out everything, even the guilt. Dominic's eyes blazed with a heat she'd never seen before. His touch on her was searing. He'd seduced himself with his own words. They were far from home in an opulent fantasy world, and she wanted this, not the man, but the mindlessness, the pure physicality of it.

"I want to watch her," Winter murmured, his eyes on her, burning right through her dress.

God help her, she hoped and feared that Dominic would tell her to do it.

BRIGHT SPOTS COLORED HER CHEEKS, AND HER FLESH WAS HOT TO the touch, her breathing shallow, her focus narrowed to the curve of Winter's lips.

All Dominic had to do was say the word, and she would lift her skirt right there. The enormity of that power made him rock hard in his slacks.

With mere words, he'd raised her to this level. His heart roared in his chest. This was better than two strangers watching them from afar. This was up close and personal, Winter imagining every move, losing himself in the description, wanting her.

"The way she caresses herself." Dominic went on, playing her, watching her, the heat in her eyes, a shot of fear that he'd make her do it. "Her abandon, as if I'm not even there. The way she rises and falls, her come all over her fingers." He imagined he could scent her right now.

"Christ," Winter choked out, "you're making me crazy."

"Sometimes I lean close and breathe her in. She's intoxicating." Dominic was so hard, his cock felt like it would explode with one touch. Her breasts rose rapidly, her skin flushed, then she bit down on her bottom lip. "It's all I can do not to throw myself on her and fuck her."

She moaned. He was sure she didn't even know and couldn't have stopped it. "Nickie," she whispered.

He couldn't wait for her another moment. He'd go crazy if he didn't get inside her. But not here, despite all the fantasizing they'd done. He didn't think she was ready. He didn't trust that she wouldn't balk at the last moment, and he wasn't willing to risk it. Gathering her hand in his, he rose, tugging her with him. Winter's eyes followed the move.

"If you'll excuse me, I have to go fuck my wife." Beside him, Erin stepped into the high heels she'd kicked off earlier.

A light danced in the other man's eyes. "Thank you for the brief moments of pleasure. I don't think anything else will prove quite as entertaining tonight." He didn't seem the least disturbed by the blatant cock tease. "I'll be imagining the look of her while you ride her hard."

"Perhaps she'll ride." Then he pulled Erin along behind him, shouldering through a group blocking the sunroom door.

"I can't believe you did that." She didn't resist, though. He assumed her words were for show.

"It was hot."

"You treated me like I was a piece of meat."

He crossed the marble lobby, turning at the first stair. "I told him exactly how beautiful and perfect you are."

Everything about her seemed brighter, sharper, as if she'd been sleepwalking through the last year, and he'd suddenly shaken her awake.

"Fuck me," he whispered, aware of eyes on them, a couple of newcomers arriving, a small group passing from the living room to the buffet. Then a raucous surge of laughter from the open room at the back caught their greedy attention, something better than a married couple heading upstairs to fuck in private.

"Why didn't you do it in front of him?"

He thought about picking her up and taking the steps two at a time like Rhett carrying Scarlett. "You're not ready."

Something sparked in her eyes. "I'm ready for this." Then she was the one pulling him up the stairs, taking the left fork. At the top, she started opening and closing doors. Until she found what she wanted and dragged him in.

7

"DO IT HERE," SHE DEMANDED.

The aliveness of her emotions swamped him, reflected off the mirrored bathroom walls. She was everywhere, all around him, back, front, side, black velvet dress, stockings, high heels, red hair, scarlet cheeks and lips. He hauled her up on the pale blue marbled countertop between the twin sinks with gold taps. Amid fancy hand towels and baskets of soaps in the shape of dolphins, he shoved her skirt up her thighs, thrusting his hand between her legs.

Question answered: thigh highs and thong panties. He pulled aside the crotch. "Christ, you're wet."

She gripped his forearm with one hand and cradled the bulge of his cock. "And you're hard."

He circled her clit, watched her lids drop. "You wanted to spread your legs for him."

"I wouldn't have done it even if you'd begged me," she challenged, the belligerence in her tone part of the game, an element of the seduction.

He fit two fingers in her channel, found her G-spot, reveled in the gasp that fell from her lips. "You drooled looking at his cock. You wanted it."

She yanked his belt, unzipped his pants, and freed his cock.

"You were afraid I'd say yes, then you wouldn't have known what the hell to do."

He loved the fight in her and didn't care why it enflamed him. "What if I'd told him to pay me to have a go at you?"

She flooded his hand with moisture, her breath puffing. "He wouldn't have enough money for what I'm worth." She squeezed his cock, spread her legs wider, wrapped her calves around his ass to draw him in.

"You would have done it for free, that's how hot you were for him."

Fire blazed in her eyes, rushed across her skin. "You have no idea how hot I am." She tugged his hand from her pussy and snugged his hips close, the tip of his cock grazing her clit. "Be a man," she ordered. "Take care of my needs." She narrowed her eyes. "Or I'll go downstairs and find the man who can."

"He's already found someone to replace you." There would be no one ever to replace her.

Hands on her butt, he impaled her. She gasped, and her head fell back, hair caressing his knuckles, eyes closed. The warmth of her enclosed him, filled him, renewed him.

Bracing her hands on the counter behind her, she met his thrusts, forcing him deeper. "You can do better than that."

Part of him wanted to laugh. He'd needed her to talk to him, say something, anything, and, holy hell, she was, insulting him every which way. It was fucking hot for no apparent reason.

"You can't take it harder," he growled.

She wrapped one arm around him, pulled him close, and bit his shoulder through his shirt. "Excuses, excuses."

The mirror steamed with the close heat of their bodies. Someone knocked on the locked door. Her skin smelled like sweet champagne as if it oozed from her pores, and he felt his orgasm build in his balls.

"You can't do it," she whispered as if it were a sweet nothing. "You can't take me. You can't make me come." Yet she moaned, breathing harsh, eyes closed, and her fingers fisted in his hair so tightly his scalp ached. In that moment, her body squeezing his cock, his orgasm damn near shot out of control as the tremors of her climax threatened to drag him with her.

But there was one last thing he had to have. Hand in her hair, pulling her head back, he took her mouth, forced his tongue past her lips, steeped himself in her taste, kissing her, devouring her.

For the first time in over a year, she melded her mouth to his and kissed him back, deep, hard, breath-stealing, heart-pumping. And when he filled her, it was beyond giving her his essence, it was his heart and soul.

THE NIGHT WAS SURREAL. DOMINIC HAD TOSSED THE KEYS TO THE valet, and when the car arrived, he'd bundled her inside as if she were a porcelain doll.

Some other woman had hurled those insults at her husband. Some other person had sat speechless while Dominic told a stranger that she loved to masturbate for him. Someone else had let those words turn her inside out with heat and desire, had let Dominic take her on the cold tile countertop, fucked him, kissed him, climaxed, and begged for more. Some other woman had loved every moment.

She wanted to say it was the champagne. She turned her head on the seat to tell him she was sleepy and drunk and she couldn't remember exactly what she'd done tonight, but his profile was crystal clear.

She reached for Dominic, laying cold fingers on his warm arm. He covered her hand with his palm. "That was hot, baby."

She absolutely could not deny it. Or that she needed more of it, the mindless sex that kept the rest of her life at bay.

WEARING ONLY BRA AND A THONG PANTY THAT OUTLINED HER firm, heart-shaped ass, Erin leaned over the bathroom counter applying her makeup. Already showered and dressed—they'd agreed he'd leave for the exhibition hall early, and she would meet him later—Dominic leaned against the doorjamb watching. After that hot episode in Miterberg's rented mansion, he'd had the nerve to reach for her in the night. She hadn't turned him away. She'd let him kiss her again. It wasn't the sweet melding of lips in the early dawn of attraction and desire, but nor was it the perfunctory swap of tongues in a relationship's fading twilight. He couldn't assign a name to it, only acknowledge that she allowed it, just as she had last night in the opulent mansion bathroom. That had to mean something, a step forward.

She moved from her brows to her lashes, whisking them with a mascara wand. She always worked from the top down, brows, eyes, cheeks, then lips. Why not up, lips first? He'd been present for the process countless times, but he'd never stopped long enough to take it all in. Until Jay morphed from baby to toddler, she'd done her makeup in her panties, like now. When he started running around and hadn't learned to knock, she'd taken to wearing a robe. At home, she still used the robe, yet here, despite the hotel garment hanging on the door, she wore only her underthings. For the life of him, Dominic couldn't remember what she'd worn yesterday morning as they were getting ready, or if the change in her had come about during the night.

"Why are you watching me?" she asked without smudging the stroke of her eyeliner.

Because last night was kinky and hot, and her reaction to that scene with Winter made him hope they'd passed a threshold. What threshold would they cross if he pushed her into action rather than fantasy and talk? Because really, that's all last night had been. Fantasy. She'd fucked him, yet that was still part of the fantasy. No one had seen a thing.

"Would you have done it if I'd asked you to?"

Her hand jerked, leaving a tiny smear on her eyelid. She hissed and grabbed a cotton swab to wipe it away. "Done what?"

A rumble of tension snaked through his abdomen as he recognized the signs of shutdown. When you don't want to answer, pretend you don't understand the question.

If he didn't force the issue here, he'd never get the chance at home. "If I'd told you to masturbate for him, would you have done it?"

She screwed the brush back into the tube of liner, then smoothed a finger over the eye shadow on her lids. She had her routine, always did it that way. Yet he detected the pulse at her throat, its beat faster than it should have been as she weighed the consequences of a lie. Or the truth.

Finally, she pulled out her blusher compact and swept the brush over her skin, adding color to her cheeks. "Yes."

A rush of adrenaline hit his bloodstream. In one moment, he was hard, cock aching with need. Yet his skin felt clammy as if he'd stepped off the curb before looking only to suddenly see the bus bearing down on him—too late.

She turned, leaning back against the counter, totally unselfconscious in her near nakedness. "Did you really want me to do it? Or would you have punished me for it later?"

The hotel bathroom seemed suddenly smaller. He'd needed her answer, craved it. Now it hovered on the precipice of being a huge mistake. She'd asked him last night if he was jealous that

Winter was checking her out. He'd gotten away with a fence-sitting answer.

What the fuck was the truth anyway? He thought he wanted it, believed he could handle it. In his fantasies, it made him hot as hell. He pulled away from the door, bracketed her with his body, arms on either side of her, leaning close, nose-to-nose. The scent of her shower made him dizzy. The proximity of her lips twisted his insides.

"I would be mindless. Then I'd have to have you while he watched. Yes, I fucking wanted it. More than you can know."

Her breasts touched his chest as she breathed. His shape filled her pupils.

He was beyond jealousy. Everything was about her reaction, forcing her to see him, look at him, touch him. He wanted that moment in the forest when the hikers turned the corner, and she'd whispered, *"Don't you fucking stop."* The tension in her body, the need, and everything else fell away but that primal act. It defied logic, yet she had been his more than at any other moment in their lives.

"Tell me how much you wanted it." He needed her confession, too. It was nothing so noble as making an intimate connection or fixing what had gone wrong or healing or finding a way to live with each other after what they'd lost. It was visceral.

Her pebbled nipples branded him with each breath she took. Then she pulled his hand down to the outline of her panties. The thong's crotch was soaked with her desire. "This much," she whispered.

He could have had her then, fucked her on the counter like he'd done last night. He merely stroked her cleft, absorbed her shudder, then pulled away to reach into his back pocket.

He laid a business card beside her cosmetics bag.

She trembled. "What's that?"

"His phone number. He gave me his card while you were prettying up in the bathroom before we left." While she was erasing the remnants of her ravishment.

"I'm not going to call it," she said.

"I am."

"Why?"

"To tell him to come here tonight."

HOT AND COLD WASHED THROUGH ERIN LIKE A FEVER. SHE WANTED to masturbate for Dominic now. She couldn't wait. Needed the relief. Yet she wondered if she'd been lying to both of them when she said she'd have done it for Winter. "I didn't bring my vibrator."

He laughed low in his throat. "You have time to shop."

Her skin buzzed with aliveness, but her blood rushed with nerves. "What if someone finds out?"

"He's not going to tell anyone."

He lifted her chin, and she realized she'd been staring at that card. Winter, winter. The winter of discontent. God, the last year had been so much worse than mere discontent. But Shakespeare had really been talking about the turn, from winter to glorious summer, from bad to good. Even if for a fleeting moment.

"I want it," Dominic said.

And . . . and . . . Jesus. "I can't do it."

His eyes didn't change; they still burned. "You said you could."

"That was last night. The heat of the moment." She swallowed. "You shouldn't have asked me. You should have just brought him here." Okay, that was abdicating responsibility, but it was the truth. As wet as she was at the thought of it, she didn't have the courage to execute.

"Fine. You need to make it up to me," he stated flatly, but that glow remained in his eyes. He wasn't angry. He'd wanted Winter in their room tonight, but he was adapting to her whim.

"What do you want me to do?"

"I haven't decided yet." He held her chin in his hand. "Maybe I should have you get down on your knees and suck me off like that woman did for her man last night."

She trembled, her nipples hard, her pussy wet. "What about *my* orgasm?"

He smiled cruelly. "You don't get one. That's your punishment for not doing what I told you to."

She wanted to snicker because cruelty was so not Dominic's nature, yet it was another phase of the game he wanted to play. When they were young and hot, sometimes she'd send him off to work with a blow job, the taste of come lingering with her. It had been exciting, the drop to her knees, then pushing him on his way, knowing he'd think about it all day. The power in that.

"You can swallow me and taste it for hours while we're in the booth, knowing what you did to me," he murmured, eyes gleaming, as if he were guessing the direction of her thoughts and the memories suddenly vivid in her mind.

Oh, yes, there was power in sucking a climax from a man, making the very act almost as good as having an orgasm herself.

"Then again, maybe I'll go to my knees and lick your hot little snatch," he went on seducing her. "You'll have the reminder all day long while I'm talking to customers." He swiped his tongue along her cheek. "Remembering how good my mouth felt on you as I'm introducing you to the people you've talked to on the phone, your customers. What would they think if they knew what a dirty woman you are?" He trailed a finger down between her breasts, over her abdomen, to the elastic of her thong.

Her belly fluttered with need. "Too much talk," she said, a slight catch in her voice. God, yes, she wanted it.

His mouth followed the path of his hand as he slowly went to his knees, then he breathed in the scent of her arousal, exhaled with a puff of warm air. "You smell good."

She gripped the bathroom counter, her legs suddenly weak.

Pulling aside the thong's crotch, he drew in another deep breath. "You're pretty, too, all plump, pink, and moist."

His voice drove her crazy, the sight of him down on his knees for her, like a slave forced to do her bidding. Then his tongue dipped between her folds, and she closed her eyes. "Oh yeah," she murmured.

He swirled against her clit. She throbbed low in her belly. Then he spread her legs wider, put both hands between her thighs and cupped her butt, bringing her flush against his mouth.

"God, that's good. So good. Put your fingers in me."

He didn't let up on her clit for even a beat, simply drove two fingers up inside her. She clenched the countertop so tightly, her knuckles turned white. "Right there, yes, please, don't stop." Her body began to undulate with the rhythm of his mouth and fingers, and she tried to think of what he'd been saying before, what he'd wanted. "Every time I look at you today"—she gasped as he rode that perfect spot inside—"I'll remember you on your knees licking my pussy." Her legs trembled. "When you introduce me as your wife—oh Jesus—" She squeezed her eyes tight against the pleasure. "I'll think about my come all over your tongue, how you'll smell like me, taste like me."

He took her with fervor, as if her words were as important as the sex, making him hotter, driving him higher. The climax started as ripples flowing out from his touch, his tongue.

"I'll know how you're thinking about licking me, sucking me, fucking me, every time you look my way." She moaned, and any other words were lost in sensation. Her body bucked against his mouth. Then she wailed, orgasm roaring over her like a train.

Coming down from the peak, she was still on her feet, though her knees were weak. Dominic gazed up at her, his lips wet with her juice, then he licked his fingers.

"Taste," he said, rising, cupping her nape, taking her mouth with the musk of her own come on his tongue. "Good," he whispered. "I'll taste you all day."

"But—" His cock was hard against her belly. "That."

He rotated his hips against her as his dark eyes glowed like hot coals. "I'm going to be crazy by the time we get out of there. Then I'm going to fuck the hell out of you the minute we walk back in this door. You can think about *that* all day long," he drawled, "every time I touch you, every time I look at you."

Then he held her chin and put his lips to hers, a sweet kiss still piquant with the taste of her come. "And one day, you will masturbate for another man while I watch." He reminded her about Winter. "I'll keep asking until you do."

She could barely move as the outer door clicked shut.

Yes, he would keep asking. She'd started something with agreeing to this weekend, and Dominic wasn't going to back down.

Gazing at herself in the mirror, her skin glowed and her lips were full and sensual. She looked so sexy and wanton, she didn't recognize herself.

8

CHRIST, IT WAS GOOD. TRUE TO HIS WORD, AFTER HE'D MADE HER come in the bathroom, he'd touched her, stroked her, whispered sex talk in her ear all day, in front of customers, when they were alone. He'd driven himself mad with desire, had pounced on her the moment they were back in the room, just as he'd promised. It had been so fucking unbelievably good. He hadn't even needed to take her to another party on Saturday night to seduce her. They'd had sex all weekend. Erin had kissed him, blown him, fucked him, bantered with him. Now, on the plane, she slept beside him.

Dominic dared to let himself hope. He wasn't an idiot; he knew they had to talk. They needed a counselor to help them through all the things they hadn't managed to say or feel since the day Jay fell ill. But he felt a surge of optimism that she would at least talk to him.

He lifted her hand, laced his fingers with hers. She didn't wake. He kissed her fingertips, stroked a soft tendril of hair back behind her ear. He breathed her in, the sweet scent of lotion and shampoo.

After months of despair, he had hope.

*   *   *

ERIN WOKE WITH HER HEART POUNDING. SHE WAS IN HER OWN BED again, night, dark, Dominic's quiet breathing beside her as the dream began to fade. No, the nightmare. Jay. She remembered every moment of the nightmare. She felt the reality of it every day, yet it was so much worse reliving it in the Technicolor of her dreams. She covered her ears, trying to block out the sound of her own voice shouting those awful words at her son.

When she was able to sleep, her dreams of Jay were usually sweet. She would wake longing to return to them. But then, in the dark, the bad thoughts would begin churning, and she couldn't sleep again. She wanted to reach for Dominic now, with her hands, her arms, her whole being. But Dominic was out of reach. It didn't matter what had happened between them this weekend; if he knew the things she'd said to Jay, he'd never forgive her. She would always see what she'd done mirrored in his eyes. She was the one who wasn't able to forgive, not herself, not Dominic.

Yet the trade show had changed something. She couldn't seek the solace of sex now. After everything they'd done over the weekend, their own bed was . . . different. She now knew she could step outside of herself, move beyond the perimeter of her guilt. She could forget for a time, live for a time, and it didn't take all that much pretending. They'd woken in Orlando this morning, showered, dressed, packed, driven to the airport, and returned the rental car. She'd let Dominic hold her hand on the plane, though he'd thought she was asleep. She couldn't remember the last time they'd simply held hands like that.

She craved his warmth now, yet too much of a good thing for too long a time was almost like betraying Jay's memory. That was the problem. The guilt tortured her, yet without the guilt, it was like forgetting Jay. God, she hadn't thought of him all weekend. And that was sacrilege. The constant pain she felt was the only thing that kept him alive. Tonight's nightmare was her punishment for forgetting that.

She knew she was addicted, knew she'd do it again, have hot sex, play Dominic's dirty games. She craved them. But not tonight. And not in this bed. It was the only thing she could promise her son.

Sliding from beneath the covers, she made as little movement as possible, keeping the blankets mashed down to avoid a rush of cool air that might wake Dominic.

She couldn't remember where she'd left her slippers and rather than turning the light on to find them, she padded barefoot down the hall. The house was split-level; four bedrooms, one was a guest room that never got used and another served as her office. Dominic had remodeled the workshop attached to the garage as his pseudolab and home office.

Her feet were cold by the time she'd booted up. Pulling her legs up onto the chair, she folded her fingers around her toes to warm them as she waited for the Internet. Her computer was old, a castoff from work, and websites with more sophisticated graphics took longer to load. She'd never been able to throw out stuff that still functioned. Though she couldn't afford to lose the time at work, it didn't matter at home. Dominic was different; he loved state-of-the-art.

The desk faced the door. She'd read that was some sort of feng shui thing, so that you could always see when someone was coming into your space. It gave you control. She did the same thing in her office at DKG. She'd also set the computer to erase her history whenever she exited the Internet. Dominic would never check up on her, but she couldn't take the chance he might see something by accident. So she always made sure she shut down her browser before she left her desk or if Dominic's shadow darkened her door.

Finally, after the tap of a few more computer keys to open the photo gallery, her son's beautiful face blossomed on the monitor. She touched the screen as if she were touching his face.

Dominic would be pissed if he knew what she did tucked away in her office late at night, if he knew the things she'd kept hidden from him.

And she wouldn't blame him for that.

HE AWOKE WITH A START. HE DIDN'T KNOW HOW LONG HE'D BEEN alone, but when he ran his hand over her side of the bed, the sheet was cold.

This was bad. In her worst moments, Erin didn't wake him up for sex. Instead, she closeted herself in her office. He figured that was better than if she'd gone to Jay's room.

Dominic shut his eyes, concentrated on slow, steady breathing. They'd cleaned out Jay's stuff last February. She hadn't cried, simply put everything in cardboard boxes, taped them up, and marked them for the Salvation Army. He'd piled the boxes into the SUV and taken them to the drop-off. But before he discarded them, he'd cut open the tape and removed the things he needed to keep. A baseball mitt from Little League. A kite they used to take out to the park on Sundays. Stuff. Memories. Picking and choosing had left a hole the size of a fist in his chest. He'd kept some things for Erin, too, for when she was ready. The clay handprint Jay made when he was six, glazed a bright blue and fired in the school kiln. The animals Leon had whittled for his birthday. He'd been working on the Noah's Ark scene, having made it through the giraffes, the elephants, the sheep, and the lions. Dominic had kept those and other special things. Erin would be sorry, he knew, when she thought of all the treasures she'd let go.

Rising from the bed, Dominic donned his briefs. He couldn't

go hunting for her with his dick dangling. A swath of light swept across the carpet from beneath the closed door at the end of the hall. He had to pass Jay's room to get there.

She hadn't changed the bedspread on the twin bed. He didn't know why. It was still Speed Racer. On Saturdays, as if it were penance, she dusted and vacuumed his room along with the rest of the house. It just wasn't lived in anymore.

Outside the door to her office, he leaned both hands against the doorjamb, his head hanging, wanting to knock, yet incapable of it. The only sound was the steady throb of his heart against his chest. He'd been on the outside looking in for over a year. Shut out, shut down. Christ, he needed to talk, sometimes so badly that the words choked him. About Jay, how he died, the pain and guilt, his belief that Erin blamed him, and how goddamn much he missed his son, how the hole in his chest was growing ever wider. All the things he couldn't say were like boulders between them that they had to walk around to see each other.

What did she do in there that she didn't want him to see?

Fuck, fuck, fuck. They'd had such a damn good weekend. A step forward. The closed door was two steps back. What had gone wrong? Maybe she'd wanted him to be jealous and he'd failed the test. Was it that he'd wanted her to masturbate for Winter? That he could give Erin to another man and feel only excitement at her pleasure? Perhaps she thought it meant he no longer loved her? The truth was he'd moved into an entirely new territory, where the only thing that mattered was connecting with her on any level he could find.

Dominic straightened, detecting the click of the keyboard.

They had connected this weekend. It worked for seventy-two hours despite the two steps back she'd taken tonight.

He would not give up on her. He would make it happen again. The more he forced her to see him, the easier it would get each time he tried. He had to think of the right thing to tempt her with. Something better than Winter.

Dominic backed down the hall. Something was coming to him. And it was going to be good.

MONDAY MORNING ERIN LEANED BACK IN HER OFFICE CHAIR, GATHered her hair in her hand, and slipped a scrunchie around the thick hank to keep the mass of it out of her way. It had taken several phone calls with Wrainger over the last couple of weeks, both before the Orlando trip and two more calls this morning, but she'd managed to raise DKG's discount percentage. It went against just-in-time principles, increasing quantities so they'd have more parts on hand, but the cost-benefit analysis she'd had Bree run proved they'd come out ahead. And they had the stockroom capacity.

She'd been able to tick one thing off her to-do list. She still hadn't done anything about Leon and the transducers. She'd considered moving the fabrication in-house, but with the loaded labor rate, which included benefits, not to mention the learning curve, Leon was still much cheaper.

She needed to take him out for lunch and ask what he was going to do with all that extra time on his hands. He'd go stir-crazy. He needed them as much as they needed him. She didn't have a decent explanation for why she hadn't already invited him. Maybe she couldn't stand it if he said no. Maybe it was because she hadn't seen him face-to-face since Jay's memorial.

Her e-mail beeped, and she flipped tabs on the monitor.

Dominic. Was he suddenly getting too lazy to walk over? They hadn't talked much this morning, not about the weekend, and not about the week to come. He hadn't said anything about the fact that she'd been holed up in her office last night either, but she knew he wasn't asleep when she'd gone back to bed.

She clicked on the message. It took her a moment to realize it wasn't a business e-mail. Warmth spread across her skin, and a kernel of heat sprouted low in her belly.

"Eight o'clock tonight, meet me at Rudolpho's on Santana Row. I want the skirt short and the heels fuck-me high. Do you understand?"

The tone of command in the words raised her pulse, goose bumps pebbled her arms, and her breath quickened. He wasn't in the room, and they were only words on a screen, yet she felt an overwhelming rush of desire followed by the oddest need for a little banter. "Forget it, dude." That should get him going.

She waited, tingling inside. He didn't disappoint her, an e-mail popping up on her screen in less than thirty seconds.

"You will be there, or you'll pay the price. If you're into a little punishment these days, that can certainly be arranged."

They'd never been into BDSM or pain. So what kind of punishment did he have in mind? Sitting in her office last night, she'd known she was addicted to this new sex game of his. Nothing was going to stop her from playing. Not even her shame or her guilt.

"Maybe I'll be there. Maybe I won't." She wrote, punctuating with a smile to herself. Then she waited for his comeback and hoped it was exceptionally naughty.

9

"YOU GOTTA TALK TO THE KID, ERIN."

Erin jumped, slamming a finger down on the mouse to switch the screen she had open on the computer, the reaction automatic. Just as it was if Dominic surprised her at home.

Steve, her quality control guy, completely blocked her doorway, the lewd tattoos on his arms flexing in agitation. His parents obviously hadn't taught him the art of knocking even when the door was open. After all, a person could be on the phone, in the middle of important business. Or exchanging kinky e-mails. So what if she had an open-door policy?

"Which kid are you referring to?" She already knew.

"Matt," Steve said with a very hard *t*. "I gotta reject seventy-five percent of his assembly work."

Erin was head of operations, and her bailiwick included assembly, quality, repair and return, shipping and receiving, production control, purchasing, and employee therapy. She was sure she was missing one of her roles in there, but that was all that came to mind at the moment. Matt was having girlfriend problems. Obviously the talk they'd had a couple of weeks ago hadn't solved them. He'd jumped from a 60 percent failure rate to seventy-five.

"I'll take care of it, Steve."

Steve pursed his lips in old-maid fashion. It was the strangest look on a five-feet-eleven beefcake, former Hells Angel, especially when the naked-lady tattoos on his arms started to . . . undulate. "It's time and money, Erin."

"I appreciate you pointing that out to me, Steve. And I said I'll talk to him."

He stood straight, hands on his hips. "You gonna fire him if he doesn't shape up?"

Erin rose from her desk and crossed her arms. In his steel-toed boots, he was taller than her, and much wider, but she was still the boss. Steve was a good guy, he took his job seriously, and he didn't like anyone messing with his accuracy percentages. And Matt was afraid of him.

"I will to talk to him again. That's all you need to know," she said with a bit of a hard edge.

Steve might be eight years older than she was, but sometimes, she was big sister to them all. And the truth was that taking care of them had gotten her through the last year.

Steve hung his head on his thick neck. "All right, Erin, you haven't let me down yet."

He hadn't let her down either in the six years he'd worked for her. Despite his badass bald head and tattooed arms, Steve was hardworking and conscientious, with an endearing little-boy grin when he smiled. Even with the gold front tooth.

She shooed him away with a flap of her hand. "Now get back to work."

Okay, what had she been doing? Reorder point. No, sex. Hot sex. What did Dominic have planned? What should she wear? Short skirt, high heels, yeah, but which short skirt and which sexy high heels? She had a pair of red shoes and a matching red suede skirt stuck somewhere at the back of her closet.

The rap on the door frame was so light she almost thought it was footsteps on the carpet outside her office. This time, Atul darkened her door, though a hell of a lot less of it than Steve had. Atul might be a couple of inches taller than Steve, but he had far less bulk.

"Erin, you must help me work with that Cam Phan." He slicked his dark hair back off his forehead with a nervous hand.

Cam Phan was too quiet to cause trouble. "What's the issue, Atul?"

"I believe she makes her accent heavier when she speaks to me so that I cannot make out what she says without much deliberation." Atul spoke with a lyrical East Indian accent.

He was responsible for their documentation, the instruction manuals, product catalogues, and website design, and therefore worked closely with the engineers, which would be Cam Phan and Dominic. Starting at DKG when he was twenty-five, Atul had been with them over four years, whereas Cam Phan had joined their team only fifteen months ago, when their original software engineer, Reggie, had gotten pissed off. The episode still left a bad taste in Erin's mouth. She liked a happy family. Reggie had stirred up a lot of animosity before he left.

"Atul, you both need to be a little more patient with each other."

He puffed, his nostrils flaring. "She speaks much more clearly to Dominic."

Which was probably true. Erin herself had never had any problem understanding Cam. Though Vietnamese was her first language, Cam had an extremely good understanding of English, and she spoke quite well. She'd immigrated to the United States when she was ten, had been educated here, graduated from college here, and at thirty-three, had worked in the industry for over ten years. Erin had a feeling that the language barrier was between Atul and Cam only. Atul could be condescending when he thought he knew more about a subject than someone else. He'd wanted the software design job, but he wasn't an engineer. While Erin believed in allowing people to stretch their capabilities, she'd known that giving him the position would only increase the burden on Dominic. Cam was a few years older than Atul, with the experience and the education that Atul didn't have. Like Steve, though, they were both good workers. Erin had to figure out how to get them to work together instead of at cross-purposes.

"I'll mediate," she said. Which would require Atul to be respectful and Cam to clean up her language, so to speak.

She should have called Dominic in on the mediation, since, technically, they worked for him, but she knew what he'd say. She babied them, not only Cam and Atul, but everyone. She wouldn't dream of saying they were acting like children who couldn't get along on the playground. Dominic would simply tell them to grow up. They had very different management styles. She believed involving employees in the solution had a bigger impact on behavior.

"Let's get together tomorrow," she said.

"That will be acceptable," Atul agreed, then left.

She sat down, then clicked on her e-mail to see if there was anything new from Dominic. Nothing. She felt a tick of disappointment. She'd wanted more banter. The weekend's sex had somehow brought her to life again. She needed more of her drug addict's fix.

Now, the red high heels and suede skirt? Or all black?

"HERE'S YOUR MAIL."

Rachel laid a stack on Dominic's desk amid all the other stacks of . . . stuff. Trade magazines, schematics, miscellaneous parts, pamphlets and brochures he'd brought home from the trade show and giveaways, pens, Post-its with company logos, key chains, laser pointers. There was even a plastic toothpick holder. He liked the more ingenious stuff people came up with to stamp the company name on. It gave him ideas for next year's trade show on what he could have made up with DKG's logo.

"Need a mouse pad?" He held out one with a team race car on it.

"Thanks. That's nice and colorful."

Rachel was a pretty woman, but she always seemed to try too hard, as if she were expecting to piss off somebody if every word out of her mouth wasn't perfectly sweet.

He smoothed a hand over the crap on his desk, spreading it out so she could see better. "You want any of this junk?" In years past, he'd always given Jay first dibs. Jay had loved the freebies. He would have thought the mouse pad was cool.

"No thanks." Rachel flapped the pad. "This is enough." Then she left him alone with his junk and his mail.

Most of the general mail went to Erin, but if anything looked vaguely technical, Rachel gave it to him. He opened one envelope after another, junk, junk, junk. Until . . . What the hell was this? He scanned the letter, cocked his head, then scanned it again.

He sat there for five beats, his teeth clenched.

Goddammit.

It was a cease-and-desist letter from WEU Systems for patent infringement. On the through-coat gauge. God*dammit*. WEU stood for Worldwide Excellence in Ultrasonics. The name was a crock, and not merely because WEU was DKG's direct competitor. Their CEO, Garland Brooks, was an ass. He was a bottom-line man, and ethics be damned. He'd been known to grind smaller companies to dust with the power of his money. WEU manufactured an ultrasonic through-coat thickness gauge, but Dominic and Reggie had checked out the patents from every angle. Yes, there was a patent, but it shouldn't have been granted because there was clear prior art by two different companies before WEU rolled out their gauge at last year's PRI show. Prior art meant that someone else had come up with the basic process you were using, but had never gotten the patent on it. Companies did that all the time if they didn't want to reveal exactly what their process was. Like Coke not wanting to reveal its recipe. A patent was on the process, not the product itself.

Now WEU wanted him to take the gauge off the market, or pay them an outrageous royalty fee. Fuck. Dominic slammed his fist down on the letter, then stood, sending his chair rolling until it hit the wall. Pacing, he shoved his hands through his hair, pulling on the ends.

That goddamn gauge. It had been nothing but a fucking nightmare getting it on the market. He laid his hand over his mouth, closed his eyes. He'd wanted to take it to the last PRI show, didn't want WEU to outgun him. He pushed it through the engineering, through manufacturing, and when there were issues, he'd spent hours trying to figure out what was wrong. Not just hours, but days, weekends. The day Jay went on that school trip. Dominic should've gone with him. He was scheduled to be one of the parent chaperones. But time had been running out; he'd needed to fix the problem. So he let Jay make the day trip without him. There were other parents, teachers. It wasn't as if Jay was alone out there. That's what Dominic had told himself.

Leaning over, fists clenched on the desk, he squeezed his eyes shut so tightly it hurt. He thought of all the minuscule decisions that had led to that day. If Reggie hadn't quit, leaving Dominic in a bind with the gauge's software. If Dominic hadn't felt compelled to have the damn thing ready for the trade show just so he could compete head-on with WEU. If he'd decided to pull Jay out of the school trip instead of allowing him to go. If he'd thrown the goddamn gauge to hell and gone anyway, because time with his son was so much more precious. In the end, he hadn't gone to the show, hadn't released the product until the first quarter, and that hadn't cost DKG much of anything.

But it had cost him his son.

A shiver racked his body, trembled in his very bones. *This* was why Erin couldn't talk about Jay. She could never say she hated him for not being there that day. He didn't know if he could survive hearing it from her either. There were so many fucking things they couldn't talk about. He wanted to tell himself the lack of communication and connection was her fault, but he couldn't say what needed to be said either. Stalemate. All he could do was come up with kinky sex acts to indulge in, a way *not* to think about what really lay between them. Fuck.

They'd have to involve their patent attorney, document the research, send letters, all the while paying an exorbitant hourly fee.

Brooks was probably hoping this would drive them out of business. Dominic would fight him on it. Because if he didn't, he would lose Erin. No matter what he'd told himself about their recent bouts of hot sex, DKG was the only real glue that held them together.

He passed a hand over his face, suddenly feeling years older.

Then he grabbed his chair, pulled it to the desk and sat down. Screw WEU and Garland Brooks for now. He wouldn't tell Erin about the letter, at least not today. Let her leave him tomorrow, but tonight, he fully intended to blow her mind.

10

THE TWINKLING LIGHTS OF SANTANA ROW AT CHRISTMASTIME sparkled on the wet concrete, casting prisms of blue, green, and red. The decorations didn't upset her; after all, she wasn't shopping. She had a totally different mission in mind. It had started raining that afternoon, dwindling to a light drizzle by evening. Erin hadn't bothered with an umbrella, just her full-length hooded raincoat. She hadn't worn the red suede skirt or shoes so they wouldn't be damaged by raindrops. Instead, she chose a Lycra top, black and tight, and a black pencil skirt with a slit from shin to mid-thigh. Her black high heels tapped on the concrete.

The small sign for Rudolpho's blinked in neon blue. It was a bar, not a restaurant, but she'd snacked as she'd dressed—carrot sticks and apples—and wasn't hungry. Dominic hadn't come home. He'd worn jeans, tennis shoes, and a black button-down shirt to work. She wondered if he'd show up in that, or maybe he'd cruised the mall, though Dominic had never liked shopping.

She opened the door, warm air rushing over her. The furnishings, and probably the prices, too, were high end, the servers well dressed in black and white, and the lighting dim. Monday night was a big night for whatever reason, many of the tables full; couples, groups, people coming in for a drink after work, even though it was eight o'clock. A young dark-haired man played the piano in the corner, a lilting jazz melody she didn't recognize. Despite the number of people, the talk and laughter, the noise level wasn't intrusive. You could hear yourself talk; even think. Erin removed her coat and slung it over the back of a seat at the end of the bar closest to the door, where she could survey the full room. The bar stools were comfortable, with a thick padded seat and a back to lean against. She left two empty seats between her and everyone else.

Dominic had been sending her e-mail instructions all afternoon. He'd tell her to do this, then change his mind, and tell her to do that. She was sure it was part of his plan, to throw her off guard, so she couldn't guess what he'd really do in the end. His basics were few; she was to wear sexy clothing, sexy heels, sit at the bar, and pretend she didn't know him when he arrived. Other than that, all bets were off. Maybe he'd send a man to try to pick her up. Now that could be fun.

"What can I get for you?" The bartender had finally made his way down to her.

"Do you have ice wine?" Ice wine was made from grapes that were frozen on the vine. It was sweet, and she felt like something very sweet tonight, but it was only carried in classier places. Of course, it was very expensive, too, but tonight she was splurging.

He grinned beneath his neatly trimmed mustache and beard. "Of course. Coming right up." He bent to a small refrigerator under the bar, and she noticed the toned muscles of his butt and legs. She smiled to herself. Maybe Dominic would want her to pick up the bartender. He was older, midforties, a smattering of gray in his hair, mustache, and goatee. Very much like Winter except for the facial hair. The bar stool she sat on was high off the floor, but she estimated him to be over six feet.

She twisted in her seat so she could cross her legs, the skirt falling open over her knee and thigh. Setting the wine in front of her, the bartender stood taller, looking over at her bared leg with a smile before he was called away by a waitress. Erin wasn't one of those who considered an ogle disrespectful. If the way she'd reacted to Winter meant anything, she considered it a compliment. There were perhaps ten stools, most of them filled, all by men. She was the only woman seated at the bar, and the only one seated alone, which, if the glances her way meant anything, seemed to make her fair game.

So, where was Dominic? And what did he want her to do?

She sipped the delicious ice wine, savoring each tasting as she looked over the bar's occupants. Having given her plenty of up, down, and sideways glances, a younger guy picked up his glass, swirled the ice cubes, then slid off his stool. He rounded the bar to her end, set his glass down right beside her. He wasn't bad-looking, brown hair, brown eyes, an angular face, but thirty was a little young, especially when she had a preference for the over-forty set. Then he smiled—"Hi, there"—and dropped several notches. The guy desperately needed to see his hygienist.

"Thank you, but I'm waiting for somebody." She smiled to take the bite out of it.

"I can keep you company until your friend gets here." He sidled slightly closer.

"That's not necessary." She didn't smile, but blinked slowly, sending a message.

He didn't get it, and he didn't leave. "Every lady needs company."

She drummed her fingers on the bar, a signal of her irritation. She decided politeness was no longer required. "I don't. Go away."

The bartender approached. "Do I need to get your tab, sir?"

Mr. Bad Teeth grimaced, picked up his drink, sloshing amber liquid over the lip, and returned to his seat.

"Thanks." She smiled her appreciation at her knight in shining armor.

He mopped up the spilled drink. "Part of the service, helping out pretty ladies."

Oh. He was hitting on her. It amused her. What did Dominic expect her to do? Wait until the guy got off work and follow him home? Or maybe Dominic was going to show up, sit across the room, and see if she could get the guy to *ask* her to follow him home as a test of her sexual prowess.

An elbow on the bar, she brushed her fingers along her throat. The position gave him a view of her cleavage. "You're good at coming to the rescue of damsels in distress."

"You looked like you were handling him fine." He shined a clean glass with a cloth, staying to talk as if he didn't notice the waitress beckoning him from the other end of the counter. She shot Erin an exasperated look.

Erin pointed. "Someone's waiting on you down there."

He tipped his head, smiled slightly. "Yeah. Duty calls." Then he turned back to her. "Are you expecting a fictitious friend or a real one?"

She laughed. It was an odd way to put it. And her real answer would have been just as odd, because she didn't know who or what she was supposed to be waiting for, so she anticipated what her husband would have wanted her to say. "Fictitious."

His eyes gleamed. "Don't go away then. Things will slow down in about an hour."

Without giving an answer, she watched him. He had a nice rear. She could have him. It felt powerful, as if it were something she hadn't thought herself capable of. She was forty years old, and yet she'd still turned a head. Two heads. Even more. *That* was what Dominic wanted, for her to see she was still attractive, to Winter, to other men, younger men, to Dominic. Maybe he thought she'd somehow lost confidence in herself. She just hadn't noticed other men or bothered to see if they noticed her. Yet it was a nice feeling now that he'd opened her eyes.

But how far did he expect her to take it? She tipped her wrist to look at her watch. Eight thirty. She surveyed the room, her eyes finally landing on a single man seated at a small round table tucked in the back by the piano. Black suit, white shirt, red tie. Dominic. When had he put on the suit? She wondered how long he'd been observing her and why she hadn't noticed him.

Picking up his glass, he rose, wended through the tables, and took a seat at the bar, leaving one empty chair between them. "Your glass is almost empty. Can I buy you another?"

The bartender watched her from the middle of the counter as he poured two highball glasses. She studied the dregs of her ice wine. "I don't let men I don't know buy me drinks." She eyed Dominic. "But I'll pay for my own, and you can move over to this stool." She patted the stool right beside her.

"Why thank you, ma'am." And Dominic moved in.

She signaled the bartender.

She felt good, powerful, alive. The heat on the inside was all for the game Dominic was making her play.

HE'D WATCHED HER FOR HALF AN HOUR, SITTING BACK AS SHE AT-tracted men like a Venus flytrap, gathering them to her, making them salivate for her in that black skirt with the amazing slit up her thigh and a formfitting top that outlined the sweetness of her nipples. She smiled and made her admirers hard. She leaned forward, and they drooled.

They'd driven separately to work, always had. Erin liked the quiet before everyone else arrived. He'd nipped home in the afternoon to fetch his rarely used suit—he figured it would add a nice touch to the evening—then changed after she left for the day. He'd gotten to Rudolpho's before she did so he could choose an out-of-the-way table. Cheesy as it sounded, he'd held up an appetizer menu to cover his face when she'd first taken a seat at the bar. He'd gotten hard watching her antics, flirting with the bartender, crossing her legs to show off her thighs.

The bartender brought her a fresh glass of wine, pushed it across the bar with two fingertips on its base. He watched her with dark, assessing eyes, his glance flashing to Dominic, then back. "Shall I run you a tab?" he asked.

"That would be wonderful." She graced him with a slow, sultry smile. "Thank you."

The guy backed off when a man four seats down tapped the counter to get his attention.

"Are you waiting for someone?" Dominic asked.

Her gaze followed the bartender's backside. He was older, reminded Dominic of Winter, maybe it was the approximate age, the sprinkling of gray, or simply the way he looked at Erin.

"I'm waiting for him," she said, indicating the bartender with a jut of her chin.

"Your boyfriend?"

She shook her head, smiling.

"Your brother?"

She laughed, and Christ, he hadn't felt her laugh quite that way for years, visceral. The first time he'd heard her laugh, he'd wanted her. And he'd never stopped.

"He'll be less busy in an hour," she said of the bartender and shrugged. "I guess he wants to talk to me some more."

Dominic had outlined a list of things for her; how to dress, where to go, and when to arrive. But there was only one rule that mattered; she was to pretend she didn't know him.

His job was to hit on her. Not that he'd told her.

There'd never been anything about what the outcome was supposed to be. So she'd upped the stakes, pitting him against the bartender.

"Did you let him buy your first drink?"

"No. I paid for my own wine."

"Well, that makes me feel better." He moved his knee so that it brushed her thigh. "What's a beautiful woman like you doing out all by herself?" He glanced at her finger. She hadn't removed the wedding ring.

"Christmas shopping," she said, sipping her wine. Her lipstick was a deep plum. It wasn't her usual shade.

"What did you buy?"

"A bustier, garters, stockings."

His heart skipped a beat imagining her in the getup, but he played out the moment. "Who'd you buy it for?" After all, she'd said she'd been Christmas shopping.

She put her fingers to the swell of her breasts above the low-cut neckline, drawing his gaze, drawing the bartender's. "My husband."

"Your husband wears women's lingerie?"

She shot him a cheeky smile. "I'm going to model it for him. That's the present." She fluttered her eyelashes. "The next present is what he'll get *after* I model."

"And that is?"

"S-E-X," she spelled for him.

The bartender read her lips, too, drifting closer to grab a couple of glasses off a shelf, absorbing every word.

"That's an extremely nice Christmas present," Dominic said.

"It's the appetizer. His *real* present is much better."

Dominic quirked one eyebrow, urging her on.

She laid a hand on his knee, raised her voice just enough to include the bartender. "I'm going to give him his biggest fantasy."

His biggest fantasy was right here; his wife's hand on his thigh, that sexy skirt and fuck-me heels, and letting the bartender think she was flirting with a complete stranger. "Are you going to make me ask or just tell me?" he drawled.

"Ask." She puckered her lips at him.

The bartender took extra time mixing a Bloody Mary and a cocktail with too much bourbon. "I'm dying to hear what your husband's biggest fantasy is."

"A threesome," she said with barely a sound, but exaggerated pronunciation that left neither him nor the bartender in doubt.

Christ, she was maniacal. He loved it. "Isn't that every man's fantasy? Two gorgeous women to fulfill his desires."

She playfully slapped his hand and shook her head. "Don't be silly. Two men to fulfill all *my* desires."

The bartender sloshed tomato juice down the glass.

"I've always wanted two men," she said sweetly. "And as my husband says, my biggest fantasy is his biggest wish." She gave him a tinkling laugh, not her real laugh, but he felt it in his belly just the same.

A flash of heat surged through his body. Christ. His wife was amazing. He came up with a plan. She did him one better, one hundred, even one million better. The bartender couldn't have moved if someone pulled out a gun and said, "Stick 'em up." Erin had him in thrall.

"So that's what I'm really shopping for tonight."

"A third?"

She blinked a yes, then pointedly looked at the bartender. "I just haven't made up my mind who." She smiled, glancing between the two of them. "Convince me it should be you."

Holy hell. He'd created a monster. But what a way to go.

11

SHE WAS A COCK TEASE. MEAN AND CRUEL. THE POOR BARTENDER. But God, it was fun.

The bartender cleared his throat, then spoke, his voice cracking like a teenage boy. "Maybe you should consider bringing home two men and letting your husband watch."

Dominic narrowed his eyes. "Don't you have a drink to serve? The waitress is snapping her fingers at you."

"Don't be rude," Erin said, liking that the bartender was trying to find a compromise that worked for all three of them. "What's your name?" she asked.

"Shane."

She liked his brown eyes, but she loved the hot gleam in Dominic's. "Nice to meet you, Shane. I'm"—she allowed herself only the slightest hesitation—"Laura." Because *Laura* from the 1940s was one of her favorite movies, and the title character was elegant and sophisticated and all the men were in love with her. She tipped her head at Dominic. "What's your name?"

Dominic smiled. It was a game. She didn't know him so she didn't know his name. "Nick."

She traced his wedding ring, wondering if Shane noticed the match to the one on her finger. "Does your wife call you Nickie?"

Dominic's grin threaded through his voice. "At the right moment, yeah."

"Then I'll call you Nickie, too."

"Shane," the waitress hissed. She'd moved down the bar, her face tarnished by tense lines, her hair a darker, unenhanced shade of blond. "I need drinks here."

Shane shot Dominic with a finger pistol. "Don't take advantage while I'm gone."

Dominic merely snorted.

"He's very protective," she explained after Shane strolled to the other end of the bar.

"Proprietary is more like it. You must come here often."

She shook her head, her hair feeling like silk as it caressed her bare nape. "My first time. How about you?"

He swirled the contents of his glass. He hadn't drunk much of it. "I've entertained clients here."

"Are you a lawyer or something?"

He shook his head. "An engineer."

"Interesting."

He propped an elbow on the bar, leaning his temple on his fist as he faced her, giving her his total concentration. "What about you? What's your line of work?"

She thought of all the exotic careers she could pretend she had. And decided she was happy with what she was. "COO of a manufacturing company." Chief operating officer. Dominic was president. The titles were meaningless, but they sounded good. "So, no more sex talk after our audience has walked away?"

It was a strange sensation talking to him as if she knew nothing about him, as if they were brand-new to each other. Even his aftershave smelled different, more tantalizing. Or maybe it had just been so long since she'd taken the time to notice. Her body reacted as if this weren't a role-play, heating, getting wet and ready for the conquest of a new male. The way he smiled was like a caress, setting a tingle loose along her skin. She actually felt breathless.

"Oh yeah," he drawled, "we're going to have more sex talk. I just wanted to know more about who I'm talking to. How long have you been married?"

"Fifteen years."

"You've got one very understanding husband."

"He's got one very understanding wife."

"Touché. Not many men would be so lucky." He didn't touch her, but his look, his voice, everything about him was almost physical. "Can you test out the goods before the big date?"

"Of course. What if I found out my choice wasn't properly equipped?" She winked. "Or didn't know how to utilize his equipment effectively."

"That could be disastrous," he agreed, unbuttoning his suit jacket so she could assess his package through his pants.

She glanced down. "On the face of it, you don't seem to have any equipment problems." Obviously hard beneath the material, she didn't have to touch to gauge how big he was.

Shane made his way back down to them. "What did I miss?"

Dominic tipped his head without moving his fist from his temple. "Equipment assessment. I passed."

Shane guffawed, glancing over his shoulder when he realized he'd attracted attention. The piano player played louder—unless that was her imagination—and the only man still paying attention after that was the one who'd tried to buy her a drink. Shane stepped back then, legs slightly spread, hands at his hips, pelvis jutted.

"Oh my," she murmured.

He beamed, shooting Dominic a triumphant smile.

"But size isn't everything," she said.

Dominic and Shane snorted simultaneously.

"Men." She sneered gently. "It's not the size; it's what you do with it. And not just *it*." She arched one brow. "But all the other stuff that goes along with *it*."

Shane leaned in to brace both hands on the bar and dropped his voice. "I think she's talking about foreplay."

She leaned closer, too. "The term was invented by men. As if it's be*fore* the real play. To a woman, it can be everything."

Shane regarded her a moment, then looked pointedly at Dominic. "Well, Nick, I do believe we have to convince Laura here that she needs to make her husband watch, because it sure sounds like the man's got a lot to learn."

Erin felt her smile stretch. "Yes, Nickie, what do you think of that? Does my husband need some lessons?"

His mouth quirked. "Oh, I think you have a lot to teach your husband. I bet there's stuff you've never told him."

She enticed them both with a low, husky voice that didn't sound like her at all, yet felt so right. "Maybe it's time for him to find out."

"What do you want us to show him how to do?" Shane kept his voice low. His body vibrated with sexual tension, but his eyes danced with humor.

Her skin was flush, her heart racing, and her nipples peaked against the Lycra. This was new and exciting and the slightest bit frightening. But God, she loved the banter. "This is still only hypothetical, remember," she warned.

"Of course," they recited in unison.

She thought about what would make them crazy. Oh, for sure, this was going to be fun. "So do you want my fantasy. Or do you want my husband's?"

*   *   *

SHANE ROLLED HIS EYES. "YOURS. WHO CARES ABOUT HIS?"

"I want yours, too," Dominic agreed.

Erin's eyes widened slightly. Dominic figured she'd been expecting him to say he wanted it from her husband's point of view, but it didn't matter how long they'd been married or how often they'd fantasized, he knew there had to be something she hadn't told him. Some dirty secret, something she wanted but had never revealed.

The waitress growled through gritted teeth. "Shane."

He glanced over his shoulder at her, then turned back. "She's a spoilsport. I'll be right back." He pointed at Dominic. "Do not get her to talk without me."

"Don't hurry on our account," Dominic answered. Although he did want Shane to return. The other man seemed to up the ante for Erin. He heightened her interest, her pleasure, her excitement, if the light sparkling in her eyes meant anything.

"So tell me, have you done anything naughty like this with your husband yet? Or has it all been fantasy?" Sure, he knew the answer, but he wanted to hear her describe Miterberg's party, her feelings about it.

Her lips curved in a sexy, sultry smile, setting his libido buzzing. "If I'd met you a week ago, the answer would've been no. But . . ." She left the word hanging.

"Then I assume something very interesting happened this weekend. How did you feel about it?" It wasn't what a guy trying to pick her up in a bar would ask, but this was no ordinary pickup.

She sat straighter, drew in a deep breath, and put her hands behind her neck, her breasts thrust out, as if she were working out a few kinks. "It was marvelous. I felt . . ." She hummed lightly in her throat, thinking, deciding. "I felt free. So alive." She brought her hand down, sliding it along her thigh. "And so in charge. It was exhilarating."

It was the last that surprised him, being in charge, as if that was something new for her. Erin never really gave up her control. "So you like a little dominance?" he queried.

She shook her head, her hair shifting over her shoulders, the light glinting in the red. "I didn't mean it like that. More like being in charge of the situation, of what you're doing. Not having people depending on you to make decisions when you know they're not going to do what you tell them to anyway."

He should have realized that, but it wasn't something he'd really thought about. Despite the fact that she gave orders at work, kept everybody going, she'd been in charge of nothing, at least not in her own mind. She couldn't control anyone's actions; therefore, she was not in control. Her control had been stolen from her over a year ago. He didn't know how to help her with that. Christ, he didn't even know how to help himself. All he could do now was file the knowledge away for later.

He wanted her to tell him what she and her "husband" had done, but the recitation would be so much more effective if the bartender were there to hear it. Dominic glanced down the bar where Shane was setting the last of five drinks on the waitress's tray. He shot Dominic a devilish smile as if he assumed they were a team, working Erin together, which was certainly the impression Dominic had given him.

What if he invited the bartender home? What would Erin do? He didn't want to lose her by pushing the night too fast. For now he wanted to know what she'd say in front of Shane, wanted to test her, find out how explicit she'd get. It had been different with Winter; she'd never acknowledged him. They'd talked over her, about her. She'd been the observer. This was different. Shane was bound to ask questions, egg her on.

Then Shane was ambling down the bar, a towel in one hand, three clean glasses on the fingers of his other hand. He set them upside down to drain. "What did I miss?"

"I was about to ask"—damn, what had she called herself?—"Laura what naughty things she's done with her husband."

Shane dried a glass slowly, painstakingly, keeping his hands busy should anyone be watching. "Hell, glad I didn't miss that answer. But what was Laura's biggest fantasy? That's what I walked out on."

Erin bit her lip, her gaze floating from Dominic to Shane and back again. Dominic gave her a nearly imperceptible nod. "Don't mind us," he coaxed. "Get as explicit as you want."

Shane smiled, nodded.

Erin leaned an elbow on the bar, propped her chin on her hand, and fell into the game. "Well, my biggest fantasy was what happened this weekend."

"Don't keep us in suspense," Dominic said. Was she going to make something up, revealing her fantasy that way? Because what they'd done in Orlando hadn't been her idea; it was his.

"We went to a party."

They both looked at her. "And?" Shane prompted when she didn't continue in the very next moment. The guy was impatient, but Dominic figured Erin liked his intent interest.

"We met an extremely handsome man." She tipped her head. "In fact, you remind me a little of him."

Shane pumped the air with a fist. "Score one for me, dude." He grinned at Dominic.

"You're slowing the pace of her story, man."

Erin crossed her legs the other way, giving them a view of her shapely thigh, then flashed Shane a sultry smile. She obviously liked the tug-of-war for her attention. "As I was saying," she went on, "he was a handsome man with some gray in his hair"—hell, Winter was *all* gray, but Dominic wasn't going to quibble with her description—"and he seemed . . . interested."

"Interested in what?" Shane wanted to know.

"Duh. What do you think he was interested in?" Dominic muttered. "We're talking to a very attractive woman here."

"Thank you for the compliment." Erin sipped her wine. She was drinking slowly now, with more than half a glass left. "Anyway, I think he was interested in sex," she lowered her voice for the last word.

Shane finished drying a glass. "With you or your husband?"

Dominic laughed out loud and slapped the bar with his hand. "Man, you are insane." Several pairs of eyes turned their way, but the audience was dwindling. It was after nine, and as Shane had said, the bar was starting to clear out.

"Sorry." Shane smiled sheepishly. He zipped his lips. "I'll shut up now, promise."

Erin liked him and his little interjections. He made things fun, and she didn't have to be nervous. "He was interested in *me*," she said.

"I knew that," Shane answered.

Erin leaned over and put her fingertips to his lips. "Shh."

Shane deliberately licked her fingers. A rush of warmth spread through her, then Dominic put his hand on her knee and slid it up her thigh. She was suddenly hot everywhere.

"Tell us what you did," Dominic urged. "Everything."

She subsided into her seat. Shane's gaze on her was scorching. Dominic's touch made her wet. Her breath came faster, sharper. She skipped the in-between stuff and went for the only thing that mattered. "My husband invited him back to our hotel room to watch me touch myself, make myself come. A performance."

"Shit," Shane breathed. "Did you do it for him?"

"Yes, I did." She put both hands on the bar, leaned closer, voice low because this time she didn't want anyone to overhear. "And I loved it. Every moment. The way he looked at me. How hard he got. I've never been so wet. I've never come so hard."

As she spoke, Dominic's hand slipped up her thigh, to the edge of the skirt's slit and beyond. She moved, and the slit rose higher, almost to her crotch. She felt his heat through her panties. He rubbed her thigh, the edge of his pinkie caressing her pussy right through the material.

Shane dropped his gaze. He knew what Dominic was doing. "Did you fuck him?" he murmured.

She flexed her fingers on the bar, breathed deeply, trying to maintain control, but God, Dominic's touch, Shane's gaze, her own voice, the moment Dominic had told her he wanted Winter to watch, how badly she'd wanted to; it all threatened to overwhelm her. "I wanted him to fuck me." She moved her hips, bringing Dominic's touch closer. "My husband did it instead. He fucked me right in front of the man after I was done masturbating for them both." If she hadn't been afraid, that's what she would have done. Everything she described.

They could have been alone in the bar, her, Shane, and Dominic. The waitress no longer hissed her orders at Shane, there were no greedy eyes drinking in everything, and the piano was nothing more than music drifting on the air. There was only her, her husband, and another sexy man.

"Was he too jealous to let the other guy do you?" Shane asked with a kind of reverence for her story.

"No. I don't know." She couldn't remember what she'd wanted, Dominic's jealousy or his desire. Maybe both all wrapped up together. "I don't think I told him he could let the man do me if he wanted to."

"But that's what you wanted, isn't it." Dominic's fingers pressed harder against her, his voice insistent.

"That's what I wanted," she said, her voice sounding breathless and excited even to her own ears. "All of it, exactly as I told you."

Good God, she was letting Dominic touch her in public, even if the lighting was dim and his moves were below the bar and out of sight of everyone except Shane. Her ears buzzed. Her body vibrated. She didn't care about what she *should* do, she only cared about what she needed. Here, now. His fingers slipping into her panties, testing how wet she was, playing her, stroking her, circling her clit until his heat became her heat. That was having complete control, taking what you wanted no matter what.

Shane's voice seemed to come from very far away. "Some day he's going to let it happen. He's going to sit back and watch while another man does all the things he's done, tasted you, sucked you, fucked you."

Then even his voice was silent, only his lips moving, talking dirty, mouthing how much he wanted to be that man. And Erin came so hard, her head seemed to burst.

12

DOMINIC THREW BILLS ON THE BAR TO COVER BOTH THEIR TABS, then gathered her coat around her.

"You're a very lucky man," Shane said.

"Yes, I am." He didn't press for more, but he figured the bartender knew he was the husband. He wasn't sure what had given them away, didn't care.

"When she's ready, come back." Shane tipped back a shot of whiskey he'd poured himself.

No one else had noticed what Dominic had done to Erin, not even the guy who'd tried to pick her up earlier. Dominic settled her lapels, tightened the tie of her coat. Her climax had been so fast, taking him by surprise. She'd been primed, ready, hot and wet when he'd touched her. With only a few more words, his fingers in the perfect spot, a sultry exchange of glances with the bartender, and she'd gone off. She'd bitten her lip, clenched her fingers on the bar, and sighed. But beneath his hand, she had trembled, and he'd felt the quiver of her body deep inside his own.

Nothing had ever felt so exciting and over the top. She *had* wanted the evening with Winter, the one she'd denied herself. She'd wanted it badly. Somehow, Dominic would give it to her when she was ready. He hoped to God he recognized the moment.

With a glassy, unfocused look, she let him lead her out. He tucked her under his arm as they hit the street outside. "Where's your car?"

"I can't believe you did that," she whispered, a note of awe rather than anger in her voice.

He hadn't intended it. "I was just stroking your thigh." Then he'd let her carry him away.

Half a block down from Rudolpho's, she stopped. A couple skirted around them. "I don't know what happened. I was suddenly—"

He planted his lips on hers, kissed her hard, backed off to breathe. "Zero to sixty, baby." She gotten off on telling Shane what they'd almost done. They'd been so close, a yes versus a no from her lips, and Christ, the fantasy-telling had been sexy. He was so hard right now, his balls ached. "Come on, where are you parked?"

"In back." She pointed. Street parking had probably been full when she arrived, but there was space in the overflow lots behind the stores.

He folded his fingers around hers and turned the corner with her. "Tell me how good it was."

She shot out a breath. "I don't know."

He thought of the things she'd told him. "You said you felt free. And in charge."

She seemed to think about that for a few steps. "I felt completely in control of the whole thing. Until you made me come."

He put his arm around her shoulders. "I didn't make you, baby, you just went off."

"It was kind of nice, Dominic," she said softly, almost in wonder.

Nice? He wouldn't have used that word. Hot, dirty, sexy, but not *nice*.

"He wanted me, but he let me play the game. He didn't push. He let me call the shots. He could have gotten mad that I was teasing him, promising stuff I wasn't going to deliver on, but he didn't." She tipped her head back to look at him. "But the whole time you were there in case things went wrong."

He'd been there to protect her. If Shane had gotten out of hand, Dominic would have beaten him down. She was so self-reliant, handling her responsibilities, her guilt, her grief on her own, for better or worse. She had never let him take care of her. Except tonight when she allowed him to be her enforcer. It was sexy. Endearing. She'd let him share her control.

She frowned and put her hand on his chest. "Stop analyzing. It was good. Fun. I liked the surprise, not knowing exactly what you were going to make me do tonight. I thought about it the whole time I was getting ready, and I was wet and excited before I even got there." Then she turned, grabbed his hand, pulled him into the parking lot. "And right now, you're going to get in the backseat of my car, and I'm going to suck you until you can't remember your name."

Until he couldn't remember anything. That was what this was all about, forgetting, pretending, being other people with other lives, a couple who hadn't lost the glue holding them together.

He let her seduce him into the backseat. He wanted to forget as much as she did.

DOMINIC FOLLOWED HER HOME IN HIS CAR. THE SALTY SWEETNESS of his come still lingered in her mouth. Her body still vibrated with that incredible silent orgasm in the bar. It hadn't been powerful in and of itself. Physically, she'd had better orgasms, harder, longer. But it was different, exciting because of the time, the place, the strangers around them, the kinkiness of letting him touch her in public, the unexpectedness of it. And Shane, of course. Knowing Shane wanted her was a huge part of the high. It was almost like having two men at once. She'd been seated next to the wall at the end of the bar, and really, no one could have seen exactly what Dominic was doing except for Shane. But some of the patrons probably guessed.

It was the combination that made it explosive, that she'd have liked Dominic to tell Shane to come back to the house. And it was the way Shane had said, "*When she's ready, come back.*" The promise in it, the possibilities. And all her choice, no one else's. Then she'd sucked Dominic in the backseat of her car beneath the parking lot lights. It was risky, and sexy because of the risk. Yet even as she pleasured him, Dominic was watching. If anyone had come close, he would have stopped her.

She'd been totally in charge of what she was doing, yet totally out of control, a delicious dichotomy she couldn't have explained to anyone. It was doing what she wanted even when she knew everyone else except Dominic would tell her it was wrong. And God, she loved it.

What would his next plan be?

Oh, but wait. Why not come up with a plan of her own?

ERIN COULD BARELY CONTROL HER SHAKING HANDS. "WHY DIDN'T you tell me yesterday?"

Dominic closed the lab door when he heard her voice rising, and that pissed her off, too. "Because we had a date last night," he said, "and I knew if I told you, you'd freak out and call it off."

How could twelve hours bring such a radical change in emotion? Erin's whole body trembled with anger. He'd wanted to get fucked so he lied. She was so pissed she didn't even give him points for being honest about it. "Of course, I would have cancelled. This is huge, Dominic." She shook the WEU letter at him. "And they want royalties in arrears? Can they even do that?" It didn't matter. It was in writing; now they'd have to fight it. "That's a year's worth of sales, and the through-coat gauge has been our biggest seller this year." That gauge, that goddamn gauge, the bane of their existence. She wished they'd chucked the prototype in the bay and let it sink.

"I'm aware of that," he said.

"How can you be so calm?" Irritatingly calm. As if she were the one who always had hysterics.

"Because it's bogus."

She threw the letter on the lab counter. "They have the patent."

"I told you the patent should never have been issued. We're fine." He blithely dismissed everything.

She wanted to scream at him. God, she'd felt so good last night. But today came the inevitable flameout, as if she just couldn't maintain a good feeling. "You should have told me all about this up front when we first started working on that gauge. We should have hired the patent attorney then."

His lips thinned. She'd gone too far, criticized his business capabilities. But damn it, they were talking about a hell of a lot of money and all the lawyers' fees it would cost even if they won in the end.

"I'll take care of it," he said flatly.

Just like a man. *I'll take care of it.* Fuck that shit. Last night she'd trusted him to take care of her. What had it gotten her? Just this. A lie.

Jesus. She couldn't think straight. Her heart was racing, head aching, it was hard to breathe, and honestly, she was seeing stars, too. Like a panic attack. She leaned her fists on the countertop and struggled to calm down.

"Erin." Dominic touched her shoulder.

She shrugged him off because if she wasn't careful she'd say something they'd both regret. Yet she wanted to strike out with words, vent all her frustration. Like that day with Jay, before she knew he was sick, when she hadn't know his behavior was a symptom of what was eating him alive. Instead, she'd been so angry and frustrated. And she'd let it out. Then Jay was gone and she could never, ever make it up to him.

Oh God, the things she'd said. How could she have gotten *so* angry with a little boy? A bad day? She couldn't remember. There were so many bad days after that she couldn't separate them all.

But dammit, if Dominic had done his part, if he'd taken Jay on the outing the way he was supposed to, she never would have had to say those things to Jay. She wouldn't have needed to. But Dominic had made that decision without consulting her, too.

She had to stop, needed to stop. Because if she let herself go, everything inside would come tumbling out. And she'd never survive it.

She pulled back, tried to keep her voice neutral. "Just fix it, okay." The way he hadn't fixed *any*thing else. She barely kept herself from adding the last bit, but it was there, so close to the surface.

"Sure, whatever you want," she heard him say, his voice dripping sarcasm, as she headed out of the lab. It was all she could do not to slam the door behind her. Obviously he'd seen through her neutral tone.

She stormed across the roundhouse to her office.

"Omph." Rachel bounced back after colliding with her.

"What are you doing there?" Erin snapped.

"Wa-alking," Rachel stammered. "I'm sorry."

Erin merely growled and marched into her office. She *hated* this place. She was buffeted around by what other people did, what other people wanted.

She crossed to her desk, slumped down into her chair. She'd felt good when she got to work this morning. Then it had all gone to hell. And she still had to do mediate with Atul and Cam about their language barriers. If she didn't get some semblance of control, she'd blast one of them. Or both. Plus she had to confront Matt about his failure rate and his girlfriend troubles or whatever the hell was going on with him this time. Why did *she* have to do it? Why couldn't they act like adults? God. She'd just treated Rachel like crap again. The thought made her inexplicably close to tears.

If only Dominic hadn't lied to her.

She was losing control, going totally ape. She closed her eyes, wanted to cry, just let it all out. Was a day's delay in telling her about the WEU letter really that much of a crime? Of course not. She'd gone overboard. And she didn't even know why. A delayed reaction to Orlando? Or last night? Because they'd *both* gone overboard last night?

She put a trembling hand over her mouth and breathed deeply. *Okay, get a grip.* She wasn't going to take her crap out on her people. That was for sure. Leaning over her phone, she hit the intercom button. "Rachel, can you come in a minute?"

She opened the door before Rachel even had a chance to knock and motioned her in. "That was my fault out there, and I'm sorry I was rude to you."

"Oh, that's okay. I know you're busy and all."

"No, it's not okay." Rachel let her get away with too much. "I was wrong."

Rachel tapped her fingers on the doorjamb. "You know, Erin, you have this habit of taking the blame for everything. You're always apologizing. It's okay to have a bad day sometimes."

It was *not* okay. But she took another deep breath instead of shouting again. "That's the kettle calling the pot black. You always apologize, too."

Rachel shook her head ruefully. "We both need to stop."

Erin gave a soft snort. "Agreed."

Having turned on her heel, Rachel stopped just outside the door. "I promise not to apologize anymore if you run into me, or if your husband makes arrangements behind your back." She smiled, not too bright or phony, just genuine, and fluttered her fingers genially as she left.

Erin picked up a pencil, then threw it back down on the desk. Shit. She probably owed Dominic an apology, too. Why was it so much easier to apologize to her employees than to her husband? True, he should have told her about the letter yesterday, but he'd done his due diligence on the patent issue, and they *had* discussed it. She'd agreed with moving ahead. WEU coming after them wasn't his fault. But with an apology, he'd want to know why she'd flipped out, and if she couldn't exactly explain it to herself, how was she supposed to tell him?

FUCK. HE SHOULD HAVE KNOWN LAST NIGHT WAS TOO GOOD to last.

Dominic ground his fist into the letter on the countertop, then crumpled it and threw it viciously at the wall. Goddammit. He had checked it out with their patent attorney before they started the design on the through-coat gauge. There was prior art, and in theory, nothing should have gone wrong. But if anything ever got fucked up, he was the one to blame.

WEU was playing hardball with them. *Just fix it.* Erin was so good at issuing orders. Sometimes he was just another one of her minions, like Rachel, or Yvonne, or Steve. He could not fix everything for her. He could not go back and change what he had done. There were so many goddamn things he couldn't undo. If he could, then when he got home tonight, Jay would be in his room doing his homework.

He scrubbed a hand down his face. He should have called Hansen yesterday. He'd chosen a local patent attorney, not one of the big guys but someone who charged reasonable rates, yet nevertheless knew his stuff. He made the call now.

Hansen wanted the letter faxed. He'd have to smooth it out.

"I'll send the bastards a response and tell them to take a flying leap," Dominic said. He'd tell Garland Brooks to shove it up his—

"Leave it to me, Dominic. I'll handle everything as your attorney. We'll have to do some searches, find the support for your case, and hopefully make this all go away."

He hated leaving it to Hansen. But the man was right, this thing needed to be handled methodically and documented all the way. That was the part he'd skipped. "Fine. Thanks. I'll send the fax. Give me a call when you've got something."

It was as Erin said, time and money, how much, and whether they could afford it. But his blood pressure had eased in the time it took to talk to Hansen. He saw things from a new perspective. Erin's moods had been bouncing all over the place since he'd first arranged the trip to Orlando. It was the holidays, the memories, everything, but after having been almost completely emotionless for a year, maybe her new emotionalism was actually an improvement, a good sign. Maybe it would force her to deal with him on more than a superficial level, to deal with Jay, and after that, maybe they could find a way to deal with each other without sex or anger as an excuse.

13

ERIN SIGNED THE RETAINER CHECK TO HANSEN. DOMINIC NEVER seemed to consider how hard she worked to make sure they had operating cash. It flowed out more easily than it flowed in, and December was the worst month for coming up with extra. Companies put off purchasing until the new year and the new operating budget. Nevertheless, Bree had added it to the Wednesday morning check run, silently laying the backup folder on Erin's desk. Bree was always quiet, but she'd been more so lately.

Erin didn't have time to think about it. "Why now?" she asked Dominic. "WEU only *just* realized we were selling a through-coat gauge?" Yesterday morning, when Dominic showed her the letter, she hadn't been in the correct state of mind to consider it. And last night, well, they didn't talk at home.

"Because we're small potatoes to them." He stood in her doorway, arms folded across his chest. "Until they noticed their loss in market share. It's just bottom line."

"We should send them a letter and tell them *our* bottom line; that they don't have a leg to stand on."

Dominic shook his head, his mouth grim. "The letter isn't a legal threat. It's a shot in the dark. We're not engaging them in a pissing contest. We'll let Hansen do the legwork. That's what we're paying him for." He held his hand out for the check.

"I don't like it." She should have insisted on talking to Hansen with Dominic.

"This is the best way to handle it," he reiterated.

"All right, fine. Just don't leave me out of the loop this time."

He bared his teeth. "Yes, Erin."

Yeah, she'd sounded petulant. But he was dictatorial. And she had work to do. She'd gotten through the mediation with Atul and Cam yesterday afternoon. They'd smiled, nodded their heads and agreed they'd work better together. She hadn't believed them for a minute, but she'd give them a chance to prove her wrong before she took it another step. She hadn't dealt with Matt, though. He'd gone home sick before she had a chance.

So she went in search of him. DKG's factory was one big room with polished concrete floors, work benches set apart by cloth partitions, shelving equipped with bins for parts storage, and a roll-up door at the far end for shipping and receiving. Heaters hung from the ceiling.

Matt hunched over his bench. She didn't think for a minute that he was so engrossed he didn't hear her. He was a skinny, lanky kid with big ears, and he didn't smile much, but he'd been a good worker until the last three months when his girlfriend moved in with him. He'd said it was to share expenses, but Erin had a feeling it was more about his girlfriend wanting to take the next step and Matt not knowing how to say he wasn't ready.

"Let's grab a smoke," she said. She didn't smoke, but if someone else wanted to, it was up to them as long as they did it outside and didn't toss their butts on the ground. The picnic table sat in the middle of a grassy area between their building and the one next door. Thankfully it hadn't rained and the bench was dry. Facing out, she crossed her legs. Matt sat next to her. The sun warmed her. Monday and Tuesday had been rainy, but today was in the low seventies. The Bay Area was like that; every day a surprise.

"Spill," she said, "and don't tell me nothing is going on because I checked Steve's report and he's turning back three out of every four units you work on."

Matt lit up and blew smoke in the opposite direction. "I'm not happy."

She wanted to laugh. Who the hell *was* happy? "You'll be a lot unhappier if you don't have a job."

He grimaced. "She just never lets me have anything my way." *She* used to have a name, which had been said with a dreamy, boyish sigh. No more.

"Are you making any compromises on your end?"

"On *everything*. She even makes me smoke outside."

"*I* make you smoke outside."

"But *she* smokes, too."

"Maybe she doesn't like how the smoke gets into everything, the curtains, the couch, the carpet." Not to mention the ashtrays and the burn marks on the coffee table.

"Whatever." He shrugged his bony shoulders. "There's other stuff." He pulled on his earlobe, a nervous habit.

"What else?" she prompted. It wasn't her business, but from experience, she knew Matt had to get things off his chest before he'd start making changes.

"She put slip covers on the sofa and chairs. Even the dining room chairs. Like I'm going to get them dirty."

"And?" It was best not to say that Matt's jeans did look pretty dirty.

He tugged on his other lobe. "She makes all the decisions, like what we're going to have for dinner"—she wondered if his girl-

friend did the cooking, in which case, she had a right to decide—
"and what we're going to watch on TV, and I *hate* shows like
The Bachelor and *Dancing with the Stars* and all that crap."

She did not laugh. Because it was what every couple did, fight
about stupid crap. Until you weren't talking at all.

Until you were so far apart you couldn't even talk about your
child.

Erin stuffed down the thought. "Why don't you tell her you'll
watch her show if she watches one of yours?"

He stubbed his toe on the grass beneath the picnic bench.
"She doesn't listen to me."

"You have to take the bull by the horns, Matt, and *tell* her
what you want, make sure she hears. Maybe you'll find out there
are things you're not listening to either."

He made a scoffing sound in his throat.

"Sometimes you have to figure out what it is they want and
give it to them. Once they're happy, you get what you want."

"Uh-huh," he agreed, though he clearly didn't get what she
was saying.

Fine, whatever, he needed to think about it for a while. "Only
you can fix it, and only you can fix your work performance. We
can't have this kind of failure rate."

He stabbed his cigarette into the ashtray next to the table. "I
know, Erin. I'll do better. Thanks for listening."

He was easy to please, though she wasn't sure she'd done a
bit of good. His work would improve, at least for a few weeks,
but if he didn't do something about his home life, she'd be having
the same talk again. She didn't want to have to fire him.

She stayed in the sun after Matt returned to work. *Figure out
what they want, give it to them, then you get what you want.* Her
problem was that she wasn't sure what she needed. She wanted
Dominic to handle his end of the business, but when he did it his

way, she got pissed off over the results. It hadn't always been that way. She used to butt out of his stuff, but now she'd developed her own dictatorial side. It wasn't all him.

But he sure could make demands when he wanted to.

With her eyes closed and the sun's warmth on her legs, images that had nothing to with Matt played across her eyelids. Dominic had been the one to set up all their dates, telling her what to do, what to wear, where to meet him, calling all the shots, giving her the orders. A stray thought made her smile, a naughty little idea. Maybe Dominic needed to be taught a lesson about *his* dictatorial side. Maybe he needed to be on the receiving end of a few orders. Just the thought made her hot. The irritation that had swept over her was vanquished by the lick of sexual heat. Sure she was trading one emotion for another, but this one was better, more powerful than anger.

Dominic needed to be punished. And that could be so much more satisfying.

HIS BLACKBERRY CHIRPED WITH A TEXT MESSAGE. HE READ:

"I will book a hotel room for you on Friday night."

A room for just *him*? Dominic knew better than to question good fortune. Erin wanted to play a game. She had forgiven him. He typed back. "Okay."

"You will arrive at seven o'clock. You will shower and lay on the bed naked."

Wednesday. He had two days to wait. He didn't know if he could make it. He wanted to ask her to book the room tonight, but he couldn't risk spoiling things. She'd made a date. She'd engaged him. She wasn't coming along for the ride; she was directing. He'd thought it would take weeks to get her to that point, especially after her blowup about the patent. Christ, she'd been furious. Now this. Another sample of her changeable moods and rocketing emotions. But this *had* to be a good thing.

"I'll be there." He didn't ask where, hitting the keypad so fast he got some of the letters wrong and had to retype.

Then he read her swift reply. "You will do everything I say, no questions asked. Do I make myself clear?"

He smiled. His blood heated. He would do anything. For her, he had no limits. It was as if they were newly married again, hot for each other, as if he'd never fucked up their lives.

He could never hope she'd forgive the unforgivable. But he could live with pretending.

STANDING AT HER WINDOW THAT LOOKED OUT OVER THE PARKING lot, Bree wiped her eyes. Rachel could see her tearstained face in the reflection.

"You need to tell Erin," Rachel said in a soft voice.

"No," Bree answered without turning.

"You're going to have to tell her sometime."

"I won't need to say anything." Bree's voice was a little stronger now.

Rachel knew it was none of her business, but really, she couldn't ignore Bree's tears. All she'd done was walk into the office and point out that the address wasn't complete on one of the checks. Running everything through the mail machine was Rachel's job, and she double-checked the work.

"You can't avoid it forever." She was becoming a mother hen, telling Erin not to blame herself for everything that went on at DKG, now offering Bree advice. It wasn't like Rachel had her life in order. She barely made enough to cover the bills even with child support to help.

"Oh, yes, I can." This time Bree was adamant. She flipped her long black hair over her shoulder, turned. The only thing left of her tears was a small smudge of mascara below her eyelashes. Her dark eyes were clear. "I'm sorry about that. I just had a bad moment. It won't happen again."

With that, she shut Rachel out, pulling her chair away from the desk and sitting down to tap on the keyboard. "I'll correct the address in the file right now. Thanks for showing me."

Rachel backed out the door. She couldn't help Bree if Bree didn't want it. Turning, she took three steps and almost collided with Yvonne. How long had she been standing there? More important, how much had she heard?

"Everything all right?" Yvonne asked. Suspicion flickered in her brown eyes.

"No, no. Everything is fine. Just a wrong address on a check." Rachel flapped the envelope as evidence.

"That's not like Bree to make mistakes." She glanced past Rachel to Bree's open door.

Rachel wanted to shake her head. All she'd tried to do was offer help, but she'd made a mess. Now Yvonne was trying to put her nose in Bree's business, too. "It was just a missing number on a ZIP code, Yvonne. No big deal."

"Excuse me for worrying about people," Yvonne snapped.

Rachel realized she'd hurt her feelings, thought of something to make it up. She forced a lighter tone. "Hey, Yvonne, are we going to decorate the office, maybe organize a holiday lunch?" Christmas was only two weeks away.

Yvonne's eyes widened in horror, then she shot a stark look at Erin's office. "Don't *even* mention that," she said, her voice dramatically low. "We're not celebrating Christmas at DKG."

Then Yvonne turned, moving with amazing grace for a woman her size, and reentered her office, sitting down behind her desk with a huff.

The roundhouse was empty. In her office, Erin's phone rang, and she answered in a quiet voice. Rachel had forgotten. When she'd asked for the week off between Christmas and New Year's, Erin had merely nodded. Rachel hadn't connected all the dots, but of course Erin wouldn't want to think about Christmas.

Rachel puffed out a breath. DKG was becoming a minefield she was having trouble negotiating.

14

FRIDAY NIGHT. ERIN HADN'T TOUCHED HIM ALL WEEK, NOT SINCE Monday at Rudolpho's. There'd been no after-midnight sex since they'd returned from Orlando. But since Wednesday, sexual tension seemed to sizzle between them, permeating every word, every look. At least it did for him.

Dominic lay flat on his back on the hotel bed, naked, hands stacked beneath his head, staring at the ceiling made of swirled plaster accented with a small teardrop chandelier. The mattress was high off the floor, the comforter thick, the pillows down. It wasn't a big high-rise San Francisco hotel right on Union Square, but it was expensive, exclusive, and luxurious. Erin had chosen well.

Over the past two days, she'd sent him a laundry list of instructions. He'd followed every one to the letter. He'd driven to the city by himself, showered, shaved, cranked up the wall heater, and laid on the bed completely naked. She hadn't said he couldn't improvise, so he brought champagne for her, a couple of bottles of beer for himself, and two glasses. They might be drinking different beverages, but they would both be sparkling.

Rain pattered against the window, drowning out the sounds of traffic from below. She'd booked the room in his name, and he'd asked for the highest floor he could get. He ended up on the eleventh.

His skin sizzled with anticipation. He'd been waiting for ten minutes. He felt his breath, in, out, accompanied by the shifting air currents across his body. A muffled sound drifted from the room next door. The hotel was older, the pipes louder.

His cell phone vibrated on the side table. Identifying a text from her, his heart actually skipped a beat. The games they played added a new element of excitement, as if she were some mystery woman who'd shown up in his life, fucked him, then disappeared again. In a way, that's exactly what Erin did, a different side of her coming out to play, a side she wouldn't give him at home or work.

He opened the message and read. "Stroke your cock. I want you hard."

He wouldn't put it past her to leave him alone in a hotel room to jerk off by himself as punishment for not telling her about WEU. But Dominic did exactly as she instructed, closing his eyes, imagining it was her hand on him until the blood pulsed in his dick.

Another vibration, another text. "Lube it."

She'd ordered him to bring a tube. He poured the cool liquid over the tip of his cock, let it drip down to his trimmed balls, massaged it in. He didn't text her back. She knew he'd do whatever she ordered him to. Ah God, his cock ached for her. If she didn't come to relieve him, he'd die. He'd done plenty of jacking off, had no problem with it, but he needed her here.

Once more the phone vibrated. "Unlatch the door but don't open it. Then get back on the bed."

In two seconds flat, he'd returned to his position in the middle of the bed. He enjoyed the step-by-step instructions, the anticipation in each vibration of his phone, the mystery of what she'd demand.

"Close your eyes and keep stroking" read the next text. "I'm sending someone to you. You will allow this person to do anything."

Sending someone? He wondered . . . but, no, it was a trick, another part of the game. Eyes closed, fist stroking idly, five minutes later, he felt the waft of air over his body as the door opened, the hall cooler than the room. The chandelier over the bed clicked off, and she turned something else on, perhaps the bathroom light. The sensuality of darkness washed over him. Blind, he could scent her better, a subtly sweet, exotic aroma he didn't recognize.

She said nothing, but he heard her movement about the room, the rustle of clothing, the slide of silk against skin. Then he sucked in a breath as a thick liquid splashed over his cock and hand. In moments, it heated, a tingling that spread from his crown down his shaft as he stroked in the warming gel. He groaned. The mattress dipped beside him. Two fingers massaged his balls, then a hand cupped his sac with the caress of satin. She wore gloves.

Lifting his head, she slipped a satin-lined blindfold over his eyes. Elastic holding it in place cut out even the dim light from the bathroom. Sliding something with the rough texture of nylon around his wrist, she pulled it tight. She wiggled a finger beneath it, then, with the tear of Velcro, clasped it more loosely. Grabbing his other wrist, she secured that one, too. Nylon cuffs. She'd taken a long lunch yesterday. Obviously she'd gone shopping. But he needed more than a few props.

"Touch me," he whispered, begging, his cock aching for her.

She answered by pulling his arms over his head and fastening them to the head of the bed. By the feel of it, she'd slipped a rope through the cuffs.

Then she crawled to the bottom of the bed and went to work on his feet, securing him spread-eagled with more ropes and cuffs. The bed shifted once more. The door opened, closed.

He waited. "Erin?" Unease trickled down his spine. He had no phobias, but being tied, blindfolded, and naked did leave a man vulnerable. He couldn't even hear her breathe.

The door reopened.

"Erin?"

No answer. Just a light tread across the carpet. Something soft trailed over his foot, up his shin, along his thigh, then tickled his balls. He was completely exposed, and when he tugged on the cuffs and ropes, his range of motion wasn't more than a couple of inches.

After a crackle of plastic, a tearing, she lifted his dick and rolled on a condom. Expertly. Tantalizingly.

Where had Erin learned the technique so skillfully? They hadn't used condoms beyond those first fumbles back in college. Why a condom now?

Unless it wasn't Erin at all.

His heart thumped faster as the unease became something more. She straddled him, soft inner thighs along his hips. Then she stroked his cock between her legs, the heat of her pussy searing the tip.

It was her. It had to be her. But she didn't smell right, not like Erin. It was good, but it was more fragrant, hotter, sweeter, as if she'd rubbed another scent on herself.

He felt suddenly as he did when the clock flipped past midnight and she fucked him without a word. When he lost himself in her, yet hated the things she held back.

"Stop," he murmured.

She put a satin glove to his lips. Then she took him, his cock sliding into heat and wet. Christ, it was good, his hips surging without conscious effort, driving deep. He groaned.

The gloved fingers tweaked his nipples, pulled until pain mixed with the pleasure. Behind the mask, his eyes rolled back.

"Say something, baby." He couldn't beg for her voice in their bed at home, but he could beg here.

Yet she said nothing, gave him nothing but the sweetness of her body. God, yes, it was punishment. It ripped his guts out. He wanted to shout, shake her, force her to talk to him, but he couldn't stop his body's reactions, jamming his feet into the mattress for better leverage. She rode him, fucked him, took him. Part of him feared it wasn't her, that it was some nameless, faceless woman she'd sent to torture him. Without her voice, her words, he couldn't be sure. Yet *how* could he be unsure if this was his wife? Shouldn't a man *know*?

She leaned back, changing the angle of penetration, robbing him of thought, turning everything into sensation. It was hot, and it was terrifying, shooting adrenaline through his veins like a fear-threat reaction. Yet nothing could stop the build in his balls, the throb, the ache, then the hot pulse through his cock, reverberating through his body, his extremities, finally working up his throat with a shout. And mindlessness.

He barely registered the untying of the ropes, the slither of clothing being rolled on. Then the soft snick of the door.

She was gone. Like a ghost. Or a soul-stealing succubus. He felt drained. Something vital had been missing. Her. He hadn't *felt* her.

She'd turned the game against him. And Dominic didn't like it.

ERIN LEANED AGAINST THE ELEVATOR WALL AS IT PLUMMETED TO the lobby.

For a moment, when he'd said her name, she'd actually believed he didn't know who she was. Or that he had his doubts.

She'd planned it that way, no talking, the gloves, the condom, the scented oil he wouldn't recognize, yet she hadn't gotten the kick out of it she thought she would. She'd wanted to tie him down, have her wicked way with him, and show him what it was like to take orders. Ultimately it was supposed to be fun, and when she'd thought it all up, she figured he'd love every moment of it, even the niggling doubts about her identity. But she wasn't sure he'd enjoyed it. She wasn't sure *she* had.

There was something wrong, something missing. She'd needed a boost, a relief, an escape; she'd needed to take all her chaotic emotions out on him. Yet it hadn't worked the way she'd wanted it to. She hadn't felt triumph, or even power.

Give them what they want, then you get what you want. That's what she'd told Matt. The problem was she still didn't know what she wanted. Was sex with Dominic really nothing more than a shot of heroin or a snort of cocaine?

The elevator hit bottom with a slight drop of her stomach, and the doors whooshed open. As the wall of voices in the lobby crashed over her, she suddenly grasped what had been missing up there in the room. The banter, the sexy dirty talk. Even when Dominic had been talking about her, over her, not just to her, she'd thrilled to that. He filled her up, made her feel desirable, wanted, needed. She'd *liked* being a sex object. Before Orlando, the sex act had driven out all the bad thoughts. Now she needed the words, too. It might not be the final answer, the final need, but it would do for right now, for tonight.

No one boarded, and the doors closed again, but the elevator sat when she didn't select a floor. Then it began to move as if someone from above had pushed a button.

She'd unfastened his restraints before she left. Maybe it was him, pushing the button for her, waiting for her, wanting her. Her pulse actually started to race. Then her stomach sank when the elevator stopped at the fifth floor and an elderly couple stepped on. The man pressed the lobby button, and the car dropped once more before Erin had a chance to do anything.

At the bottom, the wife got off, and the man held out a hand to let Erin precede him. She felt like an idiot. "I forgot something upstairs." Then she hit eleven on the pad.

The gentleman smiled politely, and the door closed after him.

Minutes later, standing outside the room, she put two fingers to the door and listened. Complete silence. Not wanting him to be sure she was gone, she hadn't latched the lock when she left. With a gentle nudge, the door snicked open. Light fell across the carpet from the bathroom just as she'd left it.

Inside she let her eyes adjust to the dimness. She didn't see him at first, then finally made out his bare feet on the carpet, where he sat in a chair. He'd pulled on his jeans, but not his shirt. The ropes, nylon cuffs, and blindfold lay heaped in the middle of the bed.

"Where did you find her?" His voice was rough gravel.

He really thought it was another woman. No. He was just playing along. Wasn't he? There was a certain delicious thrill in having to wonder. "I'm not telling you all my secrets," she answered.

He rose, stalked her. Even in his bare feet, he made her tremble with his height and size.

"She was good," his voice whispered over her. "Her pussy was tight, and so wet. She flexed around me, milked me." His voice dropped low, lower, and he crowded her up against the bed. She almost toppled, holding on to his arms to steady herself. "And Christ," he said on a mere breath, "I wanted to come inside her without that fucking condom on."

Her pulse pounded against her eardrums. This was part of the game. He'd known it was her. Right?

Then he shoved his hands beneath her armpits, picked her up, and tossed her on the bed. "Your turn," he whispered, then crawled after her, all carnal, all predator.

This was what she'd ached for, the animal in him taking over.

15

HE WRAPPED ONE NYLON CUFF AROUND HER DELICATELY BONED wrist. "Tell me to stop."

She stared up at him, said nothing, her eyes wide. To see her better, he snapped on the bedside lamp. She trembled beneath him as he straddled her hips. He'd never seen the navy blue leggings or blousy, white button-down top, the material thin and sheer. The black bra beneath was a front-clasp.

He fastened her other wrist, then, with the rope around the center of the cuffs, he secured her by the wrists to the headboard just as she'd done to him. "You still have a chance. Just tell me to stop." He put his face right down in hers. "Better yet, tell me who that woman was," he murmured, his lips on hers.

"Do your worst. I'll never tell." Now her eyes sparkled wickedly in the light.

He wanted to laugh. They sounded like Snidely Whiplash and Nell. "Last chance." Then he shoved his hands beneath the long shirt, grabbed the top of her leggings, and pulled them off her hips. Her thong panties came with them, baring her pussy. As he yanked the clothing all the way down her legs, her high-heeled shoes slipped off, too, hitting the carpet with a soft *pffft*.

Then he gazed up the length of her body. "God, you're so

pretty." The awe lingered in his voice, but he didn't let that stop him from slapping a nylon cuff around her ankle and securing her leg to the bed with one of the ropes she'd used on him. "She set my blood on simmer," he said, pulling her legs apart, and tying her spread-eagled. "You're going make it boil." He inhaled the sweetness of her pussy, then lifted his head to look at her. "You're going to make me come hard. You're going to make me scream. You're going to prove how much better you are than she was."

Her breath puffed. Her pussy glistened, beckoned. He shimmied up her body, covering her, then reached between them to undo a shirt button, slowly, then one after another.

She wrapped both hands around the rope above her head. "I don't have to prove anything. I *am* better than her. But the only way you can get a piece of my ass is if you tie me down." She wriggled beneath him, making him hard.

"I hear a challenge. You're going to beg to come." He rubbed his pelvis between her legs. "You're going to beg me to take a piece of your ass."

She closed her eyes, and though he felt her resistance in the fine tremors of her body, she couldn't stop the involuntary sigh of need and pleasure. Yet she fought him. "No man makes me beg."

He smiled devilishly as he unhooked the bra and pinched her nipple. "I will," he promised.

She squirmed, moaned, then smirked at him. "You're going to have to do better than that."

This was so much sexier than the earlier silent episode. He craved her feisty comebacks, the tease, the challenge. In the dark and the silence, she'd fucked him in anger, he knew that now. Residual anger over his lie of omission. Those emotions had been all wrong. But despite her words, she wasn't angry anymore. She wanted, needed, enjoyed the fight and the tug-of-war. She was engaged, part of the act, not just an automaton fucking him for physical release. This was what he'd craved, her total involvement with *him*.

"What's your biggest fantasy, the one you've never told me?" he demanded. He'd asked in the bar with Shane. She'd never answered, and dammit, he needed to know, now, right now.

"It sure as hell doesn't include you." She bucked, tried to throw him off.

"Feisty little bitch," he muttered.

She bared her teeth, then kneed him. It landed on his thigh, doing little damage.

"Do whatever you want," she jeered. "It doesn't matter to me," she added when the physical didn't have any effect on him.

Her fantasy suddenly became as clear as if she'd said it aloud. To give up her control, to let him have anything he wanted. That night in the bar, she'd been in control with Shane, teasing them both, egging them on, yet there'd been an underlying need fulfilled when Dominic took over, made her come.

This, tonight, was one step further, allowing him the right to decide how to push her limits. If she hadn't wanted it that way, she wouldn't have come back. She might never admit it, maybe she didn't even know it, but she was entrusting him with her body and her spirit, challenging him to give her what she couldn't ask for aloud.

He held her chin, forced her to meet his eyes. "Struggle all you want, but you're taking whatever I dish out."

"I'll scream," she whispered.

"In ecstasy," he replied, then took her lips. Everything was about taking, forcing. He plunged his tongue deep into her mouth, tasting the heady sizzle of peppermint as if she'd been sucking a candy. She moaned, pressed her body into his. Then she backed off and nipped his lip.

It wasn't hard, a sexy love bite, while at the same time upping the stakes of their skirmish.

Her panties were gone, her breasts bared. He slid a hand down between them to her pussy, their battleground. "Bet you're hot and so fucking wet."

"It's nothing more than a natural physical response." Her lips were moist, full and red from the heat of that kiss.

"Let's see what else is natural." He slid the tip of his finger between her folds to find the button of her clit. It was full, plump, needy. He circled, watching the dilation of her eyes. "Aren't you going to scream?"

She loosed a breathy sigh as he slipped deeper, finding her creamy and warm. "What's there to scream about?" she muttered.

He chuckled. She wouldn't scream even when he made her come. She'd fight him all the way. And they would both get off on the game. Still pinning her to the bed with his body, he shifted slightly for greater access between her spread legs. "So you're saying that doesn't feel good." He caressed, rubbed, circled, taking in the heightened color of her skin.

"I can do better with my vibrator."

He had to admit he loved her vibrator. The abandon with which she'd used it for him in the past made his blood sizzle. "Did you bring it with you?"

She hesitated a moment too long. "Why would I bother?"

He glanced over his shoulder at the bag she'd dropped in the middle of the carpet in the short hallway by the bathroom. Big enough to hold a few tricks such as a box of condoms, rope, restraints. And a vibrator.

Sliding off the bed, he padded to the bag, stared at it, then back at her, smiling. "What surprises do we have in here?"

"Don't you dare touch my things." She growled in her throat, but it came off sounding closer to a purr.

Flipping on the overhead chandelier, then crossing once more to the bed, he upended the bag. Everything tumbled out between her splayed legs.

"Bastard," she said.

"A vibrator." He held it up just in case she missed seeing it. "And what did you plan on doing with that?"

"Using it on your ass," she snapped.

He turned the vibrator this way and that. "That's an interesting thought." Then he pointed it at her. "But it would be so much better to use it on *your* ass."

"You wouldn't dare." She glared, her eyes sparking in the light from the chandelier's teardrops.

He clucked his tongue. "Another challenge." He pointed to her bound wrists. "You're not in a position to issue any challenges. Tied up the way you are, you'll lose."

She shot him a careless grin. "I might be now, but at some point, you're going to let me loose. Then you better watch out."

"Promises, promises," he mocked as he poked through the other items. A bottle of warming gel. She'd used that on him, the liquid heating on contact. He held it up, watching the play of light through it. "I wonder how that will feel on your clit?"

"It won't do a thing," she sneered.

Everything she denied was something she wanted. He would give it all to her. Then he spotted a rapid transit ticket. "You took BART?"

"I didn't want to hassle with parking in the city."

She'd planned to drive home with him in the morning, he was sure. Or . . . He wondered what had been in her mind? Later, when the game was over, he'd ask. Then again, the mystery of it might be fun.

He laid the vibrator beside her on the bed. "For the right moment," he said, setting the gel on the side table.

She gazed at him with a skeptical eye.

He wanted to say he loved her, wanted to tell her this was the perfect scenario, that he would make everything good again.

Instead, he stripped off his jeans and briefs and climbed between her legs. "Prepare to scream when you come."

Then he blew warm breath on her pussy.

Erin trembled with need, his dark head and broad shoulders so miraculous down there between her legs. "Only in your dreams," she scoffed.

Dominic was capable of making her scream, but she wouldn't, mainly because she didn't want the people next door complaining to management. Besides, it was more fun to fight him.

But when he put his tongue to her pussy, she forgot about the desire to fight. There was only sensation, the caress of his smoothly shaven chin against her thigh, the swirl of his tongue, then the thickness of his fingers entering her. He licked and rode her G-spot in tandem. It was more than double the heat. Then he was gone, leaving her gasping for the unattainable peak.

"Bastard," she muttered.

"I thought you said you wouldn't like it."

"I didn't." Which wasn't a lie. She'd loved it. God, yes, she was glad she'd come back for more. Her original plan had been to do him in the dark, go home, and pretend she'd sent him a woman. She'd even thought about getting angry with him, acting jealous.

This was so much better. Since they hadn't mutually agreed for sure that it was her in the dark, she could still do the jealousy thing later. There were so many possibilities. He made her feel like a different person here in this room.

Maybe feeling like someone else was all she needed to set her free.

She snapped her eyes open when he drizzled the warming gel

on her pussy, letting it drip down over her clit. It heated, tingled, and when he put his finger to it, she almost shot off the bed.

She couldn't help the moan that escaped. Oh God, this was delicious.

"Like that, don't you?"

"I can take it or leave it." If she agreed, he'd stop. If she said she hated it, he'd force it on her. "And licking me with it on your tongue isn't going to do anything either."

He laughed, a hot, sexy sound that thrummed along her nerves endings. In the last couple of weeks, he'd laughed more. It had all been about sex, but maybe that was okay.

"I'm not going to put the gel on my tongue," he said, a gleam in his eye. Then he held up a tin. The mints from her purse. "I'm going to use these." He slipped one on his tongue.

She bit her lip to keep from smiling. They were extra strength and made her mouth tingle. God, what would it be like on her pussy in combination with the warming gel he'd already poured on her? She shuddered in anticipation.

For a moment, she had the crazy notion of thanking him. For this, the sex play, the game, taking her out of herself, making her feel, making her forget, but she didn't want him to know how hard it was just to get up in the mornings sometimes. She didn't want to remind him. Or remind herself.

"It's not going to do a damn thing for me," she groused.

"You'll sing, you ungrateful little bitch." He sucked her before she had a chance to form a comeback or an insult.

"Oh God." Her head lolled on the pillow with the exquisite torture. The mint sent a zing through her whole body, hot, sizzling, overwhelming. He swirled it all around her, and for a moment, she truly went mindless. When he thrust two fingers inside her, hitting her G-spot unerringly, she capitulated and screamed out his name.

The orgasm shot through her like a starburst.

"You screamed," he murmured, idly stroking her cleft, a smile of supreme satisfaction curving his lips as he crunched the last of the mint between his teeth.

"I was yelling for you to stop." She yawned. "I'm really not interested." There were no thumps on the wall. Hopefully she hadn't screamed too loudly.

"You came"—he blew on her, eliciting a shudder—"you screamed"—he swiped his tongue one last time over her clit—"and now you're going to beg me to fuck you."

She snorted, but she needed to feel him inside her. What she'd done to him in the dark hadn't been enough. *God, make me feel,* she whispered only in her mind.

Dominic slid slick fingers along her pussy, down beneath her, then stroked her ass.

"Don't you dare," she murmured. They'd never done ass play, though sometimes he'd tried, especially after she'd had a margarita or two. But it was taboo. She couldn't say why. Then she had to smile. So ass play was taboo, but letting Dominic make her come in a bar was just fine?

"You're smiling. I know you want it."

"I'm not smiling." She lifted her head to look at him down between her legs. "I'm smirking because you're so transparent."

"Liar, liar," he chanted softly, and probed her gently, not entering, just slow, rhythmic circles, pushing lightly.

She wriggled and dislodged him. "I'm done. I'm going to sleep." She closed her eyes.

She didn't know if she wanted it. She didn't want to decide. She just wanted him to do it, make her come, make her scream, make her feel.

16

DOMINIC SHIFTED, HIS FINGERS BRUSHING HER SHIN JUST BEFORE the Velcro around her ankle ripped. He stretched to free her other leg. Grabbing her hips, he flipped her to her stomach, the rope between her wrists, which tethered the cuffs to the headboard, turning with her like meat on a spit.

Erin squeaked. "What the hell are you doing?"

He covered her, all that sleek, male flesh, his weight feeling so good on her, his cock along her ass, and one leg between her thighs. "I'm going to fuck you."

"Oh, no, you're not, not like this."

"Oh, yes, I am. You want it." He slid to one side, then traced a finger down the crease of her ass. "Exactly like this."

"It's disgusting." Her heart beat faster, in anticipation as much as fear.

"You want to feel me stretch you. You want me to take you to heights you've never been."

"You're not good enough." He was silent a moment, and she feared she'd gone too far, shot off one too many cruelties she didn't really mean.

His tongue teased the shell of her ear, his breath caressed her, and his words made her crazy. "Your ass is mine, baby. I own it. I'm going to fuck it. And you're going to love it."

Warm liquid trickled between her cheeks. She shivered as he rubbed in the lube, playing with her tight hole, massaging. She clamped down to keep him out and turned her head to glare over her shoulder.

"Let me in," he whispered. "You'll feel better than you ever have in your life."

He seduced her with his naughty touches and soft words. But it wouldn't do to give in too easily. He might think she wanted this, had fantasized about him forcing her to take it this way. That was giving him far too great an advantage. "I'm going to hate it."

He licked her cheek, kissed her ear. "But I'm going to love it, so who the fuck cares what you want."

Oh, he was really enjoying the role of pirate. "Asshole," she murmured. Of course, it didn't take him down at all because her ass was exactly what he wanted.

He probed, then breached her with the tip of his finger. Oh. Oh God. It was different, unique. Maybe even good.

"No," he muttered at her ear, "*this*"—he rotated his finger slowly—"is a pretty little asshole." Then he worked his hand beneath her belly, stroked down to her clit and played her from both sides.

She gulped, suddenly beyond words. He caressed, slid deeper, backed out, stretching her, all the while taking her clit, making her burn hotter.

"I want this," he whispered, pushing deeper once more. "I need this." His cock was hard and pulsing along her thigh. Body half covering her, he buried his face against her neck. His skin was musky with testosterone and spicy with a hint of aftershave.

As if she weren't even in command of her own body, her hips tilted, giving him better access to her clit and her ass. She rocked with him, rolled, let him take her with his finger in the most intimate of places.

"How does it feel?" he whispered against her ear.

"Oh God." She couldn't have come up with an insult if she'd used every functioning brain cell.

"It'll be even better with my cock in there."

She was just nerves, skin, heat, wet, grinding with him. He very well might be right about how good it would be.

"Beg me." It almost wasn't his voice, just an elusive tendril of smoke wafting by her, a drug beckoning her.

"Fuck me," she whispered.

"Fuck you where?" he pushed.

"Fuck me there."

He didn't let up, massaging her back and front, turning her boneless.

She couldn't hold out against the sensations. "Please," she begged. "Force me, make me do it. Just do it."

"Soon, baby," he murmured. "Feel how deep my finger is."

She felt him inside, outside, everywhere. "Now" was the only other word she could manage.

She felt him ease away, pad to the bathroom, water ran. He returned with a warm washcloth, cleansed her, soothed her, warmed her.

Reaching above her head, he tugged on the Velcro at her wrists, freed her. Her arms ached slightly. Molding his chest to her back, he folded the vibrator into her hand, his words just a breath against her ear. "Use it." Whether he ordered or urged didn't matter. He wrapped an arm beneath her breasts, hugged her close, then raised them both to their knees.

Her heart galloped. Her pussy pulsed. He slathered them both with lubricant, then she felt the nudge of him.

"You're too big," she whispered, suddenly afraid.

He leaned over her. "I won't hurt you. You want it, you need it, take me, please." He eased a fraction deeper until she felt full, but not good yet.

"The vibrator," he urged, tugging her wrist.

She turned the vibrator on one-handed, the buzz filling the room.

"That's it. Use it on your clit."

He rocked gently with her, moving their bodies together, getting her used to him. With the first touch of the vibrator on her clit, she moaned, sensation swamping her. She eased back, taking a little more of him.

"That's it, baby. That's good. God, yes."

He covered her, surrounded her, and inside, she felt him pulse, throb. "Oh yeah," she murmured, tipping her head back.

He leaned in to suck the flesh of her neck, licked the perspiration off her skin.

"Fuck me," she whispered. "Make me do it, force me."

He surged forward, and she took him deeper. "Christ, you feel so good, baby, so tight." His groan rumbled against her back, her ear, setting free an answering tremble inside her.

It *was* good, unlike anything, something new, something beyond. Her legs shook, her body quivered. "Harder."

She let him take control, deeper, faster, harder inside her. The pain was past, the pleasure overpowering, the vibrator and his cock working magic.

"Oh God, oh God," she chanted, over and over, until finally the voice seemed to be coming from someone else.

"Baby, baby, baby."

Her orgasm rushed up and over like a tsunami. There was only his flesh quaking inside her, heat streaking through her, swamping every sense, then the roar of his climax.

She was lost. Or maybe, in this moment, she was found.

* * *

AT NINE IN THE MORNING, DOMINIC WAS STARVING. HE WANTED bacon, eggs, hash browns, the works. He sidled into the booth overlooking Powell Street. Cars, circa 1950s, had been cut in half lengthwise and somehow fastened into the plaster high on the diner's walls: a turquoise '57 Chevy, a Buick, a yellow roadster. Outside, the streets were festooned with garlands and Christmas bells, the sidewalks teeming with shoppers looking for bargains and specials. Inside, voices and laughter echoed off the high ceiling. The booths were red, the table tops Formica, and the food was as American as baseball and apple pie. And just as good.

But last night was better, so good his blood was still singing. It was beyond the physical, it had grabbed hold of his heart, soothed something deep in his soul. He didn't think she was ready to hear that, though. "What'll you have, honey?"

Erin studied the menu, then raised just her eyes. "Half your bacon and half your toast."

He snorted. "Forget it. Order your own."

"Tightwad," she muttered.

"Hey, I'm springing for breakfast."

"Right, and I paid for the hotel. So that makes you"—she stabbed a finger in his direction—"a *complete* tightwad." Then she went back to the menu.

An eavesdropper would think they were fighting, but after last night, there was an easy camaraderie between them. She'd even held his hand on the two-block walk from the hotel. Like normal people. He felt ridiculously warm and content.

When the waitress came, Erin ordered her own bacon and toast. "Well," she said when they were alone again, "that was an exceptionally naughty evening."

"Over the top," he agreed, trying to downplay so she wouldn't realize how truly immense it had been for him. He was surprised she'd actually mentioned it. In the light of day, she usually pretended the nights of sex didn't exist.

Despite the bliss of a great orgasm and fucking fantastic sex, he'd lain awake with her in his arms, thinking, analyzing. It was an engineering term, but it was how he approached problems, whether business or emotional.

"But did you like it?" he asked. "Do you want to do it again?"

Pouring creamer and sugar into her coffee, she didn't answer right away. Time to think, time to decide.

Sometime during last night's musings, he'd hit on the idea that she wanted him to force her to feel. It wasn't the sex, so much as it was the emotions she wanted. It hadn't been that way in the beginning, when she'd first started reaching for him silently in the dark. Then, she'd sought mindlessness. He understood that. But something had changed. Maybe in Orlando; maybe it had begun even before that. The idea had been rolling around in his mind after she'd gone ballistic about the through-coat patent. *Just fix it*. There'd been something desperate in her words, more than a way to end an argument. The more he thought about it, the more meaning he ascribed to it.

"I don't know." She used the end of her spoon to trace the silvery swirls in the Formica.

"You don't know if you liked it or you don't know if you want to do it again?"

She shrugged, still tracing patterns on the tabletop.

She was reaching out to him even if she didn't know it. That's what she wanted, for him to fix things. His heart ached that what she needed most was something he could never give her. He couldn't fix losing Jay. He only knew that making her feel emotion, any emotion, was better than letting her go on like a robot. He'd taken her that way because she'd never let him do it before, and her acceptance of it, even as she fought him verbally, her awe-inspiring orgasm, was a testament to her desire to push her limits. *Force me. Take care of me.* They were the same thing.

Propping her elbow on the table, she laid her chin on her hand and looked at him. "Maybe now that I've had it, I need something else."

Didn't she feel the enormity of what had happened between them in that hotel room? Yes, he believed she did. That's what drove her crazy. She wanted him to help her, fix things for her, take care of her, but she was terrified of actually letting him do it. Wanting desperately yet being equally afraid. He gave, she threw it back. He couldn't help her with that, couldn't force her to hold on to any steps forward they made together.

But he would not give up. He'd push at her until she had to give him something to work with. "Trust me with what you want next then." He used the word intentionally, specifically, because he couldn't be sure how much she truly trusted him to provide for her. There was so much difference between what you wished for and what you thought you had.

Before she could answer—and he was damn sure she was glad of it—their waitress arrived, tray balanced on her hip, and slid their plates onto the table.

After the waitress was gone, Erin slathered marmalade on her sourdough toast. He picked up a crispy piece of bacon. "Come on, Erin." He leaned in, dropped his voice. "You know what dirty, nasty thing you want next. You've been thinking about it, fantasizing about it, and now you're crazy with wanting it."

She stared at him, toast halfway to her mouth. "You think you know me so well. You think you have me all figured out."

He smiled, swallowing the bite of bacon, the smoky flavor delicious. "I do know you, baby. I know exactly what you had in mind last night, what you were trying to do when you blindfolded me, tied me down, and didn't say a word." Luckily the noise around them seemed to seal them off, and no one paid attention.

She snorted. "Oh yeah? You knew? You had no idea."

He wondered if *she* had any idea what she'd been trying to accomplish. "You wanted me to doubt that it was you. You wanted me to think it was some other woman you gave me to, wanted me to say how hot it was doing someone else, just so you could slam me down in the end."

She stared at him a long moment. "Yes. You're exactly right," she agreed mildly, then added without a missing beat, "can I have a bite of hash browns?"

He laughed. "I didn't expect you to be honest about it." He shoved his plate toward her.

Chewing the forkful of hash browns she'd scooped off his plate, she wriggled her shoulders. Then she put a finger to her lips, swallowing. "I wasn't sure about it being a test and all until after I'd done it and I was back in the elevator."

"So you were going to get back on BART and leave me up there to spend the night alone?"

She raised a brow, nodded her head, and smiled. "I thought the whole silence thing was very sexy."

It would have been if she hadn't fucked him silently in the night so many times before. She didn't have a clue how that tore him apart. "What made you come back?"

She stabbed a small cube of toast with her fork and dipped it in his egg yoke. His chest tightened. She hadn't eaten off his plate like this in a long time, not since they used to go down to the corner Denny's for Sunday breakfast, where kids could eat for free. It used to piss him off how she always stole his food; now, he relished it, wanted to shove his plate at her and tell her to take everything she wanted, everything he offered.

"I came back because I didn't have"—she glanced around—"the big O," she mouthed.

She'd returned because it hadn't been enough. She'd needed more than a silent quickie just as he had. But she wasn't going to admit it.

He'd learned something essential though. "Delightful as what you planned was, from now on, I'll be in charge." They both needed his dominance. That was the simplicity of her greatest fantasy, to let him take care of everything.

Elbow on the table, she propped her chin on her hand. "You're free to *think* you're in charge."

Still feisty, that was good, but she hadn't challenged him by saying she wouldn't play at all. Even better. "You're free to give me suggestions," he prompted.

"No. No suggestions." She stole more of his hash browns. "That way if I don't like it, I can blame you."

Once again, she was being completely honest without even realizing how close to the truth she was about their entire relationship since they'd lost Jay.

17

WHAT DOMINIC HAD DONE TO HER FRIDAY NIGHT WAS NAUGHTY and taboo. And completely fantastic. In the heat of the moment, the primitive act was perfection.

Erin saw things more realistically on a Monday morning, the start of the week, all the work ahead, the shipping preparation, year-end barreling down on them. And she knew she couldn't keep on expecting perfection. She couldn't keep on ordering Dominic to find a way to give it to her or they were both bound to be disappointed.

For now, she would relish Friday night as extraordinary and Saturday morning breakfast at Lorie's Diner as rejuvenating. But this was Monday and the real world.

"Hey, Bree, can you do a quick analysis on how many of the through-coat gauges we've sold?" Erin wanted some idea of the cost if the patent problem wasn't resolved. If Dominic found out she'd asked for the report, he'd think she was checking up on him. Erin didn't care. She needed to know.

Bree was watering her philodendron. Statuesque, she didn't have to stand on a stool to water it. The plant was massive, leafy green vines wrapped around the pot, trailing down both sides of the bookcase. The philodendron had been in a five-inch plastic pot when Bree started at DKG.

"Sure." Bree didn't ask when Erin wanted it or why. She would just do the work and have the figures on Erin's desk, probably before lunch.

"Thanks." Then Erin noticed her eyes, or rather the dark circles under them. "You okay?"

Bree smiled. Somehow it made her look more fragile. "Sure."

Wow, she was a fountain of conversation today. Slender and waiflike despite her height, with long black hair and pale skin, Bree was five years younger than Erin. Erin had always thought of her as ethereal and oddly childlike. She'd worked for a big accounting firm before DKG, but she hadn't liked the pressure, the lack of routine, or the fact that she never had her own workspace. She hadn't even been embarrassed when she'd revealed that in the job interview.

Erin wondered if she should push. But if Bree didn't want to talk, she wouldn't.

"Okay then." Despite feeling that was a weak excuse, Erin backed out, turned, then called across the main room. "Rachel, I'm going out for a couple of hours."

Rachel waggled her fingers without saying a word, but Yvonne came to the door of her office. Yvonne wanted to know everything that went on at DKG, whether it concerned her or not, but Erin would be damned if she'd explain her comings and goings.

Besides, she didn't want Dominic to know where she was headed. He'd say she was bringing undue pressure to bear.

Half an hour later, she pulled into the driveway of Leon's house in the Los Gatos hills above the Lexington Reservoir. The house, workshop, and two-acre property were probably worth a couple of million, but Leon had lived there forever and she'd bet he paid practically nothing for it, comparatively speaking. Separated from the house by redwoods, pines, and bay trees, Leon's workshop stood in a clearing. The roll-up door was open, three rows of florescent lights blazing.

Thin and rangy, Leon's face was a mass of lines and crevices that signified years spent in the outdoors. Hunched over an inspection lamp magnifying a circuit board, he soldered a resistor. Leon was a ham radio operator, and he built his own amplifiers and other odds and ends of radio equipment. Seated on a metal stool with casters on the bottom, he was surrounded by rolling toolboxes, carts and bins of parts, pieces of test equipment, and two lazy, old mixed-breed dogs he'd rescued from the pound years ago. The black one twitched in his sleep.

"To what do I owe this pleasure, Erin?" Leon said, his eyes myopic behind his glasses.

She smiled. "I'm here to talk you out of giving up your sideline." DKG's transducers. Though that was only half the reason she'd driven out.

"I want to rebuild those old cars before I die," he said, raising a shock of eyebrows that were as white as his thick hair. A couple of ancient clunkers rusted out behind the workshop. They'd been there as long as she'd known him, and probably far longer.

"You're going to need money for the parts."

"I can get damn near everything at the junkyard."

The Elvis clock above Leon's head chimed the hour with "uh-huh-huh," Elvis's legs rocking back and forth serving as pendulum. The Betty Boop clock booped, Felix the Cat's eyes rolled, and the Popeye clock popped a can of spinach. Leon had grown up on the old cartoons, served in Korea and Vietnam, and had more stories than an Internet blogger, but his were real. He was history itself.

Sometimes she'd brought Jay up here. Most kids would have

been bored to death with an old man's stories and his vintage equipment, but not Jay. He'd been a sponge, absorbing everything. Erin breathed through the sudden ache.

Leon set down his soldering iron and pushed aside the inspection lamp. "You didn't come all the way up here to convince me to keep making the transducers."

"I was going to offer you a raise."

"I don't need a raise." He lived simply, and he'd never been married so he didn't have children to leave a fortune to. "I would have retired last year, but I figured you needed me." He removed his glasses, his eyes a clear blue without them, not even a hint of cataracts. "Now it's time I moved on."

Erin stepped back, her heart beating too fast at the obvious reference to Jay. On the workbench shelf was a whittled camel. He'd started another, this one lying down, legs tucked beneath it. A standing male and a seated female. Two by two. She knew without a doubt they were for Noah's Ark. Leon was still whittling for Jay.

"I don't want you to move on," she said without thinking.

"I know."

It wasn't merely finding someone else, paying the extra it would cost, or moving the work in-house. It was Leon. "I'll miss you." Even if she hadn't been up here to see the old man in a year. He was *there*, a part of the past, a symbol. The thought of letting him go inspired terror.

"I'll still be here when you need to visit." He hadn't held it against her that she'd avoided seeing him. He understood, she was sure. And instead of forcing her to talk about it, he dealt with the practical. "Here's what you do," he said in the rough, aged voice of his. "Get the kid to make them."

The kid was Matt. "His failure rate has skyrocketed. I can't trust him on this."

"Yes, you can. On paper, it probably looks like it'll cost you more than outsourcing with another outfit, but letting him prove himself will give you back immeasurably. He won't fail you." Leon had occasionally come to DKG to drop off parts. He knew all her employees. He was a good judge of character. "Give people a chance," he added, "and they shine for you."

She felt as if he was saying something else, something she wasn't getting. "But you can't really mean to spend your time on old cars?"

He waved a hand over his radio equipment. "There's all this, and—" He stopped, gazed at her, amazing her again with the clarity of his eyes. "I want to meet some of the old geezers I've been talking to on the ham radio. Road trip. Lots of stuff to do, Erin."

He had things he wanted to do. He'd only been hanging around because he thought he needed to prop her up. She'd taken him for granted. And she needed to give in gracefully. "Will you send me postcards?" she asked softly, her stomach aching.

"Course I will." He smiled, and it was as if the old grizzled face beamed.

She didn't like change, and she was going to miss him for more than his parts. Far more, but she'd think about that later. There was something else she'd come about. "Anything odd going on at WEU?" Leon fabbed transducers for them, too.

"WEU?" He scratched his head. "Odd like what?"

She didn't want to tell him that WEU was going to sue them over the through-coat patent. He'd only worry. "I've been hearing rumors." She didn't get specific. Theirs was a small industry; rumors were always flying.

Leon cocked his head like one of his dogs. "They've been pushing payment out to thirty and forty-five days. A couple of months ago, they tried to push me out to sixty and I cut 'em off till I got my money."

Most invoice payment terms were net thirty, but smaller vendors like Leon, one-man shops, needed payment right away. They couldn't afford to finance big companies. Erin made sure Leon got paid on every weekly check run. Yet WEU had been pushing him out forty-five days and beyond.

"I gave them notice, too, just like you." He didn't want her thinking he'd drop her but keep a bigger company like WEU, but she knew he'd never do that.

So, it was possible WEU was having financial issues, and that's why they'd jumped on this patent thing now. They were searching for different avenues of cash. All right, she had a possible reason, but she didn't know how that helped her. DKG didn't have overflowing coffers of cash to fight them with.

"Thanks for the intel." She gave the old man a hug. "I'm going to do as you suggest and give Matt a chance."

He patted her cheek affectionately. "Good girl. And you've still got two months left out of me. If you want, I can come down and show the little whippersnapper the tricks of my trade."

"You're a doll."

"Say hi to Dominic."

"I will. And don't forget those postcards when you're on the move." She didn't mention the camels.

The ache of loss burned at the backs of her eyes, but at seventy-five, Leon was moving on. She had no right to stop him, and she had the feeling he was telling her to do the same. He didn't have kids. He didn't understand that she'd never move on.

Back at DKG, Yvonne didn't even let her get as far as her office. It was just after noon. Yvonne signaled her with a crooked finger, looking in both directions like a spy worried about being overheard. Rachel was most likely out to lunch, and Bree's door was closed. Dominic's car had been in the lot, but he was probably in his lab.

"In here," Yvonne whispered loudly. She closed her office door when Erin was inside. "Something's wrong with Bree."

"Is she sick? Did she have to go home?"

Yvonne rolled her eyes and huffed. "I mean *weird* wrong, not *sick* wrong."

Erin did not sigh. Yvonne claimed she hated gossip, but she was actually the worst gossip in the office. "What exactly is *weird* wrong?" Erin asked.

"Well," Yvonne began to divulge, her eyes gleaming with an avid light, "she and that Rachel girl whisper all the time."

That Rachel girl? The term didn't bode well. In addition, she couldn't imagine Bree whispering "all the time" to anyone. Bree kept to herself, she was internal, one might even say an introvert. "You're exaggerating, Yvonne."

Yvonne narrowed her eyes. "I see things."

Sometimes Yvonne did too much seeing. She was wonderful at her job, friendly and caring with customers, great at solving problems. Getting her nose into other people's business was her downside.

"I don't like it, Erin. Maybe you should talk to her and find out what's going on."

"Yvonne, you need to butt out."

Yvonne scowled. "But—"

Erin held up one finger. Yvonne slapped her mouth shut, but a scowl creased her forehead.

"If it starts to interrupt the work flow, I'll talk to both Rachel and Bree. Otherwise . . ." She left the sentence hanging and opened Yvonne's door.

She hated being in the middle. If it was work, she could handle it, but sometimes she got so freaking tired of people's crap. There was nothing going on. Yvonne just didn't like being out of the loop, or that Bree might actually confide something in Rachel rather than telling her.

On her desk, Erin found the list of through-coat sales sorted by model number. Whatever was going on, as Yvonne put it, Bree had done exactly what she'd asked her to.

Erin flipped to the last page, and her next breath nearly choked her.

Oh my God. She did a quick calculation in her mind. If WEU took them to court and won, the amount of cash they'd have to come up with to pay the royalty would bankrupt them.

18

MONDAY NIGHT. TWO DAYS AFTER THAT FANTASTIC EVENT IN THE hotel. Yeah, he considered it an *event*. Erin rolled again in the bed, this time toward him. Dominic glanced at the clock. A little past midnight. Balls aching, cock hard, pulse racing, he waited for her to reach for him. He wanted it, needed it, her touch, physical, mental, emotional. Brief scenarios ran through his mind, all the kinky things he wanted from her.

But she didn't reach for him. Instead, she turned away. He couldn't stand it anymore. He trailed a finger down her spine.

Tossing aside the covers, she sat up, keeping her back to him. "Sorry, I didn't mean to wake you. I'm just restless."

"That's okay. I wasn't asleep." No, he'd been waiting, breath bated. Hoping, praying, just as he'd done for a year.

"I'm going to work on the computer."

Fuck. Before she wouldn't touch him anywhere but in the dark and silence of their bedroom. Now she wouldn't do it in the bed at all. When were they going to get it right?

He lay there listening to her shuffle down the hall, the closing of her office door like a gunshot breaking the quiet. Anger rumbled through his gut. She'd torn him apart every time she'd turned her back on him these last months, seeking the solace of her office

computer. Alone. Without him. He was overreacting, but he'd
thought things were changing. To find they weren't hit so much
harder. He punched the pillow. When was this going to end?
When would she fucking let him in? He was so goddamn tired
of it. Tired of her, yes, fucking tired of her shit. Christmas was
less than a week away. Did she think that didn't bother him, too?
Did she think he'd forgotten? Fuck.

Dominic breathed deeply, willing his mind to calm. But he was
so goddamn fed up of not being able to do anything right.

He missed Jay, his loss like a hole in his chest where his heart
should have been. God, how he missed him—day, night, with every
moment, with every breath. Wanting her back, wanting their life
back didn't change how much he missed his boy. It wasn't disre-
specting his memory to want more than what they had.

Was it?

Jesus. He closed his eyes, listening to the dark as if Jay might
suddenly speak to him, offer forgiveness, expiation. *Daddy, it's
okay. I know you love me no matter what.*

But he didn't hear Jay's voice. He just felt a swirling, crushing
need.

Throwing back the covers, he tugged on his briefs, then went
to the closet for his robe. God*damn* if he'd stand before her naked while he begged.

The hall was cold, tendrils of night air sneaking beneath the
folds of his robe. He didn't glance into Jay's clean and empty
room. If he did, he'd never make it down the hall.

He stood at her door a moment. No sound from within. But
he would not stop here this time. She could close the fucking
door, but she couldn't shut him out.

Her gaze shot up, eyes wide as he thrust open the door. Then
she fumbled with her mouse.

"What do you do in here?" He felt the scratchy ache in his voice.

"Nothing," she answered too quickly and without meeting his eye.

Nothing? That's all she was going to say? They were married for God's sake. They weren't supposed to have big secrets or shut each other out like this. He could feel his blood pressure rising, his heart pounding, and he wanted to smash something. He settled for rounding the desk, but the screen revealed only her vacant computer desktop, whatever she'd been looking at gone. His gut roiled with jealousy. "Are you e-mailing your boyfriend?"

She snorted, all her furtiveness and nervousness suddenly gone. "You've been trying to set me up with guys so why would you care if I had a boyfriend?"

He would damn well care. "It's still *us*," he growled at her. "You and me together. I need to watch you, to *see* your pleasure in a way I can't when I'm doing it to you." He wanted the sexiness of watching her skin flush with excitement, her breath quickening with desire, the scent of her arousal perfuming the air around him, the rise of her orgasm, her cries. That's what it was about, seeing and hearing *her*.

She gave him a roll of her eyes, a glint of anger flashing in them. "Don't be an idiot," she snapped. "I'm not e-mailing anyone. Give me my space and go back to bed."

Give her *space*? He'd given her so much fucking space and she still didn't understand a goddamn thing. He'd thought that any emotion, even anger, was better than the emotionless wasteland they'd been living in. Not that it was truly emotionless, just that everything was buried where they couldn't touch it, feel it, acknowledge it. But facing it when midnight had passed and all their defenses had crumbled was worse than the stab of pins and needles in awakening limbs.

"Go to bed, Dominic," she whispered, her tone gentled, almost as if she regretted snapping at him. "Everything'll be back to normal in the morning."

Yes, it would be, back to normal where she shut him out. He could no longer abide it.

DOMINIC FOUND HER IN THE STOCKROOM THE NEXT MORNING. HE shoved a piece of paper at her. "Just so you don't accuse me of keeping secrets from you again."

Then he walked away.

Erin glanced around. Fred, their stock clerk, was down the far end out of earshot, staging the next two days' parts kits at the bench.

She'd hurt Dominic last night, but she didn't know how to change it. She'd lain awake for hours, sick over losing Leon, scared to death about the patent thing. And the camels. She kept seeing those delicately carved camels. When Dominic touched her, she couldn't, she just could not give him anything, even as she knew he needed it. Then he'd startled her, opening the door of her office like that, and her heart galloped a mile a minute. He'd have been pissed as hell if he'd seen her screen.

So she'd turned him away again. She'd regretted it almost immediately, but she couldn't call him back. The words he'd said about watching her were actually kind of beautiful, but she'd effectively thrown them back in his face by not even acknowledging them. Dammit, she needed to start giving him *something*. If only she had it to give.

Why was it that when you met someone, in those first glorious days, weeks, and months, you told each other everything, shared every thought? Then the longer you were together, the more you shut down, shut them out. Until you stopped sharing anything at all.

Her palms were sweaty as she read the letter he'd given her. WEU. A demand for payment. This time they'd named an amount. She gaped when she saw it.

Yvonne and Steve were in the roundhouse when she barreled through, parting them like the Red Sea. In engineering, Atul and Cam worked silently in their shared office, and Dominic had hitched himself up on his stool in front of the lab computer. He'd always favored the lab over his office.

"How can they know how much the royalty should be?"

He didn't look at her. "Maybe they checked the sales rankings on the distributor sites."

Though they did have some individual customer accounts, DKG sold most of their product through distributors. Any user could access the sales rankings. It helped buyers figure out what the most popular items were.

But it still made no sense. "There is no way WEU could get this kind of accuracy from those sales rankings."

He tipped his head, looked at her, waited.

She felt her face flush. "I asked Bree to run the numbers." There was nothing wrong with that. She might as well tell him everything. "And Leon said WEU's been stretching out his payments. Obviously they're having cash flow problems, and that's why they're checking into the patents."

He didn't say anything for what felt like forever but was probably seconds. "So. You didn't think I'd handle the issue."

"It wasn't that." All right, yes, but not in a totally dysfunctional way. "I wanted to know the worst-case scenario. So we could be prepared."

He stood, held out his hand. She laid the letter on his palm, where he promptly folded it into a paper airplane and flew it right into the trash can. "That's how much it's worth." He took a step forward. She moved a step back. "It isn't even from their patent attorney. It's not even official." He leaned down, lowered his voice. "So we're following the advice of *our* attorney and ignoring them while he does his job and proves them wrong," he finished, enunciating the last three words with increasing harshness.

Okay, she'd *really* pushed a button last night. Maybe she should apologize. "About last night," she started.

He didn't let her finish, close and towering over her. "I told you I was in charge, and you agreed to that."

She glanced over her shoulder at the open door, then lowered her voice. "When I said that, we were talking about sex, not everything else."

He skirted her and closed the lab door gently. Too gently. Her pulse actually raced; her skin heated.

"Yeah, well, you didn't take care of me last night."

"You didn't ask."

"I touched you," he said as if that were enough.

She swallowed, her mouth suddenly dry. "Okay, I'll take care of you tonight." Her body buzzed with a weird kick of desire for his he-man act.

"You'll take care of me now. I want a blow job."

She gave a mocking laugh, but she was wet, her nipples suddenly hard. "We don't have sex at work. Atul or Cam could walk in. Anyone could."

Back to the door, he reached out and unerringly clicked the lock. "Now they can't."

She bit her lip. He had her going. Just like that. Like he'd flipped her light switch. As if she'd been on the hairy edge of desire when she walked in, she wanted to throw herself at him. Odd, crazy, but, yes, she wanted sex right here, right now, with all the anger and emotion emanating from him like a magnetic force. *Hell*, yes. She fought anyway because that made her even hotter. "You're trying to control me with sex."

He smiled like a shark. "Yeah. I miss it, I want it." He yanked her right up against his hard-on. "And you want it, too."

"Screw you," she said, but there wasn't any anger in it.

"No." He smiled, all teeth. "You're going to blow me. Right here, right now."

He didn't force her to her knees; she went on her own. Because she wanted it. She didn't care why it turned her on. She didn't care that he was treating her like a piece of meat; in a way she couldn't describe, he wasn't doing that at all.

"Suck me," he whispered. "Make me come."

That's why she wanted it. For all his dictatorial attitude, he needed it. He needed *her*. And his desire was her power.

She fumbled at his jeans. He had to pop the top button for her. He bulged against the snowy white briefs. Then a drop of pre-come seeped through, a dark, round spot of desire.

She tipped her head back. His eyes were deep, fathomless, burning right through her. "Beg me," she demanded.

He speared his fingers through her hair, and with the other hand, shoved the briefs down until his cock sprang free, bobbing, caressing her lips. "I'm not begging for something you can't wait to give me."

A sane woman would have walked out on him, leaving him with his cock in his hand. She wasn't sane. They both wanted to win. They both simply *wanted*.

"One cock's the same as another," she said, the smile on her face closer to a sneer. "And I want cock right now."

She took him. He groaned. And Erin knew she had him. His salty-sweet flavor burst on her tongue, his flesh hard, filling her mouth. She sucked the tip until his legs trembled. She slid him to the back of her throat until his cock throbbed. Then she grazed him with her teeth all the way out again, ending with the pulse of the thick vein in his cock against her lips. Through his jeans, she squeezed his balls.

"Fuck," he murmured. "Jesus, fuck. I want you."

She was wet, her clit hot, on fire. He held her head in his hands, fucking her mouth, fingers massaging her scalp as he moved to her rhythm.

"Fuck, fuck, fuck, baby, I need you."

He was hers. She owned him. The power of it burrowed into her very bones. His body shook, then he grunted and held her to him, filling her mouth. She drank him, like a vampire drinks its victim, draining him, stealing his strength, his power, and she felt herself liquefy in near orgasm right along with him.

For long moments afterward, he held her like that, her face to his crotch. She sucked him gently, his body still twitching for her. And hers twitching for him.

Then he palmed her cheek, pulling free, holding her face to meet his gaze. "That was all I wanted," he whispered.

What? An orgasm? Or a communion? Last night? Or today? It didn't matter because he was happy again. She was glad. And it hadn't cost her a thing.

19

HIS LEGS STILL WOBBLED, HIS MIND WAS STILL FOGGED, BUT HE
pulled her to her feet and imprisoned her chin in his hand. "Kiss
me," he ordered.

"But I just—"

"I don't give a shit. I want it." His taste on her tongue, her
arms around him. He met her lips with a hard kiss, and she took
him deep. He reveled in the ache that surrounded his heart, reveled in the emotion as much as the taste of her, the scent of sex
and sweet body lotion. He tasted the salt of his own come, but he
was almost sure there was something else, the salt of tears, her
tears. But when he pulled back, her cheeks were dry.

"What?" she whispered as if he were looking at her with a
question in his eyes.

"What were we arguing about?" he asked.

"I can't remember."

He stroked a finger down her cheek to the corner of her
mouth and her ruined lipstick. "Good."

"I'm going to remember soon and you're in for it," she said
mildly.

He would be. Because he remembered despite what he said.
She was pushing and pulling at him about the patent, about shor-

ing up his end of things, checking, questioning, as if she'd stopped believing he could handle anything.

The only thing he felt in control of was their sex life—as long as he wasn't asking for it in bed like a normal husband. Things were so goddamn ass-backward. But she'd sucked him at work, and he'd take it as a victory.

She touched her lips, a slight smile curving them. "You messed up my lipstick. Everyone's going to know we were doing something dirty."

"It wasn't dirty," he said with so much meaning.

She gave no answer to that. At least not until she'd backed away and stopped with her hand on the doorknob. "The numbers are too close, Dominic."

Ah, so she hadn't forgotten the argument either. "What are you thinking?" He knew what she was thinking, same as he was, and with the same kind of horror. Someone had revealed their financial data to WEU. An insider.

They didn't hide numbers from their employees. Everyone had access to shipping quantities. At month-end, quarter-end, and year-end, they could all go in and judge their shipping performance. All for one and one for all, share and share alike.

"None of them would do that, Erin." He wanted to believe that, needed to.

"Then how?"

He didn't have an answer, yet he knew in his gut his people were solid. But it wasn't just him Erin had stopped trusting and believing in.

"I know you like order and rational explanation," he said, "and for everything to fall into place. But none of them would give out our proprietary information."

Her lips thinned. "I don't need order. I can deal with stuff. But WEU getting that close *isn't* rational."

"I'm not going to outright accuse anyone without proof."

"I'm not saying we should." She huffed out a breath, her hand tightening and releasing on the doorknob. "We just need to be careful."

He didn't know what the hell *careful* was. Shut his employees out of the system? Watch their every move?

No. The only thing he could do was figure out how WEU got their numbers without having used one of his people to do it.

ERIN STOOD BEFORE THE LADIES' ROOM MIRROR, HER LIPSTICK tube an inch from her mouth. They'd never had sex at work. Not that the thought hadn't occurred, but they hadn't wanted their personal life to become a subject of office gossip. Now they were screwing at trade shows, and she was blowing Dominic in the lab.

She half expected Yvonne to slam through the door and ask her what the hell was going on.

Her cheeks were flushed. No reason to add blusher now. When she closed her eyes, she could still feel him between her lips and taste him on her tongue. His lingering scent made her dizzy.

It was the only time she felt real now, as if everything else was fantasy and the only real thing was endless, mind-drugging sex. Maybe she was having a mild nervous breakdown. That might be the reason for all this. Her *irrational* behavior. And her suspicious nature.

Dominic was correct. She suspected her own people. She wondered if Atul was punishing them because he was pissed off they hadn't deemed him qualified for Cam's job, if Matt was screwing up assembly on purpose, if Bree was selling financial numbers to the highest bidder, if Yvonne was trying to sabotage the family unit. All those thoughts had flitted through her mind.

God, that was so wrong. She didn't want to think that way. It was just that she felt so helpless, like she needed to do *something* to fix it all.

What she really wanted was the way Dominic made her feel in the lab when he'd kissed her with the taste of him still in her mouth. When he'd made her forget they'd been arguing.

When he'd made her forget everything.

GARLAND BROOKS DIDN'T LOOK LIKE A CEO. SHORT, GAUNT, AND bald, with wire-rimmed glasses, he had the soft features of the mild-mannered man on the beach who had his girlfriend stolen and sand kicked in his face by the body builder who stole her.

That's how Garland Brooks lulled the gullible before he went for the jugular. He'd started his campaign by letting Dominic wait in his outer office for half an hour. Dominic, however, had not let that stop him. They'd begun suspecting their own people. He couldn't let that go on. Coming to WEU wasn't the smartest thing to do, but after this morning's argument with Erin, he had to do something.

"Well now, Mr. DeKnight," Brooks said, sitting back in his thousand-dollar leather executive chair, "I can't comment on any issues our patent department has undertaken. But if you received a letter, I'm sure it's been researched thoroughly and the patent is on our side."

Dominic propped his foot on his knee. He wore jeans to this man's expensive tailored suit and boots to Brooks's handmade leather shoes. "Garland, your patent won't stand. I'm giving you the courtesy of letting you know you can't win."

Brooks smiled genially, folding his hands across his stomach. "That's why we have attorneys, Mr. DeKnight. To handle all this for us."

"But you'll be wasting a lot of money."

"So will you." He kept the genial smile as if it were pasted on.

Dominic considered this a fishing expedition, nothing more. He wanted to see if Brooks would take the bait, so to speak. Dominic started it off by laying the latest WEU letter on the desk and sliding it across. "This amount is ridiculous."

Brooks blinked at the odd folds of the page. Dominic smiled. Could the man tell it had once been an airplane?

Brooks pulled his glasses to the tip of his nose to read. "Oh my." The curve of his lips turned slightly malicious. "Now that is a great deal." He pushed the glasses back in place.

"According to my calculations," Dominic said, "that number is way overstated."

Brooks raised a brow, his scalp wrinkling. "I assure you the number is correct. We pride ourselves on accuracy here at WEU, both in our gauges and our numbers."

"How would you know that without an audit?"

"We have our ways, Mr. DeKnight." Yeah, the smile was definitely malicious.

So, they did have his numbers. Dominic didn't know how. He didn't expect Brooks to tell him. "Then you're going to have a fight on your hands, Garland."

Brooks smiled as if he were speaking to a very small boy. "If it comes down to a lawsuit, I'm afraid you'll find our pockets are quite a bit deeper than your own."

"Are they?" Dominic asked.

"Of course."

"Then why are you having trouble paying your vendors on time?"

Brooks didn't splutter. He didn't even blink. "That's a business strategy to even out the month-to-month cash flow."

"So you stiff your suppliers in order to smooth out your cash."

Brooks grimaced. "Now, Mr. DeKnight, I assure you no one is stiffing anyone."

Brooks was stiffing everyone. And on purpose. "That's a matter of opinion, Garland. But DKG is going to fight you on this. We are right and you are wrong. That patent won't stand. We know it and you know it. And we'll win in the end."

Brooks leaned forward, laid his elbows carefully on his blotter and clasped his hands, gazing at Dominic over them. "Right or wrong isn't the issue, Mr. DeKnight. The issue is who can hold out longer, an insignificant little company like yours or a world-class firm like ours. For every dollar you spend, I can spend five. Long before you prove my patent isn't valid, you will be bankrupt." He smiled like a mob enforcer ready with his brass knuckles. "So I suggest you simply pay the money now and save yourself any further trouble."

Dominic gave him a full three-second look. "That's what you did to the others, isn't it." It wasn't a question.

The other man didn't say a word. He merely smiled that enforcer smile.

Dominic rose, retrieving the letter he fully intended to ignore. "Thanks for the tip."

"My pleasure."

Dominic left WEU knowing three things. First, Brooks didn't care whether his through-coat patent was valid or not. Second, they made their money off the *threat* of a suit. And finally, no way was Dominic giving in to that asshole. He would fight Garland Brooks down to the last dime.

DOMINIC LEFT JUST BEFORE LUNCH, ONLY HALF AN HOUR OR SO since Erin had fixed her makeup after blowing him in his lab. Maybe, if he'd been there, Erin could have resisted herself.

Instead, she gave in to that need to do *something*, even if it was dumb to call Bree into her office and ask what was bothering her. It would most likely end badly, with Erin saying something stupid like "Bree, did you give someone our through-coat sales numbers?"

God, she hated that through-coat gauge with a passion. Without it, their lives would have been different. Now it haunted her. Perhaps it was poetic justice that the damn thing was going to bring them down.

"Close the door and have a seat, Bree." She pointed to a chair.

Bree sat obediently. Was she nervous, worried about Erin calling her in there?

Just be straightforward, Erin told herself. "You've seemed preoccupied the last few days." How long had it really been? She hadn't noticed anything herself, only had Yvonne's frantic diatribe to go by. Erin guessed that made her a bad boss. "Is something bothering you?"

"No," Bree said quickly without meeting her gaze.

Erin waited. Bree didn't say anything else, didn't offer an explanation, nothing. Bree had never been a vivacious, open person. She kept to herself for the most part, though she offered a smile or a laugh when it was appropriate. She'd always been a little closed.

Or was *secretive* a better word?

Okay, so what do you say when someone gives you no opening whatsoever? Accuse them of selling company information and gauge the reaction? "You can tell me if you're worried about anything."

"I know." Bree's face was carefully blank.

Erin was suddenly sure there was something wrong, that Yvonne hadn't imagined it. Bree's attitude was ... off. Never effusive, Bree was nevertheless friendly, yet now her features and her voice were completely neutral, as if she was afraid something might seep through any cracks in her facade.

Erin didn't want to believe it had anything to do with giving away DKG information. She *could* believe it; she had that kind of suspicious nature. But she didn't *want* to. "The door's always open, Bree, if you need it."

"Thanks, Erin, but I'm fine."

She knew Bree wasn't, but she also knew the other woman wasn't ready to talk about whatever it was. She might never be ready to.

But should Erin believe? Or should she suspect?

Maybe because she had to, or because Dominic had been so adamant, or because she was just plain scared of saying something she couldn't take back, Erin chose to believe. "Can you do another analysis for me?"

"Sure." The strange shadow didn't leave Bree's eyes even at the change of topic. "What do you need?"

"A cost analysis for making the transducers in-house."

Bree thought for a couple of seconds, then nodded. "I can do that." Her index finger tapped on the arm of the chair. "Are we done now?"

"Yes. I need the analysis by tomorrow morning. I want to have a meeting with the techs." Besides Matt, there was Susan and Tim. Having Steve at the meeting would be good, too. She wasn't a democratic leader in that she'd let her employees vote on important decisions, but asking for ideas and opinions helped create buy-in.

"I can have it by the end of the day."

She felt irrationally relieved when Bree left, as if by the skin of her teeth she'd avoided something huge. She didn't have proof. She didn't know how everything would have gotten screwed up if she'd accused Bree. She was glad she hadn't succumbed to it.

She thought of Dominic's steadfast belief that no one at DKG would sabotage them. There was something admirable in that. Something worth striving for. She needed to make a peace offering for shutting him out last night. What they'd done in the lab wasn't enough; he'd initiated that. No, *she* needed to give *him* something.

The question was what.

BREE DIDN'T CLOSE HER OFFICE DOOR. SOMEONE MIGHT NOTICE that and start thinking or questioning or wondering, especially since she'd just come out of a closed-door meeting with Erin.

Sitting down at her desk, smoothing her slacks over her thighs, her hands trembled when she lifted them to the keyboard.

She was so stupid. She should never have told Rachel. Rachel hadn't blabbed, but Bree had seen Yvonne launch the attack almost immediately. Yvonne was a busybody, well-meaning, sure, but still a busybody.

Which is why Bree should never have told Rachel. But the woman caught her at a weak moment, defenses down, a mass of emotions. And she'd spilled her guts. Okay, it wasn't *everything*, not by a long shot, but she'd told Rachel one teeny-tiny thing that was enough to turn a snowball into an avalanche if Bree wasn't careful.

The computer screen swam before her eyes. She closed her lids, but it didn't help; she simply felt dizzy. Scared and alone. With a dash of panic.

"Everything will be fine," she whispered. "I'm okay."

Yet she couldn't help herself. All she needed was a little relief, then she'd be better. She dug her phone out of her purse and hit a speed dial. He answered on the second ring.

And Bree said the magic words: "I need to see you tonight."

He didn't hesitate, not even a slight pause to think about it. "Seven o'clock." Then he was gone.

She always did the calling, never the other way round. It was the way she wanted it, needed it. And he always said yes.

Suddenly things felt so much better.

20

THE BAR WAS CROWDED FOR HAPPY HOUR, OFFERING GREAT APPE-
tizers, primarily deep-fried stuff, and cheap drinks. Where there
were cheap drinks, good food, and big-breasted waitresses, there
were lots of men. The noise level was therefore earsplitting, miti-
gated only by the fact that Dominic and Hansen had a small table in a corner by the front window and were spared the volume
on two sides. Dominic had set up the meeting right after leaving
WEU today, but he hadn't chosen the place, Hansen had; one of
his favorite haunts.

Short and sandy-haired, Hansen had probably been hassled as
the freckle-faced kid when he was a schoolboy thirty-five-odd
years ago. If so, it had toughened him, or maybe being a lawyer,
which was a confrontational occupation, had done it. Lawyers
moved from one battle to another, hence the reasons lawsuits
were either "won" or "lost." Because they were always a fight.

Dominic slugged his Italian soda. He had to drive. Hansen had
ordered a very expensive chardonnay, a glass of sparkling water,
and deep-fried artichoke hearts that smelled too dangerous for his
arteries.

"Is this going on my bill?" Dominic asked.

"Of course," Hansen said without cracking a smile. "Lawyers live by one rule: *everything* is billable."

"Good to know." Nevertheless, Dominic doubted the food and drink would show up on his "expense" section. He figured it was lawyer humor.

"Okay, show me what you received."

Dominic pushed the WEU letter he'd received this morning across the table for Hansen to read.

After his visit to Brooks, Dominic had half a mind to throw the letter in the trash for good, call Hansen off, and take his chances as to whether Brooks would follow through on his threat. But Erin couldn't live with that risk. He wouldn't force her to.

Hansen gave an infinitesimal nod signifying he'd finished reading.

"It's an extremely accurate guesstimate," Dominic said. "I paid Garland Brooks a visit about it today and he—"

Hansen slapped his hand on the table. "You did *what*?"

"I talked with Brooks," Dominic answered, uncowed.

Hansen put his hand to his forehead and looked heavenward. "Lord save me from my clients." Then he pointed a finger. "Don't get in my way, Dominic. You'll just make the situation worse and my job more difficult."

Dominic had known he'd say something like that, but he didn't care. "I wanted to know what I was up against. Brooks doesn't give a damn about the validity of that patent. He wants to extort money, and he figured I'd find it cheaper to pay up than spend the money to defend myself against him."

Hansen flapped a hand and went back to the artichokes. "That's standard operating procedure, Dominic."

"Yeah, well here's his mistake. He asked for too much, and he pissed off my wife."

Hansen gave a belly laugh. "Your wife scares me."

Dominic added his smile. "Me, too."

"Then let's nail his ass to the wall." Hansen tapped the letter. "This isn't from their attorney so I consider it a scare tactic, as you've already surmised." Hansen held up his hand before Dominic could interrupt. "But I'm still taking it seriously." He took off his glasses, setting them on the table as he attacked the artichoke hearts. "The biggest point in their favor is that they have other manufacturers paying them a royalty. Which gives them validity and muddies our waters."

An expletive rose to his lips, but Dominic shut himself down, letting Hansen go on.

"That will be our biggest hurdle, and we've got to have all our ducks in a row, no stone unturned, et cetera, et cetera." Those *et ceteras* were going to cost DKG big bucks. Hansen shrugged as if he could see the dollar signs flashing in Dominic's eyes and went on. "These other guys could be paying just to avoid the hassle of having to fight it. Or hoping someone else will fight their battle."

Because if DKG proved they didn't have to pay the royalty, then all WEU's leverage was gone. Dominic felt his blood pressure rising. Garland Brooks was playing the bully on the playground, and everyone else was rolling over, sticking DKG with the bill for going toe-to-toe with the big boy.

"So what you're saying is we have to sit and wait." And pay Hansen's fees up the wazoo.

Hansen nodded, his mouth full. Dominic would have scarfed an artichoke heart, but he'd told Erin he'd be home for dinner. Not that he expected they'd be talking at dinner. She was probably going to punish him for his high-handedness in the lab. He didn't care; it had been worth it. It had turned around his whole attitude from the previous night.

Hansen swallowed. "Nothing's going to happen until after the holidays anyway."

The holidays. Dominic hadn't forgotten, though this year there was no holiday potluck at work, no gift exchange. The office hadn't been decorated. Erin used to arrange all that stuff. She hadn't even brought it up. No one else had either. The whole group worked tomorrow, Wednesday, but then there was the four-day weekend for Christmas and the holiday for New Year's the following week.

Christmas might not be coming to DKG, but those four days loomed ahead of him. A huge reminder. What the hell were they going to do with four days? The twinge in his gut rose to an ache around his heart. Christmas without Jay. Jesus. Last year, they'd been so torn apart, they'd been numb to the meaning of the days. This year, the holiday season was like a chasm looming ahead of them, almost as if it were the first Christmas without him.

He didn't know what Erin would do. He didn't know what the hell he'd do *for* her.

"So," Hansen said, "who's feeding WEU information?"

"No one at DKG," Dominic said emphatically.

Hansen didn't say a word. He merely smiled as if he were looking at a completely delusional man.

"We don't put out public financial information." They had an annual report, but it was primarily for customers, and they didn't publish the P and L. "We've got the governmental stuff; property tax, sales and use tax, income tax." He waved a hand to encompass the sheer volume of forms.

"Well, the government's not giving it out." Hansen savored his chardonnay a moment. "Who does all your filings?"

"We have an in-house accountant who prepares the data, and an outside accounting firm who prepares the actual forms and submits everything."

Hansen wiped his fingers on a napkin. "Do you trust them?"

"Yes."

This time Hansen didn't say a word or make a face. "Have you applied for any loans online, any new credit applications?"

"No. Besides information is never that specific, right down to the product line level."

Hansen sighed, twisted his lips, thinking. "Dumpster diving?"

"We use a bonded shredding service." Dominic had already considered this stuff, and sadly, the most logical explanation still came down to someone in the company.

"Okay, okay." Hansen sipped his wine thoughtfully. "What about your data storage?"

"We've got an online enterprise system for all our manufacturing, accounting, sales, everything. All the data resides on their server, backed up regularly, and I already called to see if they'd had any hacking problems."

"That doesn't mean that *you* couldn't have been hacked." Hansen narrowed his eyes. "Maybe you've got some malware on one of your computers."

"But malware isn't that targeted." At least he didn't think it was. "Besides, we have virus protection."

"Some of these things can be really sophisticated and damn near undetectable coming in."

Dominic drummed his fingers on the tabletop.

Hansen smiled. "You're the one who says the numbers are too close to the real thing, so it's your choice, Dominic. Targeted malware. Or one of your employees."

Hell, it was worth the expense. "All right. I'll bring in a geek to go through all the machines." They'd need an expert. He'd tell everyone they were optimizing the computers.

* * *

DOMINIC WAS MEETING WITH THE LAWYER. WHEN HE'D INFORMED her, Erin had an irresistible urge to invite herself along. *Almost* irresistible. She'd stopped the runaway thought. Instead, very wifely, she'd told him to be home in time for dinner, which was usually whatever one of them felt like picking up.

That was the epitaph for her life over the last year; she couldn't be bothered. Even now, she cut up cheese, salami, and apples, putting it all on a plate with some crackers. After staring a moment, she added a handful of peeled baby carrots and cherry tomatoes to the plate. So it wasn't gourmet. At least she'd poured his beer into a mug. That was saying something.

She carried the plate and mug out to the back patio. The chairs and table were still covered with plastic protecting them for the winter, *last* year's winter. They'd never even uncovered them this summer.

What had been the point?

Erin closed her eyes against the ache.

Setting the plate and glass down, she removed the plastic from one chair, pulling it over to the stand-alone fire pit. The night was chilly but dry. Glowing logs arranged in a metal casing, the fire pit was gas and lit easily despite having been idle for so long. They'd used it in the spring and fall, when the days were lovely but the nights could be cool.

With the chair next to it, the gas fire would keep Dominic warm tonight until his blood heated. Standing behind it, she cocked her head one way, then the other, repositioned the chair slightly. The view was now directly into the sunroom, the rattan sofa spotlighted and clearly visible. Instead of returning inside the way she came, through the kitchen, she entered the sunroom, turning off the light as she went.

It was all about staging and good lighting. He wanted to

watch her, see her pleasure rise. It wasn't in her to say she was sorry; she didn't want to talk about last night or her feelings. Or anything. But he'd understand she was trying to make it up to him.

He would park his car in the garage next to hers as usual, and come in through the kitchen door. There, he'd find a note with instructions.

He'd gone to see Hansen because she'd told him to fix it. She'd told him to do something. He could never fix everything; it was too late. But he was trying.

She had to make an effort, too.

THE HOUSE WAS DARK WHEN HE PULLED IN THE DRIVEWAY. GLANC-ing at the dash clock, it wasn't even seven yet, so he wasn't late. But she'd turned off all the lights. He let out a breath, punching the garage door opener. Her car was inside. He parked in his spot next to it.

She'd probably left him takeout on the counter, then closeted herself in her office.

Dominic closed his eyes a moment, then yanked on the door handle. He should have eaten the artichoke hearts.

The garage was clean, neat, a lawn mower to one side, hedge clippers, various garden tools. He managed to mow the lawn at least once a month, but he hadn't been out to do the trimming. The box hedge was no longer a box.

Inside, she'd left the stove light on for him, that was all. He stood there a long moment staring at the empty counter. No take-out, not even the scent of takeout.

He wanted to howl.

Then he saw the note on the floor, and his skin chilled. He swallowed. She wouldn't. No. She couldn't. His limbs seemed to move like an automaton. He bent, the creak of his knees loud pops in the empty, soundless house.

For a moment, he couldn't see, couldn't read, spots swam before his eyes. Then his vision cleared, and he slid the note into the pool of light from the stove.

"Your dinner and beer are out on the patio. Get yourself all warmed up by the fire pit."

He didn't realize he'd stopped breathing until he gulped in a searing breath. He didn't know his heart had arrested until it started pounding in his chest.

She'd left him dinner and a mug on the patio. She'd lit the fire. She had a plan. He would never tell her the momentary fear that had seized him. She'd be horrified it could have crossed his mind. He almost ran to the patio, shoving open the back screen door, slamming it against the wall in his rush.

She wasn't there, but the fire pit glowed with warmth, and a plate of cheese, meat, crackers, and vegetables lay on the low table next to the chair. The arrangement faced the darkened sunroom.

It had been one of Erin's favorite rooms. She hadn't used it in a year, just as they hadn't used the barbecue or the patio or the fire pit.

Then the light came on inside, illuminating the sunroom sofa as if it were a stage, and his heart stopped all over again.

21

HOLY HELL. SHE WAS ALL GORGEOUS, SMOOTH NAKED SKIN. AND HE was the teenage boy next door spying on his neighbor, a hot, sexy older woman he'd lusted after all summer.

As he watched, she climbed knees first onto the rattan sofa, gripping the back with one hand, her pert ass thrust out as she spread her legs slightly. His heart rate skyrocketed. There were no preliminaries, no sexy striptease, just this, just her, hand suddenly between her legs. He didn't want the build up. It was better this way, unexpectedly thrust into it, his pulse pounding, skin tingling, balls aching, cock hard and dripping pre-come.

He could almost smell the sweet, lusty scent of her.

She tipped a finger back between her legs to stroke the crease of her ass, reminding him of the things he'd done to her in the hotel on Friday. Maybe she wanted to remind him.

She widened her spread, and the tip of the vibrator penetrated her pussy. She slid down on it, rocking, twisting, undulating, fucking it. It felt like his own cock being lured inside her. The night was cold, but he started to sweat. Without a touch, he was ready to ram straight inside her.

But he watched, savoring every move of her body, the blush of her skin. He wished he could hear her, but the fantasy of a teenage boy peeping on his sexy neighbor was too good to give up. The fire pit cast warmth in his direction, but he was heating up from the inside out.

Then she turned, fell with a fluid grace to the sofa cushion and gave him a view of her plump, glistening pussy before she set the vibrator to it once more. Her body writhed sinuously, her faint cries slipping through the sunroom's windows.

The sight made him hard and shot his blood through his veins. He saw it for the apology it was, to make up for turning her back on him. She'd planned it, set the stage, and this was her gift.

Or maybe she was torturing him because he'd forced her to her knees in his lab. Either way, he didn't care. This was perfection.

She shifted, gave him another delicious view. He knew the signs, the look of concentration, the utter focus; she was close to orgasm; straining toward it. Then she came with one loud, clear cry that penetrated the very walls of the sunroom.

He saw her laugh. Sometimes, before, she used to laugh after she came hard, as much a part of the release as the orgasm itself. The ring of her laughter, even muted by the windows, rolled his heart over in his chest. God, what he wouldn't give to hear it every time she came for him.

Then she was looking at him, head cocked, peering into the dark surrounding him, only the glow of the fire pit illuminating one side of his face. She yanked on a robe, covering herself from head to foot, clutching it to her chin.

Then she pushed the door open. "Have you been watching me, Nickie?"

"No, ma'am," he answered, feeling slightly giddy as if he truly were a teenage boy caught in the act.

She stepped down the two wood stairs, letting the door slam shut. "You were spying, you dirty boy."

"I wouldn't do that, Mrs. DeKnight."

She crossed the patio, her feet bare and probably cold against the concrete. "You're a liar, Nickie." She leaned over his chair and cupped his cock through his jeans. "You were watching. And you're hard."

"I couldn't help it, Mrs. DeKnight. You were so fucking gorgeous."

She straightened. "I'm going to have to tell your mother that you were spying and that you used the word *fuck*."

"Please don't, Mrs. DeKnight."

"Actions have consequences, Nickie."

He put his hands together as if he were praying. "Please don't tell. I'll do anything you want. Mow your lawn. Wash your car. Clean out your fireplace."

"Now that all sounds very interesting, Nickie, but right now I'm really cold. What are you going to do about that?"

He brightened. "I can warm you up."

"Yes, maybe you can." She stared down at him. "Unzip your jeans."

He did her one better, pulling his cock out as well.

"Oh my, Nickie. You have grown up." She licked her lips. It made his dick jump. Christ, she was good. They should have done a hell of a lot more role-playing over the years.

She bent to him, stroked his cock with nothing more than her gaze. "Have you ever played with any of your little girlfriends, Nickie, put your penis in them?"

"No, ma'am, I never did that."

She smiled slyly. "But you've done something, haven't you."

The fact that it wasn't a question formed his answer. "Yes, ma'am."

She raised her bare foot and laid it on his cock, a shock of cold against his hot, hard flesh. "Tell me what you've done, dirty boy," she whispered.

"I touched her pussy and licked my fingers." He dared to put a hand on her calf, running his fingers up to the back of her knee. "She tasted good."

"I'll just bet she did." She winked. "Did she touch your cock, too?"

Her robe had fallen open over her raised knee and he could scent her now, the sweet, musky fragrance of arousal.

"Yes," he said. "She sucked me."

She laughed, a naughty, sexy sound that strummed his cock. "I'm sure it's nothing compared to what a real woman can do."

"I don't know."

She rubbed him with the sole of her foot. "I think I should take your virginity, Nickie, don't you?"

He was aware they were in their backyard, surrounded by fences high enough to keep out the neighbors. But the house next door was a two-story. The family didn't have a teenage kid, but they did have a twentysomething son. He'd recently moved back home because he couldn't make ends meet on his own. The windows were dark, but Dominic imagined. He wondered if Erin had occasionally imagined. Sometimes she didn't close the blinds when she dressed, not really suspecting the neighbor son of peeping, but not caring if he did.

"Yes, Mrs. DeKnight, I think you should take my virginity right here in this chair."

"That's such a lovely cock, Nickie, I can't resist it." She lowered her eyelids in a seductive perusal. "I'm going to ruin you for all your future girlfriends." She leaned over to trail a finger down his nose. "You're going to be hooked on older women."

Then she turned, lifted her robe, enveloping his cock in her fist, and sank down on him back to front. He closed his eyes, his heart hammering, his head swimming as he put his hands beneath the robe to the warm, supple flesh of her hips.

God, he loved when she played with him. No matter the other things that had gone wrong between them, the agony, the loss, the emotional chasm that ensued, *this* helped him survive.

No matter how angry or lost they were, if they had this, there was a connection they could build on.

"Fuck me, Mrs. DeKnight," he whispered, burying his face in the hair at her nape. "Make me a man."

"You'll never find more of a woman, Nickie. You'll be spoiled." Grabbing the arms of the chair, she took charge, riding him, fucking him.

His eyeballs threatened to roll back in his head, it was so damn good, her muscles toned, her pussy warm, wet honey. Her legs trembled with effort as her body closed around him, flexing, working him from the inside. He wondered if she knew how her body moved on him or if it was an unconscious tightening, part of her desire, her need. It drove him crazy.

"Oh, Nickie, you're so hard," she sang to the night.

"I never knew a woman could feel like this, Mrs. DeKnight." She would always feel like this to him, hot, tight, sexy.

She gave him a tinkling laugh, cutting it off with a moan of sheer pleasure. The ache built, his cock throbbed, his mind grew drugged by the sensation, the wet slide of her. Then he dug his fingers into her hips and pulled her down hard, thrusting high at the same time. She quivered and groaned with orgasm, and with only two more strokes inside her, he lost himself, coming back to earth seconds later with her snuggled in his lap, arms around his neck. He wasn't quite sure how she'd gotten there when only moments before she'd been straddling him, facing the night.

"Oh, Nickie," she whispered against his throat, "you're such a young stud."

He held her close, his heart thudding, and he couldn't speak, overwhelmed by tonight's gift. Maybe she hadn't meant it that way, but it was how he chose to take it. Finally, he found his voice. "I'm spoiled for all time, Mrs. DeKnight."

She tipped her head back, a smile on her lips, in her eyes. Then she kissed him, a sweet touch of her lips, her tongue along the seam of his mouth, flirting inside when he opened to her, tasting, teasing. He thought he might die with the sheer intensity of the moment. A simple kiss, yet she hadn't kissed him in over a year. He'd kissed her, but this, it was all her.

Then she settled back in his arms again, knees pulled up, feet tucked within the bottom of the robe. "I can't believe I did this in the dead of winter."

He laughed. He felt so normal. Well, as normal as a man could feel after fucking his wife in the backyard when the neighbors could watch from a second-floor window. Next thing, he'd hear sirens. Though he couldn't imagine Harold or his son calling the cops instead of watching. Irene, though, she might.

All he said was, "Thank God it wasn't raining, hailing, or snowing." He wrapped her closer, one side of their bodies warmed by the fire pit. He wasn't willing to move yet, not even with the cold night air burrowing beneath his sweatshirt.

In this moment, he felt one with her; a part of her soul in him, a part of his in hers. Close, the way they used to be, the way they could be again if only . . . "Baby, we need to talk sometime, you know. Say what needs to be said."

Erin stiffened in his arms. He felt her tension in every muscle and knew there wasn't a shred of doubt in her what *talk* meant. Fuck, he was an idiot. They'd had good sex, that was all, nothing *momentous*, nothing changed, no epiphany.

"I'm getting a little cold." She clambered awkwardly from his lap. "I think I'll take a bath."

Oh yeah, he was an idiot. Maybe if he'd shut his mouth, maybe if they'd had more *moments* like that under their belt. But no, one kiss and he thought he'd won the war.

She wasn't going to talk to him. Maybe not ever. Maybe this—hot, kinky role-play sex in the backyard and a kiss—was the most he'd ever get.

THEY WERE FINE, THEY WERE GREAT, THEY WERE ALMOST NORMAL. Then he wanted to talk. Erin slid deeper into the steaming water, letting the bubbles rise to her chin. At least she'd resisted the urge to snap his head off. She could give herself that much credit. Traditionally it was the woman who needed to talk and the man who crawled into his cave, or something like that. But Dominic never followed the rules, that didn't suit him.

He knocked on the bathroom door. "Honey, you all right?"

Almost as if on cue, there he was. He didn't follow rules, and he never gave up. She'd always admired that about him, yet it gave her a guilty twist inside. She knew he needed to talk. Over the last few weeks, since Orlando especially, she'd started wishing she could do it for him. She knew he had his own guilt; she knew it was just as hard on him. But she just couldn't let it all out the way he was able to. She couldn't even listen to him do it, and the moment he'd wanted to talk out there on the patio, her whole body clenched against it.

"I'm fine, thank you," she called through the door because politeness was all she had to give him.

"I made you a champagne cocktail."

Long ago, that had been one of her luxuries, a bath, champagne, and dark chocolate. She wanted to climb out, unlock the door, let him in. Swear it. But she didn't. *Please don't make me talk.* If only he would let them be like they were on the patio *be-*

fore he started pushing, the sweet comfort of sitting in his lap, his arms around her. Why couldn't that be enough?

"I don't feel like one, but thanks for thinking of me."

She heard his soft footfalls as he padded down the hall, and she was almost sad. What they'd done tonight was so good, but the problem was that any joy in their lives suddenly became a sacrilege as soon as she thought of Jay. And she didn't know how that could ever end.

22

DOMINIC SAT WITH HIS FEET ON HIS OFFICE DESK, TAPPING AWAY on the keyboard in his lap. In the hallway people scurried to and fro, mostly Atul and Cam rushing to get everything done before the four-day holiday weekend. He was in no such rush. Erin would let them all go early, probably just before lunch, but they wouldn't give themselves the same luxury. In years past, yeah, but now they had no last-minute gifts to run out for, no rash of house-cleaning before guests arrived, no turkey to stuff.

He clicked his mouse and brought up another website, then plowed through several different pages looking at photo galleries, amenities, pricing, availability.

Erin appeared in his doorway, her face slightly flushed, her smile too big. He could see the tension rising off her in a haze. "Well, the meeting's over," she said.

He didn't stop scrutinizing the photo galleries, clicking through one picture at a time, getting a feel. "I trust everyone was in agreement."

"It'll all be fine," she said, hugging her clipboard to her chest. "Bree came up with a good cost estimate that's doable. The techs agreed to give it a shot." She raised a brow. "Matt actually showed some enthusiasm just as Leon thought he would."

Dominic could have gone to the transducer meeting, put in his two cents, but he'd decided to let her handle it. They had their own duties, their own areas of expertise. He hadn't liked it when she butted into the patent thing, so he wasn't about to stick his nose into her stuff. Besides, she was good at everything she did. He'd always believed that. His only meaningful thought about the transition to making the transducers in-house was that he'd miss Leon. Leon was a good guy. Erin had said he'd be in to do some training. Dominic would say his good-byes and give his well-wishes then.

"What about Steve?" Steve could poke holes in anything when he wanted to, especially since he was on the warpath with Matt.

"Dubious." She seesawed her hand. "I did agree with one thing he said."

"Bye, you guys." Rachel leaned into the doorway, one hand on the jamb for balance. "Mer—" She cut herself off, eyes wide with horror. She'd obviously been about to wish them a Merry Christmas and knew it was a no-no in Erin's world.

Yet Erin gave her an exuberant though patently false smile. "Have a great weekend."

Dominic waggled his fingers.

Rachel left, and Erin's tension eased slightly. "I told them all they didn't need to come back after lunch."

"Figured that's what you'd do. So what did you agree with Steve on?"

She blinked, coming back to the conversation. "Oh yeah. He thought we should assign the transducers to one person, with another of the techs as backup."

"Sounds reasonable. Who'd you choose?"

She smiled, and this time it was genuine. "I told them to choose among themselves. They picked Matt. Can you believe it?"

"That was bold," he said, raising an eyebrow. She usually liked to control everything.

"If someone takes on the responsibility by choice, the odds are better they'll give it a one hundred percent effort." She shrugged. "It'll be good for Matt." She narrowed her eyes thoughtfully. "It was like he was being entrusted with something and it made him proud."

"You did a great job."

He waited for her to slam him down for the compliment. He'd screwed up last night, and she'd shut him out, literally. When he'd taken her the champagne, she hadn't even unlocked the door. Today he'd expected the cold shoulder. She'd surprised him with a civil tongue, a smile, and now this, a polite thank-you.

"I'm out of here." Atul appeared in the doorway this time, the colloquialism sounding strange and clipped in his accent. He didn't make the mistake of wishing them a Merry Christmas.

Erin fluttered her fingers. "Have a good one."

With Atul gone, Dominic tapped the keyboard again, typing in another search. "I've got a guy coming in next week to check the computers for viruses and malware."

A line emerged between her eyebrows. "What for? We just upgraded the virus protection."

Cam popped in then, cutting them off, and behind her was Steve. With each new face in the doorway, the next good-bye, Erin's face grew more tense and her smile more brittle. He wanted to ease her pain, but he knew she wouldn't accept his emotional support.

So when they were alone again, he went back to the malware issue. "Hansen suggested checking all our computers, and I agree. We could have been infected with a malicious software that's enabled someone to see our financial data."

"I guess that's better than thinking one of our own people has turned against us." She stared at him unblinkingly for a long moment. "Thank you for letting me know."

Odd how in less than twelve hours they could go from the hottest damn sex to locked doors to being so fucking polite, each mindful of the other's feelings. Like courteous strangers. He'd been careful to make sure she knew what he'd planned before he had the guy show up next week. In days of old, he probably would've told her the morning of, and she wouldn't have cared.

He waved a hand at her. "Come here. I want to show you something."

She was slow to round the desk to his side. "What?"

He hadn't changed his position the entire time she'd been in his office. His feet were on the desk, the keyboard in his lap. He pointed at the monitor. "What do you think of this place?"

"Looks nice. What is it?"

She smelled sweet. Her lotion, he'd always liked the scent. "It's a resort in Napa."

"How much does it cost?"

He tipped his head back, looked up at her. "I don't care. I want to take you there."

She pursed her lips, but said nothing.

"This weekend, Friday and Saturday," he added.

"No way are they going to have anything available this week-end, it's—" She cut herself off lest she should have to say the dreaded word *Christmas*.

"Let's test out your theory." He clicked on the reservations tab, then filled in the dates for a two-night stay including Christ-mas Eve and Christmas Day. The wait was a couple of seconds, and it came back with an unusually low price. "Hah." He pointed. "At this price, we can even afford to get you a massage." He grinned. "A full-body massage."

She wasn't smiling; she wasn't even looking at him. She was just staring at the screen, thoughts he couldn't read running through her mind. "I don't know."

"Well, I do." He hit the reserve button, then hitched his hip to tug out his wallet. "We'll have a good time." They would be away from home for Christmas. Perfect. He pulled out his credit card.

"Dominic—"

Without even looking, he held up a finger to stop her. "I want us to go."

"Then why can't you ask me instead of ordering?"

He pulled his feet off the desk and twirled his chair to face her. "Will you please go with me, Erin?"

She stared at him a long moment, her features intent, her gaze moving over his face. "If that's what you really want."

He didn't want some half-assed agreement, where she could blame him if anything went wrong. "I want to be gone from here. I don't want to think about work. I don't want to think about the patent." Then he reached for her hand, managing to grab her pinkie finger. "I want to fuck your brains out."

She laughed out loud, then clapped her hand over her mouth.

"I'm off."

They both jumped at Yvonne's voice. Dominic almost dropped the keyboard from his lap.

"Oh," Erin blurted. "Have a good weekend."

"Oh, I will, I will." Yvonne's eyes sparkled. "I can almost smell the sausage stuffing." She waved her hand and was gone.

"Do you think she heard?" Erin whispered, her cheeks pink.

He didn't care. "I'm sure she's rushing out to tell anyone who hasn't left yet."

She popped him on the shoulder. It felt good, a little joke, a tease. They'd weathered his faux pas from last night. He wouldn't ask her to talk. He'd wait for her. What other choice did he have?

He started typing in his credit card number.

"I'm really surprised you can get such a great deal at such a late date," she mused.

"Luck of the draw," he murmured. Christmas week was actually very popular. Families went away together, *families* being the operative word. This resort was for adults only, no kids. Thus it wasn't in high demand for the holiday weekend. In fact, you could call it the off-season.

"What should I pack?" she said, thinking ahead.

"Oh, I wouldn't worry too much about that," he answered.

Not only was it adults only, this place was clothes optional. That was part of his surprise. But he had one more thing up his sleeve. If he could pull it off, he was going to make one of their biggest fantasies come true.

ERIN COULDN'T BELIEVE IT. "CLOTHES *OPTIONAL?*" SHE HISSED AS they followed the bellboy hauling the luggage to their villa.

It was Christmas Eve. Neither of them had mentioned it.

"I wouldn't worry about it much while we're outside," Dominic said. "It's too cold to be naked."

She punched his arm. "You could have warned me."

"You would've said no."

"You're damn right, I'm forty years old. I'm not showing my naked body in public." If the bellboy was listening, he gave no sign of it as he guided the luggage cart down a wide path bordered with rhododendrons.

Dominic put an arm around her shoulder and hugged her close, probably so she couldn't sock him again. "I bet most of the people who come here are older than us." He slid a hand down her back and squeezed her ass. "And most of the ladies sure as hell aren't going to look as good as you."

She glanced once more at the bellboy. His dark hair was short, his slacks pressed, and he was barely out of his teens. She couldn't imagine being naked around a boy like that.

"Besides, clothing is optional." Dominic was clarifying. "Meaning you can keep it all on *or* you can get naked."

"Well, I'm keeping it all on," she assured him, but she feared he'd never let her get away with it.

Their villa was a small adobe-style cottage with a patio in front, complete with table, chairs, barbecue, and a bed of flowers along the edge. The grounds were lovely, meticulously trimmed green grass, lush flowering bushes, and trees separating each of the villas. There was privacy. They'd passed a few couples and singles on the way; all were fully dressed, thank God.

The bellboy unlocked the front door, then handed the card key to Dominic before guiding the luggage cart inside. He unloaded their two suitcases, a laptop—because they couldn't go anywhere without checking their e-mail and the Internet—and a box of food and wine. She liked to have a glass or two of her favorite wine in her own room, and the restaurant was probably horrendously expensive. Though Dominic insisted they attend tonight, she didn't want to eat every meal there.

Dominic palmed the boy a bill as he left. "Pretty nice digs," he said once they were alone.

Erin had to agree. The small sitting room housed a corner sofa grouping, TV console, wet bar, fireplace, table and chairs. The sliding-glass door opened onto the front patio, and through a wide door to the right was the bed and bath. "At least we can stay in here and not go outside to see any naked people."

He crowded her up against the wall, pressing his body to hers. "You're dying to see naked people." He nipped her throat. "And you're dying to have them see you."

She had to admit to a certain thrill of the spectacle. Part of her reason for arguing about the dress code—or rather the non-dress code—was so that she wouldn't suddenly blurt out how damn grateful she was for his thoughtfulness. He'd done this to take her mind off the day, to take her away from anything that might remind her. But he certainly had an agenda of his own, too. She wasn't sure what it was, but it had to be more than getting naked in public.

"Well, they have a lot of rules," she said, hoping to draw his plans out.

He nuzzled her hair, blowing on her skin, heating her through. Maybe his plan was simply seduction. It was working. "The rules aren't so bad," he murmured as he skimmed his fingers over the outer swell of her breast.

Okay, rules, they were talking about the rules. There were places where nudity was not an option, in the restaurant, for example. *"We dress for dinner, sir,"* the check-in clerk had told them. You couldn't walk out to your car without your clothes. The hotel lobby was also off limits. Within the grounds, though, the pool area, the Jacuzzis, it was a free-for-all. *"But don't touch without permission."*

That was the rule that made her tingle. Because it obviously meant you could touch *with* permission. She wondered how much touching Dominic was going to give permission to.

"But you said I didn't have to worry about what I was going to wear, so I only brought jeans. I don't have anything to dress up in for dinner."

He trailed a hand down her arm, then stepped away. "That will give me the chance to buy you something sexy from the dress shop in the lobby." He shot her a seductive, heavy-lidded look. "Sometimes it's more tantalizing when the clothing makes a man crazy to see what's underneath."

Oh yeah. He had an agenda.

23

SHE MADE HIM ROCK HARD IN HIS PANTS. IF ERIN DID THAT TO HIM, Dominic could only imagine her effect on the other men in the dining room.

The resort's dress shop had an eclectic mix of styles, from classy to sedate to stylish to slutty. *Ultra* slutty. It was a nudist resort after all, with a whole lot of leeway on the amount of public touching that could go on. Dominic had purchased Erin a dress that drew attention to the delectable body that lay beneath the material.

It was a black drapy thing, with soft folds of material dipping low to expose a lot of cleavage, bare shoulders, and a short, flirty skirt that was little more than a series of scarves attached at the waist. When she walked, the scarves flowed around her legs, her thighs playing peek-a-boo. When she sat, the material fell apart to expose her gorgeous legs almost to the crotch. Wanting to keep something secret—and to heighten anticipation—he'd purchased her a pair of black lace panties. Yes, she was a walking advertisement for sex.

The clientele was well aware of it. The restaurant was dimly lit and classy, the tables set with crystal glassware and china with gold edging, and a gourmet menu, which meant the prices were high, the food elegantly presented, and the portions small. The average age of the diners was over forty; couples, small groups, a few men seated together dotted here and there, sipping expensive wine and demolishing rich, exotic hors d'oeuvres.

He could safely say his wife was a jewel among them.

"So, exactly what have you got planned for us?" Her eyes sparkled as much as the champagne. She bit into a mushroom canapé, her lips glistening.

Their table was small, round, intimate, his leg brushing hers because he'd moved his chair even closer. His pulse pumped blood through his veins, his eyes tracking her from throat to cleavage. "Dinner, then a stroll through the grounds, and finally a soak in one of the Jacuzzis." Then his biggest surprise of the evening.

He was equal parts buzzing with excitement and thrumming with nervous tension. If she objected, he was totally screwed. But he'd made his plans anyway.

"I didn't bring a bathing suit," she complained.

He detected the tease in her voice. "Neither did I."

She chose a spinach leaf daubed with beluga from the selection of appetizers he'd ordered. "So, naked hot-tubbing."

"You'll love it."

A couple, done with their dinner, passed behind her as they left the dining room. The man's gaze fell to Erin's breasts. Tall with short, dark hair and a workout-trim physique, he was Erin's type. There were some that were far too old, some that weren't in shape enough for her, some that appeared too lecherous, damn near drooling. Dominic wanted classier for her.

"What if someone else gets in our tub?" she asked, waiting until the busboy had cleared the empty canapé tray.

"Then hopefully we have a very nice conversation with some new people." And so much more, he mentally added.

She laughed.

Christ, he loved the sound. He'd been so damn smart for taking her away this weekend. At home, she'd have prowled the house like a caged animal. Here, her mind could play with other things. He told himself she would love everything he'd put together for her.

The waiter arrived, laying down their salads, topping them off with ground pepper. Alone again, she leaned closer, her hair brushing his cheek, her scent washing over him, and lowered her voice. "Is this a sex club?"

"Of course not. It's a nudist resort." But he'd read a few things online about the place. While not a club where people overtly engaged in sex out in the open, there were hidden groves, coves, nooks and crannies for a little discreet coupling, threesome, foursome, for seeing and being seen.

That was the reason for dinner in the restaurant and for the dress his gorgeous wife was wearing. He wanted her to be seen. Oh yeah, he wanted to advertise. He wanted to see what naughty things crawled out of the woodwork. It was about anticipation, about getting her primed and ready so that when he sprang his surprise, she'd jump at it.

"What would you do if it was a sex club?" he asked idly. As if he were doing nothing more than making polite conversation.

"I don't know." She speared a few greens on her fork and twirled them in the salad dressing.

Ah, so she wanted him to draw her out. Talk was foreplay. "How about a foursome with a hot couple?" He scanned the dining room, then moved his head slightly. "Them. I've seen him looking at you."

She glanced in the same direction. The couple was their approximate age, the woman with poufy Farrah Fawcett blond hair, the man with a few strands of gray and attractive lines on a tanned face.

"Do you want to do her?" Erin asked, her tone neutral.

"I'm more interested in watching him lick you to orgasm and hearing you scream." He trailed a hand up her thigh beneath one of the scarves. For him, it wasn't about other women. Though it defied explanation, for him, it was always about her pleasure, even with another man. Holding her face in his hands and kissing her as she moaned from another man's touch, another tongue on her, another cock inside her. "Thinking about it makes me fucking hard."

She regarded him, her eyes so dark in the dim light, they were the color of the deepest part of the ocean, only a hint of blue. "You wanted me to do Shane, didn't you?"

The steady rate of his heart doubled its beat. It had been two weeks, but she'd been thinking about the bartender. "I wanted you to enjoy yourself with him."

She studied her dwindling salad.

He pushed a little harder. "I was thinking about Winter actually. You wanted to say yes, but you were afraid. I wanted the trip to Rudolpho's that night to be a second chance for you to have your fantasy, whatever that was."

Through his slacks, he could feel the warmth of her skin along his leg. A pulse fluttered at her throat. "I was afraid at the time. It just seemed so crazy inviting a man into our hotel room."

"Is it so crazy now?" He waited, the noise of the dining room suddenly muted, his mind blanking out everything but her.

She gazed at him, her lips slightly parted, her lipstick glistening. "No. Not so crazy now," she whispered.

Relief and desire rushed through his body. His cock throbbed with all the possibilities suddenly driving through his mind. He'd put a plan into motion, taken a huge risk.

Without knowing it, she'd just agreed to the plan's execution. Yet he now saw the problems clearly, too. He'd been torn between his desires and the fear that she'd turn him down, but springing it on her was more like a trap. He wasn't sure of her, hadn't been sure for so long, and he couldn't stand losing any ground he might have gained when she'd agreed to the trip.

Holding her hand, he squeezed. "Are you willing to take a chance?"

She pressed her lips together, and her eyes widened. "A chance on what?"

"That I've got a surprise you're going to love."

"What is it?"

He clucked his tongue. "If I tell you, it's not a surprise. But I want you to know that something's coming."

His tensed muscles ached as if he'd waited forever, but when she finally let out a breath, he heard the slight shudder in it. "All right," she said. "You can surprise me."

The tension rushed out of him in a flood. He almost crushed her hand in his. Christ, he wanted this, for her, for him. It would be as first-rate as his fantasies. It had to be. "Good." The single word in no way described the emotions inside. Victory. Desperation. Desire. Fear. Relief.

She leveled a hard look at him. "But if I don't like it, I can call it off."

"You won't want to."

WALKING IN THE GARDENS AFTER DINNER, ERIN WASN'T AT ALL sure she was glad he'd told her about the surprise. Now she was all nerves, her skin jumping. He'd disappeared for a little while as she was dressing for the evening; it wasn't as if she hadn't known he was planning something. So why was this different than any of the other surprises they'd given each other over the past few weeks? That was the problem. He'd changed. Before, he'd simply tell her what to do and not allow any questions. Now *his* tension was making *her* tense.

Erin shivered. "I'm freezing." It was far too cold for an evening stroll, especially in this dress, the night breeze billowing through the scarves. In the dining room, she'd felt both exposed and sexy. Dominic, however, had been delighted showing her off in the outfit.

"Off to the Jacuzzi then," he said. Pulling her hand through his looped arm, Dominic directed her to one of the smaller pools they'd passed. It was tucked in a secluded corner fairly close to their villa and surrounded by faux lava rocks, a waterfall, and lush greenery.

He opened the gate for her, closing it behind them. The pool itself was kidney-shaped and surrounded by lounge chairs and tables with umbrellas. On one end there was a bar, closed for the night or perhaps the whole season. The Jacuzzi, enclosed within a tropical setting of lava rocks and palm fronds, steamed against the night air. Illumination was provided by twinkling bulbs in the foliage and a row of perimeter lights along the inside edge of the round spa. The water was unoccupied.

She was oddly torn between relief and disappointment. She reached for Dominic's hand before he went any farther. "Why didn't you simply surprise me the way you have the other times?"

He curled his fingers around hers, then raised her hand, setting her palm to his cheek, cupping his over hers. "I keep asking you what your biggest fantasy is. But I still don't really know, and all I do is offer up mine." He lowered his voice to a bare whisper. "I don't want to push you too far, yet I don't know how far that is."

"I don't know my own fantasies," she admitted. That's why she'd never really answered. It was so much better when she was swept along by his. As it was up in San Francisco. Tying him up and doing him in the dark hadn't worked. When she let him take over, he'd made it perfect. Although seducing him in the backyard had been pretty darn hot and all her idea. Still . . . "I want you to choose tonight." His hand was so sweet and warm over hers, his cheek firm and roughly male. "Make it good for me," she whispered.

His eyes were deep, full of an emotion that heated her. "I will, baby. I'm going to make it so good."

She felt the shadows of their nerves lift, and she was lighter, ready to flirt, ready to play. Ready for anything. "What do you want me to do first?"

He smiled, raised a brow, teasing. "Strip for me. I want to see you naked."

His desire swept over her, setting a flush to her skin.

"I'm sure we'll have visitors later," he promised, with a glint in his eye. Then he grabbed a couple of towels from a cart, throwing them on one of four chairs surrounding the Jacuzzi. Bending, he turned the timer for the jets, and the tub bubbled to life. "Go on," he urged.

The back of the dress plunged, and it was a simple matter to unzip and step out of it. "Here you go." She tossed it at him, and though she wore only her panties, she'd lost all her apprehension. For the moment anyway.

He caught the dress, laying it across the back of another chair. "Were you aware that everyone in the restaurant could see those gorgeous hard nipples of yours?"

She'd known he could, and that's all that mattered. "Do you like it when I touch them?" she purred, trying for sultry as she pinched them. The answering jolt in her clit surprised her.

Dominic's pupils dilated. She was almost sure his cock twitched in his slacks.

Then she stepped out of her lace panties.

"You trimmed, you dirty woman. Don't tell me you weren't expecting activity."

She bared her teeth in a smile, then stepped into the small pool. A moan of sheer pleasure fell from her lips as she slipped beneath the churning water. "Oh God, this is heaven." Even the clean scent of chlorine was delicious. "Your turn."

He was slower than she was, mainly because he had on more clothes, but the sight of his hard cock made her tingle. God, he was magnificent as he climbed down into the water, settling beside her.

"This is perfect," she sighed, giving him his kudos.

He laced his fingers with hers, leaning his head back against the pool's edge. "More than perfect."

They luxuriated in companionable silence broken only by the splash and bubble of the water and the hum of the jets. She was starting to believe maybe this was all he'd planned.

Then the outer gate clanged. Dominic squeezed her fingers, and her breath caught for a moment. She felt his gaze caress her, waiting, watching, wanting. Then she saw a man silhouetted in the pool lights. A sudden thrill rushed through her. She was hot and wet and it had nothing to do with the water. It was pure sex.

Shane. Dominic had brought her Shane.

24

"LAURA. NICK. FANCY MEETING YOU TWO HERE." SHANE GRINNED through his neatly trimmed goatee and mustache. He'd remembered their phony names.

He wore baggy swim trunks and carried a canvas bag, which he set on one of the chairs before he whipped his T-shirt over his head. Erin caught her breath at the muscular chest covered with a dusting of graying hair.

Beneath the water, Dominic squeezed her thigh. "What a surprise," he said to the other man.

She knew it wasn't any surprise at all, but somehow it was easier that they pretended for her. It gave her a chance to do nothing. Or anything.

"Mind if I join you in the water?" Shane bent to test the heat level.

"Of course we don't," Erin said. She wanted to ask why he wasn't with family or doing something for the holidays. But she didn't want to think about the holidays. Not tonight.

He grabbed the bag off the chair once more. "I just happened to bring some wine with me. Would you care for a glass?" He pulled out a bottle of the ice wine she'd ordered at the bar.

"I'd love one." It delighted her that he remembered.

The bottle was already uncorked, and he pulled three plastic wineglasses from the bag. "Let me be your bartender for the night," he said with a wink.

She blushed, then glanced at Dominic. His gaze traced her features. He wanted her to enjoy, and she was damn well going to do that. She took the glass Shane offered, saluted him. "Thank you." And she drank.

"It's my pleasure." He handed a glass to Dominic, poured one for himself, and she noticed that neither was filled to capacity as hers was.

"Hey, you're giving me more."

"I don't want you to run out," he said, slipping into the water without removing his trunks.

He wanted to get her drunk, she was sure. But they were making it all so easy on her. She didn't have to undress in front of him. He didn't undress in front of her. She wondered if Dominic had choreographed every detail of it.

"To the loveliest lady here." Shane saluted.

She laughed. "I'm the only one."

"Of which we're both very glad," Dominic said.

The water bubbled just above her breasts. Dominic traced circles on her thigh, moving ever closer to her pussy.

Shane laid his arms out along the tub's edge, swinging the glass in his fingers over the water. "May I be bold and tell you that I've had wet dreams about your story?"

"Which story?" She'd been a little dazed that night. She remembered telling him that she wanted a threesome with her husband.

"The one about the man your husband invited back to your hotel room."

Winter. The made-up story about the man at the party and what she would have done if she'd really let Dominic invite him over that night.

"Oh yeah. I remember that one," Dominic said, punctuating beneath the water with a slide of his pinkie into her cleft. Then he was gone.

Shane smirked at him. "I'll just bet you do." He shot a pointed finger at Dominic. "Because I'm well aware you two are married, and you were just fooling with me that night."

"We weren't fooling," Dominic said, his tone suddenly serious. "We were testing."

Shane tipped his head, eyed first Dominic, then returned to Erin. "I would have given anything to be the man in that story." He set his plastic glass on the edge of the pool, then hunkered down in the water and drifted toward the center, closer to her, the jet's bubbles flirting with the tip of his goatee.

She felt utterly taken over, by Shane's gaze on her and Dominic's light touches over her body. She felt him next to her, hot, hard, wanting her to say yes to whatever Shane suggested. She'd forgotten her wine in her hand, and now she drank from the glass to wet her parched throat.

"Tell her what you want to see," Dominic urged, voice low, intense. "Tell her what it will do to you."

And Shane did, desire written clearly on his features as he held her with the deep brown of his eyes. "I want you to get out of the water and sit on the edge of the hot tub so I can see that beautiful pussy of yours."

Dominic caressed her breasts, her pebbled nipples. She waited, one breath, two, three, then she felt herself rising from the water by the sheer force of their desire.

"Jesus, that's such a pretty pussy," Shane uttered with awe. He didn't touch, he merely looked, and yet it made her breath catch in her throat and robbed her of all self-consciousness.

"She's beautiful," Dominic affirmed.

She turned slightly to catch his gaze, and she saw her beauty reflected in his eyes. Not her image, but the way he saw her. At least for tonight.

"Her breasts are perfect, pert, firm, her nipples suckable."

She let herself get lost in Dominic's words.

Until there was Shane again. "Touch them for us." The water lapped and frothed against her thighs as he moved closer.

Her butt braced on the edge of the tub, she plumped her breasts in her hands. "You want the show, do you?"

Shane's eyes gleamed. "Oh yeah, we want the show, sweetheart."

She was going to give it to them. She needed to. She'd wanted it that night at the party. She'd wanted it when Dominic slid Winter's card onto the bathroom vanity. Only her fear had stopped her. All along, she'd been telling herself the naughty stuff was for Dominic, what Dominic wanted to see. She saw the lie. It wasn't for him. Saying it was for *his* desire was an excuse. *She* wanted. It was for *her*.

She didn't care about the fear anymore. She could be wanton. She could be anything. Dominic was there to protect her, there to allow only what she wanted. And she wanted the pleasure. She wanted the adulation, in Shane's eyes, in the eyes of her husband of fifteen years.

She pinched both nipples at once, hard. "Oh." Then she moaned, closed her eyes as sensation erupted in her breasts, her belly, between her legs, down to her toes. It was being watched and wanted as much as it was the physical.

"She's so wet," Shane whispered.

She laughed, feeling power at the note of reference. "Of course I'm wet. I'm in water."

He raised a hand. Next to her, Dominic tensed, but Shane came only to within five inches of her pussy. "I can see how creamy you are. How plump your pretty cunt is."

The word didn't bother her at all. There was reverence even in that.

Dominic's arm settled on her shoulders; he'd risen from the water beside her. "Touch yourself." His breath bathed her ear. "Spread your legs and let us watch you touch yourself."

She knew what she wanted, how the game needed to be played. She jutted her chin. "Get down there with him. I want you to see exactly what he sees." He also couldn't touch any more than Shane could.

Dominic went down into the swirling water, gazed up, wafting his hands back and forth to keep his body in place. "Do it," he begged.

Moving her wineglass out of the way, she raised her leg, set her foot along the tub's lip. And she opened herself to her rapt audience.

ERIN SLID HER HAND OVER HER BELLY, GLIDING HER INDEX FINGER down to her clit, deeper, to her opening, testing her wetness, then climbing back to her hot button.

Dominic felt his chest about to explode. The water jets buffeted him to and fro, his knees bent almost into a squat, the tips of his toes brushing the bottom. He steadied himself with the constant movement of his hands. Beside him, Shane watched Erin with a greedy yet awestruck gaze.

She played the performance to the hilt, closing her eyes, tipping her head back, stroking her plump clit in abandon.

"I envy you," Shane murmured. "I've never seen a woman more beautiful than she is in this moment."

It was the first step in a fantasy he'd had for years, a fantasy that had begun to consume him. The bartender was right. In their sexual life together, Erin had never been more beautiful to him than this moment in which she gloried in her body and the effect it had on them. "I know," was all he said.

Erin moaned and began to rock against her touch, her thigh and butt muscles tightening, releasing, giving her extra friction.

Shane shoved off on the bottom, moved a little closer. "I'd kill for woman with no inhibitions."

Dominic moved with him. "She has them," he murmured. "She's simply done away with them for tonight." They were close enough to see the sweetness of her cream, the ripe fullness of her pussy, the rosy hue of her skin, and the tight beads of her nipples as she climbed higher.

"Baby, look at us." He wanted her to see the evidence of what she'd done to them.

Opening her lids, her eyes were a glazed blue like fired ceramic, and a little dazed. Then, understanding what Dominic wanted, Shane rose, water streaming down his torso, his cock tenting his swim trunks.

Her breath puffing, fingers moving inexorably, Erin stared down at the evidence. "Oh, yes," she whispered.

Then she reached out.

Dominic's breath stuttered to a stop in his throat. He had planned, he had hoped. He'd gone to Rudolpho's on his way home from work Wednesday, the day Erin had agreed to the trip. He'd made a proposal. Shane had accepted, citing that he was alone for the weekend. His family lived in the Midwest, and no one was visiting. Dominic had offered him only the fantasy Erin had told him that night in the bar; watching. Anything else was her call.

When she slipped her index finger, nail painted a blood red, into the waistband of Shane's trunks, Dominic felt dizzy, needy, his cock damn near bursting beneath the water. Jesus Christ. He wanted this fantasy. He was terrified of it. His wife. Another man. He could lose her. He could have everything.

"Take them off," she ordered in a guttural whisper Dominic had never heard before.

Holding her gaze, Shane shoved the trunks over his hips, his cock jutting high. Erin gasped.

Even Dominic had to admit the man was damned impressive.

Then her gaze slid to Dominic. She smiled. The curve of her lips bore the slightest hint of triumph, satisfaction, power. "Tell him to stroke himself but not to come yet."

His cock surged with his own sense of power. Maybe she was punishing him. He didn't care. "You heard the lady, start stroking."

"Yes, I like that." Erin's voice was almost a purr as she put her fingers to her pussy once more. Eyes a mesmerizing blue that reflected the hot tub's tile, she watched Shane's hand on his cock.

He pumped. He grew. And Erin stroked herself to his rhythm.

"You're hot, lady." Shane's voice was rough.

"I know," she said. She believed it. In that moment, Erin understood her power over men, knew her beauty, her strength. It was something Dominic had never imagined he could give her. In ways, this moment had always been about him, about *his* need to see her pleasure, *his* desire.

With her gaze on the immense sight of a man masturbating because of his need and desire for her body, Erin gave as good as she got. She laid back on the pool's deck and raised her hips to her own touch, moaning, writhing for them.

"Jesus." Shane groaned. He didn't ask to fuck her. It was her choice, her decision.

Dominic waited, needed, willed.

She came without either of them touching her, an explosion

that trembled in her thighs, jiggled in her gorgeous breasts, her nipples peaking at the moment of her orgasm's peak.

Even before she had come down, she pushed herself up on her elbows and looked at him. "Fuck me while he watches, Dominic."

His heart damn near shot out of his chest. Then he was on her.

25

GOD, SHE WANTED, NEEDED. HER BODY STILL QUIVERED AND trembled. She had to have it, like a crazed animal.

Dominic didn't give her a chance to change her mind. He hauled her out of the water, bent her over the edge of the tub, and entered her pussy from behind, sliding hard, fast, and deep.

His cock pulsed, the angle perfect. She moaned and ground back against him. Then she turned to Shane.

He'd moved up onto the seat beside them, bracing himself against the lip of the pool, taking his cock in an unceasing stroke. Up, down, his wrist twisting, the head of his cock dripping with his desire.

"I'd love to stick my cock in your mouth and make you suck me," he said as if he were talking about the coolness of the night.

Erin licked her lips, closed her eyes a moment as Dominic found that exquisite spot inside, caressing it over and over with each thrust.

"Suck him, baby. You know you want to taste that." Dominic was inside her, hands on her, voice surrounding her. But it was Shane's gaze that held her.

"I want him to watch," she murmured. "I want him to come just from watching."

There was power in it, total, utter power. She didn't have to be afraid; this was only something to be enjoyed, nothing beyond what she could handle. And it was incredible. "I like the way you look at me," she said, her voice low, seductive, a tone she hadn't known she was capable of.

Shane's cock jerked in response, his balls growing taut. "How do I look at you?"

"Like I'm a box of expensive white chocolate, handmade just for you to eat every last bite." She gasped, letting the sound end on a moan. There was something amazing about Dominic taking her, driving her higher, making her body and her legs tremble with need, all while she talked to Shane as he watched her with greed in his eyes.

"Fuck, lady." Shane tipped his head back, groaned. "The way his cock looks in your pussy is a thing of beauty."

"He feels good," she said. Dominic had never felt more right inside her, never bigger, never harder. All made hotter by the fact that he stood behind her like a stud servicing her.

"Touch yourself while he's fucking you." Shane's face stretched, straining. "I want to see you come again."

Bracing herself with one hand on the tub's edge, she put a finger to her clit. "Oh God."

"How does it feel?"

At that moment, she didn't know whether it was Shane or Dominic who spoke. "It's unbelievable, the cock on my G-spot, over and over and over . . ." Her voice trailed off as the sensations rose, the hardness of Dominic's cock, the warmth of the water frothing at her thighs, the heat of Shane's gaze. "Yes, yes, yes," she chanted.

Then someone pinched her nipple and she was gone, nothing but her body imploding, the hot spray of Shane's orgasm across her back, and Dominic's pulse of climax inside her.

* * *

DOMINIC'S LEGS BUCKLED, AND HE TOOK ERIN WITH HIM INTO THE foaming water.

She'd felt so fucking good around him, so wet, so sweet. She was in the place of delirious pleasure he'd wanted for her, but only she could find for herself. She had to want it. He could never force her there, but she had gone of her own free will, dragging him and Shane with her.

Beside them, Shane subsided into the warm, soothing waters as well. Smiling, he merely said, "Fuck."

"Yeah," Dominic agreed, because the word said it all. The guy jerked off for her, came on her, and Dominic had felt the power of another man wanting his wife. There was nothing quite like that sense of possessiveness, knowing she was his, yet knowing he could give her away for a short space of time in which her pleasure would exceed any he could provide alone.

Erin snuggled deeper into his embrace with a hum of total satisfaction, smiled, and, without even opening her eyes, said, "That was naughty. You're both very bad men."

"Hell, yes, we are." Shane laughed. "And you're a naughty lady. I love naughty ladies."

She stuck out a toe and jabbed Shane's thigh.

Deep in his bones, Dominic felt her delight. He wanted it to last. He knew it couldn't.

Laughter drifted across the night, followed by the clang of the pool gate. It was a testament to her satisfaction that Erin didn't move, though she was seated between two men and what had been going on only moments before was evident in the way she was huddled in his lap. Not to mention Shane's wet trunks by the side of the hot tub.

The woman preceded the man, a blonde in a tight fuchsia sweater dress that looked a hell of a lot warmer than Erin's dress had been. The sheath revealed every curve of her breasts, and she had a lot of breast. She was young, maybe thirty, pretty enough, and a midlife-crisis trophy wife, Dominic surmised when he noted her wedding ring and the older man trailing in her wake, a gold ring on his left hand, too. He was on the wrong side of fifty, but he had all his hair even if it was streaked with gray, and he'd definitely spent time in a gym to keep up with his younger wife.

And Shane was noticing the blonde.

"Mind if we join you?" the man asked politely.

Time to go. Another woman spoiled the moment. She couldn't compare with Erin in his eyes, but it was Erin's eyes that counted. He couldn't chance any competition right now.

Dominic gave an equally polite smile. "Not at all. We're just leaving anyway. Come on, honey." He pulled Erin up just as the timer ran out on the jets and the surface fell smooth. "I need to get you back to our villa ASAP." His meaning was clear, and he noticed both men's appreciative glances as water streamed down her gorgeous curves.

"Shane, good seeing you," he said as he wrapped Erin in one of the thick towels he'd thrown on the chair.

The newcomer cranked the jet timer and the water began to bubble and foam again. He wasn't leaving Shane in the lurch. The fun in that Jacuzzi was only just beginning.

As for him and Erin, they hadn't crossed the line yet. They hadn't touched anyone but each other. He had a gut feeling they would cross that line soon, not tonight, but soon enough. And whether Erin was truly ready or not, she would be the one to initiate it.

He didn't want her to be able to blame him later.

* * *

DEAR GOD. SHE'D MASTURBATED FOR SHANE, A MAN SHE'D MET IN A bar, and let Dominic fuck her in front of him.

And it was out-of-this-world hot.

Christmas Eve, she'd slept the sleep of the sated and woke Christmas morning with her body feeling deliciously used. They did not exchange gifts in their room. They did not acknowledge the significance of the day over breakfast. Oh God, for a moment though, she remembered all they'd lost, and an almost crippling pain shot out from her heart. Even her joints suddenly seized up as she reached for her mimosa. But she looked at Dominic across the breakfast table, and she knew what it would do to him if she gave in to the ache and the guilt. He'd given her this trip so she would have no reminders, and she owed it to him not to allow any bad thoughts in, no guilt, no anger. So Erin ruthlessly tamped everything down. She could keep it at bay. At least until Monday.

They'd gone for a long hike, then visited a few wineries in the early afternoon. It was a fifty-fifty mix, some being open because times were tough, some closed for the day. They all, however, shut down early. Instead of dining at the resort, Dominic had taken her into St. Helena for dinner. They'd returned to the room to watch a movie. She'd subjected him to a chick flick; then he'd chosen a war movie that had won an Oscar.

She had to admit that she'd loved masturbating for Shane and Dominic, loved having Shane jerk off as Dominic fucked her, the hot spray of his come across her back. She hadn't done it to forget what day it was or to blot out her pain. She'd done it simply for her own pleasure. And God, it was good.

In the dark sometime past midnight, she'd reached for him and fucked him until sleep had simply overcome her, before she could let herself feel guilty about any of it.

* * *

AL WAS TALL AND AROUND THIRTY, WITH WAVY BLOND HAIR AND A nose that ended in as close to a point as a nose could get and still be real. "So, dude, here's how I work," he said, smiling at Dominic, his teeth straight but with a large gap front and center. "You stop hanging over my shoulder asking questions, and I run a bunch of diagnostics on all your computers and solve all your problems. Got it?"

Dominic had to laugh. Yeah, he'd been hovering. "Do your thing then. Let me know after you finish each computer." Al had started with Rachel's machine, not because of anything suspicious, but simply because it was free.

"Will do, dude." Al gave him the thumbs up.

It was Monday morning and Erin was annoyed he'd brought the techie in the last week of the year, when she was trying to finish shipping. New orders were down during the holiday season, especially the last couple of weeks of the month, and Erin figured the more she shipped before year-end, the earlier she pulled cash receipts into January. True, he'd told her he was bringing in someone to look at the computers, but he'd done it when everyone was leaving for the holiday. Her stress was up, her attention span down; she hadn't keyed on the words *next week*.

As far as Al tying up computers was concerned, Rachel and Yvonne were out, having taken the week off between Christmas and New Year's. Cam was here, but Atul was gone. Bree was finalizing all the new overhead rates so the standard costs could roll in the year-end update over the weekend. Only one of the assembly techs was working, plus Steve for QC and their shipping and receiving kid. There were plenty of unused computers to move to if Al was working on one, and the whole exercise wasn't as big a deal as Erin made it.

He hung in her doorway. "I'm making a trip out for some office supplies. You want a chai tea?" The coffeehouse was right next door. He didn't need supplies since Rachel kept the cabinet well stocked, but he wanted a peace offering.

"No," she snapped, her gaze focused on her monitor. He knew damn well she wasn't going to give up her computer no matter what.

Then she puffed out a breath, stilled her fingers on the keyboard. "Sorry, I take that back," she said as if she'd suddenly heard how bitchy she sounded. "I'd like a chai. Thanks." She *was* trying for him.

She'd been companionable on Saturday. The day had been good, even watching movies together. She'd laid a pillow in his lap, then snuggled up against him to watch. It was so damn perfect, his eyeballs ached with emotion. She didn't have a freaking clue how much that meant, how it eased the tension in his chest when he thought about Christmas without Jay, about all the Christmases ahead without Jay.

Then she'd turned to him in the night. The sex was hot and in several positions, and maybe she hadn't said much, but it was good. On the drive home Sunday, he'd wanted to ply her with questions, pull out her every reaction, relive the experience with Shane all over again. He wanted to tell her how he'd planned it, every step he'd taken, share the fun, but he was smart enough to keep his mouth shut. Next time, he'd push her to tell him everything, share everything, but for now, he'd let her get used to it on her own. Then he'd start working on her again, a new plan, something even hotter. Ultimately, he needed that connection, the sharing afterward. For now, though, he was simply grateful that she hadn't turned her back on him and closeted herself in her office on Sunday night.

Al came to him after lunch. "No little buggers detected yet." He went on to say he was working the vacant computers simultaneously, running diagnostics on one while optimizing another.

Rachel's desktop was fine, so was Yvonne's. He'd done Dominic's while it was free during the coffee run.

"Have you called your system's techs?" Al wanted to know, lounging in Dominic's doorway.

Dominic hadn't kept the patent issue from his people, but he didn't mention the possibility that someone had gotten their numbers. With Al, however, secrecy was antiproductive. He'd told him he was worried about a security breach of their data. Al had started the checks on the computers, but he'd said the problem most likely wouldn't have come from any random malware. *Inside job.* Dominic still refused to believe it.

"I called," he told Al. "They haven't had any security issues, and they assured me my data was safe on their server."

Al rolled his eyes. "Like you expect them to tell you they'd had a breach?"

"Yes, I do."

Al looked at him as if he were living in a fairyland.

"I did some searches, too," Dominic said. "I don't see anything on any forums or boards about any problems with them."

Al raised a brow, his respect rising. "Good job, bro."

He'd moved from *dude* to *bro.* He figured that was a plus.

"What about people working from home computers?"

"Me, my wife, Yvonne, Bree, Atul, Cam, we all do stuff from home. You think one of those computers could be infected?"

"Searching for answers. Our motto: no stone unturned."

Dominic was surprised the motto wasn't in some geek-speak metaphor. "We can look into that next."

"Okay, back to the diagnostic grind."

By late afternoon, Al had cleared all the computers not in use, plus Cam's and Dominic's. Now he needed access to those in manufacturing, then Erin's and Bree's.

Fists on Dominic's desk, Al leaned forward. "You have to tell your wife she needs to give up her computer," he whispered conspiratorially. "*I* ain't gonna tell her."

Had Erin been terrorizing the help?

"You can have it in the morning. She can work from home for a bit." He paused. "So everything's good so far?"

Al flattened his lips and shook his head. "Nothing yet. Your protection software's good, but someone in the know, like me"—he put a hand to his chest—"could get through it. But that's why I can ferret out any baddies. I cleaned everyone up, too, so you should be running more efficiently." Then he hooked a finger over his shoulder. "The one in there," he indicated the office Atul and Cam shared, "don't know how that chick works. No amount of optimizing is gonna do any good. It's way out of date for what she's doing, dude."

Ah, he was *dude* again. A notch down. Dominic made a mental note to talk to Cam about her computer. She was quiet, didn't complain, and lived with what she was given. Jesus, people needed to speak up for themselves.

"Fine, see you tomorrow," he told Al.

On the one hand, it was good Al hadn't found anything. On the other, it still left the door open to their leak coming from inside.

26

PARKING IN THE ONLY AVAILABLE SPACE A COUPLE OF SHOPS DOWN from the coffeehouse, Erin climbed out of her car. Of course, she should have saved herself the parking woes and gotten the chai at the place next to DKG, but she'd wanted the hot drink for the drive in.

It was eleven on Tuesday, and Dominic had kicked her out of her office for most of the morning, the last shipping week of the year, for God's sake. And it was a short week at that. She was trying, *really* trying not to be pissed about the whole thing. After all, he'd given her a perfect weekend away from home, just what she'd needed exactly when she'd needed it. So no, she would *not* get mad. Not today.

A man held the door of the coffee shop open for her, and damn if the line inside wasn't horrendous. You couldn't fool her and say the economy was bad when people still paid close to four dollars for a coffee drink. She idly thanked the man.

"Laura?"

For a moment, she didn't realize he was talking to her. Then . . . oh my God. That knowing smile. Holy shit. It was Shane.

Her immediate reaction was to run, but she stopped herself. She was in a public place. He couldn't do anything.

He fell in line behind her. "Did you enjoy your weekend surprise?"

See, that's why you didn't get kinky and fool around with someone who lived or worked nearby. Sure it was fun and sexy when you were out of town and your husband was egging you on. But then you run into the man back home. *Without* your husband.

Her face heated. What the heck was she supposed to say? "Umm" was all that came out.

She suddenly felt him too close behind her. "Yeah," he said softly. "That good. Leaves you feeling kinda speechless."

She almost jumped away. God. What if someone she knew saw them? They'd think she was having an affair. Yet he smelled like cloves, like spice and Christmas cheer, and his voice at her ear made her wet. She moved forward in line, her heart pounding, her nipples brutally hard against her jacket.

He was right there again, unnervingly close. "Next time I want to be the one fucking you while he's jerking off." His voice seemed to boom out the damning words, yet she knew they couldn't have made it farther than the two inches to her ear.

She could feel it, his cock entering her, his fingers on her nipples, his tongue on her pussy, licking, sucking, making her come, making her scream, and Dominic whispering how sexy she looked with another man's cock in her.

She felt faint with need. She was almost sick with it.

"There will be no next time," she whispered harshly.

Shane laughed softly. He heard the lie.

Suddenly she broke out of line. "I forgot something I have to do," she said, then practically ran for the door.

In her car, she started the engine, rammed the gear into reverse and backed out. Leaving the parking lot, her tires squealed. A block away, she pulled into a mini-mall and let the car idle.

Their marriage was totally messed up. They couldn't talk. When they tried, they fought. Her first instinct was always to get pissed at him; she had to think hard in order to control it. As far as sex, their kinkiness was growing, their limits expanding. It wasn't normal. In fact, after seeing Shane in the coffee shop, it was starting to freak her out. What would people *think* if they knew what she and Dominic had been up to?

Yet, the next time Dominic offered her a man, Erin knew she was ripe for fucking him while her husband watched. It could be Shane. It could be Winter. It could be someone else.

She couldn't let Dominic know. He'd arrange it at the snap of his fingers. Once they'd done it, there would be no going back. Everything would change.

She laughed, the sound without an ounce of humor. What was she thinking? Everything had changed a year ago when she lost Jay. He was gone forever and they could *never* go back.

Really, all they had left was fighting or kinky sex.

SOMETHING WAS WRONG; DOMINIC HAD NO CLUE WHAT. ERIN SAT at her desk. She talked to her monitor instead of him. "And my computer was fine?"

"It was fine," Dominic confirmed.

Her back was ramrod straight. "Good."

"Bree's was fine, too."

She finally looked at him. "That's good news."

He realized that Bree was at the top of her suspect list, and Erin probably hated herself for the disloyalty. "We should have the home computers checked, too," he added.

She turned back to her screen. "Fine." She flexed her fingers as if she was barely restraining herself from wrapping them around his neck, and her knuckles cracked. "Everyone can bring their laptop in rather than sending that kid out."

Al might look like a kid, but he knew his stuff.

Then suddenly *the kid* was standing in her office. "Dudes," he said. "I got a massive brain implosion."

Was that a good thing?

"What if it's as simple as someone accessing the system through a valid user ID that's been hacked?"

"What do you mean?" Erin's mascara had smudged beneath her eyes as if she'd been rubbing them, and the dark circles were deeper than usual.

"There'll be a log of every user. Unless he or she back-doored it somehow, the user log will show it." Al hunched forward, his eyes gleaming. "We can match the user ID with the IP addresses and see what kind of fallout we get."

"I still don't get it," Erin said.

But Dominic did. "If someone hacked in, retrieved a user ID, then started using it from another IP address, that IP won't match the valid user ID. And we can detect the port of entry into our system."

"Bingo." Al grinned. "Unless they're really clever and wiped the trail."

"It's worth a try." Dominic felt a slight measure of relief. Another avenue to investigate that didn't finger one of his own people.

"You'll have to talk to your system techs and get me authorization to access the logs." Al shot him with a pointed finger. "Can you handle that, dude?"

"Yeah. I'll call them."

"Awesome. I'll finish scanning and optimizing the other computers first."

"How much is this going to cost, Dominic?" Erin asked after Al sauntered out the door.

Erin was all about the money, but it was his people that gave him the bigger headache. He didn't want to believe someone in his group would sell their proprietary information.

"I don't care how much." He spread his hands. "We need to put the issue to rest."

"It doesn't put everything to rest. We still have the patent to worry about."

Garland Brooks was blowing smoke. He wanted money for nothing. Dominic wasn't going to let that asshole win no matter how much it cost. He leaned his fists on her desk. "Stop worrying all the time."

She pursed her lips. "Somebody has to."

He wanted to throw his hands in the air. He did his own worrying; she just never gave him credit for it.

"Dominic . . ." She didn't go on. And she wasn't looking him in the eye.

Whatever she wanted to say had nothing to do with the patent or the computers. "What?"

She waited a beat, staring at him. "Nothing." She turned back to her keyboard.

Dominic wanted to pound something. Especially after the great weekend they'd had. He hated unfinished sentences, stuff hanging in the air between them, but it was the way they lived these days, everything unsaid. He raised his hands in defeat and backed out. "Fine. Whatever."

Damn. She was doing it again, taking him on that roller-coaster ride, fucking fantastic sex, then shutting him out. He needed something to shake her up, put her off balance again, right back into the zone he'd had her in over the weekend, where she'd do whatever he wanted.

They had the three-day weekend ahead of them. He'd have to come up with something to top Friday night in the hot tub with Shane.

* * *

EVERYONE WAS SO TENSE, BREE COULD FEEL IT LIKE COLD FINGERS on her skin. Okay, not everyone, just Erin and Dominic and that geek they'd brought in.

She stretched her arms over her head, reaching with her fingertips, one hand, then the other, working the kinks out. She'd been sitting at the computer too long without moving.

She had to tell Erin. She couldn't stand it anymore. There was no way out of it, none at all. Things were coming to a head. But God, she couldn't even begin to say the words.

Of course, there *was* another way out. She could ignore all the calls. Pretend. But the calls would just keep coming, pushing, prodding, driving her crazy.

She strode purposefully to the door of her office. She'd tell Erin. She had to. She owed it to her.

Bree stopped before she made it out the door.

Erin would ask all sorts of questions that Bree couldn't face answering.

The phone rang on the desk. She ignored it. Immediately afterward, her cell phone started to ring. She closed her eyes and ignored that, too. She knew who it was. Only one person would move immediately from her work line to her cell phone, and Bree didn't want to talk to her. She could ignore those calls for a few more days. Then, maybe it would all go away.

God help her, that was the worst thought of all.

TWO DAYS LATER, THE WEATHER HAD TAKEN A RAPID TURN, FROM sunny but cold, to stormy and even colder. The forecasters were predicting snow in the Santa Cruz Mountains overnight. Rain beat against the window of Erin's office.

Her mind itched to do something, anything about the spy or the mole or the hacker or whatever you wanted to call the person who'd given their numbers to WEU. Letting some computer whiz pour over their equipment searching for viruses or clues made her feel helpless. Dominic was running around like a chicken with its head cut off trying to prove the leak was an outsider. They'd barely spoken over the last couple of days just so they could avoid the fight about it.

Swear to God, she hated to think it was one of her people, but wasn't the simplest answer the correct one? Like cops looking to the family when there's a murder. The most logical choices were Yvonne, who had been with them the longest and knew shipping numbers inside and out, or Bree, who had all their financial data at her fingertips. Sure, Erin hated to think it, but the suspicions hounded her regardless.

She clacked away on the keyboard, queuing up the morning's shipments even as her mind whirled around in circles. Today was the deadline, actually this morning was, because she intended to let everyone go after lunch just as she had last week. She'd pulled in as many shipments from next week as she could, which would give her a week's jump on cash receipts in January.

She punched a button on her phone.

"Yo," Fred from shipping yelped at her a moment later.

"The packing lists are ready to print."

"Cool."

She clicked off, then hit another button. Bree's phone rang next door, and when she picked up, Erin got her voice in stereo. "Yes, Erin, what can I do for you?"

"Invoices are ready to print. They need to go out today."

"Sure."

Erin clicked off again. The packing lists would go with the equipment, the invoices separately. She'd tried sending them together, but invariably receiving lost the invoices or never bothered to send them to accounts payable.

She sat back, listening to the rain a moment. It was almost peaceful. Even Dominic was too busy playing with the computer geek to bother her.

Last night he'd holed himself up in his lab at home, enraptured with his computer screen. That was fine with her. That way he wasn't asking her what was wrong. Of course, she could have said it was the patent, the cash, the year-end, any number of work things.

But it was Shane. Not Shane per se, but what Shane represented, a man Dominic wanted to watch her have sex with. Later, she'd lain awake. Did that mean Dominic didn't want her anymore, didn't love her? Hell, did the fact that she was actually turned on by whole idea mean she didn't love him?

She'd spent the sleepless parts of the night thinking about sex, Dominic, and Shane, and somewhere toward morning, she'd experienced a sudden stab of guilt. She'd forgotten to think about Jay.

The outer door opened. She couldn't imagine who it was. Deliveries were made in receiving, and it was way too early for the mail.

She leaned over her desk to look out.

A courier wearing a white baseball cap. "Erin DeKnight?"

"That's me." Rising, she rounded the end of her desk and met him halfway across the roundhouse.

"Sign here." He passed her a clipboard.

She did, then he handed her a registered letter. Her heart started to beat wildly. The return address was WEU. A registered letter from WEU. Oh God, WEU was taking them to court over the damn royalties. She wanted to scream. Everything just kept going downhill.

Back in her office, her heart pounded more loudly than the rain beating against the window. Her hands shook as she tore the envelope. She scanned the letter, and one sentence stood out . . .

"We'd like to meet to make a formal offer to buy out DeKnight Gauges, Inc., and, frankly, we don't think you can refuse."

27

WEU WANTED TO *BUY* THEM? WHAT THE HELL FOR?

Erin snorted. They hadn't reacted to the royalty demand, and WEU wanted to get them one way or another. Dropping into her chair, she read the letter again with more focus. They were willing to discuss having Dominic and Erin stay on to run the company, a separate division of WEU. Of course, the royalty issue would be null. Nothing would have to change except the paperwork; they could go on the same as before, yadda, yadda. What a crock. You let a big company in, everything changed. You were forced to adhere to their company policies, then all of a sudden they were siphoning off your profits. It was a scam.

One line grabbed her, flashing at her like neon. "Due to your difficult cash position, we know the relief you will feel having the patent issue off the table."

Their difficult cash position? How would WEU know *anything* about their cash? They made payroll, paid their bills on time, and had no outstanding debt. She managed the cash scrupulously. WEU was having the cash problem. They were stretching out Leon's payment terms. So what the hell were they talking about?

She glanced at the signature on the letter. Their CEO, Mr.

Garland Brooks. DKG was a very small fish in the pond WEU ruled. In fact, to them, DKG was pond scum. Except for the market share WEU had lost to them on the through-coat gauge.

But how would WEU have any clue about their cash position? Unless someone at DKG told them.

A queasiness started in her belly, spread up through her torso, then into her throat, choking her. Bree had been acting strangely. Yvonne had noticed it. Rachel had seen it. Even Erin agreed that something was bothering her.

Bree wouldn't do that. She couldn't.

Erin clenched her teeth. But look at the timing of the offer. Year-end. Which was always harder because companies put off purchases and decision making until the new year and a new budget. Year-end and the holidays. The holidays, which was the hardest time of year for Erin personally.

The letter actually shook in her hand, its crackle and rustle filling the office.

What if someone had told Garland Brooks this was the perfect time to hit them with the royalty demand, then follow it up with an offer, a mere pittance of what DKG was worth, to buy them out when their defenses were low?

"Frankly, we don't think you can refuse."

A threat? Why would he phrase it that way unless he knew something, unless someone at DKG had betrayed her?

Maybe, if Bree hadn't suddenly appeared in her office door, Erin would have controlled herself, thought about it first, talked to Dominic, considered it all rationally. Maybe she could have controlled her emotions the way she so scrupulously controlled them with Dominic so she didn't bite his head off.

But Bree was there, holding a stack of envelopes, the invoices. "Erin—"

Erin didn't let her finish. "Shut the door, and sit down."

Bree's face blanched. "Sure, Erin." She closed the door and sat.

As if her anger had been bubbling beneath the surface for days, weeks, her emotions were suddenly so high there was nothing except the letter in her hand and the woman in that chair. Erin rose, rounded her desk and stood over Bree. Her skin was hot, her voice cold. "How did WEU know our sales numbers?"

Bree's eyes went wide. "What are you talking about?"

"WEU. How do they know the through-coat sales? How do they know about our cash position?" Erin took one step closer, glaring down at Bree, her breath like glass in her throat. "Only you and I know about that."

"I didn't tell them." Bree's lip trembled.

"Then why have you been acting so secretively?" she snapped. "Yvonne saw it. I saw it. I offered you the opportunity to come clean the other day and you just stood there and said nothing was wrong."

Bree perched on the edge of the chair, her hands clasped. "It's not about WEU. It has nothing to do with work at all."

Erin was so angry, she shook the letter before she could physically strike out. "Then what the fuck is wrong with you?"

Bree stared at her, her cheeks two spots of bright red in her otherwise white face, her pupils so wide, Erin could see herself in them. "I—I—" she stammered.

"You what?" Erin spat out. Her vision was red-rimmed, her chest so clogged with emotion, she scared herself.

Bree shifted her eyes, and her body rocked with tension. She dropped her voice to little more than a whisper. "My—my father's dying of cancer and my mom wants me to come home and help her take care of him. And I'd rather die than do it."

Bree's words smacked her in the face and drove her backward. Erin stumbled two steps, clutching the letter to her chest. A tear trembled on Bree's eyelash but didn't fall. It simply seemed to get sucked back inside.

"Oh," was all Erin could manage.

"My mom wants me to ask you for time off, but I didn't want you to think I was a terrible person because I—I *can't* do it."

Erin swallowed. Oh my God. She didn't have any words. What could she say anyway? She'd yelled at Bree, accused her. And the woman's father was dying.

She said things when she was angry. She always regretted them, but only when it was too late. Just like she had with Jay.

Oh God, what had she done? What had she said? What was wrong with her? She could only stand there, trembling, hearing her anger, her own voice, shouting at Bree, screaming at Jay. *God forgive me. Please forgive me.* She was always begging, but saying awful things anyway.

Erin cleared her throat. "I'm sorry." She owed Bree more than that. "I don't know what came over me. I got this letter, and I just freaked out." It wasn't even a good explanation. It was just a pitiful excuse. "I'm so sorry."

"That's okay," Bree said softly. Color was returning to her face.

"It's *not* okay." Erin struggled to breathe. "What I did was unforgivable."

Bree blinked. "You just asked me a couple of questions."

"I said *fuck*." It was the least of what she'd said.

Bree stared up at her. "I've heard worse," she said almost calmly. "It's not a big deal. I was just worried that I'd done something wrong. And if I'd told you when you asked me the other day, then I wouldn't have seemed so suspicious."

Erin came down off the adrenaline high, suddenly drained. Shuffling behind her desk, she collapsed into her chair. "I don't deserve your excuses. I was wrong. I don't know what came over me." She apologized to Bree the way she never could to her son. It would never be enough. "And you can have all the time off you need to take care of your dad. I'm so sorry he's ill." So sorry he's dying.

"Thank you."

There was the other thing Bree had said, too. "I don't think badly of you for being ambivalent about taking care of him." Erin drew in a breath, forced the words out. "Dealing with death is hard."

Erin should know, she hadn't dealt with it at all. She wouldn't even let Dominic say Jay's name. She couldn't say it now either, not even when Bree needed her empathy.

"Please forgive me," Erin whispered. She should have said it to Jay. To her husband. But she couldn't. She would have had to tell Dominic what she'd done, the things she'd said.

"It's okay, Erin. Honestly. I'm over it now. And I'm glad you made me tell you because I feel a lot better. Really." Bree rubbed her hands on her pants as if her palms were sweaty.

"You're not a terrible person for having feelings you don't know what to do with." Erin wished she could say the same thing for herself. But she *was* to blame.

Bree suddenly waved the stack of envelopes. "I was just going to let you know everything's ready to mail. I ran them all through the mail machine."

"Thank you." Erin paused. "I really am sorry, Bree."

Bree stood. She was statuesque, lovely, but there was still a shadow in her eyes. "Don't worry about it, okay?"

Erin stopped apologizing. She couldn't fix it anyway. "If you need to talk, my door's always open." Erin didn't think Bree would use it, especially not after what she'd just done to her.

For a long moment after Bree left her office, Erin stared at WEU's letter.

She'd been so good controlling herself the past few days, hardly snapping at Dominic, sounding like a reasonable person, even having a lovely time with him up in Napa, seeing Shane in the coffeehouse notwithstanding. Then she'd completely lost it with Bree. She closed her eyes. God.

More than anything in the world, she wanted to pick up the phone and call Garland Brooks. *Yes, please, take it all. Take everything. I don't even care how much you pay for it. I'm so tired, I just want it all to go away.*

"HOW DID IT GO WITH AL? DID HE FIND ANYTHING?" SEATED AT THE kitchen table, Erin's voice was neutral, not enthusiastic but not tuning him out either. A case of mild interest.

They'd let everyone go after lunch. All the shipping that could be done had been, the invoices were in the mail; there was nothing else to be done this year. Erin had remained in her office the rest of the afternoon checking and rechecking the rates, routings, and raw materials before the standard cost roll. Dominic spent the afternoon working with Al.

"Nothing yet," Dominic said as he opened the pizza box he'd set on the kitchen counter. "The computers all checked out. He's going to work the logs over the weekend."

"Doesn't he have a life?"

He was surprised she hadn't asked if he'd be paying Al holiday rates. "It's a puzzle. He wants to figure it out."

She waited for him to put her pizza in front of her. He'd offered to get the takeout on his way home. She hadn't protested. She'd been listless with a "whatever you want, I don't care" attitude. He'd gotten half combination and half Hawaiian because she didn't like so much sausage and pepperoni.

Jay had taken after both of them, wanting a slice of each.

Jesus. Maybe he shouldn't have gotten pizza.

The silence was loud in the kitchen. He didn't ask her what was wrong. She wouldn't tell him. Instead, he hitched his hip and pulled a sheet of paper from his pocket, unfolding and sliding it across the table.

"What's this?" She didn't bother to read it for herself.

"Train tickets." They were will call.

"For where?"

"Reno. I want to ring in the New Year up there." It had taken him hours on the Internet over the last two days to come up with the idea. He'd gotten them tickets to a New Year's party at one of the big casinos, two nights' accommodations included.

She closed her eyes a moment, swallowed, then opened them again and looked straight at him. "Okay. That sounds like fun." Her voice was so flat, it was scary.

She didn't protest, didn't ask why the train, why Reno, nothing. He didn't know what he'd been expecting, but it wasn't total acquiescence.

"It's supposed to snow tomorrow, and driving over Highway 80"—which was the fastest route through the Sierra Nevadas to Reno—"would have been a bitch. So I picked the train."

"That was a good choice." She rose. "Do you want another piece?" she asked, though he still had a full one on his plate.

"No, I'm fine." He didn't trust her politeness. Something was going on in that mind of hers. She was pissed . . . or remembering stuff. Just as the pizza had reminded him.

But all she did was come back with another slice of Hawaiian. "Is it a fancy party? Should I bring the dress you bought me in Napa?"

He hadn't thought about what he wanted her to wear. But then he smiled. "Yeah. That dress and—" He stopped, waiting for her to look up at him. When she finally did, he finished. "No panties."

"None?" she asked without even raising a brow or putting up a fight.

Yeah, scary. Like she was saying all the right things, but feeling absolutely nothing.

"None." He bit into the slice of pizza, the spicy sausage sizzling in his mouth. He smiled again, despite the tension in his gut, and added, with his mouth full, "Thigh-high stockings, too. Black. With those little seams down the back."

"I don't have any," she said, shaking her head slightly.

"Then we'll buy you some." He grinned wickedly.

She didn't react at all. "What are you going to wear?"

"It doesn't matter." He rose and hit the counter for another piece. When he turned back, her gaze was on him, her eyes a pale, washed-out blue in the overhead kitchen light.

He slid his plate onto the table, but leaned over her. "Tomorrow night is all about you." He gripped her chin, her skin warm, smooth, kissable. "I'm going to find the perfect man for you."

She didn't say anything, didn't move a muscle. Damn her.

"And I'm going to watch him fuck you."

"What happens in Reno stays in Reno," she murmured without inflection, without any clue to her emotions.

"Yeah. Something like that."

Her lips parted, her breath puffed, and finally she said, "All right."

28

THEY HAD TO BE UP EARLY THE NEXT MORNING TO MAKE IT TO THE train station in Emeryville on the other side of the Bay Bridge. The morning was overcast, but the rain had taken a break. Thank God the traffic over the bridge was light. The Zephyr's route began in Emeryville and ended in Chicago. It would take over seven hours to get to Reno.

What happens in Reno stays in Reno. A variation on the Las Vegas slogan. Erin had every intention of giving Dominic what he wanted.

She didn't tell him about the letter from WEU. She didn't mention how she'd accused Bree in that awful, near hysterical tone. She was ashamed. She couldn't say it out loud. Couldn't bear for him to look at her. Or hear his words. *What were you thinking, Erin?* Of course she hadn't been thinking, not at all

It was better to give him what he wanted. New Year's Eve in Reno and her in another man's bed. She'd masturbated for Shane. He'd watched them fuck. This was just one more thing, one further step so she didn't have to think about Bree. Or Jay.

"He's gotta be hot," she'd said last night in bed. "I don't want some smelly, skanky old guy."

"I don't want to watch you with some smelly, skanky guy."

"So if I say I don't like him, don't push me into it."

"I won't." Dominic had leaned over to blow warm breath in her ear. "We're going to find the hottest, sexiest man who makes you wet just looking at him." He'd licked the shell of her ear. "I want to watch you take a big cock between those gorgeous lips of yours." He could have been talking about her pussy or her mouth. "I want to hear you make him groan, then scream." He'd rubbed his hard cock against her. "I want to taste you with another man's come all over you, inside you."

It had all once been his idea, his growing obsession, but he'd succeeded in making it hers. With his body wrapped around her in the dark, she'd started getting into it. That was the moment she'd blotted out the argument with Bree, the things she'd said, the moment she put aside every other thought and started thinking hot, kinky sex in flashing neon letters. She wanted it as much as Dominic wanted it for her.

There was something to be said for living for the moment. Sometimes, it was the only thing a person had to offer and the only way to survive.

HIS WIFE WAS HOT. DOMINIC HAD ALWAYS THOUGHT THAT, THE first time he saw her wearing jeans and a baggy sweatshirt; when they'd married; when she was glowing in pregnancy. Even this past year, despite everything that had gone wrong.

She wore tight jeans, a short-waisted suede jacket, and white snow boots with fake fur around the tops that hit just below her knees. For whatever strange reason, the boots were fucking sexy. He wasn't the only man who noticed.

Among the constant stream of people up and down the train's aisle, male gazes followed her when she sauntered back to the powder room or down to the lower-level snack bar for a glass of wine. He'd immersed himself in the sway of her hips in those tight jeans as the train rattled along. The car pitched, throwing her off balance, and her hand automatically reached out, connecting with a broad shoulder. She smiled an apology with ruby lips, moved on, leaving the man with a stunned and heated expression.

Dominic had staked out two seats in the panoramic car, the windows curving up and over them for a spectacular view. Though less comfortable than the reclining seats in their booked car, these chairs faced out for watching the countryside race by. The groupings of two were separated by small round tables for drinks and snacks while larger parties played cards, board games, or ate lunch in restaurant-style booths at the rear of the car. Dominic preferred the scenery here versus the regular compartments, which had only side windows, the daylight partially blocked by the curtains even when they were pulled back.

The sky had been moody and overcast as they passed through Sacramento and the tracks climbed. Cityscapes morphed into marshland, then to rolling pastures and finally to the sandy earth of mountain slopes. Oak and ponderosa pines were surrounded by the greenery of incense cedar and Douglas fir, the deep-red earth itself littered with the scrubby look of manzanita. Outside of Colfax, they'd gotten their first sighting of yesterday's snowfall still sticking to the ground.

"Here you go, sweetie." Erin handed him a beer and plastic cup. She'd purchased a bottle of chardonnay for herself.

"Thanks."

Sweetie. The endearment rang nicely in his ears. He tried to remember when she'd so easily used a term of affection in the last year and couldn't. Except when they were deep into one of their games. Just as the scenery morphed before his eyes, so had she, from the expressionless automaton of last night in the kitchen to this woman he barely knew but wanted badly.

She reached down to her carryall between them and pulled out a can of roasted nuts, shook it at him. He held out his hand for her to pour several into his palm. Leaning back, she propped her feet on the low windowsill, throwing a few nuts in her mouth. "They've got premade sandwiches and hot things like hamburgers and hotdogs," she told him, "but they get warmed up in the microwave." She wrinkled her nose in distaste.

"Let's do the dining car."

"Sure." She hadn't fought him on anything he wanted.

"Cheers," he said, tapping his plastic cup to hers.

She smiled. This was how he wanted her, easy, loose, whatever the source of her recent ennui now gone or at least buried. For the moment, they were comfortable, amiable.

"Snow on the trees." She pointed to the cedar limbs bending slightly beneath the weight. The red earth was covered in a layer of white dappled with animal prints.

Her interest permeated his senses. The train was a good idea. He didn't have to concentrate on the driving or the traffic. There was just her. And God help him, he wanted this woman back for good, not just fleeting glimpses of her. Turning, he stretched his arm along the back of her chair, playing with the ends of her hair.

She hadn't noticed the guy four seats down, but Dominic did. The man glanced away quickly as if caught in the act.

"What's your age limit?" he asked under cover of the train's clatter.

She didn't dissemble. "Fifty." She sipped her wine. "Unless he's something extraordinary."

"What about the low end?"

She tipped her head to him. Beneath the dark, moody sky, her eyes were a contrasting light blue. A flame began to burn in the depths. "Twenty-five."

"That's daring."

She sat straighter, preened. In the heated car, she'd thrown off the suede jacket, and her long-sleeved teal T-shirt was tight across her breasts. "I'm worth it," she murmured.

Christ. His cock throbbed. He saw her splayed out with the firm young body of a twenty-five-year-old between her legs, her face aglow, skin flushed with desire. "I have someone in mind."

She settled back against the seat, her hair once again within reach of his fingers. He stroked it as if it were silk. "Describe him for me," she demanded soft and low. "Tell me why I'm going to want him."

His pulse kicked. Oh yeah. She was tumbling into his fantasy, feeding his nasty obsession, where everything was about her pleasure, her release of inhibition, plummeting into a state where she was all emotion, completely open to him and anything he asked of her.

Tomorrow, the next day, the one after, she might tear it all away from him, the sexy smiles, the laughter. Whatever. He'd ache for the loss then. Right now, she was here for the taking.

He assessed their target, using her as the smoke screen. "Thirty or so. He's alone, I haven't seen him with anyone. Reading a book—I can't tell what—hardbound, no dust jacket."

"A reader is good." Boots balanced on the sill, she let a knee fall, parting her legs slightly, her thigh caressing his as the train car rocked. "I like intelligence."

"His hair is short. And dark, almost black."

"Short hair screams sexy executive." Then she pointed at the foliage streaming past the window. "Look, it's snowing."

He'd been aware of the shifting light, a darkness descending, but now he recognized the softness of snowflakes against the rising slope of the mountain.

Without turning her head, she continued the low murmur of their conversation. "Describe his body."

"Jeans, blue shirt. Good shape, broad chest as far as I can tell. Legs are long so he's probably tall."

Raucous laughter erupted from one of the booths, and their quarry glanced up from his book, his gaze lighting on Erin's profile, then flicking to Dominic, then finally to the noisy group beyond them.

"Maybe he'll get up," Erin said softly. "We all have to use the restroom sometime. What about his face?"

"Decent looking. Clean-shaven."

"Thank God. I hate that scruffy look. It's so unkempt."

He didn't know how to judge handsomeness except by comparison. He tried to think of her favorites. "He reminds me of that doctor in *Grey's Anatomy*."

She smiled, lowering her lids as if she were seeing a vision. "Patrick Dempsey is hot. Even better when he's had a fresh shave." Twisting in her seat, her eyes glancing off the guy, she ended by gazing out the opposite window and raised her voice slightly. "Look over there. All that snow."

Dominic turned as well. The view from the right side of the train, what he could see of it that wasn't obscured by the unused minibar standing in the way, was of the mountain's downward slope, and off into the swirling snow.

Erin rose, sidled past him, and stepped across the aisle. The opposite seats were filled so she leaned over the minibar's console to watch, leaving enough room for people to walk by her.

Jesus, in the tight jeans, she had a heart-shaped ass that made his mouth water.

"Isn't it cool?" she said, her gaze sliding over the thirty-year-old before landing on Dominic.

"You'd think you never lived in a place where it snows," he mocked.

"That was ages ago." She shifted from one foot to the other, one cheek plumping, then the other echoing the movement.

The Patrick Dempsey look-alike stared at her, mesmerized, his book forgotten in his lap. He swallowed, his Adam's apple sliding up and down his throat.

Dominic had a sudden vision of what his wife could do to this young man, the heights to which she could take him in the last seat in the last car of the train. He didn't consider the two porters that wandered back and forth between the cars almost constantly. No, in his fantasy, no one noticed a thing.

The loudspeaker crackled. "Last call for lunch in the dining car. You have ten minutes to get your reservations in."

Facing him, Erin leaned back against the bar, hands braced behind her, breasts thrust forward. "I'm starving. Go put our name in, sweetie." She smiled, then crossed to his side of the car and leaned down, pert ass in the air, to give him a smooch.

Damn. She was playing to their audience. When Dominic rose from his seat to pass her in the aisle, he cupped her butt briefly, the caress obvious to the man sitting only a couple of seats away.

By the time he'd returned, Erin was in her seat, boots once again propped on the sill, picking one peanut at a time from the pile in her hand. "How long will it be?"

"Ten, fifteen minutes. It's community dining."

"What's that?" She held out her hand. He took several nuts.

"We sit with other people so the tables are filled up."

"That's fine." She sat forward, twisting in her seat as if she were stretching kinked muscles. "I love meeting new people."

She was such a damn liar. And so good at it.

Their man rose, heading toward the dining car.

"Now *that's* a tight end," Erin murmured, slouching back against her seat to watch.

The guy was tall, lean, with a decent breadth of shoulder. Dominic dipped down to her ear. "I can imagine that tight end with your legs wrapped around it."

"You are so dirty," she whispered, but her eyes sparkled. Right now, it was a stress-free fantasy. "I wonder if he's getting off in Reno."

Dominic laughed. She was falling into the whole innuendo of the thing right along with him. "Now who's being dirty?"

She clucked her tongue. "It's *your* mind conjuring up double entendres."

"He's back," Dominic singsonged to her, and she gave a full-throated laugh. "I love the way you laugh," he whispered without thinking before the words were out.

She laughed for him again as if she didn't get the gut-wrenching importance of his words. "Why?"

"Because it's sexy, and it makes me so damn hard I can't think of anything else but doing you."

"Sweet talker."

A garbled announcement sputtered through the loudspeaker. "I think that's our name," he said.

"That was quick. But thank God"—she rolled her eyes dramatically—"I thought I was going to faint from hunger." Rising, she pulled on her jacket, leaving it unbuttoned. Taking her purse from the bag she'd had at her feet, she laid the carryall on her chair. "There's just a book and some water and the nuts in there. I'll leave it to save our seats." Then she pulled out the book and tossed it on his chair.

"That better not be a romance. It'll wound my manhood."

She glanced at his jeans. He was semihard. "I don't think you have any problem with your manhood, sweetie."

The book, he saw, was a managerial how-to tome and way too dry. No wonder she hadn't brought it out of the bag. But Erin was still smiling over her comment as they headed down the aisle to the dining car. She gave a slight tip of her head as they passed the young man. At the same moment, he looked up, their gazes meeting briefly. Ah, eye contact. Unspoken signals. Dominic didn't expect anything to come of it, not on the train anyway, but at least she was flirting. He was hoping the guy would get off in Reno. In more ways than one.

In the dining car, the waiter led them to a table midway through the car. They both took the window seats of the booth, sitting opposite each other, and ordered coffee to start.

"This is a nice setup." Erin opened the menu. The food already served to the other diners actually looked appetizing and smelled good, too. The snow-laden countryside rushed by, but inside, they were warm, the tablecloth was white, the napkins cloth instead of paper, and by the window, a little vase of daisies danced to the train's rhythm. The drone of voices blended with the whoosh of the wheels on the tracks, making other conversations virtually impossible to distinguish and isolating them at the same time.

Their waiter was heading their way. "We have another diner who will be joining you, if you have no objection."

Erin's young admirer slid into the seat next to her.

29

ERIN BREATHED DEEPLY OF THE MAN SEATED NEXT TO HER. HE smelled wonderful; not something she could identify in particular, but an expensive, spicy, male-dominant scent.

"Hi. Craig Miller." He laid his book on the edge of the table, then stuck his hand out first to Dominic.

They shook. "Dominic"—he touched his chest, then extended his hand—"my wife, Erin." He didn't provide a last name.

Hmm. Coincidence that Craig made his lunch reservation right after Dominic had gone forward to make theirs? He took her hand, his grip firm, his touch dry. Thank God he didn't have sweaty-palm syndrome. "Nice to meet you," she said, dropping her voice, shooting for low and sexy. "Are you going to Reno?"

"No. A little farther." He didn't offer additional information, but his smile was as warm as his touch, his eyelashes lush for a man.

Okay. No Reno. Playing with him a little was safe then. Craig Miller was totally hot with those movie-star looks, dark hair, brown eyes, and a deep voice a woman felt on the inside. "I noticed your book out there," she said, letting him know she'd seen *him*, not just his book. "I love to know what others are reading."

He blushed. It was kinda cute.

Dominic shot her a look, not quite a smile, more of a smirk because, number one, it wasn't like her to question people, and number two, she'd openly admitted she'd been watching.

"It's a biography on Joseph Goebbels," Craig said.

"Oh, you're a historian. How interesting." She smiled brightly, laying it on thick. That would get Dominic going.

Craig's color deepened. "Not exactly. I write historical fiction, the World War Two period."

Dominic set down his menu, his attention grabbed, but he let her do the talking.

"That is *very* interesting," she enthused. "World War Two spy novels?" Being a writer, he'd love talking about what he did.

"Yeah, you could call them spy novels." He picked up his menu as if he were embarrassed and needed a distraction.

Their waiter arrived with coffees all around and to take their orders. He looked at Erin first. She leaned a little over Craig in order to point around the waiter at a plate on the next table. "What's that? It looks delicious."

The waiter stepped back to see. "Goulash, ma'am."

"Is it good?" she asked the man across, raising her voice so he could hear over the incessant clatter of the train. He nodded, mouth full, surprised someone would interrupt.

Under normal circumstances, Erin wouldn't have done anything like it. But she was the woman whose husband wanted to watch her have sex with another man, and this Erin had a lot more freedom. This Erin was downright bold. "I'll have that."

"It comes with a salad. What kind of dressing would you like?"

She let her eyelashes sink a moment, her lips curving as if she were reviewing each individual taste. "Blue cheese. It's so tangy, but sweet at the same time." Like come, she thought.

Craig grinned. "I'll have what she's having."

It reminded her of that movie *When Harry Met Sally*, when the woman ordered the same thing after Sally faked an orgasm in the restaurant.

Under the table, Dominic tapped her leg with the toe of his shoe. She bit her lip to keep from smiling. She felt like a hot little tease. And she didn't have to do anything either. The train was too crowded, and she was *not* doing it in the john. It was a game. And it was fun.

"I'll take the burger," Dominic said when it was his turn.

"You're so boring, sweetie," she teased. "You should try something with pizzazz."

"I'll let you have all the pizzazz." The glance he shot Craig was deliberate with subliminal messaging.

"So," she said when the waiter was gone, "back to your spy novels. Do you use your own name? Would we have seen your books in stores?"

He shrugged. "Yeah, I use my name, but it's no big deal."

She noticed the blush again and began to suspect he was embarrassed. She didn't recognize his name from anywhere either. Maybe he felt the prick of not being a household word. Then, without a clue how the idea popped into her mind but knowing it was brilliant, she said, "It's a total coincidence that you're a writer because we have something in common."

He raised a brow. "Don't tell me. You've written a novel, and you're trying to get it published." Erin detected a hint of disgust in his tone.

She flapped a hand, laughed at him. "I've already had several novels published."

Dominic choked on his gulp of coffee before catching himself. She got the biggest kick out of leaning closer to Craig and dropping her voice to a sexy note. "Don't tell anyone, but I write erotica. And I *don't* use my real name." She leaned back, making sure her jacket was open wide enough so that her breasts were fully visible—and inviting. She smiled at his gape. Hah, he believed her. She held up her hand. "Don't ask me what it is. I have to keep my anonymity."

"Don't tell me you're Zane," he said with an ounce of awe.

Zane? Honestly, she'd never read erotica and didn't know any of the writers. Was that Billy Zane? No, he was an actor.

"Honey," Dominic interrupted, "we're incognito this trip." He raised one devilish brow.

She glanced from Craig to Dominic and back to Craig. Then she patted his hand. "Dominic's right. I shouldn't have said anything. This is just a . . ." She paused for a heartbeat, then puckered up to add, "pleasure trip."

Craig was young enough to let his eyes widen at the innuendo. And it was definitely an innuendo. "It's your secret. I'll just"— he cut off, waited a beat—"fantasize about it." His eyes traveled from her to Dominic, gauging her husband's response.

Dominic merely smiled, cool, smug, and knowing.

Her pulse began to buzz. Craig was falling in with the program, flirting back, picking up on the fact that Dominic was fine with it all. Oh yeah, erotica writer was perfect. She didn't have to wonder how to bring sex into the conversation. She'd put it right out on the table, and he'd taken the bait. "And I absolutely love my job."

Beneath the table, Craig's leg brushed hers. A purposeful touch. A flash of heat. Warmth rushed through her body, her clit suddenly pulsing, her breasts tingling. Beneath the thin bra and tight T-shirt, her nipples peaked. Dominic saw.

With the young man's thigh resting against hers, she smiled wickedly at him across the table.

* * *

DOMINIC SHOT HER A LOOK. ERIN BATTED HER EYELASHES AT HIM.

You dirty little slut. He had no doubt she knew exactly what he was thinking. She was goddamn perfect, opening the door to sexual banter with a stroke of genius. Her jacket framed her breasts, and damn if her nipples weren't completely suckable right through the T-shirt.

"I bet you love the research." Craig grinned, fixing Dominic with a direct gaze.

The game was on, and the kid wanted in. "You have no idea," Dominic said.

He was sure Craig would have asked for specifics if their lunch hadn't arrived at that moment.

Erin tried the goulash before the salad. "Oh my God." She let out a sexy moan of pleasure that made him hard as granite.

She was on a roll. He loved it.

"That's to die for." She waved at the opposite table. "Thanks for the recommendation." The guy merely nodded.

Then she bumped Craig's shoulder with hers. "Try it. I have to know if you adore the taste as much as I do."

Craig seemed a little stunned, aware of the sensuality in her words, her touch, and the fact that she had no compunction cozying up to him with her husband sitting right across the table. He was starting to realize he'd bitten off more than he could chew, so to speak.

"It's great," he said after swallowing a forkful.

Dominic waited. He had no idea what his wife would say or do next, and the uncertainty had his blood hot and his cock throbbing. He was dying for her next word.

Elbow on the table, she leaned her chin on her fist a moment, toying with her fork in the goulash as she gazed at Craig. "How do you do your research?" she asked, eyes wide, innocent. "Reading books and cruising the Internet? Or more . . . hands-on?"

She had the pause just right. Even Dominic felt it in his groin.

Craig matched her look. "Hands-on is the only way."

"I agree." She took a bite of goulash, savored it, turned a smile on him. "I'm very tactile," she purred. "Writing spy novels, do you have to go out and . . . play with your gun?"

Christ. Dominic wanted to kiss her. Or fuck her. Both.

"Occasionally I have to do that. You've got to keep it primed, you know."

She nodded with all sincerity. "Dominic keeps his primed, too." She smiled sweetly. "A man never knows when he's going to have to whip it out on the spur of the moment."

Dominic sputtered, chuckled, then couldn't help himself. "You are so bad."

She pouted charmingly, then patted Craig's arm. "I'm teasing. That's what we"—she lowered her voice with a quick look at the opposite table—"erotica writers do. Everything is a sexual innuendo." She laughed sweetly. "We can't help ourselves. It's in our genes."

"Is that your DNA genes?" Craig asked, "or *these* jeans?" He dropped his hand beneath the table, and he had to be touching Erin.

Dominic's heart kicked into high gear. He was suddenly so goddamn hard, he didn't think he'd be able to stand straight.

Then Erin's hand disappeared under the table. "It's always in these jeans."

Dominic could swear he heard every single snowflake hit the ground. What were they doing under there? Though the angle of their arms and bodies wasn't right for it, he had the distinct image of Erin holding Craig's fingers to her hot pussy.

Then everyone's hands were back on the table, and Erin leaned forward. "I do believe this young man is capable of a few innuendos himself."

"I'm sure he is," Dominic agreed, damn near lightheaded with all the testosterone zipping through his blood. "After all, he's a big boy."

Erin gave Craig a sidelong glance. "I have a feeling he's a *very* big boy."

Craig smiled but said nothing, filling his mouth with goulash. Erin had said it all for him.

It seemed only moments of cock-hardening sexual tension in which Dominic wasn't aware how he'd done it, but his burger was gone and so were most of his fries.

The waiter cleared their dishes. "Dessert?" he asked, plates stacked along his arm.

"I couldn't fit another thing in," Erin said, then tossed a glance at Craig. "At least not dessert."

Damn. She was daring, flirting outright in front of their waiter. Dominic didn't have a chance to feel even a spark of jealousy that he was on the other side of the table. He didn't have a chance to think. There was just the thrum of his blood, the ache of his erection, and Erin's heat arcing across to him beneath the table. She was his sex object, the fantasy woman that drove him wild, and the images in his mind were crazy, taboo, exciting, dirty, nasty, and enthralling.

"I could use a glass of wine." She tipped her chin and stroked a finger down the smooth column of her throat. "I'm parched." She managed to make everything she did and everything she said sensual, sexual.

Christ, this was what he'd dreamed of when he'd told her tales over hot phone sex. "I'll get something from the snack bar." It was the cue to invite Craig to join their party in the panoramic car.

Maybe they could convince him to get off in Reno after all.

The waiter brought two checks, laid one in front of Dominic, the other next to Craig. Dominic tossed his credit card on top of his bill, but Craig merely signed.

"Sleeper car," he said when they both looked at him.

Holy shit. The kid had a goddamn bedroom on the train.

Suddenly, the possibilities were endless.

ERIN'S HEART STOPPED MIDBEAT. HE WAS IN THE SLEEPING CAR. HE had a private room.

He had a bed. Oh my God.

Dominic gazed at her, a slight tilt to his lips, and she knew she wore that squirrel-in-the-road look.

Craig shifted his leg against hers. "I've got some wine in my cabin. If you like chardonnay. The accommodations are pretty nice." He smiled widely as if he'd trapped a fly in his web.

She blinked rapidly. Okay, back up, breathe. She'd flirted. He'd flirted back. That didn't mean she had to sleep with him just because they had wine in his cabin.

Then again . . . her heart beat faster, and her skin flushed.

Dominic smiled at her, all sweetness and light. "We should see it for the research value"—his eyes sparkled and she knew exactly what kind of *research* he was talking about—"in case you decide to set one of your stories on a train."

Bastard. She had to laugh at him; he was in hog heaven. She'd done this to herself, flirting, sexual innuendos, allowing Craig to put his hand on her thigh, and even covering it with her own, giving him a squeeze of encouragement.

Erin, you're an idiot.

But she'd enjoyed the flirting. And she was wet between the legs, turned on by it all. So what if they went to his compartment? She could still say no. Maybe sex wasn't even his intention.

Duh. She couldn't be that stupid. Of course it was. And she'd egged him on.

Craig stood, picked up his book. "I'm in the last compartment in the first car when you leave the dining room." He pointed to an older woman in a white blouse and navy slacks standing sentinel at the sliding door to the sleeper cars as if she were keeping the unwashed masses from entering the citadel. "I'll let the porter know you might be coming through." Not *will*, but *might*. "Thanks for letting me join you for lunch. The goulash was a great recommendation."

He left. She appreciated his politeness and the fact that he didn't push too hard. All he'd done was invite them.

"It's just a glass of wine," she told Dominic, toying with her cup, the coffee now cold. "No big deal."

"He specifically reserved lunch in order to sit with you." Dominic signed the credit card slip the waiter had just brought.

"That was a coincidence." But the thought had already occurred to her.

He shook his head slowly. "No. Before they opened the dining car for lunch, there was announcement that all sleeper-car passengers were given first seating. He wasn't going to eat lunch in here." Dominic smiled until it hit his eyes. "He came for you."

She shrugged. "All right, so it wasn't *all* coincidence."

"It's just a glass of wine," he echoed her, then lowered his voice to a slow, seductive whisper. "No big deal."

She pointed her finger at him. "Don't push."

He held her gaze across the table for a long moment. "I don't have to because I know you want it."

Did she want it? What about tomorrow when it was over? Could their marriage really survive something like this? Maybe their ability to do it meant their marriage was over anyway. It might have been over the moment they lost Jay, and they just hadn't figured it out yet.

Maybe it didn't matter anymore.

"Let's get our stuff," she said. "I don't want to leave my bag in the panoramic car." She'd see how far Dominic let it go before he stopped her.

If he stopped her.

30

CRAIG MILLER HELD UP A WINE BOTTLE. IT WAS A VERY GOOD LABEL. "I snagged some real wineglasses from the galley." His face lit with an endearingly boyish smile as he poured.

Erin stood on the threshold of his compartment. She thought of Shane. He'd seen her naked, watched her masturbate, sat next to her as Dominic took her. He was a known quantity. But this man she would never have to see again. He wouldn't surprise her in coffeehouses, wouldn't pop up in other areas of her life. He was safe. He was attractive. And this was what Dominic wanted.

So, with her husband in the aisle behind her, she adjusted her limits, and stepped fully into the sleeper. Fuck everything else. She was going to have fun no matter how it ended.

"Wow, this is pretty cool. Thank you." She took the wine Craig offered—it tasted expensive, too—and gazed around the compact room. On the left, the lower bunk was neatly made up, the head of the bed by the door, indicated by the pillow. Above, the closed upper bunk slanted out slightly from the wall, the release handle in the center.

"The bed can be folded up into seats, but since I'm alone and there's another chair over there"—Craig pointed to a single seat in the corner—"I just left the bed down."

"You're in the lap of luxury." She dropped her carryall down by the window seat and did a one-eighty, noting the sink and mirror and a door that read TOILET and SHOWER in small lettering.

Dominic remained just inside the compartment's opening. "We should have gotten one of these, sweetie," she told him.

"It's only a seven-hour trip to Reno." He took the wine Craig had poured. "Thanks."

Erin slid onto the corner of the bed by the window, pushing the curtain back to gaze out. "Look, there's a ski lift." The chairs were full despite the snow flurries, the riders bundled up, skis dangling in the air. "I wonder which resort that is."

Before either of them could answer, if they even knew, an announcer came over the PA to say they were about to enter the oldest, longest tunnel still existing over the mountain pass. Suddenly plunged into darkness, the compartment door closed with a discernible click over the whoosh of the train. She was alone with them.

It gave her the oddest sense of power.

Like the letter in her desk at DKG. She could say yes. Or she could say no. Thumbs up or thumbs down. The power of the emperor in the gladiator ring. She was in charge, and these two men would do what she said. There was awesome control in that. Just as there was a weird sense of power in knowing she could dial the number in that letter and tell the CEO of WEU that he could take her company off her hands, lock, stock, and barrel.

She didn't think Dominic would even object. And he wouldn't object to anything she did in this cabin.

Her eyes adjusted to the light from a row of thimble-size bulbs running along the outer edges of the ceiling. Dominic was a tall shadow by the door. A sentinel. A protector. A symbol of her freedom from restraint.

She fluttered her eyelashes at Craig and patted the bed beside her. "Sit."

Craig shoved the half-empty wine bottle into an ice bucket beside the sink and sat. She hadn't given him a choice of which seat to take.

She hadn't given Dominic a choice either. He took the single seat across from her.

The train burst into light, and they were once again surrounded by the overcast sky and evergreens laced with snow. She started to tuck her feet beneath her. "Do you mind if I take off my boots so I can put my feet on your bed?"

Craig shook his head. She pulled off her jacket, tossed it at Dominic as if she were doing a striptease, then toed off her boots. "So," she said, "how far are you traveling?" She'd assumed when Craig said he was going a little farther than Reno that he'd meant within the next couple of stops like Elko or Winnemucca, but obviously he was riding the train overnight.

"Denver. I have a book signing."

She gaped. "That's three days of travel time."

"It's part of a conference, then I'm doing some local signings." He shrugged. "And I don't fly."

"Why not?"

"Remember that flight into SFO that dropped ten thousand feet?"

"Yeah. Everyone was okay except for bumps and bruises."

"I was on it."

She puffed out an amazed breath. "You're kidding."

"It lasted about ninety seconds. Do you know how long ninety seconds is?" He paused, letting her imagine. "I've never gotten on another a plane."

Ninety seconds that could alter a life. How quickly things could change. How utterly. She looked at Dominic. He was staring at her, waiting, not a muscle moving, not even a breath. Ninety seconds could lead you to a stranger's room while your husband waited with bated breath for you to do something kinky and taboo.

She knew then that she was going to do it.

"WHY'D YOU GET SUCH A BIG CABIN?" ERIN ASKED, CURLING COMfortably in her corner of the bed. She looked like a sleek cat. Dominic was dying to hear that sweet, sexy purr of hers.

"I don't share my shower." Craig grinned. The guy had a wickedly hot grin Dominic knew had Erin's panties wet and warm. "At least not with unknown people in there before me." Then he swept a hand out. "I can write in here undisturbed." He stuck a thumb over his shoulder. "You close the door on one of those two-person cabins and it's claustrophobic."

"Yet you were up in the panoramic car."

He gazed at her a long moment, then smiled. "I liked the view better up there."

She blushed, realizing Craig was talking about her, and Dominic knew she was pleased.

"In here," Craig went on, "I've got room to entertain."

Christ, this was better than anything Dominic could have dreamed up. A good-looking man ten years younger, curtains open, the white world rushing by outside, and Erin. She was chatty, asking and answering questions. It wasn't like her, not the usual nervous chatter she made in crowds and with strangers, but comfortable, easy, probing. She'd once told him that her mother said it was rude to be nosy; you should let people volunteer what they wanted instead of prying. He didn't agree, but it had been standard operating procedure for Erin. Yet now, she pestered Craig about his writing, how he'd started, where he was from, how big his family was, if he had a girlfriend.

It was fascinating, like a fly on the wall, watching a woman he didn't know. He let them talk, said nothing beyond the occasional murmur when she turned to him. Sometimes it was with shock in her eyes, as if she'd forgotten he was there.

"Tell me about your research?" The kid wasn't even trying to be sly. He was opening the door to sex, and they all knew it.

This time when Erin looked at him, there was complete awareness. Dominic gave her an imperceptible nod, the hairs on his arms suddenly on alert. What would she say now? How much would she reveal? His breath became shallow with anticipation, as if he'd miss something essential if he breathed too loudly.

"My last story took place at a nudist colony."

Craig laughed. "So you had to find out if nudist colonies really exist."

She nodded, then flashed a sexy smile that wormed inside Dominic. A flush zipped across his skin.

"Of course." She dropped her voice to that seductive note he was getting used to. "And they're very real."

"What did your characters do in this nudist colony?"

"A foursome. I wanted to explore the whole foursome dynamic," she said as if she were a real writer.

"That must be an interesting story." Craig raised a brow. "You really have to tell me your pseudonym."

He'd somehow moved closer, shifting, one knee pulled up carelessly next to hers, within a hairsbreadth of touching, an electric current arcing between them as she told him different scenarios she'd written about; flirting with men in a bar with her husband by her side, watching people at sex parties, masturbation, threesomes with two men. His skin a ruddier shade, breath faster, she commanded Craig's attention. The man couldn't tear his gaze away from her. Dominic felt the same sizzle of electricity along his own skin.

He experienced an uncanny sense of being outside himself, as if he were sitting in a bar observing a hot chick he'd never seen before, watching her work her wiles, picking up the most desirable guy in the place. It was sexy, fascinating, as erotic as the stories she spun for Craig.

For the first time, Craig spared a single glance for Dominic before turning back to Erin. Then he rested his hand on his knee, his fingertip brushing hers. The first touch in front of the husband, no table obscuring the view. "So what's the premise for your WIP?" he asked as if he didn't have his hand in plain sight on Dominic's wife.

Jesus, the anticipation was combustible.

Erin tipped her head, a tiny flash of confusion creasing her brow. "WIP?"

WIP was an inventory term to her, an unfinished gauge sitting on her tech's workbench, not a writer's incomplete manuscript. That wasn't how she thought.

"I choose the premise," Dominic said.

Craig gave him a long look. "That's an interesting way of doing it."

"On old writer's trick for stepping outside yourself," he improvised.

"And what did you pick for Erin this time?"

Dominic stared him down. "A voyeur watching another man take his wife."

Even the train seemed to hold its breath for a long moment, silent as if it were coasting on air, then the sounds returned.

Craig cocked his head, his eyes a dark brown fastened on Erin. "And I'm the research material?"

Dominic leveled a steady look on Erin. If she wanted to stop it, all she had to do was speak for herself. She didn't. So he said everything for her. "You most certainly are."

Craig's gaze flickered between them. "Are you two really married?"

Dominic smiled, pinning Craig with a look. "Yeah."

"Have you done this before?" Craig had no illusions now. This was real, not a premise.

"You're the first."

Craig's eyes bore the keen interest of a writer, a journalist, a scientist needing to figure out the cosmos. "How can you actually want to watch your wife with some other guy?"

Dominic felt Erin's scrutiny, the air suddenly crackling with intensity. He couldn't remember if she'd asked as directly as Craig. He thought of all the reasons Craig couldn't possibly know, about Jay, about forcing Erin to see him again as a man, as her husband, about sex being their only connection, and the odd logic of this whole thing being about *them*, not the man who was fucking her. All the things he wasn't sure he could explain even to himself.

He could say his brain was wired differently, which he believed was true, but it was also the flippant answer one man would give another. While that was good enough for Craig, it wasn't good enough for Erin.

"Because she's the most beautiful woman I've ever known and I want to see her pleasure. There's the excitement of the first sex session with someone new, someone attractive and desirable. It's like reliving something we had years ago. And it's something we can share together later."

Erin shifted on the edge of the bunk, pulled her legs closer to herself, and he knew he could lose her this way, that even as he pushed her to see him, to connect with him, to share with him, he risked pushing her further away rather than dragging her closer. Yet he wanted this with her, no one else. With another woman, it would be like watching porn. He wanted to feel it with her, share it, come back to it again in those dark hours past midnight when she usually shut him out with silence.

"That's all very nice," Craig said, "but man is inherently territorial. He doesn't share what's his." The guy was a writer, all right, looking for the motivation in everything.

"I'm not territorial."

Craig snorted. "Everyone's territorial. What if I'm better than you? What if I make her hotter, make her come harder, longer, make her scream my name instead of yours? What then?"

Craig really was a boy. He had no clue how utterly fucking hot it was for Dominic that his wife was another man's fantasy. Craig's younger-man definition of marriage and love and sex had nothing to do with fifteen years together, tragedy tearing you apart, loss, real life, growing up together, living in each other's pockets, at work, at home, things that couldn't be found in a chance meeting on a train.

But did Erin know? Or did she see only the tragedy that had destroyed them, feel only the pain? Would he lose her to something that was merely physical?

He willed her to meet his eyes. When she did, he spoke only to her. "It's about Erin's pleasure, not your prowess or mine."

"But wouldn't it make you totally crazy?" Craig pushed.

"Yes, it'll make me crazy," he agreed. "That's part of the emotion, making it hotter, making me *feel* deeper. And that's why I'd love it." He stopped short of saying he loved her. He needed her to feel the emotion without the words, to know it was there, unspoken and waiting for her.

"Excuse me," Erin broke in, turning both their heads at the same time, "but maybe you should both shut up and let me be the judge." Then she curled her fingers in the open collar of Craig's shirt and yanked him close. "Put your money where your mouth is." Then she smiled, as sexy siren as they come. "Or maybe you should put your mouth where it'll prove your point."

Holy shit. They were in for a hell of a ride.

31

"YOU SHOULD START WITH MY BREASTS," ERIN SAID SOFTLY, HOLD-
ing Craig's deep brown gaze. Then she let her eyes slide to Dominic. "Tell him what I like, Dominic."

Dominic rose from the seat opposite, took a mesmerized step
closer. "Pinch her nipples. Hard."

Equally enthralled, Craig raised a hand, then tweaked her nipple through her T-shirt. Heat zapped from her breast to her clit.
Her head falling back, eyes shut, Erin moaned. She was wet. Though
it was only verbal and oh so diplomatic, they'd fought over her
like rams. That's how sophisticated men waged a war, a battle
of words and wills, not horns.

Because she's the most beautiful woman I've ever known. That's
when Dominic truly won her over.

She had no intention of letting him stand back to watch. If a
woman had two men competing for her, she would damn well
use them both.

She rose up on her knees, legs spread for balance, and putting
a hand to the back of Craig's neck, she held him to her breast.
"Suck me," she ordered. "Lick me."

He bit her right through her T-shirt and bra. She gasped, feeling the zing straight down to her pussy. Then she crooked her finger at Dominic. "Come here."

Kicking aside her boots on the floor, he leaned over her, bracing a hand on the lip of the closed upper bunk as the train swayed and rolled. "I can smell you, you're so fucking wet."

She reveled in the heat of his eyes and the flush of need along his cheekbones. "Tell him what I want," she murmured. He would know. In sex, he knew everything about her. It was everywhere else that he didn't have a clue.

"Stroke her pussy through her jeans," he ordered Craig.

Ah, the perfect thing. As he played her nipple with mouth and tongue, Craig put his hand between her legs, running two fingers along the seam of her jeans with precision pressure. Her body liquefied. The train rocked her gently. She left the next step to Dominic. He would be her choreographer.

Even as Craig licked, sucked, and stroked, Dominic cupped the back of her head and covered her lips. He tasted of the mint that came with the dining check. He tasted of desire.

Her body started the rocky climb to orgasm. She clenched and unclenched her butt cheeks, doubling Craig's action between her legs with her own movements.

Then Dominic backed off, his eyes glittering like obsidian in sunlight. "Not yet." He'd known how close she was. "Take off her shirt."

Craig yanked the material from her jeans, shoving his fingers beneath, sliding slowly up her torso, then dashing the T-shirt over her head. As her hair fluttered down over her shoulders and back, he buried his face between her breasts, his breath heating her skin.

Dominic cupped her nape once more. "Now the bra," he demanded, as if he had a drone to do his bidding.

When her breasts were free, Craig took her nipple in his mouth again.

"Beg me to pinch your other nipple." Dominic's words were so low she had to read his lips at the same time.

"Please, Dominic. Pinch me hard. Make me moan."

He held her gaze as he possessed her between thumb and forefinger. She thought she'd die caught between pleasure and pain, the opposing sensations carrying her higher than each could separately. She felt her moan only as a throaty purr.

Dominic had been right. There was something tenfold with two men. She dropped her gaze from Dominic's blazing eyes to the blackness of Craig's hair against her breasts.

"I want his touch on your pussy," Dominic demanded. "No clothes."

"Yes, God, yes."

Fisting his fingers in Craig's hair, Dominic pulled his head back. His eyes were dazed, as if he'd forgotten the challenge he'd issued Dominic about who would be better. That he'd lost himself in her body, her breasts, and her taste was even hotter, sexier than the challenge itself.

"Remove her jeans and panties." The command in Dominic's voice thrummed through her. They'd had so many different kinds of sex in the past month, he in charge, she on top, both of them lost in the sounds and sight of sex and bubbling water. This was different yet again, the two of them vanquishing Craig.

"Fuck, yeah," Craig said, fumbling with her belt, tearing at the button, yanking on the zipper. His eagerness was unbearably exciting.

Then he grabbed the top of her jeans, tugging them over her hips, the force pulling her down onto her back. When he tossed the clothing aside, he was between her naked thighs and Dominic was on his knees beside her.

"Make her come hard." Dominic pierced Craig with his gaze. "Just like you advertised, harder and better than she's ever come in her life."

Craig's eyes glittered with male triumph. "She'll be begging for seconds and thirds." Then he cupped her butt in big, hot hands and put his mouth to her.

"Oh God." Her body involuntarily bucked, strained closer, begged for more. No other man had touched her, tasted her, or taken her in seventeen years. She arched her head back into the bunk's stiff mattress, driven by sensation.

It was utterly terrifying, and it was so good, oh God, so fucking good. But it wasn't Dominic, Jesus, it wasn't her husband. She writhed against the unfamiliar tongue, the newness of another's style, texture, and feel between her legs. When he sucked hard on her clit, she couldn't feel it, but when he circled and licked, she was close to madness.

She opened her eyes, breath puffing from her parted lips, and Dominic's features were stark, avid, greedy, his eyes stormy. He fisted his hand in her hair just as he had with Craig and slammed his mouth onto hers. His taste exploded against her tongue, his scent invading her head. He licked, sucked, took, just as Craig did between her legs.

She was taken over, mauled, crushed, and the orgasm was simply there, roaring through her without preamble. She screamed into Dominic's mouth. Her body pitched and rolled with it.

And his voice was everywhere. "How good? Better than me?"

"Fuck," was all she could manage. What was she supposed to say? What did he want to hear? Craig's hands tensed on her ass, then he blew a warm breath on her still quaking flesh.

What the hell did she care what they wanted? This was about her, all her, the body they had to please, the woman they needed to fight over, to win over.

She pitted them against each other. "Yeah, he's way better than you, sweetie."

CRAIG PUNCHED THE AIR. "YES."

Fuck. Dominic didn't know what he wanted or expected. His heart beat hard, fast, his dick throbbed with need. He'd felt her go off, and a thrill raced through his blood just as a warning bell rang in his brain.

Sex, love, and connection. What if she really couldn't separate them all? What if she actually found connection, and it wasn't with him?

He'd thought to enjoy and get off, go crazy and love it. It was all of those things. But it was more; it was worse. It was frightening.

"My turn," he whispered to her, hoping he masked the strain in his voice. He knew her body, her buttons, her likes, her needs. But he wasn't new, he wasn't different; he was the same thing she'd had over and over since before they were married.

Craig crawled from between her legs with the gleam of victory in his eyes. "She should suck me while you're licking her, and we can compare that way, too."

"Go stroke yourself," Dominic growled.

Erin stretched sinuously on the bed, her skin flushed, her nipples a taut, delicious red, her pussy glistening. His need choked him.

She smiled at him, and he hated the smile. "I want to suck him."

He knew it was punishment. He wasn't sure for which crime. Yet his heart rolled in his chest. It had been so fucking hot seeing another man between her legs, feeling her body quiver with the lick of another tongue, taking the cries of orgasm into his mouth, holding her as she was racked with climax. Fuck yes, he wanted to see another cock in her mouth, to watch her suck and know exactly how it felt to be Miller.

Punishment or not, he would have his fantasy. So he took his rightful place between her legs and inhaled the sweetness of her pussy as Craig popped his button fly.

Dominic eased two fingers inside her as the kid shoved down his jeans and briefs, and his cock sprang free.

"Oh my," she murmured, then glanced down between her legs to gauge Dominic's reaction.

Craig was decently proportioned, but he wasn't bigger. "Suck him," Dominic urged, stroking inside her, riding her G-spot.

Craig kicked off his shoes and shucked his jeans, and Dominic's heart flamed out as he watched another man's flesh slide between her lips. First the plum-colored crown, then she short-stroked him with her mouth for several beats before finally taking the hard, thick flesh deep.

Craig groaned. Knees bent, his thigh muscles bunched and strained as she sucked.

Christ yes, it was everything Dominic had imagined and more. He could feel the heat of her mouth as if it were on him, the suction, the ache and need in his balls. She was so goddamn good at it. They'd shared oral-only nights, mixing up their sex life. Sometimes hands only, sometimes a long, hard fuck.

Now he would always have this, the sight of her lips wrapped around Craig Miller's cock. The kid was as clean-shaven down below as on his face. He wondered how the smoothness of his balls felt against her lips.

Then Craig leaned over, laid a knee on the bunk beside her and cupped her head, steadying her as he forced his cock deeper.

Dominic heard her moan amid the moist sounds of the blow job.

He admitted to competing for her on a purely sexual level, like wild animals fighting to prove they were the better choice. He bent to her clit. She loved the slow ride of her G-spot as he circled the hard, plump button. She didn't need her clit sucked; she craved friction. Because she was his, he knew another secret. She wouldn't come while she was sucking cock. He could build her higher and higher, but in the sixty-nine position, she always had to back off before she came. The advantage was his. He would be able to lick her longer, keep her on the edge longer, and her climax would be harder because of it.

Her spicy flavor burst in his mouth. He licked and circled, teased her inside and out, all the while watching her suck, her eyes closed, one hand gripping Craig's bunched thigh.

With the snow and trees rushing by outside them, it was a sight like no other.

She bucked and writhed beneath his ministrations, her body hot and needy, quivering, her breath coming in little pants and moans as Craig drove his cock deep between her lips. Then she backed off suddenly, sucked Craig's balls into her mouth, and stroked his shaft in her fist.

"Fuck, wait, shit." The kid arched with a guttural groan. "I'm gonna come, don't make me come." He stumbled back.

Dominic hit her hard with his tongue and fingers, and her sweet juice filled his mouth. She bucked, cried, climaxed, and it was hard, momentous. He knew, he reveled, keeping at her until she squirmed away, her breath a series of gasps, her eyes wide, lips moist.

He didn't ask.

But she answered. "Better," she whispered.

A purely male pride surged through him. "Let him fuck you. Let him try to top me." He'd win; he fucking knew he would. He had to, because if he didn't . . .

He rose, his fingers trailing along one splayed leg, her skin smooth. Then he reached in his pocket and tossed a condom at the other man.

Erin eyed it. He'd come prepared. Just in case. Though he could only have dreamed he'd find what he wanted sitting in the same train car with them.

"Put it on," he ordered the kid. "I'll give you first crack at proving who's better."

Naked and not giving a damn, Craig raised a brow at him. "I think she was pandering to your ego about who gave her the best."

He glanced down. Erin hadn't moved, one leg bent at the knee, her pussy plump, wet, gorgeous, her nipples hard, her lips glistening, one arm above her head like an artist's embodiment of beauty. She was his sexy, sultry fantasy woman.

"She's never pandered to me," he said, gazing down at her. "She doesn't have to." Then he stripped off his clothing.

Looking at him, Erin purred. He didn't believe he'd ever been this hard, this aching, or this impressive.

He would enjoy winning.

32

ORGASMS RAISED TO THE POWER OF TWO LEFT HER LANGUOROUS but not sated. A month ago, she couldn't have imagined herself taking two men. All right, she'd thought about it. Being married to a man with a rich imagination and as sexually charged as Dominic, of course, she had. He'd enticed her with it.

She'd just never believed they'd go this far. It was a hot fantasy. After they lost Jay, there was no more sex talk, only desperate fucking when the hour was already past midnight.

Until some switch inside Dominic had suddenly flipped. He'd made her want it, too. He'd made her revel in having that hard young cock in her mouth as he lay between her legs and shot her to orgasm.

I'll give you first crack. His words should have pissed her off, as if she were his possession, something he could give away. Yet she loved the male posturing, the need to prove who was more virile. It was all about wanting her, vying for her.

She rolled up, curled her legs beneath her, then rose to her knees on the bunk. Craig unfurled the condom along his length. "I want to ride him," she told Dominic, touching the tip of his cock; her husband was hard, magnificent. "And I want to suck you while I'm doing it."

His nostrils flared, the stallion ready for mating.

Then she stood and pushed Craig back into the single seat on the opposite side of the compartment. Outside, the snow had given way to red earth, rocky outcroppings, fewer trees, and more scrub, the mountains behind them now as they followed the Truckee River.

She climbed aboard Craig, fitting her bent legs along his sides, bracing herself with one hand on his shoulder as she rose above his cock, teasing him with the closeness of her pussy. His eyes burned. "Then you're going to watch me fuck my husband," she told him.

He took hold of his own cock, thrusting up slightly to stroke her pussy with the tip. "You'll be too worn out."

Dominic slipped into the space between the seat and sink, anchoring his fingers in her hair. "She wants two men. Would you deny her that?"

Erin didn't know what she'd started out wanting. She only knew she was caught up in the touch of bare skin, the scent of pre-come, the salt of it still on her tongue, and two men desiring her.

Craig slipped an arm across the small of her back and jerked her down. She gasped at the delightful intrusion. "Oh God, Dominic." The words slipped out, because, yes, it was good. Another cock, another sexy man. She tipped her head back to meet Dominic's hooded gaze, a flush racing through her whole body. She licked her lips, glanced down to see her pussy pressed against the young man, his cock deep. He was thick, he was hard, he was long, but the fit was different, less of a stretch. Yet she could feel him pulse inside her. She couldn't always feel Dominic.

"Let me see more," Dominic said, his words a mere breath. "Let me see him fuck you."

She was his object, his fantasy, and, yes, she savored that. She reveled in what he claimed was her beauty. Leaning back, hands on Craig's thighs to brace herself, she began to rock.

"Jesus, that's so fucking hot." Dominic twirled and tangled his fingers in her hair. She saw what he saw, her pussy lips parted, her clit burgeoning, and that thick cock between her plump pink folds.

"Oh God, he feels good." Her body heated as she took him, forcing him to long, slow strokes over her G-spot. Craig became the object, the tool to fuel their needs.

Dominic licked his index finger and put it to her clit, caressing her with the give and take of her own body. She forgot to suck his cock. She simply closed her eyes and rode for the sheer physical sensation of it.

"Holy hell." She heard the catch in Craig's voice as she squeezed him inside her, flexing her muscles. "She's doing something to me. Christ."

"She's hot," Dominic murmured. "She'll make you crazy."

She shuddered with the friction inside and the sizzle of Dominic's touch on her clit. Craig thrust deeper, his hips surging, taking more, forcing more. She became nothing more than a body, fucking, needing, the pressure building, shooting out, spiraling back, all heat, all wet. Someone chanted Dominic's name, and she knew it was her, but the voice came from so far away.

She started to come and Dominic held her in place, stroked her as that lovely, delicious cock plunged, hard, her body squeezing, quaking. She cried out with the intensity, the pleasure, and she fell over the edge when his climax throbbed deep inside.

"Fuck. She's milking me." Craig's voice was thick, guttural. "Holy mother."

Her cries mingled with his. Then Dominic's hands were under her armpits, hauling her off, damn near tossing her down on her knees in front of the bunk, and he thrust into her from behind. This time she screamed, long, loud, the sensations going on and on until she felt tears on her cheeks, gumming her eyelids together, and still she came.

Her hands in fists, she held on to the bunk and let him take her, his cock slightly thicker, filling her in a way the stranger never could. She heard Dominic shout, couldn't make out the words, could only feel the hot spurt of his come inside her, her body taking his essence.

Then he laid her flat on her back on the cabin floor. She heard the snap of fingers by her ear, his voice demanding, "Lick her now, lick my come out of her, make her climax again."

Craig didn't need another invitation. She lay with her head in Dominic's lap and Craig between her legs, lapping her husband's come from her pussy. It was the most intensely erotic, taboo, dirty thing she'd ever done in her life.

This time when she came, she didn't know whose name she cried out. It might even have been her own.

ERIN STOPPED IN THE AISLE OUTSIDE A CLOSED COMPARTMENT.

"What are you doing?" Dominic paused, waiting for her.

She leaned slightly toward the door. "I want to see if you can hear anything inside?"

"Worried someone might have heard you screaming?" Dominic felt particularly pleased with himself. It had been better than hot. She'd been wild; they both had.

She made a face. "No. There's too much train noise out here. Which means no one could have heard."

Her words confirmed she'd been worried; not while she was in the throes of climax, but after she'd put on her clothes. It hadn't taken long to come down off the high.

He intended to put her right back at the pinnacle by reliving the whole experience. He'd passed up that delight with Shane; he wouldn't let it go this time.

The dining car was empty of patrons as they passed through, the wait staff setting up for dinner. In the scenic car, all the seats and booths were taken.

"Damn," Erin muttered. "We'll have to go back to our own seats."

"We'll be fine. It's only a couple of hours to Reno." They'd pulled into the Truckee station while redressing in Craig Miller's compartment. The stop lasted five minutes at the most. As Reno passengers, they'd been assigned to the last car, and Dominic had snagged them two seats at the back so they could see out the rear door.

The best part, he could sit her by the window and lean close to whisper encouragement. He needed to know how she'd felt, what she'd been thinking, every step of the way.

The last car was sparsely occupied, most passengers having moved forward to the panoramic car, which had the snack bar on the lower level. Or they'd taken empty seats in the forward cars since it was hotter back here, the train's air circulation getting worse the farther back you went. Erin's T-shirt, though long-sleeved, was thin, and she would appreciate the warmth. Dominic herded her into their seats, throwing their stuff on the luggage rack overhead. They'd checked the suitcase they shared for the two-night trip.

She gazed out at the rushing torrent of the Truckee River as they passed an old line of water flumes no longer in use.

He raised her hand, kissed her knuckles. "That was fucking hot," he murmured, leaning in to smell her. The light fragrance of her arousal still clung to her as did the faint aroma of come. "How did you feel having that hard young cock in you?"

She smiled, still looking out the window. "You are so filthy. I can't believe you made me do all that."

He leaned down to kiss her shoulder. "You loved it."

She sighed. He watched her reflection in the window, but it was too distorted to read.

"Tell me how much you loved it." It was his whole reason for doing it, wanting her satisfaction, giving her the newness of first sex and the excitement of sex with a handsome stranger. It was so many fantasies all rolled into one.

"He was good," she finally said. "But you were better because you know what I like, how I like it, exactly where to touch me."

He'd let himself be pulled into competition and fallen down on the job. It could have been so much hotter for her if he'd kept up the banter, telling the kid how to touch, where, her G-spot. But Dominic had to admit he'd gotten off on the rivalry, too.

"You came hard, though." He needed to make sure of that.

She turned, cocked her head. "When you made him lick the come out of me, it was so nasty." Her eyes glazed a moment. "And somehow it was so wrong," she finished in a whisper.

Yet he knew she'd loved it. It had been a masterful, spur-of-the-moment decision.

"Why'd you tell him to do that?"

"Because it made me top dog." It debased Craig, and Dominic became all-powerful. It was the ultimate cuckold, to be forced to lick another man's come from a woman you'd just fucked. He didn't think he could explain it to her without making himself look bad. He had triumphed and humiliated.

Not that Craig had seemed to mind at all. So where was the harm in it?

It had been hot, powerful, and he'd staked a claim. Yet he also realized it was the first time since before they were married that he'd felt the need to compete for her on a sexual level.

"I'm sleepy," she said, pulling out the pillow she'd stuck in the seat pocket in front of her when they'd boarded. She stuffed it between her ear and the window and closed her eyes.

"Erin?"

She mumbled something, then she was gone. Truly asleep?

It didn't matter. As quick as that, she'd shut him down. He wasn't sure what he'd said wrong. Perhaps it was her own rising guilt about the taboo nature of what they'd done. You crave something, yet hate yourself for wanting it. You can get off on some kinky sexual act, yet sense the wrongness of it later. He wanted to talk and relive. She wanted to forget and pretend. She could ruin something amazing in less than fifteen minutes.

It was the story of their life. She didn't want to talk about something, and he simply rolled over in the bed, falling into the quiet the way she wanted him to. She wanted silent, emotionless sex, and he merely took off his clothes, laid down in the bed, and waited until she was ready. He was pathetic.

She was top dog in their bed, the all-powerful, leading him by his dick. That's why he'd needed to win in that sleeper car, why it had become about besting the kid rather than her pleasure. He never won with her. But he could win over that kid.

Dominic rose and slipped out of the seat. He'd tried to keep her by shutting up, by only saying what she wanted to hear when she wanted to hear it. Like a pussy-whipped wimp. He'd buried the truth to keep her happy, never telling her of his own guilt and fears, never crying in her arms because he couldn't forgive himself for letting Jay go that day, never letting her tell him how much she hated him for doing it, too.

This is what I did and I hate myself for it. Tell me you hate me, too, because I know you do. Let's get it over with.

Then he could have told her how he hated her for shutting him out, for blaming him without words, for changing, for stealing his memories of Jay because she wouldn't even talk about him anymore, ever.

For God's sake, let me say all these things. Then maybe we can find a way to forgive each other.

She never let him. She kept him trapped in his own guilt, scratching in the dark for a way out, any way out, reduced to begging for a touch.

That was what he could never forgive her for.

33

IN SILENCE, THEY WAITED FOR THEIR SUITCASE TO BE UNLOADED from the baggage car. The lights of the sleeping compartments illuminated the station platform. There was no snow on the ground in Reno, but it was freezing at a little after five, night having fully descended. Erin watched her breath puff in the cold air as she wrapped her jacket closer around her.

Dominic spotted the case and yanked it upright, then pulled out the handle. He rolled it away without saying a word to her. Erin had to skip to catch up. They entered the crowded elevator with the other passengers, then followed them off and headed out of the station like cattle. Dominic marched right past the cab stand.

"Aren't we getting a cab?"

He pointed as he reached the corner and punched the WALK button on the traffic light. Their hotel's sign glittered half a block down, close enough to walk.

Before she'd fallen asleep on the train, she'd felt him get up. When she woke, they were pulling into the station, and Dominic was wordlessly yanking their belongings from the overhead rack.

Why was he so angry? She'd had sex with another man just the way he'd wanted her to. He'd had a fantastic orgasm, too.

The light changed, and he started across the intersection, the suitcase bumping and rolling behind him.

She'd been tired, a little weirded out at what they'd done, and she was afraid someone had heard. Walking through the train cars to get back to their seats, she'd felt as if everyone was staring. Like the couple that comes out of the same bathroom on the plane and everyone knows they've just joined the mile-high club. Okay, *she'd* never seen anything like that, but it had to happen. Otherwise there wouldn't be a mile-high club. And well, she felt strange about having just fucked another man. About letting him lick her husband's come right out of her pussy. About *liking* that he did it and having yet another mammoth orgasm. But she'd had fun and she'd told Dominic so.

It wasn't enough for him. He'd wanted more; he'd wanted it all right then. They were so different. She needed time to process, come to terms with it, *handle* it so she didn't completely freak out later on. But he wanted it now. God, their timing was always so *off*.

She followed him through the casino to registration. Everything was flashing neon and indistinguishable noise, and though there were separate smoking sections, a haze permeated everything. The old-style slot machines with handles were gone, replaced with electronic ones, where all you did was push a button, but there were still flashing lights and bells and the sound of coins chinking everywhere.

At the reception desk, they had to wait five minutes for an available attendant, then Dominic tossed his credit card on the counter. He was polite, but not his usual friendly self. Dominic could talk anyone into anything, always getting extras, just because he was nice and chatty and good-natured. Tonight, he was Mr. Stone-Face.

Okay, in the room, she'd be ready to talk about it, to give him exactly what he wanted from her, to tell him that the whole episode was hot and sexy, that she'd do it again if he wanted her to.

Erin closed her eyes a moment as she waited a foot or so to his left and one pace behind. It had definitely been hot, exciting. If she tossed out all the shoulds and shouldn'ts and had-anybody-heards, it had been incredible.

She could feel Dominic's mouth on her, his fingers inside her, and all that sleek, hard flesh pumping her mouth. The salty taste of pre-come. Craig had smelled like soap, and the smooth feel of his balls had been amazing. She wanted Dominic to shave just like that.

Then the actual sex, first riding Craig, slowly over her G-spot until he couldn't take anymore, Dominic's fast hard fuck against the bunk, the differences in their textures, their scents, their tastes, the feel inside her. Finally, Dominic's touch on her as they'd watched Craig lapping at her pussy. Oh, yes, it had been out of this world.

"Are you coming?"

Dominic's voice jerked her out of the reverie. He was already walking toward the bank of elevators.

She'd done what he wanted. Fucked another man, sucked him, laid herself bare. She shuddered. God. She'd really done those things. *All* those things over the last few weeks. Total debauchery. Her breath seized in her chest as if she'd been living in a dream and suddenly found herself thrust back into the real world.

She'd done it *all* for him. Because he'd wanted her to. Because he'd sanctioned it. But, dammit, she never seemed to get it right, never gave him exactly what he needed. Why couldn't they get this right? Was it her never giving enough? Or him always expecting more than what she had.

The elevator dinged just as she reached him, and he entered the empty car without holding the door, forcing her to throw out her arm to catch it herself.

The tiny cubicle was so quiet, she could have shattered eardrums with a scream. On the fifth floor, he exited, glanced at the packet with the card keys and room number, then followed the signs. Halfway down a hall, he stuck the plastic in a lock and shoved the door open with his foot.

Through the open curtains, neon flashed across the darkness of the carpet and bedspread. Dominic punched on the overhead light. The room was just a room.

Then Erin saw herself in the mirror on the closet door. God, she hadn't even combed her hair back in place. Her lipstick was gone, her mascara smudged beneath her eyes. There was a light stain on her shirt right over her nipple.

Jesus, what had other people thought?

Dominic tossed the suitcase on the bed and unzipped it. Still without a word to her.

She couldn't stand it anymore. Turning, she threw up her hands. "Aren't you even going to speak to me?"

He looked up. "See how it feels to be shut out?"

"I did not shut you out. I've been trying to talk to you since we got off the train."

He gave her a look. They said women were so good at the *look*, but Dominic had it down. A weaker woman would have withered, but she was starting to get pissed off.

"You damn well know I'm not talking about the last fifteen minutes. I'm talking about the last year."

She didn't want to discuss the last year. "Let's talk about *now*," she ground out. "I did exactly what you said you wanted. I fucked him. You wanted to see it, and I did it." She marched to the bed, trying to be strong, and grabbed stuff out of the case, her cosmetics bag, pajamas, underwear.

"You wanted it, too, Erin. You had the best orgasms of your life." Carrying the sexy scarf dress he'd bought her at the resort, he hung it in the closet, stood staring at it for a long moment as if remembering everything they'd done in the hot tub. "You loved it, you know you did," he said softly. Then he glanced up at her. "But you want to blame me for making you do it because it's easier than admitting you wanted to."

She stomped past him in the small narrow hallway and dumped her vanity bag on the bathroom counter. "I've never blamed you for anything." But she *had* blamed him, not just for this. She swallowed, prickles of unease raising goose bumps along her arms. She wasn't going there with him, though, not now. "Look," she said, much more gently. "Let's not fight. It's New Year's Eve. We should try to have a good time."

He stood at the bathroom door, his face a dark glower. "We can't have a good time. We can only have highs followed by deep lows."

"That's not true." She took things out of the bag, laid them by the sink, her lotion, moisturizer, hair spray.

When she turned, he blocked her way out. "You blame me," he stated flatly.

She swallowed, gritted her teeth. "I don't blame you. I enjoyed what we did in Orlando, and with Shane, and on the train. Everything." She drew a deep breath, knowing it wasn't what he meant, but hoping he'd accept it. "But sometimes after doing a thing like that, you step back and actually look at yourself and wonder how the hell you could have done it. I just need to process this, that's all."

"That's not what I mean."

But she went on as if he hadn't interrupted, staring at all her personal sundries on the countertop. "I have to assimilate everything, get used to, accept it. That always takes me longer than it does you." She stopped long enough to suck in air, then jumped in again without giving him an opportunity to talk. "You're always ready to rehash and relive and analyze, but I need to be quiet for a while and think without being disturbed or pushed." She was rambling. Everything she said was true, but she was talking over what she knew he really needed, thinking the whole time, *I can't do this, I can't do this.*

She knew the things his guilt had done to him, the terrible ache. She understood how hard it was. His pain tore her apart. But she couldn't give him what he wanted. She hated herself for that, but she couldn't talk about it, couldn't think about it, let alone listen to his feelings.

"Don't you think I blame myself, too?" he said, his voice low, harsh, and full of . . . something she didn't dare think about. "That I wish I could do it all differently."

"It was fine," she answered as if he were talking about today. "I enjoyed it. I'm not saying we can't do anything like it again, and in fact," she rushed on, "I'm sure we will do it again."

"I shouldn't have let him go by himself."

Something let loose inside her so fast she couldn't control it. "Will you shut up?" she screamed at him, covering her ears.

But he grabbed her hands, pulled them down, held her. "It was my fault. I wanted to finish the gauge, get it out the door, I didn't have time, and his teacher said it was fine, they'd take him, they had plenty of other parent chaperones."

She jerked away, her boot catching an uneven edge of tile, and she went down hard on the toilet lid. "I'm not talking about this." All she could hear were the words *she'd* shouted at Jay. Not Dominic. Her.

He hunkered down in front of her. "I miss him, too, goddammit. And I want to talk about him. I need to talk about what happened."

"Stop it." She kicked out with a boot, hit his knee hard, sent him sprawling. "Just fucking stop it. He's gone. He's dead. He's not coming back, and talking about it won't change anything so just shut up." Her ears started to ring. "Shut up, shut up, shut up."

He braced his hands on the tile floor behind him. "No. He's my son. There isn't a day that goes by that I don't miss him so much my guts get twisted up. I'm so fucking tired of not being able to say his name or have his picture out or say how fucking sorry I am or much I miss him. He's dead, but you've stolen even his memory. I fucking hate that." A single drop of moisture leaked from his eye, rolling down his cheek, leaving a long wet track. "And I can't forgive myself if you never let me talk about it."

She did not cry; she would not cry. If she did, she'd never stop.

"Don't you see you're robbing yourself of his memories, too?"

She didn't deserve any good memories. But she knew there was one way to end this. "I forgive you. It wasn't your fault. I don't blame you."

He swiped a hand across his cheek, seemingly surprised when it came away wet. Then he settled a steady gaze on her. "Don't you fucking pander to me."

Her heart beat so loudly it drowned out every other sound. There was only his face. She didn't know that face. She didn't know that man. In that moment, she knew he hated her.

She rolled her lips between her teeth, held her breath. Yes, she'd blamed him for not taking care of Jay. If he'd taken care of their son the way he was supposed to, she would never have said those things, the last words she ever said to her son while he was still coherent enough to understand.

"Say it," he whispered. "Tell me you hate me, too."

"Why are you doing this?" The words hurt, barely making a sound as they passed her lips. Her temples pounded as if someone were driving a nail right through the soft tissue.

"Because I can't live like this anymore."

"I'm tired," she whispered. "I want to go to sleep."

He shook his head. "You can sleep after we talk."

She blinked. Her eyelashes stuck together for a moment. "No," she mouthed.

"Please," he begged.

If she talked, she could help him put an end to his misery. She could help him forgive himself. She'd known all along that he'd blamed himself, that he'd died the day Jay had, knowing he'd left their son alone with strangers, even if they'd been his teachers and his friends' parents. Dominic had made that decision, but in his place, she'd never been sure she wouldn't have done the same thing. It should all have been so easy, a school day trip, that was all, and Jay had been on other day trips, everything fine.

"Erin. We're dying here. Can't you see that?"

She knew what he needed. She wasn't strong enough to give it to him. She couldn't talk about it. Not ever. Without a word, she got up, stepped around him. And shut him out.

Their marriage had died a year ago. They just hadn't buried it yet.

HE COULDN'T MOVE FOR LONG SECONDS THAT TICKED INTO MINutes.

He'd bared his soul. She'd walked away.

His heart felt dead in his chest. His head pounded as if someone had tightened a vise around it. His cheeks were dry and cracked, his lips too brittle to speak with.

When he finally rose from the bathroom floor and stepped out into the room, he found her silhouetted against the dark, neon sky of Reno.

As if they weren't a part of him, his feet moved to the desk against the wall. His hand picked up the phone, dialed. "I need the first flight out to San Francisco."

She didn't turn, didn't say a fucking word to stop him.

It had taken him a year to get here. Now he'd finally given up.

34

ERIN DIDN'T KNOW HOW IT WAS POSSIBLE NOT TO SAY A WORD TO someone for over forty-eight hours, but it was. They'd silently repacked the few things they'd removed from the case, checked out, taken a cab to the airport, gotten on a plane, and flown home, all in silence.

She wasn't sure exactly when Dominic remembered that their car was in the Emeryville Amtrak parking lot, but it was somewhere between the time he'd booked their flights and when they'd signaled the cab at SFO. She hadn't thought about it until he told the driver to take them to Emeryville.

She didn't feel real. She didn't feel as if she were sitting next to him, reachable, touchable. Would he file for divorce on Monday? She didn't have enough emotion left inside her to know how she'd feel if he did.

She cleaned the house on Saturday, scrubbed toilets as if it were penance. She didn't even go to bed, staying in her office until long past midnight, long after he was asleep. Ditto for Sunday night.

"What do you do in here all the time?"

Torture herself. That's what she did. Dominic accused her of robbing herself of Jay's memory. But all her memories were right there on the computer, and she tortured herself with them every night when she couldn't sleep. And now she could torture herself with the fact that she'd stolen Dominic's memories, too. He was right about that, one more injustice she'd done him, one more thing to feel guilty for. If she could just *talk* to him the way he wanted, give him what he needed.

She touched the computer screen. "I'm so sorry, baby," she whispered to her son's photo, squeezing her eyes shut before a tear leaked out.

Monday came. Work came. She didn't care about that either. When she pushed through the front door of DKG and saw Bree in her office clicking away on the keyboard, her belly crimped. Another reminder of all her mistakes. She didn't consider apologizing again. After all, apologizing was only to assuage your own guilt, to force the other person to forgive you. It didn't actually make *them* feel better.

She should have asked how Bree's father was doing. How Bree herself was. But even the thought of doing that tightened something in Erin's chest, cutting off her breath.

Amid the chorus of "Happy New Year" and "Good morning" and "Hey, there" Erin opened the middle drawer of her desk. The WEU letter lay there. It still called to her. *Give us a jingle, and we'll buy you out of your misery.*

"Happy New Year, Bree." Rachel, next door, her voice cheerful after a week off. "You okay?" If Bree answered, Erin couldn't hear.

Erin closed the drawer ever so slowly, just in case her fingers jerked and she accidentally slammed it. Rachel's voice was the mirror of her guilt. She couldn't even find the guts to speak to Bree.

Just like she couldn't tell Dominic what she'd done even after he'd stripped himself bare for her. She could tell him she was sorry, but it wouldn't fix her inability to talk about Jay.

"Okay, hon, I'll check on you later," she heard Rachel say. Rachel would now come to her office. Erin steeled herself.

Sure enough, she was the next on Rachel's list. "Happy New Year, Erin." She wore a sweet smile and a new dress, a leopard print with a high waist and calf-length skirt.

Erin jumped on the new dress before Rachel could ask anything she didn't want to talk about. "That's snazzy." She pointed at Rachel's outfit, inserting a cheery note that felt totally alien. "New for Christmas?"

Rachel held the skirt out and twirled. "Isn't it great? My kids picked it out all by themselves."

"Wow! They've got great taste." The talk was easy, idle chit-chat. Erin could handle that.

"But the best part was that they got it at the Salvation Army. It was only four ninety-nine."

"You're kidding."

"I swear. They left the tags on to prove it."

Erin had been referring to the fact that Rachel's kids shopped at the Salvation Army for Christmas. But she'd made enough judgments recently, so all she said was, "Amazing."

"I've been trying to teach them about the value of a dollar, since their father just hands them money on a platter."

"That's a great lesson." There was something to admire in the fact that Rachel was more concerned about the lesson than the material thing.

"Well, I've got lots of stuff to catch up on, but let me know if there's anything you need."

Erin needed to know if Bree was okay, but if she wanted the answer, she'd have to find the nerve to ask for herself. "I'm fine for now, thanks."

"Find some courage," she muttered to herself after Rachel left.

Dammit, she would do this. She was so good at putting her feelings above others, avoiding anything that made her uncomfortable or brought up her own bad memories. Not this time. She owed it to Bree.

Erin stood up, straightened her jacket, girding herself, then she rounded her desk.

The girls were planted by the coffeemaker. The girls, that's how she thought of them, Yvonne, Rachel, and Bree, who'd left her office to follow the scent of fresh coffee as if it were brewed by the pied piper.

"Oh my God, Yvonne. That's so great." Rachel threw her arms around the older woman, hugged her tight.

Rachel was so . . . solid. A great mom, a good employee, a decent friend. Erin admired her, envied her.

"Did you hear?" Rachel said, suddenly seeing Erin and pulling her into the circle with just her voice.

Erin didn't used to feel like an outsider. DKG had been her home and everyone who worked there part of her extended family. Now, she was just the boss. She didn't know how to retrieve the sense of family.

Like Jay, it was gone forever.

"No, I didn't hear the news." She infused her voice with enthusiasm. "What?"

"Yvonne's going to be a grandma." Rachel gave her another quick hug.

Erin gulped. "Congratulations. That's great." She'd known the holidays would be bad, but *after* the holidays almost felt worse, probably because of what happened with Dominic in the hotel room. But she would not let Yvonne or any of them see it. "I'm so happy for you."

Yvonne beamed, eyes glittering with unshed tears. "My youngest daughter wrapped up a 'welcome baby' card in a box, and that was my Christmas present."

"Oh, that was the best present you could have had." Rachel's excitement knew no bounds.

Even Bree gave Yvonne a hug. "When's the baby due?"

"July."

Jay had been a July baby.

She saw the moment Yvonne remembered, the moment the sparkle in her eyes dimmed. Her gaze flashed to Erin as if she'd done something terrible, as if she'd personally made sure her grandchild would be born in July so that Erin could feel the punch of it.

"Oh, wouldn't it be fun if the baby was born on July fourth," Erin said, forcing a bubble of excitement into her words.

"Yes," Yvonne answered, then clapped her hands. "But let's get to work, girls. There's a ton of work to catch up on."

What was it that Rachel had said the day she drove Erin to the airport for the Orlando flight? That she knew she wasn't ever supposed to mention Jay or even sympathize. It wasn't just Dominic's memories Erin had stolen. It wasn't even her own. She'd taken them from everyone at DKG. She'd even managed to put a blot on Yvonne's happiness over her grandchild with her inability to face her guilt and pain.

Life had stopped for her so she'd made sure it didn't go on for anyone else. If only she'd let Dominic talk long ago. She felt sick. If only . . .

"Bree," she said as the girl headed back to her office with a fresh cup of coffee.

"I'm running the inventory revaluations now with the new standards." Bree tucked a fall of dark hair behind her ear. "I'll have the change calculated for you in couple of hours."

"Thank you." Erin took a deep breath. She could have let it go at that. She didn't. "How are you doing? How's your dad?" She could hear the loud beat of her heart in her ears over the sound of her own voice.

"Fine, just fine." Bree stared at Erin's throat instead of meeting her gaze.

Erin had used the stock phrase so many times herself when Dominic tried to get her to talk that she knew exactly what it meant. *Nothing* was fine. "Well, if you need anything, please come to me."

"Sure, Erin, thanks," Bree said to the carpet.

Erin touched her arm. A deep pain had blossomed in Bree's eyes when she looked up. "Bree, you *can* come to me. I spoke out of turn last week, and I want you to know that I believe in you. I'll help out in any way I can." It didn't make up for the tone of her accusations. "Let me know if and when you need time off, and we'll take care of everything. I'll support whatever you decide to do."

"Yeah. Thanks. But it's okay for now, Erin."

Erin had to let her go. She didn't feel better, but at least she'd found the courage to say something.

She stared across the room at the hallway leading to the engineering offices and the lab. Dominic had been in the shower when she left this morning. Now he was half an hour late. She was part terror over that, part glad for the reprieve.

It was one thing to face Bree and Yvonne. She wasn't ready for Dominic. She might never be ready for Dominic. And yet, he was the one she most owed an apology to. If only . . .

"Hey, Erin, come here." She was concentrating so hard, she jumped when Al suddenly appeared in the hallway.

"What?" That was all she could manage.

He smiled, waggled his eyebrows. "I think I've got it, but Dominic's not here yet, so I gotta show you or bust a seam." Then he disappeared.

She trailed him to Dominic's office to find him playing with the computer. He signaled her around to watch over his shoulder.

All she saw were listings of random numbers and letters, dates and times.

"Okay," he said, pointing. "See this user ID?"

"Yes." The seeming randomness coalesced into a recognizable name: ycolbert. He was looking at Yvonne's user name. Her stomach sank.

Then Dominic appeared in the doorway, and the bottom fell out of everything. His thick hair was dry, his jaw smooth with a fresh shave. Even standing behind his desk with Al, she could smell her shampoo on him. He always used whatever she had in the shower, yet this morning, the scent on him turned her inside out.

What had he been doing between his shower and arriving at work? Why was he late? Where had he been? She was afraid to ask.

He looked at her, his face expressionless, then spoke to Al. "What's up?"

"Dude, I have answers." Al pressed his lips into a flat line. "Actually, I have more questions, but it's all leading in the right direction." He tipped his head, glanced up at Erin, and, as if sensing something was off, added, "You weren't here so I was showing it to Erin."

"Fine. Now you can get me up to speed." Dominic moved around the desk so they were flanking Al in the chair.

Al filled him in. Dominic didn't say a word as he deciphered Yvonne's user name.

"Now most of her logons are coming from DKG's IP address." Al tapped the screen. "It's her work computer."

"Okay, I see that," Erin said.

"Here's her home computer. I verified the IP address." He sat back, bobbed his head. "And I did a cursory check of when she claims she logs on from home versus the data you see here. It checks, mostly when she's trying to get shipments out the door at a crunch time."

Why was he drawing this out? Her head was starting to ache. She'd already blown a gasket and accused Bree. She wasn't about to turn around and do the same thing to Yvonne.

"But see this?" He pointed to a completely different IP address, but didn't wait for anyone to answer him. "For the last six months, Yvonne's user ID has been logging on from this address the first week of every new fiscal month. It could be her using another computer somewhere . . ." He trailed off, shooting them both a dubious look that asked why Yvonne would bother with a third computer and only use it once a month.

Erin stared at the numbers and dates which were suddenly not so random at all. It wasn't the first day of the new month. It was the fourth. After Bree had compiled all the month-end reports. "But that means—"

"Yeah. It means someone's been logging on to your system once a month. They've been monitoring your cumulative sales figures. And your financials."

35

"HOW WOULD SOMEONE GET HER PASSWORD?" DOMINIC STARED AT the damning screen, sick, tired, and all the rest of it. He and Erin had barely spoken over the weekend, the house covered in a silent pall. And now this. "The system requires that it's changed every month."

"She could have a malware on her home computer that's tracking her keystrokes," Al offered up.

Erin shook her head, her finger to her lips. "If someone was going to track her keystrokes, they'd be better off stealing her credit card numbers or banking password." She narrowed her eyes at the monitor. "No, this is directed at us specifically."

She was all professional and studious, dressed in a black blazer, black slacks, and a white blouse. She didn't show a trace of what they'd done on the train. Nor a trace of any emotion for what he'd said to her in the hotel room. Nothing. Over the long weekend, he'd accepted that she was no longer capable of any real emotion.

It had died with Jay. Their marriage had died. The woman he'd loved was gone for good.

Al threw up his hands. "I've got a brilliant idea." He flashed a look between them as if they were dunces. "Let's ask her."

For a moment Dominic thought Al was referring to Erin. *Let's ask her if she's got any anything left for you, Dominic, or is it really all dead?*

He'd gotten the message loud and clear in Reno.

But of course, Al meant Yvonne. "I'm not going out there and accusing her," he said, his voice tight.

"We won't do that," Erin said so earnestly he wanted to break something. Why couldn't she be that earnest for him, for their life? "She's upbeat right now about her daughter's baby. I don't want to bring her down."

"I'll talk to her," Dominic said. He knew how to be diplomatic with his employees.

"We'll do it together," Erin answered.

He stared at her over Al's head. Together? Was he supposed to read something into that along with her steady gaze? They weren't together. They were nothing. His bitterness swamped him. "Fine, whatever. I'll do the talking."

When Al rose with him, Dominic pointed to the chair. "You stay here, and try to figure out the origin of that IP address. A name would be great." The main thing, though, was not making Yvonne feel they were ganging up on her.

She was in her office running her finger along a line she was reading on her computer screen. "Hey there, Dominic, Happy New Year." When she saw Erin right behind him, her welcoming smile froze. "What's up?"

Dominic struck a casual pose, leaning his hands on the back of the chair in front of Yvonne's desk. "You know we've been having this patent problem on the through-coat gauge, right?"

"Yeah, Dominic." Her eyes grew darker, wary.

Best way to handle it, get right to it, no questions, no accusations. "We've been wondering why the royalty they want to extort out of us so closely reflects our real sales numbers. Lo and behold, Al found a third IP address accessing the system through your user ID, and the only thing they were looking at was financial information." Once a user logged on, the system tracked all movement.

"It wasn't me," Yvonne said immediately, her tone harsh, defensive.

"We know that," Erin said just as quickly. "What we can't figure out is how they got your password. Any ideas?"

"I don't give my password to anyone." Yvonne crossed her arms beneath her ample bosom.

"We know that, too." Dominic pulled out the chair and sat. They were losing control of the situation. He leaned forward, put his elbows on his knees, clasped his hands, and looked at her over the top of his laced fingers. "But has anyone been in the office, a vendor or someone"—he shrugged, trying to put them on the same baffled level—"looking over your shoulder? It would have to be someone that comes by regularly. Because they've got to see it every time you change your password."

"People sit over there." Yvonne jabbed a finger at the chair he occupied. "Besides, Erin talks to the vendors, not me."

He glanced at Erin; she returned the look. They had a moment of silent communication that said they were fucking this up royally. He resented that he needed her, but he did.

Yvonne's office had only the one chair, so Erin leaned against the wall. "We're stumped, Yvonne. We need your help because someone's jerking us around and we don't know who."

We. They weren't a *we.* His bitterness grew, choking him.

Yvonne tipped her head, stared at her monitor for a long moment. Then she licked her lips and swallowed. "Here's the thing about my password," she said so softly he had to hunch forward to hear. "I don't change it."

Dominic sat back with jerk. "But the system prompts you to change every thirty days."

She pressed her lips together. "I know, but I was always for-getting it. The new password, I mean." She huffed out a sigh. "So after I changed it, I'd go back in and reset it again to the old password."

He stared at her.

"How long have you been doing that?" Erin asked.

Yvonne glanced from Erin to him and back again. "Almost since the beginning."

Jesus. They'd been using the system for two years. He didn't yell. He would *not* yell.

"Well, that was silly," Erin said mildly. Too mildly. She was as close to an explosion as he was. Yvonne had been with them from the start. She knew better than that. But he supposed she'd gotten complacent, comfortable. And negligent.

"I sure as hell hope you change your bank password more of-ten," he said grimly.

She remained silent, and Dominic scrubbed a hand down his face. "Jesus, Yvonne." He knew she didn't like taking the Lord's name in vain, but how could she be so unaware?

"I will from now on, Dominic, I swear it. I'll change the pass-word right now." She blinked, close to tears, he thought.

He wanted to be angry. It suited his mood. But he couldn't take it out on Yvonne. He couldn't even take it out on Erin. "All we can do is have Al keep working on the IP address and see if we can come up with something that way."

"I'm sorry, Dominic. I didn't think it was a big deal."

Yvonne's words stabbed him straight to the heart. He'd thought the same thing the day he let Jay go on that school trip. Getting slowly to his feet, he felt a hundred years old.

Outside Yvonne's door, the troops had scattered, keeping their heads low and out of the battle lines. Erin crossed the roundhouse, turning when he didn't follow her. "I have something to show you."

Whatever it was, he didn't want to see it. Yet he entered her office just as she pulled out the middle desk drawer. The sheet of paper she held out to him shook in her hand.

It took him a moment too long to read and understand, to assess the full impact, so she told him what it said. "WEU wants to buy us out."

He stared at her expressionless face, and something shot up from the deep pit of his anger, grief, guilt, and all the other stuff she wouldn't talk about. "You want to sell DKG?"

"That's not what I mean."

He knew what she fucking meant. She was done. It was over. She wanted out, away, anywhere without him. He folded the letter, shoved it in his back pocket. "Let's do it. Let's get the fuck out of this thing."

"Dominic, would you just listen—"

He cut her off. "I've listened enough." He turned. "You can come with me, or you can sit here and wait it out." He left without her.

He actually enjoyed that she ran after him, that she had trouble catching up. "But they didn't even name a price," she said as he slammed through the front door, the glass rattling in the heavy metal frame.

"I don't give a damn."

HE WOULDN'T LISTEN TO HER, NOT WHEN SHE TRIED TO POINT out that they didn't have an appointment, that Garland Brooks might not even be there, that they should strategize about what they would say.

Hands tight on the wheel, knuckles white, he ignored her.

Erin finally shut up. She'd only shown him the letter because it made WEU's campaign strategy very clear. Squeezing them for ridiculous royalties, threatening them with a lawsuit, it had been about eliminating the competition. DKG was stealing their market share; the solution, eliminate DKG. Weaken them with threats, hit them when cash was vulnerable, then offer to put them out of their misery by buying them. WEU could pocket their cash receipts the moment the sales contract was signed. Voilà, instant market share.

There was a part of her that wanted to say yes. *Let's just take it, let's get out.* She was so tired of fighting. But seeing the evidence of WEU's dirty tactics, the fact that they actually had someone steal Yvonne's password, she was suddenly as pissed as Dominic. They were on the same side, she'd tried to tell him, but he wouldn't listen. To him, they'd been on opposite sides since they'd lost Jay. And everything she said or, more aptly, didn't say, only cemented that.

She pushed back into the corner of her seat to watch him, the lines of his face tense, stark, his brows slashes of anger. They had done this to each other. It couldn't be undone. It had gone too far, the tear in the fabric of their lives irreparable.

There was one space left in the guest parking outside WEU's headquarters. Dominic rammed the gear into park. She had no clue what he was going to say to Brooks. In this mood, she didn't put it past him to start a fight, fists and all.

He shoved through the lobby door and marched to the black-and-chrome receptionist's desk. "Tell Garland Brooks that Dominic and Erin DeKnight are here to see him."

She was a pretty brunette, her eyes wide with apprehension as Dominic hit her with a glower. "Is he expecting you, sir?"

"Please"—his face was strained, the courtesy costing him— "let him know we want to speak to him."

Never taking her gaze off him, the brunette punched some numbers into her state-of-the-art switchboard equipped with Bluetooth. "Please tell Mr. Brooks that he has visitors in the lobby, Dominic and Erin DeKnight." She listened a moment. "Thank you. I'll let them know." She disconnected. "He's finishing up a meeting right now, but he'll be down in a few minutes if you'd like to wait." She pointed to a couple of black leather lobby chairs. "There's coffee."

"Thank you," Dominic said with tight politeness.

Erin smiled her thanks at the woman. The floor of the lobby was expensive marble shiny enough to see her reflection in, the leather furniture top quality, the feel of the place posh and world-class. And overextending the cash flow? WEU management obviously subscribed to the policy that in a cash crunch, you didn't stop spending, you just stretched out your payment terms. Or maybe accounts payable was so busy paying off the lobby remodel that they couldn't pay hardworking, small-fry vendors like Leon. The coffee service had everything imaginable, even an automatic espresso machine on a granite countertop, all of it top of the line.

She pressed the button for plain coffee to soothe Dominic's savage beast. She was actually surprised at his muttered *thank you* when he took the cup.

After settling in the chair next to him, she said, "We need to talk before Brooks gets here."

Dominic turned his head slowly, his gaze sliding to her. "You want to get rid of DKG, we'll get rid of it." He leveled her with a dark, hooded look.

She eyed the receptionist and dropped her voice. "That isn't why I showed you their letter. I wanted you to see how they were trying to make a move on us."

"Then why didn't you tell me about it when you got it?"

Okay, so he'd seen the date was from last year. "For the same reason you didn't tell me about the patent infringement when you first got *that* letter. We were supposed to be going away. I didn't want to spoil the fun."

His eyes were sharp, narrowed. "I didn't tell you about the trip I'd planned until the evening. *After* you must have gotten the letter."

Shit. Yes, she'd wanted to keep it to herself, think about it, hold it close as if it were a way out of her guilt and turmoil. Then, with everything they'd done, the hellish weekend, she'd forgotten about it until the moment Al showed them how their numbers were being stolen. It wasn't just Jay she'd stopped talking about; it was the business, their lives, everything.

Dominic gave her a small smile that never reached his eyes. He wasn't fooled. She'd told him so many lies, shut him out so many times, he no longer had faith in her. Why should he? She hadn't given him anything to have faith in. Not for a long time.

They sat in silence, except for the brunette's soft, polite tones as she took calls and the beat of shoes along the hallway off to the left.

"Hey, Denise, can you give this to the FedEx guy when he gets here?" A man's voice echoed across the lobby. A very familiar voice.

Erin knew it in a heartbeat. So did Dominic.

At the same moment, Reggie recognized them. Reggie, their ex-software engineer, the man who'd worked on the through-coat gauge, the one who'd helped Dominic research the patent.

What the hell was he doing at WEU?

36

"HEY, YOU GUYS, HOW ARE YOU?" REGGIE'S VOICE WAS TOO LOUD, falsely genial, and nervous. "It's been ages. How ya been? How's everyone at DKG? Wow, I really miss the old gang. You can't imagine how impersonal it is working at a big place like this." He flapped a hand in the general direction of the building's back end.

Oh yeah, real nervous. Dominic had known Reggie almost since they'd moved to California, fifteen years, and Reggie telegraphed jitters with his fast-talk, wide eyes, and the way he shifted foot to foot like a kid who had to go to the bathroom. Tall, gangly, with a thin nose, and a pocket protector, he was the archetypal nerdy engineer.

"I'm sure you know exactly how we've been, Reggie."

Reggie nodded, his head bobbing on his neck like one of those bobblehead dogs. "Man, it's been so busy around this place"—he waved his arm to demonstrate—"I haven't had time to poke my head out." He laughed tensely. "Like a t-turtle."

The brief stutter was a dead giveaway. Dominic smiled with the acrimony burning inside him. "Then let me tell you we've been doing great. Sales of our through-coat gauge have gone through the roof."

"Cool." Reggie's eye started to tick.

Dominic had been consumed with Erin, that she wanted to sell, she wanted out of DKG, out of their marriage. He hadn't stopped to consider the implications of the letter itself. Escalating everything at year-end, then a sweet little note saying, *oh, hey, we'll take your company in settlement, help you get out of the mess you got yourself into.* It was so convenient. His visit to Garland Brooks had played right into the scheme, making them think he was nervous. Brooks was still playing them, as evidenced by the wait in the lobby rather than inviting them to the inner sanctum. Mind games.

He'd *let* himself be played, and that made him all the more pissed at Reggie. "But you already knew how well the gauge has been doing." Dominic crossed his arms over his chest, smiled maliciously, like a predator ready to pounce. Beside him, Erin smiled, too, as if they were suddenly a team again. "Trying to get your profit sharing out of us any way you can, Reggie?"

Reggie's gaze flashed between them like a Ping-Pong ball. "What are you talking about, Dominic?"

Reggie had managed their software system, worked with the techs, added the user IDs. He knew how each module worked. He would know how to obtain the pertinent data. He probably knew that Yvonne circumvented the password change. Dominic didn't need to test the theory, he felt the rightness in his gut. "Are they paying you a bonus for our financial data, Reggie?"

"Dominic, I—"

Then Dominic laughed. "Holy shit. The royalty scam on the patent was *your* idea." He didn't even make it a question.

Reggie gaped, but couldn't get a word out.

"I'm sure he knows about Leon and the transducers, too," Erin added, staring Reggie down. Yeah, Reggie would have assumed their costs would go up, putting them in a deeper bind, but Erin had it under control. She'd implemented a plan.

Dominic suddenly felt a burst of pride completely at odds with the crap they'd been going through personally. He wanted to touch her, hold her hand in solidarity. They'd lost so much, but they still had DKG. He would not let her throw it away.

Reggie was saved from sputtering and stammering by a strutting Garland Brooks making a grand entrance in his slick suit. "Well, the DeKnights. How wonderful to see you." He didn't extend a hand.

In her high-heeled shoes, Erin was slightly taller. "Nice to meet you," she said politely, though she knew of the man's ethics, or lack thereof.

Brooks pushed his wire rims up the bridge of his nose as if that would help him see better. "I had no idea you were talking to Reggie here about our offer"—yeah, right—"but why don't we go to my office to discuss the particulars?"

"We're not here to discuss particulars." Dominic didn't give the man the benefit of a smile. "We're here to tell you that DKG isn't for sale, and you can sue us over the patent but you'll lose." He turned on Reggie. "Isn't that right, Reggie? You understand since you helped me do the research on it."

Reggie spluttered. If he was getting any sort of bonus out of backing DKG into a corner, he'd lose it now.

"It's going to cost you a lot to fight us." Brooks punctuated the threat with a scowl.

"It will cost you more." Seeing Reggie in the enemy territory put everything in perspective. WEU knew they couldn't win, which is why the original patent infringement letter hadn't come from an attorney. Garland Brooks was blowing smoke. "I wonder what would happen if the other manufacturers paying you a royalty were to learn your patent's validity is questionable?"

"Well . . . well—" Brooks blustered ineffectually. He was losing confidence.

"Don't worry." Dominic waved a hand and gave them a conspiratorial wink. "It won't come from me." It wouldn't have to. Like magic, the industry grapevine would transmit the news. Dominic clapped Reggie on the back. "But hey, Reggie, hacking into a competitor's system is illegal. You should cover your tracks better." Al hadn't pinpointed the culprit, but Dominic didn't have to be a betting man to know it was Reggie.

Reggie cringed, stammered, nothing came out. Garland Brooks glared, but even backed up by his thousand-dollar suit, the look didn't carry the punch he wanted.

"Thanks for the coffee." Dominic drained the last of the brew, crumpled the cup, and tossed it in the trash. Then he drew WEU's letter from his back pocket. "Guess we can throw this in the old round file as well." He tore it and let the pieces fall into the trash can, too.

Dominic had won not just the battle, but the war.

"My dear?" He held out his hand as he turned.

Erin put hers in it.

ERIN DIDN'T KNOW IF THE CLASPED HANDS WERE FOR SHOW, BUT she held on tight. She'd never admired him more. Dominic hadn't gotten angry. He hadn't yelled. He stated the situation in good-old-boys terminology, a simple "Don't mess with me or mine."

"Do you really think they'll back off?" She wasn't sure how stubborn Garland Brooks could get.

"They will. I'm right about the patent. This is over."

His hand around hers was warm, solid. She'd forgotten how solid he was, how she could count on him. He hadn't given up on DKG. He wasn't the type to give in without a fight.

And he'd fought for her for a long time now. She'd shut him

out, punished him with her silence and her distance, yet he'd bared his soul to her. She'd been too afraid to give him the same in return. She was still afraid. If only . . . there were so many *if onlys*.

If only they hadn't let Jay go that day. If she'd gotten him to the doctor sooner. If she hadn't screamed at him. And even later, after they'd ruined their lives, if she'd let Dominic talk, if she'd talked to him. Maybe she could have at least stopped hurting them both. For a year, she hadn't thought about losing him. Now, she was actually afraid of it, about what that meant, how it would feel.

If only. Maybe she had some control over that. *If only* she could talk to him? It was just a matter of opening her mouth and doing it. Giving him what he needed instead of considering only her own stuff, her own feelings, her own fears.

She tugged on his hand as he headed to the car. "Walk with me for a minute. I'm not ready to go back yet."

WEU was at the end of a cul-de-sac, the street tree-lined, the sidewalks edged with flowerbeds now dormant in winter. He followed her, but his fingers tensed in her grip.

She was afraid to talk, but afraid to lose him if she didn't. She opened her mouth, closed it, started again. "I did blame you," she said, and the words actually carried a physical ache with them.

"I know." He didn't have to ask if she was referring to Jay; she heard the softness of heartbreak in his voice.

"Not for the reason you think."

"Why then?"

The words stalled on her lips. She'd spent so long trying not to say it, hiding it, hiding *from* it. But Dominic had been right, she'd robbed them both. When that was all they had left, denying Jay's memory was like losing their son all over again. She needed those memories back. There was only one way to get them. "I blamed you because if you hadn't let him go, then I never would have said those things to him the day we took him to the hospital."

A squirrel chattered as it scurried along a wire, and birds twittered in the trees, high tweets, musical chirps, the caw of a crow. And there was Dominic's hand tight on hers, then his deep, torn voice. "What did you say to him?"

"He was being a pill." Even now, she could see Jay's cheeks bright with splotches of anger. "He threw his oatmeal, broke the bowl. Then he started shouting at me. I couldn't stand it anymore, and I yelled right back. I called him a stupid little asshole." Later, so much later, when it was too late, she'd learned that the combativeness was a symptom. The knowledge hadn't made her feel better.

"He could be a pill when he wanted," Dominic said gently, almost as if the memory were fond.

"Yes," she whispered. "But it was worse. I was so angry. I punished him by not speaking to him the rest of the morning, while I drove him to school." Just as she'd punished Dominic by not talking.

Their footsteps had grown to near nonexistent. She no longer heard the birds. She could hear only her thumping heartbeat. She could feel only the tightness in her chest, the prick at the backs of her eyes. "He kept whining that his neck ached, and I still didn't talk to him because I thought he was playing the sympathy card so I'd forgive him without making him apologize for his behavior." Later, the school called to say he was sick. "Every mother knows," she whispered, "that when a child has a neck ache, you take them to the doctor." She didn't realize she was crying until she tasted a tear on her lips.

Dominic put his hand to her cheek, brushing away a teardrop with his thumb. "It was already too late."

She'd hated herself every moment since, every time she woke to the sound of her own words in her ears. She hadn't kissed Jay good-bye that day. And she would hear the things she'd shouted at him until the day she died.

Maybe, with Dominic's help, she could also remember the sweetness of her son's smile, or how much he'd loved to be read to at night, even when he was old enough to read for himself.

This was what she denied both herself and Dominic for that last year, all the sweet things. She wanted them back, even if they were only memories.

EVERY BREATH FLAYED DOMINIC'S THROAT, EVERY WORD ERIN spoke stripped his flesh from his bones. She had punished Jay with silence, and she had punished him. But for herself, she'd reserved pure torture.

As much as he'd loved and hated her in the last year, he understood why she'd shut him out. "Hating yourself won't bring him back, and it won't make the pain go away." Nothing could.

She raised her gaze from the open throat of his shirt to his eyes. "That's why I need to start remembering all the good things. I need you to help me do that."

She had never asked him for anything. Until now.

"We can help each other." That was all he'd wanted. For them to comfort each other. It wouldn't end the pain. It wouldn't even stop the guilt. But it was better than dying inside all alone.

Beneath a bare dogwood tree that wouldn't bloom for another three months, he pulled her against him. She slipped her arms beneath his jacket, and her tears seeped through his shirt.

"Do you hate me for what I said to him?" she murmured in a child's voice.

She'd feared all along that he would. But no, not for that.

"That's only a reflection of your own feelings." He'd hated her for other things, but then you couldn't love someone if you didn't sometimes hate them, too.

"I forgive you for letting him go by himself and not telling me." She waited a beat. "I would have done the same."

"I would have let him do a cannonball in the hot springs."

She sighed, sniffed, and finally smiled just a little. "You would have been the first to do it."

"Yeah." He wouldn't ask now, but he knew when he did, she would finally agree to talk to someone with him, a professional. "I forgive you." He breathed in her sweet, cleansing scent. "And I love you."

He led her back to the car, but when he drove her away, he didn't return to work. He took her home. Once there, he carried a box in from his lab, where he'd hidden it away since February. Setting it on the floor of her office, he opened the flaps.

She came down on her knees beside him. "You kept some of his things."

"I knew someday you'd wish you still had them."

She pulled out the much-loved stuffed green dinosaur Jay had slept with for so many years until somehow it made its way to the back of his closet. Rubbing the grubby material against her cheek, Erin fingered the tail. Her eyes misted. Then she rummaged through the other favorites, touching each one for a long moment as if she could see Jay in her mind's eye. She gave the baseball glove to Dominic, dug deeper.

"Noah's ark." She traced a giraffe, an elephant, Leon's painstaking detail. "He was carving the camels."

For a moment, Dominic couldn't speak, then he swallowed past it. "Maybe he'd let us have them to put with these."

"I'm sure he would." She pulled something else from the box. "My mug." She wrapped her palm around the ceramic "World's

Best Mom" mug Jay had given her that last Mother's Day. He had the matching Father's Day mug in his lab. There wasn't a day he didn't drink from it without equal parts pain, guilt, and love. He could still taste the burned toast and the overdone bacon his son had made him for breakfast on Father's Day. He would take the hard memories because with them came the good ones, too.

"He didn't burn your bacon the way he burned mine." His throat ached; his cheeks were wet.

"That's because I was the world's best mom." She laughed, choked it off. "And you were just his dad," she whispered.

He lifted her hand, kissed her knuckles.

She drew in a breath, held it. "There's something else."

His heart pounded. There would always be something else, a memory that would slice him like shards of glass. "What?"

She rose, let him follow. Her computer had finished booting while they'd gone through the box. She opened a photo gallery.

Jay's face bloomed on the screen in picture after picture. Dominic's heart stopped beating. He'd thought she'd purged these.

"I believed that if I looked at him enough," she murmured, gaze fixed on a photo of Jay in his baseball uniform, "that he'd forgive me."

For a moment, he wanted to hate her all over again for hiding those precious moments of Jay from him, for keeping them to herself for a year. His vision blurred, yet in the next breath, he knew they'd hated and punished each other more than a lifetime's worth. He needed it to end. "This is what you did every night?"

She nodded. "Can you forgive me for this, too?"

She'd tormented herself with them. They were her penance. "Yes," he said, "because I love you. And because I can't do this anymore without you."

37

DOMINIC HELD OUT HIS HAND. "COME WITH ME."

In the bedroom, he cupped her cheek with the most tender of touches, his lips on hers feather light. When he backed off, angled his head the other way, she murmured, "But we have to get back to work."

"Screw work." He licked the seam of her lips, her taste as intoxicating as if it were the first time. "I need this. I need you." He needed all the things he'd craved, her kiss, her touch, her laughter, her voice whispering to him. "Kiss me."

When her lips parted for him, he held her as close as he could without pulling her right inside his skin. She tasted of sunlight. Up on her toes, she wound her arms around his neck, opened everything to him. He took her with his mouth, his tongue, his need. She took him with her heart. The kiss lasted until he couldn't breathe, until his pulse pounded and his blood rushed through his veins.

Then he lifted her, tossing her into the middle of the bed. She laughed. Christ, her laugh; it bathed his senses, turned him inside out.

"What the hell are you doing?" Her smile swallowed any bite in the words.

"I'm going to fuck my wife in the middle of the day in the center of my bed." He yanked his shirt over his head. "What are you going to do about it?"

She stared for a long moment, a hint of shadow passing through her eyes, then she got to all fours and crawled across the bed to him. She laid her hand on top of his as he tugged his belt loose. "I'm going to suck my husband's big, fat cock."

This was what he'd craved in those hours past midnight. Her laughter, her banter, her dirty talk, when making love was hot sex and so much fucking fun. She'd given it to him during their games, but she'd denied it to him in their bed. "Strip first," he ordered, "or you don't get any cock."

"Hah. You're dying to give it to me." But she pulled off her jacket, tossed it, slipped the buttons of her blouse loose, shoving it off her shoulders where, still tucked in, it dangled over the waistband of her slacks. Her bra was utilitarian cotton and oh so sexy. With one finger, he slowly pushed the strap off her shoulder, then down her arm until her nipple popped free.

"You're so beautiful," he whispered, the backs of his eyes aching, his breath catching in his throat.

She held his palm to her breast. "I love you."

He raised his gaze to hers. It had been so long. "I never stopped loving you." They would never stop missing Jay, but there could be moments like this, where they felt the connection like the beautiful, delicate threads of a web, unmistakably there yet so easily broken if you weren't careful. They had not been careful with each other for so very long.

Putting a knee to the mattress, he knelt before her. Slowly, with care and deliberation, he unsnapped the back clasp of her bra. Holding her with his gaze, he slid the fabric from between them. Her nipples brushed his chest.

"So good," he said, then pushed the thick luxuriance of her

hair back from her neck. Breathing deep of her sweet scent, he licked the shell of her ear.

She shivered, then laid her palm flat, taking his nipple between her index and middle finger, squeezing. His cock jumped. "Even better," she murmured. Bending to his chest, she licked him, bit his nipple lightly, then soothed the skin with her tongue. "You taste perfect."

They removed the rest of their clothes in fluid, synchronous motions as if they performed an intimate dance. He was sure it would never happen that way again. He didn't care.

Face-to-face, breast-to-breast, she stroked his cock. "I love how hard you get. That amazes me."

It was always how he'd been for her. How he always would be. "You know what I want?"

She shook her head, her hair brushing him. "Tell me."

"Missionary."

She laughed. "You're kidding."

"That's how I want it." He trailed a finger down her side, then between them, tracing her pussy, testing. She was wet. "I want your arms around me, your lips on me. I want to see you."

She laid back in the center of the bed, spread herself for him. "Take me, I'm yours." Despite the quip, there was a momentousness to her words, a glow in her eyes.

There were no preliminaries, no foreplay. He simply filled her and filled himself with her. She tangled her fingers in his hair, pulled his head down, took his lips with a long drugging kiss. Slow, steady, sweet, hot, he made love to her until she writhed beneath him, moaned into his mouth, her pussy working him from the inside.

Someone whispered "I love you" over and over. He took her to the rhythm of that chant, their chant, loved her with the sweetness in those words. When he came deep inside her, she became his again, finally.

*　*　*

SHE COULDN'T MOVE TO LOOK AT THE CLOCK. IN FACT, SHE DIDN'T care. The work would be there tomorrow.

"We should do this more often," she whispered against his neck, her body, hot and marvelously sweaty, plastered along the length of his. He was all smooth, hard muscle, the phantom feel of him inside her, his scent all over her, her own body-wash aroma sweet but changed, becoming his, utterly masculine.

He rolled, pinned her beneath him. "We should do it at work." His dark eyes sparkled as he raised a devilish brow. "In fact, I have this fantasy of you walking into my office, closing the door, sitting in the chair, and lifting your skirt." He dropped a kiss to her nose. "Then you whip out your vibrator and let me watch."

She laughed. "You're so filthy." Then she cupped his face, held him, her heart beating loudly in her own ears. "Is that over? All the kinky things we did?"

He searched her face, his gaze moving from her left eye to her right, down to her lips, back up. "I loved watching you come. I loved your pleasure. I loved holding you while he licked my come out of you and made you climax all over again." Even now, against her, she felt how much he'd loved it in the hardening of his cock. "But all I really needed was this, you in my arms, seeing me, loving me. I don't need the rest the way I need you."

"I don't know if I want those things again. Maybe. Maybe not. Later. I don't know. Can you wait?" She wasn't ready to think about it now.

He kissed her soundly. "I can wait forever."

He already had waited. She moved sinuously beneath him. "What we really need is some time off, a long vacation."

"Good God." He waggled his eyebrows. "You? Take off more than a day from work, especially in January."

"Maybe we should do it in February. Valentine's Day." She burrowed her face against his shoulder. "Maybe I work too much." She didn't say *we*. The problem had never been Dominic. "We need time to learn to be together again."

"Yes. We do." He kissed her ear. "I love you. I have always loved you. I always will love you. But things are different now."

She knew he meant Jay. She knew he meant their life without Jay. They'd said so many things today. There were so many things left to be said. They had to admit to each other that the ache would never go, but they would have to go on anyway. "I never stopped loving you. I just forgot how to show you."

He wiped a tear from her cheek she hadn't realized had fallen. Then he rolled with her once more, pulling her astride him. "Do you know how I survived?"

She leaned down, pressed her body to his. "No."

"Past midnight," he murmured, his eyes as deep, dark, and soulful as the hour of which he spoke. "I lived for when you touched me then."

When things seemed their darkest, when she didn't think she could go on, she'd always turned to him, and it had always been past midnight. "You were the only way I survived, too."

"Don't ever stop touching me like that in the middle of the night," he whispered.

She put her lips to his. "I never will." Then she kissed him.

Keep reading for an excerpt from

THE FORTUNE HUNTER

by Jasmine Haynes.
Now available from Berkley Sensation.

"FAITH. OVER HERE." TRINITY GREEN WAVED FRANTICALLY FROM the other side of the ballroom, her voice falling into a sudden hush as the dance number ended.

Faith cringed as she suddenly felt every eye on her, the party-goers around her stepping back slightly so that she was in a little circle all her own. The indisputable center of attention.

Trinity would never understand why any woman in her right mind *wouldn't* want to be the center of attention.

Faith, obviously not in her right mind, loathed it. Her friend was now skirting the dance floor, a dark-haired man in tow. Faith smiled. Men loved being towed by Trinity. In addition to her blond hair, Aphrodite looks, and flawless body, she was quite a lovable person.

They'd been best friends since the seventh grade when Trinity had rescued Faith from a spiteful group of girls. Middle school girls could be terrors on anyone different. Though their fathers had known each other for years up to that point, Trinity hadn't seemed to notice Faith existed. Yet Trinity stood by her that day, and Faith would forever love her for it.

"Sweetie, there's someone I'm dying for you to meet." Trinity grabbed Faith's hand, then seized her companion's, and forced their handshake. "This is my best friend in all the world, Faith

Castle. And Faith, this is Connor Kingston. He's working with Lance at Daddy's company." Lance was Trinity's brother and heir to the Green company throne.

"It's nice to meet you, Miss Castle."

Out of force of habit due to her short stature, Faith tended to look at hands instead of faces during introductions. But something in Connor Kingston's voice, the husky quality of it, like a rhythm guitar strumming a deep chord, made her look up. And up. She was five foot four in the heels she wore tonight, five foot two without them. Connor was over six.

He had the blackest hair she'd ever seen, so black the chandelier lighting gleamed off it. Charcoal eyes gazed down at her— though charcoal seemed such a boring color. His were the shade of a moonlit midnight.

He and Trinity made a perfect couple.

"And it's nice to meet you, Mr. Kingston."

Trinity snorted. "Give me a break. It's Faith and Connor, okay? No more of that *Mr.* Kingston and *Miss* Castle stuff."

Faith almost laughed hearing the names said so closely together. His king to her castle. Like a chess move. Or a statement on male to female relations.

Introductions done, Trinity stroked his black tuxedo-clad arm. "Connor, would you get us some champagne? I'm parched." Not that Trinity would drink the whole glass. Too many calories.

Connor smiled. A wolf, tamed for the moment, grinning at a cute little bunny. "Of course." He turned the smile on Faith, something flickered in his eyes, then his mouth crooked a little higher on one side.

If she didn't know better, she'd have thought she'd made the wolf comment aloud.

"Isn't he divine?" Trinity whispered as they watched him until he was swallowed up by the crowd at the bar.

"Absolutely."

Then Trinity sighed. "It's too bad he doesn't have a cent to his name other than what Daddy's paying him."

"At least he has a job."

Their small community of Silicon Valley elite, those left after the dot-com crash and the economic downturn a few years ago, could be broken down into two categories: those who had, and those who didn't. Most of the didn't-haves lived off the did-haves, not by working but by being charming and getting their entertainment written off as a tax-deductible business expense by the other half. Or, they married into the class they coveted.

"That's the worst part," Trinity moaned. "Everyone *knows* he works. Daddy would have a hissy fit if I even *mentioned* marrying an employee." She tapped her chin thoughtfully. "But we could have a wild affair." She fluttered her eyelashes. "You know, all that unbridled passion, the fear of being *caught*." She shivered dramatically. "It sounds so intense."

Agreeing completely, Faith wanted to shiver herself. With his dark good looks, Connor Kingston incited many a delicious fantasy. Trinity winked, and they scanned the crowd for him.

Faith spotted the back of his head. My, his shoulders were broad in the tuxedo. "I'll leave you alone to work your magic."

Trinity grabbed her arm. "You can't run off. He wanted to meet you since I talk about you all the time."

Faith gasped. "You do not."

"Close your mouth, sweetie. I told him you're the only one in the whole dissolute lot of us who has a calling."

"What calling?"

Trinity huffed. "As a kindergarten teacher, of course, shaping young minds. You're producing a better next generation."

Faith taught because she loved children. And because she was sometimes terrified she'd never have any of her own. She was twenty-nine years old, thirty by the end of the year, and unless she married one of the didn't-haves looking for a did-have wife, teaching might be the sum total exposure she had to children.

Yet Trinity was right, being a teacher was her calling. Which reminded her. Faith smiled to herself. "Do you know what little Roger Weederman said the other day?"

"That's what I adore about you. You *love* the little monsters. When I have children, you have to quit your job and become their nanny. You'll raise them to be little presidents." Trinity spread her hands. "President of the company, president of the United States, president of the United Nations."

Faith laughed. Heads turned. She sometimes laughed too boisterously, but when she was with Trinity, she couldn't help herself. Trinity didn't mean half of what she said. She liked to talk, especially at big bashes, saying outrageous things to anyone who would listen. She had, however, graduated from college with honors and would one day make a perfect first lady.

But Faith wasn't going to be anyone's nanny. She wanted children of her own.

Over the crowd, Faith spied Connor fast approaching. She wasn't jealous of Trinity's sleekness when matched against her own relative plumpness, but for some reason, she didn't want to watch *him* do the usual mental comparison. "I really have to go before Mr. Stud-Muffin returns. He's all yours."

"I can't have him. Unbridled passion doesn't outrank one of Daddy's hissy attacks. And Connor got you champagne." Trinity clasped her hands. "Come on, Faith. Pretty please, don't go."

"Ladies' room," Faith whispered as she slipped away.

"Spoilsport," Trinity returned, just before creasing her lips with a smile any man would die for.

Handsome men made Faith nervous. Connor Kingston did

worse. For the first time, he made her wish for cosmetic surgery to turn herself into a Trinity clone.

FAITH GRIMACED. THIS WAS A HUMILIATING POSITION TO FIND herself in, sitting in a ladies' room stall, minding her own business, while being forced to listen to mean-spirited gossip.

"Lisa is so dumpy, she deserves to have him cheat. I mean, really, she wore stripes. No one wears stripes to a formal."

"Not only that," the other girl joined in, "they were going the wrong way. Everyone knows stripes make you look fatter when they're horizontal instead of vertical. What possessed her?"

Poor Lisa. Faith commiserated though she was secretly thankful she wasn't the subject of the nasty gossip. She'd chosen a basic black cocktail dress for the evening.

One of them sighed without an ounce of sympathy for the hapless Lisa. "Well, he got exactly what he wanted. A frumpy little heiress and all the afternoon delight he can handle."

Faith couldn't remember the husband's name, only that he was one of the have-nots before he married Lisa. *Afternoon delight*. What a lovely term for adultery. Poor Lisa.

"Do tell. Who's he doing the do with?"

"Kitchum's wife."

Gasp. "That slut. She's twenty years older than him."

"She just had her face done and looks younger than Lisa."

"Well, that's what old man Kitchum gets for marrying a gold digger half his age."

They laughed in unison, then, thank God, their voices faded as the ladies' room door snicked closed behind them.

Faith was now blessedly alone. Which was worse? The cheating, or the humiliation of having it discussed in the restroom? Maybe she was in danger of lumping all those in her own social circle into one neat plastic baggie, but gossip did seem to be a favorite pastime amongst them.

What on earth was she doing attending one gala after another? Searching for Mr. Right? That's what her father hoped for her, bless his heart, though he did seem to find something lacking in the few prospects Faith had brought home.

To tell the truth, she didn't need Mr. Right. She only needed children. Her heart ached she wanted them so badly. Yet she grew up without a mother, and she firmly believed kids needed both parents. So, being good potential father material was the only requirement on her list. Amongst her peers, she had serious doubts of finding a man who fit the bill.

Slipping out of the now empty ladies' room, Faith headed into the club's gardens for a respite from the activity. Blooms perfumed the spring night, the garden resplendent with camellias and azaleas, and the crescent moon reflected off the still waters of the man-made lake in the center of the club grounds.

She wandered down the incline through the trees and bushes, and she would have made it to the water's edge if she hadn't suddenly heard a voice on the other side of the hedge.

"Suck it, please, honey. I'm dying here."

Dear Lord, with another few steps, she would have passed the hedge and stumbled right on top of the couple. Faith knew she should find another route to the lake, but something, a devil on her shoulder perhaps, kept her rooted to the spot.

The woman didn't say a word. There was only the rasp of a zipper on the night breeze.

Faith, that devil whispering in her ear, peeked around the end of the hedge. Seated on a stone bench, the woman had a firm grip on her partner's penis, slowly pumping him as his head fell back in total ecstasy.

"Christ, yes. Suck it, sweetheart."

"Don't rush me." The voice was soft with seduction, husky with desire, sultry with power.

The couple cavorted in the shelter of the overhanging trees, and Faith couldn't make out faces. Somehow, their very anonymity fueled her own fantasies.

"Please," he begged.

Faith's nipples beaded against the soft fabric of her dress, and a throb started low in her belly, streaking down between her legs. In an instant, she was damp.

Oh yes, she could almost feel her own hand wrapped around his erection, hard flesh begging her to caress the tip, to suck the tiny drop of come.

She wasn't a virgin. She'd had moments when she'd almost believed she was desirable. Those moments hadn't become anything lasting, and the few men she'd been with had gotten bored quickly. Or they were after her money. Just as her father said.

This, however, was the stuff of her sexually explicit fantasies, where she could have everything done to her and do everything in return. Where she asked for what she wanted without fear of rejection and indulged in all the erotic, sensual acts she'd never done but wanted desperately to experience.

The woman bent her head. Faith could almost taste him, feel him between her lips. Without conscious thought, her hand lifted to her breast, her palm fondling one tight nipple as she watched. Watching was naughty but so incredibly sexy.

Then the woman took his penis all the way, her mouth fusing to him, his fingers tangling in her hair. Whispers, groans, sounds all around her, making Faith almost a participant in what they were doing. Her hand slid down the front of her dress, over her abdomen until her fingers lightly pressed her mound.

She should have walked away. But her feet wouldn't move. Nothing on heaven and earth could make her stop watching.

* * *

CONNOR FOLLOWED FAITH CASTLE INTO THE MOONLIT GARDENS, giving her plenty of lead to disguise the fact he was tailing her. When he caught up, the meeting would appear accidental.

Over the past few weeks, as he'd dutifully squired her around town, Trinity Green told him everything there was to know about Faith. She was almost thirty, a schoolteacher, and she loved children beyond anything. She also happened to be the heiress to Castle Heavy Mining. According to the Trinity gospel, Faith was a paragon. Could there actually be such a thing? Trinity had extolled her virtues as if she were putting the woman on the auctioning block. The question was why. What was the benefit in touting Faith?

Whatever her reasons, Trinity had told him everything important about Faith. Or so he thought. She hadn't mentioned Faith's abundant body. Far from a model-thin beauty queen, Faith was round and curvy. A man could hold Faith in his arms and not worry about breaking her. Her breasts were a bounty. Her derriere begged for a man's caress. Her hair, cascading past her shoulders, was the color of an exploding sun, all reds and golds.

Faith lacked the classic aristocratic features revered in today's world. Her face was round, her nose a tad snub, and her mouth small, but beauty was so much more than bone structure. It was the whole package, inside and out. Trinity had given him a hint of Faith's soft center, but her full impact hit him when she laughed. From across the dance floor, the throaty sound shot straight to his cock. That's when he started imagining her on her knees taking him into her mouth, when he'd envisioned sinking his fingers into her hair and holding her to him as he came.

Yes, Faith Castle was a pleasant surprise. A lush creature begging for him to plumb the depths others casually dismissed. He hadn't imagined that seducing her would be so pleasurable.

Ahead of him, she stopped at a hedge, leaning forward slightly to peer around it.

Connor stole closer. Hushed voices reached him, then indistinguishable sounds. Faith seemed rooted to the spot like a statue hewn in place. She didn't hear him as he circled, coming up on her left. The fingers of her right hand found purchase in the hedge branches, as if to steady herself.

Then he saw what so fascinated her.

Well, well, well, Faith Castle was indeed a bundle of contrasts. Knee-length cocktail dress, well-hidden cleavage, moderate heels on her shoes. One thought prim and proper.

But there she was, standing in the flower-scented garden watching a woman go down on her lover. A breath whispered from Faith's lips as the man drove his cock deep. Her hand left the hedge and skated down the front of her dress, brushing her abdomen, then pressed between her legs.

The sight sucked Connor's breath from his lungs, and his cock surged. Her breasts crested against her dress. Diamond-tipped nipples begged for his mouth. That luscious body was meant for loving, and if Trinity was to be believed, Faith hadn't seen much of that lately. Fucking idiots, the men who passed her over because of a mere body-type fad. She wanted passion. Hell yes, she wanted it badly.

He wanted to give it to her. He'd stumbled onto the perfect supplement to his plan, the ideal stratagem to draw her in.

He hadn't imagined securing his future could be this sweet.

IN HER FANTASIES, FAITH FELT AN ARM WRAP AROUND HER WAIST, pulling her against hard male thighs and a raging erection. Warm, enticing breath bathed her hair.

"You like watching, don't you?"

"Yes," she murmured.

Her own voice snapped her out of her reverie. Her body stiffened in his embrace. The touch was tangible, his words real, her orgasm on the horizon.

"Let me watch with you."

Smooth and sultry, his pitch seduced her as easily as the tableau in front of them. All she had to do was permit his caress, his nearness. She didn't have to act, simply allow him to do as he would. It was so effortless. He pulled her closer, rubbing his body sinuously against her back, bottom, and thighs.

His hand slipped down her abdomen and covered her own. He moved his fingers over hers, rotating gently, caressing her.

"He's going to blow in her mouth," he murmured.

Faith's breath rasped in her throat. She was dizzy and drunk on sex, on the kinkiness of watching, of letting some stranger take liberties with her body.

Under the trees in front of them, the man groaned louder, his hips pumping frantically. He held his partner's head, taking her mouth with his body rather than the other way around. He clenched, held, then cried out.

Lips dropped to Faith's neck, bit gently. Fingers rolled her nipple, pinched. Between her legs, he guided her hand rhythmically back and forth across her covered pussy.

She almost came when he pressed up and in, hard. Ripples of pleasure shot out from her clitoris. She bit her lip, closed her eyes, and savored the sensation.

Then he yanked her back into hiding on the other side of the hedge just as the male half of the tableau before them spoke.

"Jesus, that was good."

The woman's answer was smug, as was her voice. "I know."

"Let me fuck you."

"You'll get my dress dirty. Tomorrow. Doesn't your wife have tennis lessons or something? Meet me at the usual place."

Behind the hedge, Faith's mystery man held her close in the circle of his arms.

"Shh," he whispered.

As if he knew she was about to twist away and say ... something. Such as, *How dare you?*

There was the rustle of clothing and what sounded like a belt buckle, then the man's voice again. "You're such a fucking tease."

"You love it. And Lisa doesn't swallow."

"And Kitchum wouldn't be able to fill your mouth with that much come. Don't tell me you don't love it."

God. It was old man Kitchum's wife with the face-lift and Lisa's had-none-of-his-own husband.

And just who was the man holding her?

"Thank you," he whispered, "for letting me join you."

She knew his voice then, the seductive, rough tones she'd first heard not a half hour ago.

Connor Kingston. Trinity's new dish.

She struggled a little in his arms as the lovers drifted off in the opposite direction. They'd part soon and head back to the ballroom. To Lisa with her horizontal stripes, and Kitchum, well, who knew if he was even here? Faith hadn't seen him.

"Let me go."

He shook his head as he once again dropped his lips to her neck. Did he even realize who she was? Or had he merely been turned on by the sight of a woman watching a sex scene played out in the moonlight?

Then he stroked her chin and turned her face to his. For a fraction of a second, his eyes locked with hers. No surprise, no horror. He had known exactly who he was touching. Faith almost drowned in his glittering gaze a moment before he took her lips with his. He tasted of the evening's champagne and something else—hot, hungry male. Greedy, ravenous, his tongue swooped in and stole her breath.

With a kiss like that, he could make a woman do anything.

His touch, then his kiss had her so hot, restless, and bothered, she had to battle her own needs far more than she had to fight him. She tried to wriggle away. "I have to go."

"Not before we make a date."

That made her stop. "A date?"

"Tomorrow evening."

"Why on earth would you want to go out with me?" Screw her, maybe. But a date?

He chuckled, his chest rumbling against her back. "Because I like the way you laugh."

"The way I laugh?" She was repeating like an idiot.

"In the ballroom. Trinity made you laugh."

No one had *ever* thought her laugh was special. She wanted to accept his invitation, but the whole incident was a fluke. And she was the one who'd get hurt. "You think I'm easy because of what just happened. But that was a strange combination of events, and it'll never happen again." Except in her fantasies.

"Not a date, then. Coffee."

"No." She squirmed against him once more.

"I'm not letting you go until you agree."

"Why?" It was the dumbest thing to ask, making it sound as if she couldn't understand why a man like him would want to see a woman like her again. But really, she *didn't* understand.

"I like your laugh, and I like the way you feel in my arms."

He was seducing her with just a few wonderful, tremendous, unbelievable words. He couldn't mean them.

"Meet me. Say yes. Please."

Dammit, the please did it. "Just coffee. And this will be the only time."

He sighed, his breath fluttering her unbound hair.

She said it would be the only time, but she knew without much pressure, she'd do anything he asked. That's how frighteningly hungry *she* was.

HE HAD A KING KONG–SIZED HARD-ON FOR HER. SHE'D BEEN equally affected. He could have made her come with one more touch. A woman hadn't felt that good in his arms since . . . not since he was teenager and still believed in love.

Step one complete. He'd secured the first date. Connor had a plan for Faith Castle, a mutually advantageous plan.

He'd considered Trinity Green for a few short weeks, but while she was beautiful, sweet, and loyal, she was a little too absorbed with outward appearances, not to mention she'd probably freak if she perspired during sex. Besides, he had nothing to offer Trinity in return for what he asked, and he didn't intend making a one-sided deal that benefited only him. But with Faith, he had the one thing she wanted, and, according to Trinity, the thing Faith wasn't sure she'd ever get.

Yet, instead of pulling together a strategy for his campaign, all Connor could think of was the exquisite taste of her on his lips. That was a boon he hadn't anticipated.

Oh yeah, Faith was the one he wanted to marry. The moment he touched her, no other woman would do.

ABOUT THE AUTHOR

With a bachelor's degree in accounting from Cal Poly San Luis Obispo, **Jasmine Haynes** worked in the high-tech Silicon Valley for twenty years. Now, she and her husband live in the Redwoods with Star, the mighty moose-hunting dog (if she weren't afraid of her own shadow), plus numerous wild cats (who have discovered that food from a bowl is easier than slaying gophers. It would be great if they got rid of the gophers, but no such luck). Jasmine's pastimes, when not writing her heart out, are hiking, gardening, needlepoint, and brainstorming with writer friends in coffee shops. Jasmine also writes as Jennifer Skully. Please visit her website and blog at www.jasminehaynes.com and www.jasminehaynes.blogspot.com.